Prelude to War

Maria Albert

DESCENT of KINGS Book 1

Dreamspinner Press

Published by
Dreamspinner Press
5032 Capital Circle SW
Ste 2, PMB# 279
Tallahassee, FL 32305-7886
USA
http://www.dreamspinnerpress.com/

Descent of Kings: Prelude to War

Cover Art by Paul Richmond
http://www.paulrichmondstudio.com

ISBN: 978-1-62380-357-5
Digital ISBN: 978-1-62380-358-2

Printed in the United States of America
First Edition
April 2013

Acknowledgments

Special thanks to Rachel, Ariella, and Joylyn, my beta readers, first fans and staunch supporters, and to all the folks at Dreamspinner, for enabling me to fulfill my dream.

Recovered Fragment, Journals of King Talon
~ Historical Archives, Kingshome

ELVEN & DWARVEN CALENDAR 3013

MILES
0 50 100 150 200

N

HAMMERHOME
FROMER MTNS.
DOROLINGAS
CARAMORE
MALAR IN FROMER
THE WATCHTOWER
IRONHAND
AXEMORE
IRONFORGE
FROMER MTNS.
SARASHEN RIVER
NALEA
TAHIR RIVER
WOODS
THENALON
LOST ROAD
ARALON
GOWER
FENEMAL
WESTERN ROAD
GLEN'S FORD
LOGARETH
METHIR
HELDEN
FEONOKE FIELDS
HELDEN RIVER
PVOY
ATHANARIK
CORDEN MTNS.
GELTHOR PASS
ERENIA
FALNOR WOODS
FALNOR
MERDAN RIVER
KIERNESS MARSH
ELINGOR RIVER
CORODEN MTNS.
SYLVAN RIVER
TANIERIA
LYSENIA
WOODS
RIVER

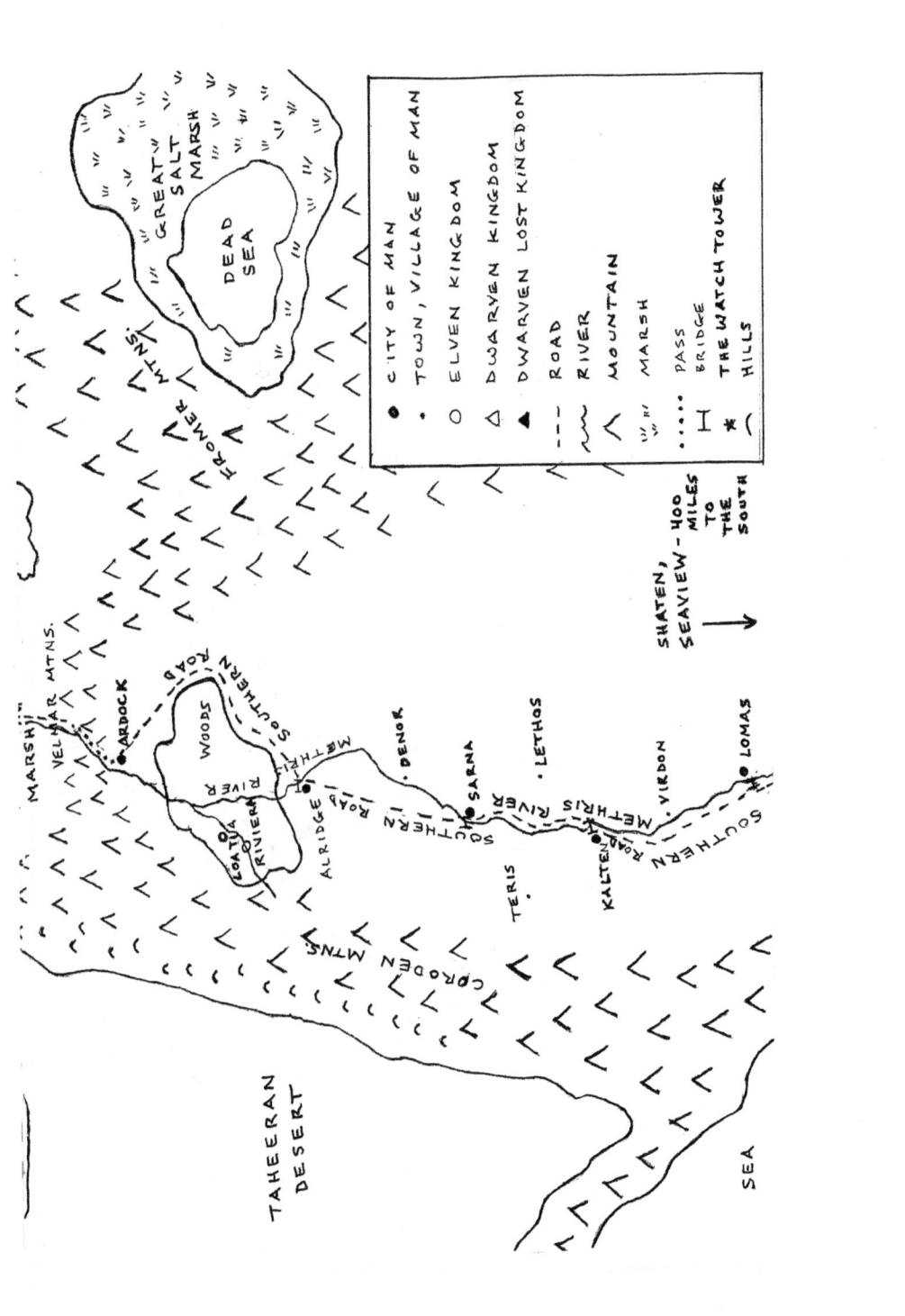

Chapter 1

River's Edge

HARDRED shifted in the saddle, trying to stretch his back muscles as best as he could without dismounting. After nine months, with five different caravans, he was at least used to traveling by horseback now. He'd almost not taken this latest job, from Logareth to Ardock, though it was supposed to be by far the shortest and easiest journey he'd faced. He'd learned the route paralleled the Methris River and that he'd be traveling downstream the entire time and then through the mountains at the end. He'd been afraid they would end at the sea, and he had no desire to ever see her again, at least not yet. Julian's death was still too fresh, too raw. He still dreamt of the storm, relived seeing the terror in Julian's eyes as the wave swept him overboard and the despair in his sister Riana's eyes, day after day, mourning for Julian and worried for him. But Beltris, the captain of the guard of this caravan, had laughed and told him the sea was nine hundred fifty miles beyond Ardock. Hardred had never known the land was so big, that there was so much of it; it seemed as endless as the sea to him.

Riding near the Methris River had not bothered him. There was no smell of salt in the air, no cries of gulls overhead. Even when they'd been right beside it, the gentle, constant flow of water had sounded nothing like the crashing roar of the surf upon the shore. He doubted Seneth was here. What need had the Goddess for such a paltry trickle, when She had the whole sea to claim as Her home?

They were approaching the river now. They'd been out of sight of it for a while, but they were breaking for lunch and they'd be replenishing their water skins and watering the horses as well.

"Hardred, you and Alnas scout ahead. Make sure the way is clear, and that the banks aren't so soft that the wagons might get stuck, or so steep that the horses can't drink," Beltris ordered.

"Aye, Captain," Hardred acknowledged. The words no longer brought the pain they had at first. He'd been surprised when he'd learned that these landers had captains of their own, both of the Guard in their cities and on the road. He'd learned a lot about landers in the past few months, too. He no longer thought the word with scorn—as he and his shipmates had in the ports they'd visited when they saw the locals—though their actions still baffled him at times.

This part of the Southern Road was dirt packed hard as stone from the countless thousands of wagon wheels that had travelled over it, heading from Logareth to Ardock and back again over the years, but it was treacherously grooved with new channels in places from the recent rains. Hardred trusted his mount to watch their footing as he eyed the forest to the right and left, keeping a wary eye out for bandits and other predators. They'd been remarkably fortunate in that regard so far, but their good fortune only served to make him more cautious: it was inevitable that disaster would strike when they least expected it.

"Hardred, we've two days left of this journey. Would it really be such a terrible thing to spend those last two days with a smile upon your face?" Alnas teased gently.

Hardred sighed. He'd tried so desperately not to like Alnas. He'd successfully kept himself aloof and apart from his fellow guardsmen on the first four caravans. But he was far from home and terribly lonely, and Alnas was impossible not to like. "Forgive me, Alnas. It's just I'm not looking forward to the end of this journey, as the rest of you are. I've never had much use for shore leave, nor for a port other than my own, and the next caravan I guard or the one after that might well bring me to the sea."

"HARDRED, surely you're joking! You can't possibly guard another caravan!" Alnas said in shock and alarm. "You've lived through five such trips already, Elmoth watch over you; we're not safe yet. I'd not meant that as a challenge, Elmoth. You know me. I say things I shouldn't," Alnas quickly added. He'd not meant to tempt the God into taking his friend from him. Normally, only half those guards who took a single caravan journey lived. Fewer still survived a second. Three was almost unheard of. Four astonishing. Five was tempting the Gods beyond all hope of survival. Alnas didn't want to see his taciturn friend perish. Hardred was a hard man to befriend, but as he had suspected, well worth the effort. It had taken him nearly two weeks to even begin to crack the armor Hardred had cast about his heart.

Alnas wondered what terrible tragedy had struck Hardred that he might be driven so far from the home he obviously loved. He wasn't wandering or looking for adventure, like some of them were, nor in it for the coin as many of the others were. He was fleeing something or perhaps someone. Alnas had heard him, more than once, awaken screaming a name, or sometimes two, as he had the night of the thunderstorm.

He wondered who Julian and Riana might be that they haunted him so terribly. His brother and sister? His friends? Was Riana his lover, or perhaps his wife, and Julian his son? Or were they his children? He was certainly old enough to have sired two or more. The thought of Hardred having a lover or a wife and children tugged at his heart. He was a fool. No matter what Hardred was seeking, it surely couldn't be what Alnas wished for. Had the Priest and Acolytes at the Temple of Elmoth in Logareth not enlightened him, Alnas would have thought his own quest a fool's errand.

"Seneth doesn't dwell in the River, does She?" Hardred asked. He stopped his horse, a look of terror flashing across his face as his gaze darted to the River that had just come into view.

"Seneth? Who's Seneth? An Elven queen?" Alnas asked, intrigued, glad for the distraction, looking out over the muddy water curiously, guiding his horse carefully, and eyeing the ground warily. The packed soil and clay banks were steep here and crumbling, where the churning, rain-swollen waters of the mighty Methris had undercut them. The roots of several trees were dangling exposed above the waters, and a number of trees lay half-fallen, their branches dragging in the water.

He and Hardred both backed their horses farther from the water's edge as one of the doomed trees, a mighty oak, succumbed to the inevitable and was yanked from the shore and dragged off by the current as if it were a mere twig.

The Methris filled Alnas with awe: it was enormous, running north to south for well over a thousand miles, all the way from the mountains to the sea. It was relatively narrow here, but Alnas had heard it was over a mile wide in some places, farther downriver. Still, he knew its grandeur was dwarfed in comparison to the sea.

The two men rode farther, looking for a place where the bank might be lower and more secure, closer to the water, where the horses might safely drink and they could refill their water skins. They'd not needed to fill water barrels for this trip, since they paralleled the Methris the entire way and the Southern Road never strayed far from it.

HARDRED sighed and exhaled in relief. If Alnas had never even heard of the Goddess, Hardred doubted he need worry, but still, he shouldn't have spoken Her name when there was even a chance She might have been so close and heard. "If you've no idea, then the question is moot. Forget I spoke it."

Alnas scowled at Hardred in obvious vexation. Hardred knew his silence was a source of frustration to his new friend. Hardred's eyes widened in fear, as he quickly looked away from Alnas. No, not friend. Surely, he'd not been careless enough to think of Alnas as his friend, right beside the water? *Seneth, I beg you, please don't take him. He's nothing to me,* he pleaded, careful not to say Alnas's name in his silent prayer.

But it was a lie; he knew it was a lie. He'd lied to the Goddess. If only Alnas was right that She wasn't here to hear it. But She'd know anyway. The next time he went to the sea, She'd hear the words he'd thought now and She'd punish him for them. It terrified him that She might take Her wrathful vengeance out upon Alnas because of him.

Alnas's eyes widened in concern, and he reached out and touched Hardred's shoulder. "Hardred, please. Can't you talk to me? Won't you ease the burden of your heart, by sharing it with a friend?"

Hardred flinched from the touch and from the words that had echoed his own thoughts, further betraying his perfidy to the Goddess. "Alnas, please, I cannot! You must know I cannot," Hardred said, anguished. Then he stiffened, his hand going instinctively to his sword hilt, when once it would have gone to his diving knife. "The River! There's someone on it," he warned, and Alnas turned abruptly away from him to face whatever danger might be there, angling his horse in front of Hardred as if to protect him from it.

Hardred eyed the boat curiously. She was not a barge, though she was loaded down with crates: she was too trim to be, and she had oars and even a single mast for a sail, though the sail was furled. She was riding low in the water, too low. The Captain never should have weighed her down so far. Though she was in the center of the River she wasn't moving at all, even though the current was swift enough to see. She'd run aground, somehow, snagged on some hidden rock or shoal.

Hardred saw the men on board had noticed them as well. There were eight uniformed men who looked to be guards—one of whom had a bow strung and at the ready, fingering an arrow but not nocking it—two others who looked to be crew, another who might be the boat's Captain, and a twelfth man, of impressive girth and loudly dressed in a bright-orange shirt, obviously a passenger.

Hardred didn't have a bow, but Alnas did, slung upon his back, already strung. "I don't think they mean us harm, but be wary," Hardred warned.

OBERAS glared at his four new guards in contempt as the latest of the series of calamities that had befallen him this cursed trip unfolded around him. "Dethrus swore to me the four of you could swim. Then again, he swore to me the pilot knew his business as well, and he's the one who's fouled us in the first place. So then, I want one of you, I don't care who, to get under this boat and free it."

"Not me! I'll not be getting in that water, not with water snakes and Elves and who knows what else might be living in there," Randor said. The others nodded silently in agreement.

Oberas glared at them and then turned to Tebras in disgust.

The pilot and captain, who was eyeing the two broken poles his men held in dismay, looked up and launched a tirade against him. "If you want it freed, why don't you jump in and do so? It's your fault we've fouled in the first place! I told you the cargo was too heavy, that you'd make us ride lower than we should. I warned you that after the flooding the river would have completely changed, that the bars and snags I knew of would be gone, but others would be in their place, that I hadn't had a chance to map it out so close to Ardock yet, but you said you couldn't wait. You merchants are all alike! You think by waving enough coin at a problem it will go away. Well, this one won't!"

"So, you're complaining about my cargo now? That I'm too good at my job, by having so much, just because you're so poor at yours? I didn't hear you complain about it when you accepted coin for five percent of the total load. You and I both know you only tried to convince me that the river was dangerous so I'd not try to haggle it down to three," Oberas growled.

This was yet another delay, in a series of many, and this idiot had wanted him to wait another three days before leaving, just so his friends could tell him how to do his job. Of course he couldn't wait until those others came upriver! Some of the cargo was already dangerously close to spoiling. That was part of what made it so valuable, that it was so perishable. He was already late returning, and here they were, still two days out from Ardock, and they were wasting more time trying to free the boat from whatever had snagged it.

He'd be more than a week late back to the City as it was. He'd lose his security deposits with at least four of his buyers, and what's worse, they'd probably go to his competitors in the future. The two guards he'd left with his shop might start getting ideas that he wasn't coming back and help themselves to his goods. Well, Devrik would certainly know better, but Curtis might not.

Also, he'd had a total of twelve boys set up to take the apprenticeship test with him, six each over two days. The test alone was five gold apiece, so that was sixty more gold he'd not see, if some of them decided not to wait and took apprenticeships elsewhere. Worse, he'd have to start looking for likely candidates all over again, and he'd already had four apprentices fail under him in the past six months. Of course, he'd at least gotten half their fifty gold apprenticeship fee to make up for all the trouble they'd caused him, and the losses. But that hundred gold wouldn't come close to what he'd lose if they didn't free this boat soon.

"Sir, someone's on the bank," Logan, one of his older guards said, quickly stringing his bow and fingering, but not yet nocking, an arrow.

Oberas looked up. Horsemen, two of them. Bandits, no doubt, with the luck he'd been having. On horseback, they might be able to cross the river and reach them. Although he saw only two, there could well be more. His hand clenched on the hilt of the dagger, which was concealed under his shirt, as he scanned the riverbank, looking for signs of an ambush. This was Elmoth's doing, the varging bastard.

"Ahoy, Captain!" one of the two riders called out loudly, his voice carrying easily across the water. "It looks like you've run aground. Are you in need of aid? I swear by the Mariner's Code we'll not seek to harm you."

Oberas exhaled silently in relief at the unexpected reprieve. He'd still be wary, of course; it could be a trick, but it sounded like his luck was finally starting to change. He studied the men more closely and couldn't help but notice that both men were easy on the eyes as well. It had been two decades since he'd wanted to do more than look, but he could still discreetly admire a fine man when he saw one.

"Mariner's Code?" Tebras asked, brow furrowing.

"Yes, imbecile, Mariner's Code," Oberas said scornfully, his brief moment of calm shattered. "You mean to tell me you float this river and have never heard of it? The man's a seaman, a mariner, obviously, or once was one. From the accent I'd say he comes from the far west, probably Delthos or perhaps even Meria. If he truly follows the Code, he means he'll aid us, and now that he's sworn to do so, he'd certainly not risk Seneth's wrath by doing otherwise. Those who swear by the Code then break it don't live long."

Those who angered the Gods often died for it, if they were fortunate. The unlucky ones like him were damned to live after losing those they loved. He forced his dark thoughts down. He had the rest of his life to remember. All that was left to him were his memories, damn Elmoth to Ragnar's fire.

"Ahoy, seaman! Seneth bless you, we are indeed in need of aid," Oberas called out loudly and hypocritically. He followed none of the Gods, certainly not Seneth, Goddess of Sailors, when he didn't even follow Mereth, God of Merchants, or Elmoth, the treacherous bastard. He hated Elmoth as much as Vargas did, though he'd never loved him half as much as Vargas once had.

"Can you perchance swim?" Oberas asked the seaman politely. It sounded an absurd question, but he knew many seamen held a superstitious fear that entering the water gave the Goddess a taste of them, and She'd hunt them ever after until She claimed them, so they never learned the art of swimming, though no doubt hundreds of men died each year for their folly, who otherwise might have lived.

HARDRED looked nervously at the water. Seneth! The passenger had invoked Seneth. And he'd asked him to swim. He knew how; he swam well, though he'd not swum for many months. But the passenger had asked him to, he'd already sworn his aid, and he knew how, so now he had no choice.

"Aye! I'll see what I can do to free you!" he called out. "Alnas, ride back to the caravan, let them know what's happening, so they'll not worry for us, then bring two more men with you, in case these men prove less than honorable. Don't have the entire caravan come; this might be a trick of some sort."

Alnas looked at him nervously. "Surely you can't mean to swim the River? There won't be snakes—it's too big and swift for them, and they prefer brackish water—but there may well be Elves or other dangers. Or what if those men decide to rob you?"

"That's why you need to bring the other two men. Preferably two who can swim, if we have any," Hardred said. "I might need their help. It depends upon how difficult it will be to free her."

"Her? Who?" Alnas asked, sounding intrigued and scanning the boat in renewed interest, apparently looking for a captive onboard.

Hardred shook his head, the right corner of his mouth quirking upward just a fraction in a hint of an amused smile. "The boat, Alnas. Boats are always 'she,' not 'it.' Call one 'it' and you'll offend...." He stopped. He'd almost said Seneth's name aloud again. "Please, Alnas, just go, and be quick returning," Hardred said, eager to get Alnas to safety.

Alnas nodded reluctantly and rode quickly away. Hardred dismounted, tied his horse to a tree branch, and then began removing his boots.

"What are you doing and where did the other man go?" the large passenger asked suspiciously.

"Removing my boots and clothes. You don't expect me to swim in them, do you?" Hardred called. "And Alnas has gone to get two of our friends, in case it takes more than one man to free you." He stripped quickly to his undergarment. He was reluctant to leave his sword behind, but he kept the dagger that was strapped to his calf, a relic from when he'd been a mariner.

The bank here was of more gently sloping clay. It squished wetly beneath his bare feet, welling up between his toes as he walked to the water's edge and began wading out to the boat. The water was cold and muddy, at least here. He hoped closer to the center of the river it might be clearer. The current was strong, but not overpowering. He'd be able to swim safely.

When it was deep enough, he swam with strong strokes, making it to the side of the boat easily, gripping a rung set into the hull and kicking steadily so he could stay beside the boat to speak to the Captain without boarding. Those on board eyed him warily.

"It looks to me like you're at least ten percent over your draft and under your freeboard, aren't you?" Hardred asked, having viewed the boat from the bank and now at the side of it.

The Captain looked surprised at his knowledge and chagrined. "Yes, I'd figured about that," he admitted, obviously impressed.

"Have you a rudder in the back?" Hardred asked.

"Aye, that's what I fear is fouled. And I liked not at all the feel of the tiller when we snagged. I think the rudder might have cracked, or, Seneth help me, even broken from the weight of the cargo," he said, glaring at his passenger.

"That's what you get for letting a lander tell you your business, now, isn't it?" Hardred asked.

"Lander?" the Captain asked, puzzled.

Hardred smiled ruefully. "Forget I spoke it." The Captain was obviously as much a lander as his passengers. Hardred had forgotten for a moment the sea was so far away. It was hard, remembering, when he was in the water, holding the side of a boat. "I'm going to go under and take a look," he said, then held his breath and dove.

The water was far murkier than he'd have liked. Hardred felt along the keel with his hands to supplement what little he could see, heading for the stern, insuring that the rudder was the only part fouled, that her keel wasn't resting upon rock or a sandbar, but it was clear until the rudder.

There was a large dark shape, holding the boat fast. Neither a rock nor a sand bar. His heart started hammering. He'd not thought there might be large beasts in the river, as there were in the sea, and now it was too late to flee from it. But the creature didn't move.

Fearfully, Hardred reached out his hand and felt hard, rough skin and soft scales. One of the scales came off in his hand, and he swam for the surface clutching it, expecting to feel the angry monster drag him down.

Hardred broke the surface, and scrambled up the rungs set into the hull, boarding the vessel for the scant safety it might offer. He dared look at the scale in his hand: it was long and smooth and green and…. He laughed sardonically at his own folly. It was not a scale at all, but a leaf! A tree: it was a sunken tree that had fouled her. "Have you a saw, or even an axe?" he asked the Captain.

"Why those?" Tebras asked, suspiciously.

Hardred held out the leaf. "Because it's a tree that has you snared. Before I free you, I mean to try to take a better look at the rudder. If it's badly damaged or broken, you'll need to dock in order to repair it, especially as it looks like you've managed to break both your poles. Or did you mean to spin off down the river without any way to steer?" he asked, amused.

Tebras looked sheepish. "To tell you the truth, I'd not thought so far ahead. Seneth bless you for coming to our aid, stranger."

Hardred's face creased in sudden pain. "Save your blessings for someone the Goddess loves, Captain." Then before the Captain could respond, he dove back over the side, from nearer the stern, but not so near that he might hit the tree.

He felt along the keel again until he reached the rudder and the tree. The rudder was slick with sea grass, or more likely moss, Hardred realized, except for one spot that felt different. He trailed his fingers along the jagged crack that ran the width of the rudder and felt the unnatural, sudden bend. It had all but sheared off. He surfaced again.

"It looks like I'm going to have to go ashore and make you some new poles. Then we'll tie a rope to your bow and I'll swim it over to our horses. That way we can both pole and pull you toward shore; we'll need to do both, with such a load. The bank there is high," Hardred said, pointing to an area slightly downstream from where he had entered the water that wasn't undercut. "The water below is deep, so you can dock there, for now, and you'll not run aground. Your rudder is cracked clear in half; it's useless."

"Cracked! What am I to do now? I can't pole her the rest of the way to Ardock," the Captain said bitterly, glaring at the arrogant-looking man in orange.

"You'll make a new rudder, of course," Hardred said, surprised he'd even think to do otherwise.

"Make a rudder? I've not the skill nor tools to do that! You name me a pilot or captain who does," the Captain said.

Hardred sighed. A lander indeed. Whoever heard of a boat without tools to repair her? "We've a caravan we're guarding. If the Caravan Master is willing to wait, I can make a new rudder for you. I've the skill, though I'd hardly thought I might ever need to use it again, and I've access to the tools I'll need as well. We've a carpenter with us."

"If he'll not hold the caravan, I'll buy the tools from them and pay you twice what they've paid you for the entire journey you've just made, and any bonus you might lose by not completing it, if you'll stay with us and make a new rudder and accompany us downriver," the passenger said.

Hardred eyed the man distastefully. "I'll not break an oath for coin. I'd not even aid a man who asked me to, were it not that I already swore upon the Code."

OBERAS was genuinely surprised and viewed the man before him in growing respect. He'd had a difficult time finding guards so principled. Most did such work for the quick and often easy coin it brought, for the adventure, and for the women. He'd been a guard like that himself once, long ago, save for the interest in women. Vargas had been the other kind, the honorable kind. Oberas cursed Elmoth silently, for the thousandth time, for taking Vargas's arm and Terhannon's life, when he should have been the one to be maimed or to die.

"Forgive me, stranger. I'd not meant to offend you, not at all. It is rare that I meet a man of principle. I'd hardly expected to find one in my time of greatest need. Please, my name is Oberas of Ardock," he said, stating his name and current city. He'd certainly not betray his true name by listing his father and place of birth, not after all he'd learned two decades ago in the Dwarven Lands about the danger of revealing your true name. "Might I ask your own?"

HARDRED eyed Oberas warily, taking in the man's portly build, his bright-orange silk shirt and billowy black pants, his finely cut boots and heavy gold ring. He was not impressed by what he saw on the outside. But the man's eyes, his face… there had been memory there, a flicker of heart-wrenching grief and bitterness, even anger, that mirrored his own spirit all too keenly. And he had apologized and had sounded sincere in it. In any case, Hardred was still bound to aid him by the Code he'd sworn.

"You're forgiven. I'm Hardred." He'd not name his city, he'd not name Meria. Meria was no longer his home port for all that his sister Riana was still there. As much as he loved Riana, his heart was no longer in Meria. His heart lay dead, at the bottom of the sea, with his best friend Julian, the man they'd both loved, the man she was to have married.

"Hardred!" an eager voice called.

For a chilling moment, Hardred thought it might be Julian, calling him to join him beneath the waters, until reason overtook him. He turned to the bank. Alnas was there, with Sadrin and Kard. He waved to them and then turned to

Oberas. "I'll go ashore now, and make you those poles at least. I'll have to see about the rudder." He dove over the edge and headed ashore.

Alnas was obviously relieved to see him alive and well. Hardred explained the situation, and they agreed that it looked safe enough to bring the caravan. Hardred was sure Roberthan, the carpenter, would let him use his tools, and perhaps even aid him. They'd spoken a few times around the fire, when he'd not had night watch.

Alnas went to tell Beltris it was safe for them to come, while Hardred started scanning the bank for two saplings of the right height, width, and straightness to make the poles.

The caravan approached, and Beltris called him over. "How long do you think it would take to make them the rudder they need, Hardred?"

"I'll start work on it as soon as we tie her to the shore and I remove the old one, so I get the size and shape right. I'll have it done and installed by morning. I'd not had night duty tonight in any case. We can't leave her rudderless, Captain. She'd founder for sure, laden with so much cargo, if she tried to pole her way downstream," Hardred explained.

"I'm surprised the merchant didn't try to bribe you away from me to help him," Beltris said dryly.

"He did, Captain. He offered me twice what you're paying for the entire journey, including whatever bonus I might lose," Hardred replied honestly.

Beltris stared at him in surprise, shaking his head. "You're too honorable by far, Hardred, may Elmoth bless you for it. Most men would have jumped at the offer.

"I'll speak with the Caravan Master and see whether he's willing. Many of the merchants and craftsmen are quite anxious to get to Ardock. We've been making good time until now, but you never know until the journey's done."

A while later, Hardred, Sadrin, and Kard swam across to the boat with the poles and the good news. "They're camping here for the night, so I can aid you. They're hoping Laneth and Mereth might favor them for their charity."

Hardred handed Tebras the poles and unstrapped the bag with the saw and axe. "Sadrin and Kard, you take the ropes to the horses, so when I free her, she'll not drift too far downstream. Captain, have your crew man the two new poles." Sadrin and Kard took the lines, one tied to the bow cleat and one to the stern, and dove in.

Hardred went over the side with the axe and saw. After feeling along the keel carefully again to find the rudder, he hooked his legs about the tree as he found the base of the first branch that needed to be cut. He began sawing, marveling at how odd it felt to be doing so while under the water.

SADRIN and Kard looped the two ropes over a strong branch and pulled them taut.

Alnas was watching the boat anxiously from the shore. He kept expecting to see Hardred bob to the surface for a breath. Alnas looked from the boat to Sadrin and Kard. "Shouldn't he have come up to breathe by now?" he asked anxiously.

"Maybe," Sadrin said. "Although I've held my breath longer than this, when my brother pushed me to do it. Still, I wasn't working hard, as he is, when I did so. It might be a good idea to check on him," he agreed and ran for the water and swam toward the boat.

Sadrin made it all the way there without Hardred having risen yet.

"Hardred!" Alnas yelled, nervously, going to the water's edge, looking helplessly at the boat as Sadrin dove under.

HARDRED felt something touch him and jumped, releasing a burst of bubbles and nearly cutting himself with the saw. He drew his knife and spun, praying it might be an Elf and not a monster, though many thought the Elves monstrous enough. From what he could see of the shape, it appeared to be a man or similar enough to one. He'd lost too much air by being startled to see more. He rose to the surface and inhaled the crisp, clean air deeply. A moment later someone bobbed to the surface beside him. It was Sadrin, not an Elf or a monster.

"What's the matter, what's happened? Why did you come for me?" Hardred asked. He could hear Alnas calling to him and looked to the shore in concern that some disaster might have overtaken the caravan. He feared the boat might have been the lure for some elaborate trap after all, and an army of bandits might even now be attacking them, but everything looked peaceful.

"I came to save you. We thought you'd drowned, you were under so long," Sadrin said.

"Drowned? Then why would Alnas call my name so loudly that the Goddess would be sure to hear him? I thought he was my friend," Hardred said, wounded by it.

"Hardred, what are you going on about? He was calling for you because he was worried but can't swim. At least he had the sense not to try to go in after you anyway," Sadrin explained.

"But if I were dead from the water, by calling my name, he'd be dooming my spirit to be lost forever to it, instead of finding rest," Hardred said, confused.

Sadrin looked at him, equally puzzled. "He didn't know that, Hardred. None of us did. It's a good thing you've warned us. Look, why don't we work at it together? Two is safer than one under the water," Sadrin reasoned. Sadrin had tried to convince him so before, but with little success.

Hardred shook his head. "It's hard to see, and I'm the one who's familiar with boats. We can't risk letting the rudder fall, if it comes off with the tree. Besides, I'll not risk you like that. Here, put the axe on board her. I'll not need it. Then go ashore and reassure Alnas and tell him not to call for me, especially if he thinks me drowned," he said and then slipped beneath the water again.

SADRIN swam back to shore and told Alnas and Kard what Hardred had said.

"I like him, but Elmoth help me, I don't understand him," Alnas said, exasperated.

"You don't need to, Alnas. Just be there for him, as you've been this trip. He's finally warmed up to you, at least. We've been worried for him. At first we'd believed he just thought himself too good to associate with the rest of us. If you'd not been so persistent, we'd still have thought so. He's a good man, deserving of good friends. I hope he finds whatever it is he's been seeking in Ardock," Sadrin said.

"He's told me he's not staying in Ardock. That he's taking another caravan. Sadrin, it will be his sixth! He can't possibly survive six! The Gods would never allow it. I fear, the next time he travels by caravan, tragedy will strike him," Alnas said, dismayed.

"He's young to die, younger than you've suspected. I heard you and Kard speaking last night, while Hardred was walking the perimeter. I thought Hardred twenty-four or so as well, when I first saw him, the age a guard normally starts thinking seriously of retiring; his face is aged enough to be. But I was there when Beltris signed him on and he swore he was eighteen. A man like him wouldn't lie about that," Sadrin said.

"Eighteen?" Alnas asked in surprise. "Surely not as young as that! I'm nineteen, and I was sure he was much older than I am. How can he have first been a seaman and then made four caravan trips as a guard and nearly a fifth and be eighteen? He can't have rested at all between them."

The boat lurched and suddenly began heading downriver again. "Hold fast to the ropes," Sadrin called, running for them. They were looped over the branch and tied to their horses, with two men to each rope for good measure.

Alnas saw the men onboard poling the boat and waited anxiously for Hardred to come to the surface as the boat approached the shore. Why wasn't Hardred surfacing yet? The horses were straining to drag the heavy load across the strong current. Where was Hardred?

Cold dread seized his heart again, worse than before. He could scarcely breathe for it. No, surely not! They'd been speaking of tragedy for him; surely they couldn't have brought it down upon him! "Sadrin! Sadrin, he's not come up for air! Surely he would this time, when there's no need to stay submerged! Perhaps the tree's snagged him, somehow. Please go look," Alnas urged.

Sadrin eyed the water, frowning, as they tied the boat securely to the shore. "That I will," he said and waded out, then began swimming.

Hardred still did not appear.

Sadrin dove down, stayed under, then bobbed up and dove again. "Curse it all, Alnas, am I in the right spot? I can't even find the thrice-blasted tree!" he swore.

"Try more to my left," Alnas called, looking out wildly over the water for any sign of Hardred.

Sadrin surfaced again, and Kard, Velson, and Ledrus rushed to join him in the water.

Alnas fought the urge to call Hardred's name. Instead, he prayed. "Mighty and merciful Elmoth, please spare my friend Hardred. He's not a follower of yours, I know. From what I've now heard the other guards, who know more of such things, say, I think he once followed Seneth, but…. Please, Elmoth, it's not right that he should die for helping those in need. What kind of lesson does that teach your children? Not that I'm criticizing you, I…. Forgive me for praying so poorly. Please, just help us find him. Please return him safely to me," he pleaded.

OBERAS had disembarked and was watching the search for the missing man grimly, twisting his signet ring back and forth on his finger. No, absolutely not. Hardred could not drown, not after freeing them. Especially not after listening to the guards remaining on shore talking and praying and learning Hardred was only eighteen.

Terhannon had been eighteen when he was killed. The pain of it knifed Oberas's heart as sharply as it had when it happened, these twenty years gone by. He remembered the terrible feeling of being overcome and then staggering to his feet, astonished and thankful at first to be alive, only to find Terhannon dead and Vargas nearly so from the loss of his arm. He remembered digging the grave, numb with shock and grief, and laying the body of the man he loved into the cold, unforgiving ground. Loessen had been the one to sever his head from his body, but he was the one to toss the first shovelful of dirt upon Terhannon's beautiful, beloved face, before he had been blinded by his tears and then looked away. They all had looked away. Terhannon had been as a younger brother to the others, for all he'd been so much more to Oberas. They had all shoveled blindly, until they thought both his head and his body completely covered, but when they'd finally looked, they'd still been able to see his right hand before they covered it.

That same look of desolation, of unbearable loss, of helplessness they'd all worn was on Hardred's friend Alnas's face. It was not acceptable that Hardred die for helping him. Oberas fingered his hidden knife and pulled it carefully from the sheath, eyeing it. He remembered the first time he'd used it and the last and every time in between. It had saved his life a number of times. Perhaps now it might save Hardred's. He scowled at the water and at the knife, moving away from the others so they'd not hear him, motioning even his guards away.

The muscle in his jaw twitched as he ground his teeth together, and then he spoke, his voice hoarse and gravelly to his own ear from his carefully controlled rage. "Mighty Elmoth, I'll not call you merciful. You've yet to show me that aspect. It's been two decades since last I spoke to you. You'll be remembering me. You'll be knowing why. It's Oberas. You've had your eye on this knife for some time now. I've felt it. Even when you took Terhannon from me… from us… and Vargas's arm from him, you were not able to wrest this knife from me. You remember trying though, don't you? It bothers you that I'm still the one carrying it, doesn't it?

"People tell me you can't haggle with a God. Pah, I say, you can haggle with anyone. Gods haggle all the time, with each other, with worshippers, with the rest of us. They barter men's lives as if they were buns at the bakers.

"Anyway, if you give that man Hardred back to us, if you return him unharmed, I'll give you this knife. I'll set foot in your Temple, when I swore I never would again, and I'll give you the knife. You won't have my love again, nor my worship, but we both know you never wanted either, or you'd not have done what you did. So that's my offer. Take it or strike me dead here and now for making it," he said and waited.

Nothing happened. "Right, then. Done and done," Oberas said, pressing two fingers of his right hand against two of his left, to seal his bargain with the God he hated.

ELADAR wondered what might be keeping Talon. He was supposed to have met him here by the bend in the River a week ago. At least that was what he thought the Marker had said. He might have misread it. The Amontiri codes were still new to him. He hoped he hadn't made a mistake in discerning the location. Elavar would certainly scold him for it. Elanara likely would as well. Eladar sighed. It was hard, them being so much older than he was. Elavar was almost five hundred fifty, and Elanara almost three hundred. They'd quite forgotten what it was like to be only forty-three, not even an adult yet.

Next year he would finally begin his military training in Nalea, and then it would be only five years until his coming-of-age ceremony. He wondered if Elavar or Elanara might take him more seriously, once he completed the training. He'd be a Reservist, of course, not a Naval Guardsman. He might only be a second son, but he was still the son of a king.

He wondered if High-Prince Aras would be training at the same time. They were almost the same age: Aras was only a year younger. Regardless, he'd see Aras again there. He might even be allowed to spend more than a little time with the High-Prince, although he was a River Elf, not a Wood Elf, like Aras, and Aras's father, High-King Laedrin, normally despised the River Elves. Still, Eladar's Father, King Laranela, was King of Riviera and second only to Laedrin in the power he wielded. Eladar again wondered what motive High-King Laedrin had for betrothing Aras to his sister, Elanara.

He grinned. Poor Aras! He'd certainly not want to marry Elanara!

He sighed and turned his thoughts back to Talon. Eladar was not looking forward to seeing Talon again. He'd done so just over a year ago and it was unsettling. Talon's eyes were surprisingly intense, for a Man. There had been more currents within him than in the River. He was an extremely complex and taciturn man. Eladar was surprised Elavar had gotten so close to him. His brother truly valued Talon as a friend. Even more surprising, he respected him. Elder Elves seldom respected Men.

Eladar eyed the water wistfully. He'd not let the River wash over him for more than a short while each day, in concern he might somehow miss Talon. Surely a few stolen moments now would cause no harm? He needed the River to live. Talon knew that. He would understand if he saw him. He'd keep a careful ear on both banks. Lord of the Watch or not, Talon would not be able to move totally silently; Eladar was certain he'd hear him.

Eladar stripped off his clothes and walked into the water. It was cold and wonderful but not clear. There had been recent storms, serious ones, and the water was still muddy from them. He inhaled deeply and then sank to the bottom, curling one hand about a submerged rock to anchor him in place.

He'd not be able to drift off with the current as he preferred, or he might miss Talon.

Eladar's long, silver hair flowed about his slender body, as the current caressed him. For a moment he imagined instead it was another Elf who did so. That was another reason to be excited about his coming-of-age. The playful flirtations he'd engaged in these years past had been a tantalizing glimpse of the pleasures he would soon enjoy.

He still couldn't decide whether his first encounter should be with a man or a woman, or perhaps with both. He'd made the mistake of getting up the nerve to ask Elavar once about what his had been and received an unbearably long lecture on how he was absolutely not supposed to even think of such things until he came-of-age. As if anyone would dare bed a child and a prince before then! At least another Elf wouldn't. A Man would, in a heartbeat, but of course few Elves would even consider bedding a Man, male or female.

His people were all so terribly aloof! Elavar was the worst. He personified every stereotype Men had of Elves. Eladar wondered what it would be like bedding a Man, either man or woman—it scarcely mattered which. He had just decided that he'd gotten himself aroused enough thinking about it that perhaps he should take matters into his own hand, as it were, when the tree hit him.

Eladar cursed, spraying bubbles everywhere, at the sharp pain in his head from the impact and the sharper pains as its branches raked across his bare torso. What was it doing down here in the first place?

Ah, he saw now. It was weighted down by a sizable mass of compressed dirt and clay about the roots, as well as by the body nestled amongst its branches. Eladar swam along beside it, curious.

The Man had been handsome in life: dark-haired, blue-eyed, and beardless. He was nearly naked. His body was leanly muscled. Eladar admired it for a moment but then realized how morbid that was.

Eladar was surprised how good he looked. Water did terrible things to bodies. Perhaps he was newly drowned? Very newly drowned. He saw the cut upon his forehead, still leaking blood. Surely not so recently that he might yet be saved?

Eladar eagerly swam closer and carefully extricated the Man from the tree, then rose to the surface with him. Freed of its burden, the branches of the tree bobbed to the surface beside them, though the roots remained submerged.

Difficult as it was to keep them both afloat and yet move toward the bank while he did so, Eladar began breathing into the Man's mouth even as he carried him to shore, knowing that every moment was precious if he was to be resuscitated. He was so light! Men weighed so much less than Elves; their bones were so fragile.

Eladar laid him down on his back upon the soft clay of the riverbank. He was not warm, but the water was cold so he wouldn't be, if he'd been in it for any length of time.

He continued breathing for the man, alternating that with chest compressions when the breaths alone proved insufficient to revive him. What if the Man had been under too long? He was not fearful that he might merely be dead. Men died all the time; it was the way of things. Their lives were so short. But what if he had been under the water long enough that he might be revived, but with his faculties impaired, unable to think or move properly? Might he not prefer death? But he must give the Man the chance.

Suddenly the Man began coughing up the water he'd both breathed and swallowed. Eladar knew the Man would have breathed less than he had swallowed; his vocal cords would have constricted, blocking entry of the water to his lungs, at first.

The Man's eyes opened, and his initial look of confusion was replaced by terror as he tried to scramble away from Eladar.

Eladar effortlessly pinned him to the ground, concerned that he might injure himself in his panic, or aggravate whatever existing injuries he might have.

HARDRED was coughing as his eyes opened. What had happened?

There was a woman leaning over him as if about to kiss him. She was naked, a vision of loveliness, her long, dripping silver hair covering her chest, torso, and groin, her blue eyes boring into his own. He remembered the river, the boat, the tree. He'd freed the boat, he was sure of it. Then there had been pain and blackness.

His eyes widened in terror as he realized who must be beside him. Seneth! It was Seneth! She'd come to claim him! Terrified, he struggled to flee from her, fighting to live, but then she pinned him to the ground with the strength of a Goddess.

"I know who you are! You'll not take me!" Hardred yelled, still struggling but held fast.

ELADAR looked at the Man, baffled. The Man was acting as if he were mad, but that wasn't supposed to happen from lack of air to breathe, was it? "Who is it you think I am?" Eladar asked in Common, puzzled.

"I won't speak your name nor my own. You can't take me when I yet live, when the water hasn't claimed me. I'll not allow you to lay with me!" the Man cried, struggling vainly in his grasp.

Eladar laughed. "Ah. I suppose this is a bit of a compromising position at that, with me unclothed and you nearly so, lying restrained and helpless before me. It's a good thing he-who-is-my-brother is not here. I can imagine I'd have quite a time trying to explain myself."

"Since your brother isn't here, you can explain yourself to me, Eladar, if that's who you really are, and not a shadow in his form," a hard voice said in Elvish from behind him. "The Elf I know would not be forcing himself upon an innocent. And this Man is terrified of you and accuses you of being other than who you appear to be."

Eladar turned, startled. It was Talon. He looked cold and hard and deadly. His sword was drawn, held in his gloved hand. And Eladar had been so sure he would be able to hear him approach! He knew he would have to proceed very cautiously. Talon might well kill him, were he to misspeak. He realized he must argue from a position of strength, rather than sounding defensive.

"You are hardly in a position to criticize my actions, Prince Talon, when I too am a prince of my people and am only here at all as a favor to you and your own people, particularly after you have kept me waiting a full week," Eladar said in Elvish. "It hardly speaks well of you. It is to your misfortune that I was the one to come and not my elder brother, whom you no doubt expected to see. I am sure he might more easily overlook the insult of your lateness."

Then he switched to Common. "After such a prolonged delay can you blame me for growing bored? When the opportunity came to save this Man's life, I thought it might only be a mild diversion. I had no idea you'd both want to kill me for it!" Eladar said, finally laughing, unable to maintain his artificially aloof demeanor at the absurdity of what he had said. As if his elder brother Elavar would easily overlook anyone's faults!

He sighed, and his smile fell. Except Elavar well might have overlooked Talon's. He loved Talon as a brother. No, Elavar loved Talon more than he had ever loved his own brother, though admitting so, even to himself, wounded him deeply. Eladar had ever been dismayed that the brother he so admired and always sought vainly to impress was far more fond of this strange Man than of his own flesh and blood.

The Man he held stopped struggling, looking puzzled. "How did you save my life?" he asked warily.

Eladar submerged his forlorn thoughts with the ease of long practice and forced himself to turn from Talon, as if he weren't concerned about him, to look at the Man beside him. "You were engaged in a rather torrid embrace with a sunken tree at the time. From the cut upon your head, I'd say it was the tree Talon should be worried about, not me, since it is obviously the one who attacked you."

Eladar released him and rose, and then flicked his long, wet hair over his shoulder to his back. The Man's eyes widened as he stared at his groin. "You're a man!" he cried out, in obvious shock.

Eladar scowled at him. "I'd take that as a compliment since I've yet to come-of-age, except it is obviously my gender to which you are referring. As I am certainly not underendowed, I will accept the fact that you have suffered a head injury and that you were dead for a time, and not take offense as I otherwise certainly might," Eladar said sourly.

Talon laughed, and Eladar turned to him in astonishment. It was a natural, joyous laugh. Talon never laughed. "Well, I can see you're not who I feared you to be either. Beryl, it's truly him. It's safe to show yourself," Talon said, sheathing his sword.

Eladar looked about in surprise in time to see someone emerge from behind a tree. He was a beautiful youth, with long golden hair down to his waist and eyes the green of summer leaves, a fine-boned face, and a slim build. He looked so like a Wood Elf that Eladar's gaze actually flicked to his ears to be certain he was not. Eladar gazed appreciatively at the boy, who grinned in return.

"Well, I'm certainly relieved you're not a Resemblant, especially considering the way you're eyeing me! I've heard so much about you. I would have been devastated if the Enemy had taken you," the boy said with a smile, in Elvish, obviously mindful of the Man who was listening to them.

Eladar looked at Talon in surprise. "Talon, whatever possessed you to bring a boy of your people so far from the safety of Caramore? And how is it he has learned Elvish so young? His accent is flawless," Eladar said, in the same language.

Talon looked pained. "Because Caramore has been lost, and it was our final refuge. My people have scattered to various Cities of Men, in the hopes that most of them might evade the Enemy by doing so. I need to make sure Beryl is safe. I've named him Heir to the Throne, after Hunter, should I fall. I'm bringing him to Riviera, to your parents. I'll tell you more later. For now, I must see to this Man you've rescued. Meanwhile, you might get dressed, Eladar, and I strongly suggest you stop viewing my cousin as if he were something you might want to eat. It will be several years before he will be anyone's lover, and I sincerely doubt he might ever be yours."

Eladar saw Beryl blush darkly at Talon's blunt remark. The boy was adorable.

TALON walked over to the Man who was sitting upon the clay bank, watching the three of them intently. "Greetings, stranger," Talon said in Common. "Forgive us for the drama, but these are dark times and we are men with an Enemy, one who is often crafty and devious. You have been injured, I see, as well as nearly drowned. I have the skills of a healer, and medicines with me. Might I tend to you?"

The Man eyed him warily and then spoke. "I would be grateful if you did. My head feels like it is about to split in two."

Talon retrieved his healer's kit from behind the tree, where he had hidden it when spying upon Eladar and the Man, before revealing himself. He removed and opened a little pouch with one of his powders, took his cup from his pack and poured some of the powder into it, and then added some water, mixing it with his knife. "Drink this."

The Man did so. Then Talon began cleaning his wound. Talon had to touch the Man's face to do so. As he did, he extended his Power carefully, testing the core of the Man before him for taint by the Enemy. Eladar certainly seemed himself, but this Man might well be a trap the Enemy had set to ensnare either Eladar or himself. But the Man's core was only as it should be, small and dark and brittle, as that of any Man without Power, with no taint of the Enemy about him.

"So, how did you come to be in the river for my friend to save, and who did you fear him to be that you reacted so strongly to him? Though I've known people to react to him that way myself, even knowing who he truly is," Talon teased.

"I heard that, Talon, as you no doubt meant me to," Eladar said. Talon watched from the corner of his eye as Eladar turned to Lunahr. "And I thought my brother was difficult, and he's only a prince, as I am. How do you put up with having him for a king, Beryl?" Eladar asked in Elvish.

Talon could see Lunahr was unsure how he should answer. Eladar laughed. "What House are you from, or am I not allowed to know?"

"Laren? It is all right to tell him, isn't it?" Lunahr asked him in Amontirin.

"Yes, Beryl. You may tell anyone in the King's family who asks, but no other. And please, Beryl, remember to call me Talon in front of others, now that we're not amongst our people," Talon said in the same language, smiling to take the sting out of it. He had not spoken Lunahr's given name in front of Eladar, just as he knew Lunahr would never have spoken his full given name, but still, it disturbed him to hear even part of it spoken here, where anyone might hear it.

Talon turned back to the Man he'd been tending. "So, who did you fear him to be?" he asked again in Common.

The Man looked at Eladar in chagrin. "I had thought he was the Goddess of the Sea. I'd not seen he was a man. I've never seen a man with hair as long as that, nor such an odd color for one so young, with arms and legs so hairless, and his hair covered his torso so I could not see his chest or groin and…." He trailed off, wide-eyed, as Eladar, who was dressing, flicked his long hair back from the side of his face, exposing his elegantly pointed ear. "He's not a Man at all! He's an Elf!" the Man said in shock.

ELADAR looked at him and laughed. "And she-who-is-my-sister calls me absurd! I would have thought that was readily apparent. You at least had the decency to think me a Goddess and not some ordinary woman. I am rather breathtaking to gaze upon, am I not?" he said, posing and laughing.

"I was quite pleased by your appearance as well. It is a shame I am not older. Our encounter might have taken an entirely different bend, were I allowed to let it," he said with a sigh. He glanced at Beryl, who was blushing darkly.

"Pay him no mind. Elves aren't nearly as bad as they pretend to be, nor as other people think them to be. He's not so lecherous that he would have forced himself upon you. I will see to it that your virtue remains intact," Talon said, grinning.

LUNAHR looked over at Laren, his eyes lit with love. It was so good to see his cousin well again! It had been years since Laren had smiled like this, and it was less than two weeks ago that he'd gone mad. Lunahr had been so frightened for Laren. He had wanted so desperately to help him. That was when the Power had flared to life within him. He'd saved Laren; he'd locked the demons that tormented him safely away as Farad had six years earlier, the first time Laren had gone mad.

Lunahr swallowed hard. Farad had not come to save Laren this time. He had not thought anything could keep him from doing so. Laren had told him that Farad yet lived; he still felt their bond, but Farad had not come to Laren's aid. Lunahr wished Farad would come home. Only now, there was no home to come to.

"You were about to tell me your House," Eladar encouraged gently, apparently seeing the despair on his face.

"Oh! Oh, of course, forgive me. I am Lord of House of Eagles," Lunahr said.

"Lord?" Eladar asked in surprise. "But surely you've not come-of-age! You hardly appear twenty-five to my eye, and I was told that the Amontir come-of-age at twenty-five, not sixteen, as other Men do."

"I'm not and we don't. I've only just turned eighteen, although I know to most Men, to those who don't live as long as we do, I'd only look fifteen or sixteen. But I'm last of my House now, although still, I wouldn't have been named Lord so young, except I needed to be a Lord, in order to be named Heir to the Throne by our laws and... but I'm afraid I'm telling you too much! I'm not really very good at keeping secrets yet, but I do learn quickly, although it's something I wish I had no need to learn."

"DO NOT worry. You will find far less need to keep secrets in Riviera than in your own kingdom," Eladar said. He honored Beryl by calling his people a kingdom. By all accounts there were a scant twenty of the Amontir left.

What a terrible thing it must be, to lose your kingdom and all your subjects. He was glad he'd never know what that might feel like. Riviera was the jewel of the Seven Kingdoms. She would always stand strong, even against the Enemy himself.

"WHAT is your name?" Talon asked the Man he tended.

"Hardred," he replied.

"If Meria is still your home port, you're far from home," Talon prodded, curious as to what a mariner was doing so far from the sea. Talon was sure the Man was from Meria. The accent was unmistakable, though he'd last been to Meria many years ago.

Hardred winced. "I have no home."

Talon looked at him in sympathy. There was such pain in his eyes, as if he was remembering a loss too terrible to bear. For a moment, he felt as if he were looking into the eyes of one of his kinsmen. "But surely you are not out here alone?"

"No. I'm a guard on a caravan. We stopped at the River, to aid a merchant who had run aground in the middle of it. His rudder had caught on that tree that nearly claimed my life. When I worked it free, either the boat or the tree must have hit me. I remember nothing, until waking and finding that Elf beside me."

"Then we must get you back to your friends. They will already think you lost. We are obviously downstream from where you were, so we will walk upstream. Which side of the River was your caravan on?" Talon asked.

Hardred looked at the Methris. "This side, fortunately. I really would prefer not to swim again, any time soon. I had no idea a river might be as treacherous as the sea, but I've heard now that the Goddess swims here as well. I am very grateful to you for your aid, and for the offer of escort, for I am poorly armed and even more poorly dressed," Hardred said, the ghost of a smile playing briefly upon his lips.

Talon eyed him critically. "You and I are near enough the same size, and you have the good fortune of happening upon me one of the few times when I have an extra set of clothing with me." He removed from his pack a burgundy shirt of Thenalonese silk and a pair of black pants that were no less fine. "Please do your best to be careful with them, though. I need to be wearing them myself in a few days' time. Unfortunately, I do not have extra boots with me, but I will wrap your feet in bandages so you may walk easier and with less of a chance of injury."

HARDRED fingered the fancy clothes in surprise. He had not thought this travel-worn man might have clothes such as these. They were as fine as what the merchant had been wearing, but far more subdued in cut and color. He thanked him and dressed. He heard a soft sigh.

"It's really not fair at all, you know, my being so young," the Elf said, eyeing Hardred wistfully. "If you were mine, I would dress you in clothes such as those so you might always look so pretty."

Hardred stared at him, unsure of how he should respond.

"You shouldn't taunt him like that, Highness. He doesn't know you're only bluffing," the boy said.

"Highness?" Hardred asked and swallowed. "You are a Prince of Elves?"

ELADAR sighed. "Yes, but it's not something one usually mentions," he said, looking pointedly at Beryl.

"Forgive me! I knew I wasn't supposed to say your given name. I thought 'Highness' well chosen," Beryl said, dismayed. "How am I supposed to refer to you, then?"

Eladar furrowed his brow. "How indeed? I seldom find a need for a traveling name, and Highness suffices for my own people." Then he grinned. "I will let you pick something for me, Beryl."

Beryl looked at him in surprise. "Me? Really? Hmm. How about Fisher?"

"Fisher?" Eladar said, crinkling his nose. "Elves don't fish, Beryl. We don't eat animal flesh."

"Well, of course not! I know that. Neither do I. It's one of the things I love about your people. But you're a River Elf and you fished Hardred out of the water, didn't you? So I thought Fisher might work," Beryl said, a little defensively.

"Ah, that's different. I did at that, didn't I? Fisher I shall be, then," Eladar said, smiling, and Beryl grinned back at him upon seeing it.

"You said before I was dead," Hardred said hesitantly to Eladar. "What did you mean by that?"

"Dead: you had drowned. Your lungs filled with water, as much as they were able, and your heart stopped," Eladar said, as if he were speaking to a backward child.

"But then how is it I now live? Only the Gods have the power over life and death," Hardred said suspiciously. "Once a man's breath has fled, he is lost to the Goddess."

"You mean to tell me that when someone drowns, you don't try to save him?" Eladar asked, astonished.

"Of course we try. We try to get to him before the Goddess takes him. We fight Her for every life. She enjoys the fight. Often it gives Her the chance to take other lives as well," Hardred said bitterly.

"But you don't try to resuscitate someone who's drowned? To aid him in breathing again? To restart his heart, when needed?" Eladar asked, amazed.

Hardred looked at him, dazed. "Such a thing is possible? Your Elven magic allows you to do that?"

Eladar laughed. "Magic? It is not magic. It is a simple thing, really. I could teach you if you'd like. So that if ever you see someone drown you might save him."

"If you can truly teach me that, then I would learn," Hardred said.

"I would learn as well, Fisher," Talon said, his gaze intense.

"I also," Beryl said, equally intrigued.

"Certainly. I will need one of you to volunteer to be the drowning victim, so I can demonstrate upon you," Eladar said.

"I'll do it!" Beryl volunteered eagerly.

Eladar smiled at him. "Very well. Lie down here," he said, and Beryl did so.

LUNAHR'S heart started hammering and he blushed darkly as Eladar lowered his mouth to his in what felt to be a kiss. He hoped Laren wouldn't be able to sense the desperate desire he felt at that simple touch across their nascent bond.

To his further shame, Lunahr felt his manhood harden instantly in response to Eladar's touch. Eladar seemed to be oblivious to his reaction as he instructed them all in how to perform the lifesaving techniques, and Lunahr forced himself to concentrate.

After he was done, Lunahr tried to get up, but Eladar pinned his shoulders to the ground. "You can get off of me now, Fisher," Lunahr said, his heart hammering wildly once more.

Eladar looked down at him, lust in his eyes, and Lunahr realized Eladar had not been oblivious to his body's reaction to him at all. "Must I?" he asked, a wealth of desire in his words.

"Yes, you must," Laren said, his voice iron.

"Ah, Talon, you cannot protect him forever. One day you will not be there to defend him. Beryl must learn to protect himself, if he does not welcome such advances," Eladar said, caressing his cheek. Then Eladar yelped as Lunahr's arm pressed against his throat, Lunahr's hand grabbed his hair, and Eladar was flipped over face down in the dirt. Lunahr straddled Eladar, pressing the cold edge of his dagger to Eladar's throat.

"I'm fully capable of defending myself," Lunahr said, stroking Eladar's cheek with his free hand, much the way Eladar had caressed him, even as his heart slammed in terror at what he expected he would find as he probed outward and prepared to fight for his life.

He almost fainted in relief when his Power did not detect the darkness he expected and feared to find. Eladar's core was, surprisingly, brighter than he expected for an Elf, certainly not that of the monster in disguise that he had feared him to be. Eladar's amorous attentions were merely playful, mischievous, harmless. Lunahr forced a laugh and sheathed his dagger as he rose off of him.

Eladar wiped wet riverbank clay from his face and leapt to his feet with a rueful smile. "I stand corrected, Oh Learned Teacher," Eladar said, bowing to him. Then he laughed along with him and grinned at him. "If you are all ready, I believe we should be heading out."

The four of them began heading upstream.

"ALNAS, I'm sorry. We tried. He must have been injured when the boat came loose. It probably hit him, knocked him out. The current is swift. It would have carried him far downriver by now. We've no hope of recovering the body," Sadrin said.

"But if we can't find his body to bury, how is his spirit to ever find peace?" Alnas asked in despair.

"The seamen bury their shipmates beneath the waves, Alnas. I've no doubt the Goddess will welcome him with open arms. She certainly wanted him badly enough," Oberas said, trying to comfort him.

Beltris came up to him. "Alnas, we want you to have this. It's Hardred's pack. You were his closest friend. It should be yours. And there's his clothes and sword, as well, although we thought we might bury those, as we've nothing else we might. The merchants paid for his horse, so they'll share in the profit when we sell him with the rest of them at the end of the journey."

Alnas nodded. At least they could bury Hardred's sword. He eyed the pack and hesitantly took it. He walked to the river's edge, curious despite his heartache. Hardred had been so closemouthed. He wondered what he might find out about his friend from what lay inside. He took a deep breath and opened it.

There was a spare shirt and pants, as he might have expected. But next he was astonished to find an inkwell, quill, sheaf of writing paper, drying sand, a stick of blue sealing wax, and a brass seal of a stylized bird. What in the world might Hardred need with those? Then he pulled out a small bundle of letters. He untied the leather thong which bound them. They were sealed with blue wax and the reverse image of the bird, and each bore writing upon the outside, the same incomprehensible scribbles. He realized in astonishment that Hardred must have written them. Whoever heard of a guard who could read and write? Perhaps Oberas or one of the merchants in the caravan might read them to him later.

Alnas was nearly at the bottom of the pack. He pulled out an oddly shaped flute. It was made of varying lengths of reeds, seven in all, going from longest to shortest, all bound together. Had Hardred known how to play it? He had never heard him do so, though he had heard him sing once, the night after the thunderstorm. His song had been so mournful it had almost made Alnas weep. It was a song about a woman losing her one true love to the sea.

Underneath the flute was something carefully wrapped in soft cloth. He unwrapped it. It was a wood carving. He looked at it curiously and then stared at it in openmouthed amazement. The detail was exquisite for so small a piece. She was the most beautiful woman he had ever seen. He felt a stab of jealousy followed by a wave of painful loss as he wondered who she might be. Riana? Hardred's wife?

There was one last thing, at the very bottom, something heavy. Alnas hefted it. It appeared to be a purse, but it was far too heavy to be, and Hardred had worn one. He opened it and stared in amazement. It was a purse full of gold! Numbly, he counted it without removing it from the pack, then dropped it back into the bottom before finishing, stunned. He had stopped counting at one hundred gold. There must have been at least one hundred fifty in coins inside! Hardred had been mad to risk his life as a caravan guard when he already had such a sum!

"Here, Alnas, I've brought you some lunch," Sadrin said.

"I'm not especially hungry right now," Alnas said, repacking the bag with the statue and the letters and flute on top. There was so much he hadn't known about Hardred. So much now he'd never know. So much now he'd never be able to say, to do. Gone. He was gone. Hardred was forever lost to him.

Blessed Elmoth, how could I have failed you so terribly that you would take him from me like this, after what you showed me in the Temple in Logareth? Alnas prayed silently in despair.

At Sadrin's look of sympathy and concern, he forced himself to ask, "Is Roberthan going to be able to help the boaters?"

"He thinks so. They've gotten the rudder off. He's selected a piece of wood from the planks of hardwood he brought with him. It will save time, carving it from a plank. Hardred swore on the Code he'd aid them. Roberthan doesn't want Seneth getting angry at the rest of us for Hardred not keeping his word, even if it is Her fault he can't. I'd never known much about Seneth before, but from what some have been whispering now, I've learned She's treacherous and cruel, as well as beautiful and loving, just like the sea herself. It makes me glad I worship Elmoth."

There was a sudden commotion at the edge of camp. Sadrin and Alnas ran to see what the trouble was and then stared openmouthed in shock. Hardred was standing before them, alive and hale, dressed like a Lord, save for his bandaged feet, and he was grinning. There was a hunter beside him and two Elves.

Alnas ran to Hardred and hugged him, unable to restrain himself. "Hardred! But... but this is impossible!" he said, then released him and looked warily at the two Elves. Elves had magic, everyone knew that, but they never used it to aid people, only to create mischief and misfortune.

"Believe me, Alnas, I'm no less surprised to be alive than you are to see me so," Hardred said, still grinning.

"Am I glad to see you," Roberthan said. "That merchant is driving me to distraction. I'm just as willing now to hit him in the head with the piece of wood I selected as to try to craft it into a rudder for him."

To Alnas's amazement, Hardred actually laughed. "Before you put me to work, let me introduce you all. This is Talon and Beryl, and no, Beryl's not an Elf, for all he looks like one." The people who had been standing back from them lost their wariness and smiled openly at the two. "And this is Fisher, who truly is an Elf. He's the one who saved me from the River."

ELADAR looked around him at all the wary faces and laughed dryly. "Don't all thank me at once. Perhaps I'd better just take to the River. I can see how nervous your friends all are seeing me here. I'd be more welcome if I were a river snake, I think! Perhaps I'll summon one or two or fifty, so they might be able to make a comparison as to which of us is worse," Eladar said, a mischievous gleam in his eye.

"Perhaps I should tell your parents and siblings you're harassing Men again. Fisher was it, this time? You really must pick your own traveling name sometimes. The ones others pick for you are so strange," Oberas said, emerging from amongst the trees.

Eladar scowled at him. "Oberas! I should have known when Hardred told us there was a merchant stranded in the River for overloading his boat that it might be you. And here I'd been so pleased I was ill and missed your visit the last time you troubled our waters! Fortunately, it is only once every seven years you plague us. I heard you've successfully graduated a third apprentice. Wasn't that six months ago? Shouldn't you have a new one by now, keeping you safely in Ardock and away from us? Or has your reputation finally reached far enough that they've learned better? Haven't you been able to find another one willing to put up with you, you fat, greedy, arrogant, loud-mouthed braggart?"

"Arrogant? An Elf calling a Man arrogant? Isn't that a little like a sea slug calling a jellyfish slimy? Aren't you still a little young to be allowed out to wander on your own without a nursemaid? Does your mother know where you've gone? We all remember what happened the last time you snuck out of the Kingdom unescorted, don't we? Or do you forget it was me that saved your life and brought you back?" Oberas taunted.

Eladar's face darkened in rage and humiliation. "No more than you have forgotten it was my mother who saved your sorry life after you killed Terhannon and cost Vargas his arm," Eladar snapped in a cold fury.

Oberas paled, and then his face darkened in rage. He took a step toward Eladar, hand clutching his dagger.

Talon stepped between them, arms outstretched. "Gentles, I'm afraid I cannot allow this to escalate further. I think you have each sufficiently insulted and humiliated the other. Fisher, you certainly don't want to risk upsetting your parents or your siblings, do you? Why don't you wait for us in the River? And Oberas, I'm sure you don't want to lose the Elves' grace, or the luxury of being one of only two merchants allowed to sail through the Elves' Wood instead of detouring around them? We both know what the stretch of road around their forest is like, don't we?"

Oberas eyed Talon shrewdly. He'd thought him a simple hunter. He'd wondered how he might have found himself in the company of an Elven prince, especially this particular one. Elves did not travel in Man's company lightly. But from the way in which he spoke, from the knowledge he had of Riviera and the royal family, it was obvious there was far more to him than met the eye. "Well spoken, sir. I, for one, certainly have better things to do with my time. If you will excuse me," Oberas said smoothly and headed for the fire.

ELADAR glared after him, then spun on his heel, stalked to the riverbank, and began walking upstream. He'd not disrobe and enter the River anywhere that a Man might see him, but he certainly needed the calm and solace of its waters. He was fuming for what Oberas had said, all but shaking in rage and humiliation that he might have said so before Talon and Beryl in particular.

"LAREN, now what do we do?" Lunahr asked Talon in dismay, softly, in Amontirin. He was feeling overwhelmed. There were so many people here! He counted at least thirty-six. They kept shifting about, making it hard to count. That was almost twice the number of Men he'd ever seen in his whole life, though he'd been to more than one Dwarven kingdom teeming with Dwarves.

His own kin numbered a scant twenty now, and they were seldom all together in one place for any length of time, and not likely to be anywhere close by each other in the near future, now that their home had been taken by the Enemy.

Lunahr felt a lump forming in his throat again. They were sending him away, exiling him to live with the Elves. It was for his own safety, he knew, because they loved him so much, not because they didn't. But it didn't make it any easier to bear.

TALON saw the look of despair on Lunahr's face and heard the loneliness in his voice. It cut his heart to the quick to see him so, when Lunahr had ever only been filled with smiles and laughter before, for all his scant eighteen years. Not since the death of his parents and so many of their remaining kin had he appeared so forlorn and distraught.

He was so young to be leaving them! By their custom, he would not be an adult for another seven years. But it was the only way to keep him safe. In the Kingdom of Riviera, he would live to reach adulthood, to come-of-age, so that he might one day fight by their side, or claim the throne should he and Farad fall.

"We need to stay here at least long enough for Hardred to return my clothes to me. We can perhaps stay a wee bit longer, but we can't stay for too long, not with Eladar at odds with Oberas like that. I was disappointed by Eladar's behavior but intrigued as well. I would like to hear the story of how Oberas might have saved his life," he said in Amontirin.

He turned to Hardred. "Hardred, if you don't mind changing, we'll be going soon, now that you are safely returned to your people," Talon said in Common.

"OF COURSE. I thank you for going out of your way to bring me and for the use of your clothes. Alnas, have you seen my pack?" Hardred asked his friend, noting it was no longer upon his horse.

Alnas blushed. "I have it. Sadrin gave it to me, when we thought... you know. I'll get it." He left and returned shortly with it.

Hardred opened it and looked at the contents in surprise. He'd left his spare clothes on top, but now his sheaf of letters to Riana, the statue Julian had carved of Riana on their last voyage, and his pipes were. He looked at Alnas curiously.

"Forgive me. I was looking through it. I'd never have done so if it weren't that we thought.... But the letters are still sealed, and I didn't harm the statue or your flute. I didn't know you played one," Alnas said.

Beryl, who had looked crestfallen only a moment ago, turned around eagerly at Alnas's words, and his eyes lit with joy as he spied the instrument in Hardred's hands. "I've never seen a flute like that before. What's it called? Do you play it? Can you teach it to me?" Beryl asked eagerly.

Hardred looked in surprise at the boy. He looked and sounded like an overeager puppy.

Talon smiled affectionately at him. "You must forgive Beryl. He has led a rather sheltered life, until now. He is a minstrel, and instruments and songs with which he is not already familiar fascinate him."

Hardred smiled at Beryl. The boy was young to be called a minstrel. His friend Talon obviously doted upon him to do so. Yet he was so like Alnas, it was impossible not to like Beryl, to want to please him.

"They're called sea pipes. Yes, I play them. In fact, I made them. It's customary to make your own. They're made from reeds that grow in the marshes along the coast near Delthos, far west of here. Although the basics are easy enough to learn, it takes many years of practice to master them, to sound anything less than shrill and raucous upon them. They're sometimes called gull pipes for that," Hardred said, trailing off.

A look of pain flashed across Hardred's face. He'd not spoken the word "gull" in ten months, not since the *Silver Gull* had sailed her final voyage. "Forgive me. I'd thought to play them for you but... I cannot," he said, his voice a ragged whisper.

"FORGIVE me for stirring up memories which cause you pain," Lunahr said solemnly. "I'm adept at not doing so with my own people, but I don't know what subjects are taboo amongst others."

"Why don't we give Hardred a chance to change, so he can return my clothes, and then I think we had best be on our way," Talon said diplomatically.

Lunahr nodded, crestfallen. He headed for the river, his pack clutched tightly in his hands. He looked out at the swift-moving waters, watching a small twig spinning helplessly downstream in the grip of the current. He was like that stick. So small in such a big world, with forces over which he had no control guiding his every move.

He pulled his own flute from his pack. It was the only instrument he'd been able to save from Caramore. He'd had to abandon the rest when they fled. He'd barely been able to save his music. Laren had told him the Elves would provide whatever he might need. But they wouldn't be his instruments, the ones he loved, the ones he knew so well.

He caressed the flute and put it to his lips and began a song so that the flute might expel the burden of his heart into the wind.

HARDRED changed quickly. As he was finishing, he heard the first strains of something so hauntingly beautiful he froze so he'd not make a sound and miss hearing any of the notes. It was coming from the River.

The Sirens! He'd not thought The Sisters might visit the waters of the River. No! The boy, Beryl, had been heading for the River! He'd be in terrible danger from them. They would not hesitate to take one so young, so innocent, so beautiful.

Hardred ran quickly to the River's edge and stopped, perplexed. It was not Sirens at all. It was the boy. He held a silver flute to his lips; it was he who was playing that haunting tune. And he'd so casually denied that the boy might be a minstrel at such a young age! Hardred stood, enraptured, his heart aching anew as he listened to the mournful melody. It had been so many months since he'd last heard Riana play, since she'd stood on the cliffs above Meria and poured her despair into her pipes.

LUNAHR finished his song, sighed, and turned, then blushed. There was a cluster of men behind him. The entire camp had apparently gathered to hear him play.

"Play us another, son. Something less painful. You can't leave us in such darkness and despair," one of the men entreated.

"Of course! Forgive me," Lunahr said, concerned by the looks of anguish all around him. He'd not meant to lace his music with his Power. Had he done so unintentionally? He looked fearfully at Laren and was relieved to see he still appeared well. Thankfully, then, it had been the song alone that so affected them.

He began a second song, lighter, but not too light. He could not bring them too quickly from where they were, or else he might lose some of them, those still trapped in the melancholy of his first song. He had not thought about the effect releasing his despair into the wind might have upon them. Then he played a third song and a fourth and a fifth.

The fifth was a sunny piece, full of light and life and hope, the diametrical opposite of the first piece. Then he lowered his flute and tucked it safely away into his pack.

He jumped, startled, at the loud and enthusiastic applause he received, and blushed again.

ELADAR swam back upstream when it became apparent there would be no more music. What an exceptional child! He would not have thought any of the Amontir might wield an instrument other than the sword or bow. He began to suspect Beryl was the heart and spirit of Talon's people and that they sought to keep him safe for reasons far less practical and calculating than succession to the throne. How could any people risk losing such a treasure?

Eladar wondered if Beryl could sing as well as he played. Surely he must be able to sing with at least some degree of competency? He was eager to hear him do so. And Talon had said he was bringing him to Riviera to stay. He might have years in which to hear such sweet songs.

Eladar rose from the water where he had laid his clothes and dressed. He had thought before he might need half the day for the waters of the River to soothe him after Oberas had so enraged him, but Beryl's songs had done so far more quickly.

He strode toward the camp, hopeful that Talon and Beryl might soon leave these other Men. He was relieved to see that Talon and Beryl were saying their good-byes to Hardred. Eladar watched silently from the trees, slipping easily past the perimeter guard, not choosing to reveal his presence. Talon and Beryl began heading for the water's edge. Eladar paralleled them. It would be fun to startle Talon.

He watched with interest as Talon and Beryl began heading downstream along the riverbank. The two were conversing in what must be Amontirin, not once looking at the River. Eladar grew annoyed. If he weren't shadowing them, they'd have left him leagues behind, apparently without even caring. He was just about to say something, when Talon looked right at the tree he was hiding behind and said, "Honestly, Eladar, I wish you'd stop playing games. We've got a lot of ground to cover before nightfall."

Eladar sighed and stepped out from behind the tree. "I don't much like you, Talon. But I've never heard anyone play the flute so beautifully, Beryl. I hope you might play it again and perhaps sing for me while in Riviera," he said, eagerly.

Beryl grinned. "You heard! And you liked it! I'm glad. I've heard so much about Elven music, I'd been afraid you might laugh at me for mine. I was hoping I might learn more of yours. I know so few Elven songs, but I feared you'd not think it worth the time and effort to try to teach me."

Eladar grinned and then looked at him coyly. "There is much I might teach you," he said, and Beryl blushed at his tone.

TALON sighed. Elves had such a strong effect upon Men, and Lunahr was so young, so innocent. He would have to be sure to stress to King Laranela and Queen Naraena what his expectations were when it came to protecting his young cousin. Amontiri Law was very strict about relationships outside their own people. Nothing must jeopardize propagating the Houses. But it was so hard now, with so many Houses lost and those few that remained already so closely related. There were few enough potential spouses for any of them, and Lunahr was the youngest of them by more than a decade.

"Laren, stop," Lunahr said, in Amontirin so Eladar couldn't understand. "It was so good to see you smile again, to hear you laugh. I'll not let you succumb to melancholy so quickly."

Talon smiled at his young cousin and replied in the same language. "Forgive me, Lunahr. You are right. I should not be so morose, especially as we are so near our destination."

Lunahr switched to Elvish. "Laren? Mightn't we stop in Ardock for even one day, instead of skirting around it? I've never been in a city, I mean a real one, with people in it, and I doubt I'll have the chance for the next seven years at least. Once I'm safely in Riviera, I don't expect they'll ever risk letting me leave again," Lunahr said wistfully. "Please? I'll be ever so careful. I'll do whatever you say. I swear I'll be discreet. I won't even sing or play while I'm there," he promised.

Talon laughed. "You, go for an entire day without singing or playing? That I find impossible to believe," he said affectionately.

"I can do it, I know I can! I might hum a little, or whistle, I'll admit, but I won't sing or play, nothing that might draw attention to me. If I could just hear music, other people's music, new music…," Lunahr said wistfully.

"Talon, if you won't bring him to Ardock, I swear I will, the moment you are gone," Eladar threatened. "I only warn you so you might be there to protect him instead. Surely you know what happens to a songbird when kept in a cage, no matter how gilded? He is such a bright light; I would not see him fade. Give him just one day to balance seven years of captivity against. Does he really ask so much?"

"You reason oddly, even for an Elf, Eladar. Or do you truly view Riviera as a dungeon?" Talon asked.

"If you knew me better, you would know better than to ask. Riviera can be prison enough that one might wish to escape her," Eladar said softly. "I was all of twenty-one when I tried. Oberas told you how well that went. It has taken twenty-two years for my parents to allow me to take wing on my own again. You have kept me waiting a week for you. I have no doubt even now my father fears me lost, that he has his men combing these lands for me, that he might never let me leave home again unescorted," Eladar said bitterly.

"Laren! Then never mind! We mustn't delay Eladar's return. It was selfish of me to think to do so. We should make haste to Riviera and you must speak in Eladar's defense. We were the ones who were late. In fact I will speak for him. It was because of me it took you so long to get here. I'm not used to traveling as you are. I know I slowed you down considerably," Lunahr said, sadly.

"Don't be ridiculous, Lunahr. Were it not for you, I'd still be writhing upon the floor in madness," Talon said in Amontirin.

"The delay was my fault, and I'll take the blame for it," Talon said in Elvish. "Eladar was arguing upon your behalf, that you be allowed to enter the City. After what he has said, I cannot permit you to do otherwise. I thank you, Eladar, for seeing and understanding my cousin's heart so well. Love often blinds us to the needs of the very person we seek to protect. Perhaps I might open your parents' and your siblings' eyes in relation to you as well. So far you have done admirably, in waiting for us, despite out lateness, when many of your kind or mine would have departed in annoyance. And you saved a life, when you were under no obligation to, a fine Man who deserved to live. You have done exceptionally well so far, and I will be sure to let your family know."

ELADAR looked at Talon in surprise. He had certainly not tried to win Talon's approval. Far from it, he had teased and goaded him on more than one occasion. "Thank you, Majesty," Eladar said, with a small bow of his head, acknowledging for the first time Talon's rank of King, though Talon yet bore the title of Prince for strange political reasons which his people had not yet been able to fathom.

"So, it is off to Ardock, Beryl," Talon said in Elvish, smiling indulgently at his young cousin.

Eladar couldn't help grinning as well, as Beryl looked in astonishment from Talon to him and back again. Beryl's face lit with joy, and he began singing, his sweet clear voice dancing upon the wind.

Chapter 2
Aspiring Apprentice

"TELL me again, Mother?" Rion urged, his blue eyes wide and bright.

Alissa laughed, setting off a fit of coughing.

Rion sat up in concern, but his mother smiled reassuringly at him and drank from the cup beside the pitcher of water by his bed.

"I'm fine, Rion," she said. They both knew it was a lie. "Honestly, you know that story by heart. I swear you memorized it the first time I told it to you, though you must not have been four at the time."

"Please, Mother? If my apprenticeship comes through, I'll be leaving next week, and I won't get to hear it again for seven years, and by then I'll be all grown up, too old to tuck in and...." Tears wet his eyes. They both knew she'd not still live. Even now, at night, it was a struggle for her to breathe. He'd heard his parents speaking about it; he'd heard the healer. His mother had taken to sleeping in her rocking chair in the family room. It was far easier for her to breathe sitting than lying down.

IT TORE Alissa's heart to see the anguish in her son's eyes, when they had always been such a laughing blue. He had his father's eyes, and his eyes were one of the things she'd always loved most about him.

"All right, I surrender, Rion," she said, forcing a smile. Then she grew serious as she began her tale. "It is such an amazing thing, to be sixteen and on your own in a city as large as Ardock. Denor is such a tiny town, on the wrong side of the Methris and too far from the Southern Road to get most travelers. Even most of the boats don't stop there. There is seldom a need to, since Alridge is always their last stop in any case. No one dares try to sail the River further, for the Elves." She looked thoughtful and wistful, as she always did, when she mentioned the Elves and thought about their River and their Woods.

Then she smiled and continued. "If I'd stayed in Denor, I'd have had to do more than sing for my supper, and I was far too virtuous and prideful to ever consider it. I'd had the fortune to be born with a pleasing voice, as well as a comely face and body, and I played the mandolin, even then. Yet there is a reason strolling minstrels are men. But I get ahead of myself. I always do, don't I?" she asked and smiled. Her smile was natural this time. The lines of worry and illness softened with it.

"Four weeks after Father died, a merchant boat came downriver and docked outside of Denor for supplies. The night the boat came, there was such an uproar in our town. As I said, few boats stopped there, and they were going on about how they needed to restock to make the crossing to Ardock because the Master Trader refused to stop in Alridge. He was boycotting them for some reason or other, for something that had happened on his last voyage.

"Old Lathrin tried to tell them they couldn't possibly sail past Alridge, for the Elves, that they wouldn't allow such a crossing. But the merchant, Oberas, laughed, not a friendly laugh at all, but a laugh at how foolish we all were, trying to tell him how to do his business. He told us he could do as he pleased, that he traveled the Elves' lands and their waters by their grace. He said he'd done so more than once.

"Oberas was neither young nor handsome, but he had height and presence, and remarkably broad shoulders. It looked like he might have been well muscled when he was younger. He still had an impressive build, though much of it was padded by fat, particularly about his middle. Still, he was intriguing. And such clothes! Never had I seen such richly made clothes in such garish colors.

"He went into the inn, the only one, the Thorny Rose. I followed. I had to. It sounded like he might speak more about the Elves." She blushed prettily. "I was besotted with the Elves even then, before ever seeing one myself, for the pictures in Father's book, the one he started to write. I've told you about it, about how he only wrote ten pages, then drew the picture of the Elf he'd seen and drew it again and a third time, until finally there were twenty-two drawings, and none was perfect enough. He never got past that point.

"When I buried him, I thought I should bury the book with him, as it meant so much to him. But I couldn't bear to put it into the ground for some reason. It just didn't seem right to bury that face he'd drawn. So I left the book on top of the grave. Then that night, I realized how foolish I was, that here I had a piece of my father I might treasure always, that I might share when I had children of my own.

"I went back to his grave the next morning to recover the book, but it was gone. In its place was a single white mourning lily, not picked, but growing from the soil of the grave. It must have been the Elves. I know it must have. They must not have taken offense at the pictures, or they'd not have left the flower."

Then she laughed. "But here I'm at Father's grave four weeks earlier, when I should be at the inn! I'd never have made a living as a storyteller, I talk all in circles when I try, don't I? So then, let's see... ah, that's where I was!

"So, I followed Oberas into the inn. But he ignored all of us and ordered his dinner. Keegan, the innkeeper, asked me to sing and play, though not to entertain the merchant. He could tell he'd be hard to please. But because the inn was filled, but they'd soon leave without reason to stay. Besides, he'd been Father's friend and he could see I needed the coin.

"I'd never been so nervous in all my life, singing and playing, as I was that night. I was so worried about what the rich merchant might think of me! So I played something safe and happy, 'The Moonlit Garden.' I'll admit, at the start my voice did warble a little, and I hit more than one false note, for the trembling in my hands.

"Oberas rose from his table and walked over to me, flanked by his four guards. He tossed a coin into the bowl at my feet and my eyes widened, for it was a five-gold piece. My heart fluttered in pride for an instant, until over the strains of my mandolin I heard his voice, cutting and cruel. 'For payment such as that, you must take requests, but I've only one to make. Cease your caterwauling at once, you bumpkin, before I lose my dinner as well as my appetite.'

"I just stared at him, astonished that he might say such a thing, when everyone else ever only had praise for me," she said, her voice still betraying her incredulity at it.

"'Ah, much better,' he said, at my silence, and returned to his seat.

"My face flushed so hotly! I was shaking, and I reached down and took the coin, more coin than I'd ever seen at one time in my life, enough to feed me for weeks, and I carried it back to him. I slapped it down onto the table in front of him. 'Your pittance cannot buy what you will now hear,' I said. And I stalked back to the hearth and began to sing and play. The song just rose up from my throat, from the strings, as if Meloneth himself were guiding me. I sang 'The Ballad of Riverwalker.'

"You've heard me sing it, though I don't sing it often; it's too sad by far. It's the one about the Elven maiden and the hunter, the mortal Man who sees her bathing naked in the river and instantly falls hopelessly in love with her. How she sees him watching her and instead of fleeing or punishing him, rises from the waters to stand before him. He is mesmerized by her, enchanted by her. She takes his hand and leads him into a tunnel within the riverbank. He spends one glorious night in her bed and awakens at the river's edge, alone.

"He at first thinks it must have been but a dream, but in his hand he finds she gifted him an Elfstone. Some people swear they are emeralds, but I think they are more, or why would the Elves value them? Then he searches desperately for the opening in the bank, only to find there is none.

"He spends the rest of his life wandering, walking the banks of every river in the land, calling to her, but never finding her, until finally he wastes away to nothing but a voice. To this day, when you call out in a river valley, you hear his voice calling back to you, hoping against hope it might be she who is answering him." Her voice trailed off almost to a whisper. Then she forced a smile. "It's an allegory, of course, to explain why you hear an echo, but also, to warn Man against the folly of ever loving an Elf.

"I don't know what possessed me to sing it to Oberas. I suppose it's because it's so complex, but also so mysterious, so forlorn, not at all something you can scoff at. And breath held, I looked at him. My eyes had been focused on the river in my mind. I only then started to see the room again, the people.

"I was amazed. It was dead silent. It was clear many of them had wept; even Lathrin's face was stained by tears. But the one that surprised me the most was Oberas. There was such a look of pain on his face, of loss, of longing. He pushed aside his plate, food still piled high upon it, and rose from the table surrounded by his guards, and left the room without a word, heading for the stairs.

"I just watched him go. I felt so odd, like I'd crossed a bridge somehow, and turned to look behind me, and then seen that it had fallen into the river, and there was no way home. But I left for home anyway, of course.

"The merchant's boat left the next morning with Oberas and all the rest on it. When I worked up the nerve, I left my house and went to Keegan, to apologize for upsetting his customers. But he greeted me with a fatherly smile and said, 'You did nothing of the kind, Alissa. Many of them stayed till nearly dawn, drinking and talking, the ones who lived alone. They couldn't bear to return alone to an empty house, after hearing your song. I made quite a profit last night. As did you,' he said, handing me a small but heavy purse.

"'What's this?' I asked, opening it and staring at the coin in amazement.

"'It's what they left for you in the bowl, after you left,' Keegan said. I just stared and stared, I couldn't believe it. Denor's not a poor village, but far from rich, yet there was at least five gold in coin, enough to make up for the single large coin I'd returned.

"'But that's not all. The merchant, Oberas, left this for you,' he said, handing me a heavy folded parchment, sealed with golden wax, with a stylized 'O' imprinted upon it.

"I opened it, not knowing what to expect. I was lucky that Father had taught me to read. I was the only one in the village who could. Father had been silly to teach me, of course. What use has a girl for learning her letters, when so few men can read? I still love him for it. Anyway, the letter was short, and to the point.

> *Honored Minstrel,*
>
> *I am a fool.*
>
> *Master Trader Oberas of Ardock*

And stuck with wax, beside the word 'fool,' was a twenty-gold piece. Twenty! I just stared at it. I couldn't believe it! Neither could Keegan, when I showed it to him.

"'Alissa,' he said, 'your talent is wasted here. You should go to Alridge or Sarna. You've the coin now to make the journey. Pay for a berth on the next boat that comes or join a caravan. If you can impress a man like that, you can impress a worthier one. You're old enough to be finding a husband, and there are few enough prospects for you here. All the young men go to the cities to find their fortunes. There's little to keep them here. Your father, may Laneth watch over him always, never meant to leave this world so suddenly, to leave you so ill-provided for. I'll help see you safely away from here. I'll make sure you don't fall in with thieves or worse.'

"And that's what I did," Alissa said, eyes distant with the memory. "Only I went overland, because I didn't want to go to Alridge or Sarna. I wanted to go to Ardock," she said, choking on the word. She began coughing again, worse than before, bending over double on Rion's bed.

Hands shaking, Rion reached for the cup she'd drunk from before and forced it into her hands, water spilling everywhere. She drank from it gratefully, but the coughing did not ease.

The tears in her eyes began brimming over, and then she lost all control and started sobbing in terror as she fought to breathe.

"Father! Father!" Rion called out, panicked, putting his small arm about her shoulder, vainly trying to calm her.

His father burst into the room and pulled her away from Rion, glaring at him. "Alarion, I've told you she can't tell you stories at night anymore! You know what the healer said! You know better than to keep her here talking!" Anorion scolded his son.

He wrapped his large, strong arms around his wife and spoke to her in a softer tone. "It's all right, Alissa, you're all right. You just have to catch your breath. Breathe, Alissa, you have to breathe. Don't try to talk," he soothed, his hand stroking her back.

Gradually, she calmed, and the coughing began to ease. She was gasping for air until slowly breathing became easier. "There, that's it, that's better. I'll get you some tea with honey. That's helped before, hasn't it?" he said and began walking out of the room with her.

"Wait," she whispered, resisting her husband's guiding arms. She pulled away from him for a moment and went to Rion, hugging him tightly. Then she pushed him gently back onto the bed, pulled his blanket up to his chin, and kissed him on the forehead.

His eyes were bright with tears, some of them escaping to roll down his cheeks. She brushed at them with her hand, forcing a smile, and turned quickly away. He could see it broke her heart to see his tears for her. Then she left with his father, heading downstairs.

Rion lay listening to the silence. There wasn't supposed to be silence. He was supposed to be soothed to sleep by the gentle murmur of his parents talking, or better still, by his mother's singing and playing. But it had been months since his mother had been able to sing and now sometimes she could scarcely talk. It was worst at night, when she tried to sleep.

There should be something he could do to help her, something his father could do, or the healer. He didn't blame his father for scolding him. Rion could see how helpless his father felt, how it tore him up inside that, strong and brave and skilled as he was as a City Guard, this time there was nothing he could do to save her.

Rion hugged his pillow tightly and began sobbing silently into it. He'd not let his mother nor father hear. He'd not add to the pain he saw in their eyes.

Rion had cried enough that he felt calmer again when he heard the door open and the light spilled in from the hall. He pretended to be asleep. He could hear his father's soft steps.

"Alarion? Are you awake?" his father asked.

Rion didn't answer.

"FORGIVE me, Alarion. It's not your fault. You must know it's not. I love you, son," Anorion said softly, leaning over to kiss his son's forehead. Anorion was startled when he felt two little arms wrap around him. His son was trembling. Alarion was small for ten. Many of his friends' sons were almost a foot taller. But for all his small size, his grip was strong.

"I love you too, Father. Please don't feel bad for scolding me. You were right, I do know better. Only she so wanted to tell me again, and I wanted to hear it.

"Tomorrow night, I'll finish the story for her, so she doesn't have to speak. I'll tell the part about the trip to Ardock and how she was playing and singing in the Square and earned so much, and how those bad men followed her. How they pushed her into the alley and how terrified she was when she realized they didn't just mean to rob her. How you were off shift heading home when you heard her scream, after she bit that evil man's hand, and the scuffling sounds, and how you ran in and took on all four of them, just you alone with your sword, and saved her," Rion said, eyes shining in pride.

"And I'll get the apprenticeship, I know I will, so you won't have to worry about me anymore, and Mother won't. I know she's been so anxious about it. She wants me to grow up to be a City Guard even less than you do. I could be a good one, though, Father, like you. I could help people. I know I'm small now, but I'll grow soon. It's just taking longer for me than for my friends."

"I think you telling the story to her is a fine idea, Alarion. And I know you'd make a fine City Guard; you'll do a fine job no matter what job you have. But the life of a City Guard's not for you, son, and not because of your size. You're smart, you know your numbers and your letters, but most of all, you're good with people. You know their hearts. You'd make an excellent merchant. I'm so glad you've the chance to apprentice, that I saved enough so you could," Anorion said.

So many of his friends had far less coin. Of course, many of them had five or six children to feed, while he only had the one. He'd been so glad Alissa had given him a son, as Alarion was the only child she'd been able to have. He wished they'd been able to give Alarion a brother. He knew how desperately his son wanted one. He couldn't imagine life without his own brother, especially now. At times the support Farion had been giving him through Alissa's illness had been all that kept him going.

"STOP worrying about me, Father. I'll be fine. You take care of Mother. It frightens me that she'll be home all alone while you're on duty," Rion said, regretting it instantly. He knew it frightened his father, too.

"I don't need to apprentice yet. I have until I'm twelve," he said, not really hoping his father would listen. He'd tried to sway him too many times already, without success.

"No, Alarion," Anorion said. "She'll not be alone. Emma and Katlina and her other friends will be taking good care of her. You know it's easier to apprentice the closer to ten you are. Besides, Oberas has an opening now. He'll not have one again for another seven years, until his apprentice is grown and on his own.

"Oberas is a hard man, a cold one; it won't be easy working under him, but he's a Master Trader, one of the wealthiest men in Ardock. He's respected by many." Reluctantly, he added, "And he travels, when many merchants don't. You'll get to see some of the world, as you've always wanted to;

maybe even get a chance to see the Elves. Oberas isn't afraid of them as most people are."

Rion was surprised. He'd not realized his father had thought about that part of it. Traveling was dangerous for merchants, everyone knew it. But Oberas had kept safe enough these eleven years past, since Mother had first met him. And Rion did so desperately want to see the world, and especially to see the Elves. He'd always been disappointed that the Elves lived so nearby but in such seclusion.

It was his secret dream that he might marry an Elf someday. He knew it was foolish, of course. Elves did not marry Men: they mocked them, tricked them, and used them. They were cold and aloof and dangerous—everyone knew that. Only Rion had a hard time believing they might be. So many spoke so wistfully about them. There must be more to them, mustn't there?

His Father smiled at him, and Rion realized he could tell he was far from the worries of home for the moment. "Goodnight, son. Sweet dreams."

Rion nodded and yawned, suddenly sleepy, and snuggled back down into his bed. Then the door closed, and within moments, he was sound asleep.

RION awoke with the dawn, washed and dressed, and then crept downstairs. He had his gold piece with him, the one Uncle Farion had given him last year. He snuck past his mother, who was asleep in her chair. Rion put on his cloak, opened the door, and stepped bravely into the street, mindful of the puddles, pulling the door shut behind him. It had finally rained last night while he slept. He was glad for the rain. It cooled the air and moistened it and washed the dust away and made it easier for his mother to breathe.

Rion looked to the left and right confidently, keeping a careful eye upon his surroundings, making sure he appeared neither furtive nor fearful. Father said it was those who drew attention to themselves or looked like victims that most often became them.

The two-story wooden houses all around him had been scrubbed clean by the rain, the worn, silvered wooden outer walls temporarily darkened to richer tones, and the rainbow of colorfully painted doors, each in a different hue, were all the brighter for it. Many of the window shutters were already open, letting in the morning sun and the cool, sweet air, some already emitting the tantalizing smells of freshly baking bread and roasting meat. Rion's stomach rumbled as his gaze flicked from the buildings to the street for a few moments. There were few horses in this part of the city, but there were still occasional piles of horse droppings, both old and new, that he needed to skirt around.

To his relief, he spotted and traveled in the wake of two City Guardsmen—two he didn't recognize, although he was sure his father would have known them. He'd been nervous about walking alone and was pleased that they walked most of the way to the Market. He felt safer for being in their presence. But four blocks before the Market, they turned left, and he had to turn right. He continued on.

Rion was only two blocks from the Market when a heavy hand came down on his right shoulder. Heart pounding, Rion spun and crouched, ready to kick his attacker and then flee, but he drew up short, stumbling, and barely kept his balance.

"Elmoth, Rion! It's only me," Matt protested, dodging from the kick that didn't come.

"Don't do that!" Rion said in relief. "You scared me out of my wits!"

Matt was ten, too, but a full head taller than Rion and broader, of the same rugged build as his father, not small and slender like Rion. Matt wasn't alone.

"How come you're out here by yourself?" Ric asked. He was eleven. His father was also a City Guard, as was Drew's. Drew was twelve. Currently, he was keeping watch for the rest of them.

"I'm buying some things for my mother," Rion answered.

"She'd not have sent you out by yourself," Ric argued.

"She didn't. I'm doing it from me, for her. I mean, I'm using my own coin. I'm buying her presents," Rion explained.

"Oh! Well, we'll come with you, then, to be sure you're not robbed. Besides, if any of our fathers saw you out alone they'd tell your father for sure," Drew reasoned.

Rion nodded, relieved for the company. He'd never been so afraid as when he'd felt that hand upon his shoulder and thought it was someone who meant to do him harm.

"So, we've not seen you about. We thought you'd already entered your apprenticeship and forgotten to say good-bye," Matt accused.

"Don't be ridiculous! Of course I'll say good-bye. I've wanted to see you all. I've just had to stick close to home," Rion said. Then his voice grew softer. "Mother's worse."

Drew looked at him in sympathy. His own mother had died last year. Her death had been sudden and unexpected. Rion knew Drew hadn't had the chance to be sure she knew how much he loved her. Drew had spoken with Rion about it a lot. Talking to Rion had seemed to help him. Rion was glad he'd been able to help. He enjoyed helping people. He sighed. Guards helped people. Merchants just took their coin.

"So, when does your apprenticeship start?" Ric asked in the sudden silence.

"I'm not certain," Rion said. "I suppose I'll know after the test. It might start right away, or in a week or even two. I'll be sure to say good-bye to you all before the test, just in case Master Trader Oberas won't allow me out after."

"He's testing you?" Ric asked in surprise. "I thought as long as your father paid the fifty gold, you'd automatically become his apprentice. What sort of test?"

"I'm not sure, really. Reading, I think, and sums, I suppose. I've been learning all I can about how much different goods are worth," Rion said, relieved his friends seemed so interested. He'd not spent much time at all with them lately, and he'd been afraid they might have been angry with him for it, or worse, forgotten about him altogether. "Father has to pay five gold just for me to take the test. Then it's fifty more if I pass. It's a big responsibility. I have to do well."

"So, what are you buying?" Matt asked.

"Flowers for Mother, to remind her of me, a plant, for her to take care of when I'm gone, not cut ones, not ones that... would wilt," he said, swallowing. *Not ones that would die*, he'd thought, but he hadn't been able to give voice to the word.

He was surprised to feel Drew's hand on his shoulder. "Don't worry, Rion. My older sister Stasia is going to help your mother when you're gone. I heard her and Father talking about it. And Ric's and Matt's mothers are going to help, too, and some of Father's other friends, ones we don't know, the ones without children our age, or worse, with girls," he said scornfully. Drew had little use for girls; none of them did yet, though Rion knew that would change.

Rion was relieved to hear Drew speak about the help Mother would get. His parents had told him the same thing, but now he could believe it better.

They were at the Market, now. The farmers' fruit and vegetable carts and wagons were already swarming with customers eager to get the freshest produce available. The fish stands were doing a thriving business as well. The wondrous aroma of fresh breads and cakes coming from the three bakers had Rion's mouth watering and made his stomach rumble again more loudly than before. But Rion knew just where he wanted to go. He'd get the plant first. He couldn't risk someone else buying the one he'd had his eye on. He was afraid it might already be gone.

Afterward, he'd buy some bread, so Mother wouldn't have to bake, and then some kakla. They'd been carefully rationing their beans, having only a couple of cups of kakla a week for months. They'd been saving all their coin for the apprenticeship fee. He'd get some citrons too, if he could find any, for Mother's tea.

Rion went to the stall of the man selling plants, hoping the one he wanted was still there. He'd seen it five days ago, and it was perfect. The flowers were blue, Mother's favorite color, and it was even in a blue ceramic pot.

Rion didn't see it at first, but after looking more carefully he was relieved to find it half hidden behind a number of white flowers in pots of different bright colors, thankful it hadn't been sold to someone else. Rion looked at a number of other plants, pretending to be interested in this one or that, asking their prices, and then, as if it were nothing special to him, he asked the price of the blue flowers.

"That one's ten silver," the merchant said. "Those flowers only grow in the mountains. It's rare we get them that color here."

Rion hid his dismay. The asking price was so high! "Really? I'm surprised. I can't imagine anyone paying more than two silver for it," Rion said, starting the haggle.

The merchant looked at him and laughed. "Why would I take such a small sum?"

"Because there's a chip on the pot, in the back, where you put the leaves over to cover it. Also, no one wants blue this time of year. They all want white, for Feast Day. Besides, you've had this plant for at least a week. I've seen it before. Most of the buds have bloomed already. In a week's time, it will be mostly green," Rion said confidently.

The merchant eyed him in surprise and dawning respect and suggested seven silver, substantially lower than the sum he'd first named. Rion had expected his next offer would have been eight at the lowest, and he'd been afraid it might be nine. Encouraged, he continued.

After a decent amount of bargaining, they agreed upon the price of five silver and three copper. "Done," they both said, and Rion crossed two fingers against the merchant's, in the universal gesture that the haggle was over. Then he opened his other hand and handed the man his gold piece.

"A gold! You talked me down so far from ten, when you had a gold!" the man grumbled.

"Yes, sir. Forgive me, but I had to. I've so much else I still need to buy, you see, and that's all the coin I have, all I've ever had. The plant is for my mother. She's very ill and I'm starting an apprenticeship next week, if I pass the test, and I wanted her to have it, to cheer her. She'll be so lonely with me gone, and I'm worried about her," Rion explained.

"If you'd told me so before, you might have gotten me to lower my price more," the merchant said honestly.

"Really?" Rion asked in surprise. "Thank you, sir, I'd not known that! You see, I'm going to apprentice to be a merchant. I'm glad to know there are other ways to haggle. I certainly don't like finding fault with people's wares. I know you take great pride in them. But I was told that's how it's done.

"It's just a tiny chip, actually, and it really is a beautiful pot. Blue's my mother's favorite color. I was so relieved to see you still had it. I saw it five days ago, but I didn't have my coin with me, and then Mother was too ill for me to go out since then. In fact, I had to sneak off today, before she woke up. I couldn't risk waiting longer. I was already afraid it might be gone and I was afraid the flowers might all be wilted even if it was it still here."

The man handed him his change, and Rion accepted it and carefully counted it, as he'd been taught, to ensure he'd not been cheated. His eyes widened in surprise, and he held out a silver. "Sir, you've given me too much."

The merchant smiled at him. "Did I now? Well, then, you'd best keep it, boy. That will teach me to take better count now, won't it?" Then he added conspiratorially, "It's lucky for me I only paid two silver for it. I got it at a discount myself for the chip in the pot. Five is the usual price for it, so I still managed to make a good profit after all. Oh, but wait, don't go. First, I've a bow for the pot. It's blue as well, the same shade as your eyes. I'm sure your mother will like it," he said, smiling broadly. "I usually charge as much as five copper for one of these, more when I can get away with it," he said, confidentially. "But this one is a gift from me. You've talent, lad, and a good heart. Good luck on your test. And may Mereth watch over your mother, as well."

Rion grinned in delight and thanked him effusively, leaving with his prize.

Ric shook his head in wonder. "Who ever heard of someone adding an item to a purchase after the price has already been agreed upon! And both sides, the buyer and the seller with such smiles! It's good to see you happy again, Rion. You were born to trade. Your father's right. You'd have been wasted as a Guard. I only wish my tongue had half the skill of yours. It might have spared me more than a few scoldings," he said, laughing. Rion laughed too, basking in the warmth of the praise and his friends' company.

Rion bought the bread, kakla, and four large citrons and still had two silver and three copper left. Then he bought some sweet buns for his friends and his mother and father, and carefully held his last silver. "Can you walk me home? I'm afraid it's taken me longer than I expected, and I'd make a tempting target so laden down, and Father would be sure to scold me for being out alone," Rion entreated.

Matt laughed. "You need not haggle with us to help you, Rion. We'd do so in any case."

Rion blushed and then grinned at the gentle teasing. But when he got home, it was good his friends had come with him, for the look on his father's face. His father scowled darkly at him, then eyed his packages. "Alarion, where have you been? I was just about to go out looking for you. Haven't I told you not to go out alone?" he scolded.

"But sir, he wasn't alone. We were with him," Ric said, in Rion's defense.

"I see, Adric. Is that so? From the moment he set foot outside the door?" Anorion asked, eyeing his friend Cedric's son shrewdly.

"Um… no, sir," Ric admitted, swallowing.

"But I was safe, Father. I followed two City Guardsmen almost the whole way to the Market and then my friends found me," Rion said.

"And what's all this?" his father asked suspiciously, eyeing the packages Rion was carrying.

"Presents for Mother," Rion said, his voice sinking to a whisper, fearful of what his father might say to him about spending his only coin.

"And how did you get them?" his father asked imperiously.

"With the gold piece Uncle Farion gave me," Rion admitted. "I bought the plant for Mother, to cheer her, and the loaf of bread so she'd not have to bake and the kakla because you've both been rationing it because of me. And I bought the citrons for her tea, because the healer said they might help, but they'd been so expensive we'd not gotten any before. Oh, and then I got the sweet buns for breakfast, for both of you. I know how much Mother has missed them. And I bought some for my friends, too, to thank them for keeping me safe." Rion turned to them and said, "Thank you all again. I'll see you later."

His friends left at his urging, though they were obviously reluctant to do so when he was still in trouble.

His father glowered. "You can't possibly have bought so much for a single gold."

"Oh, but I did! Except I've one silver left over. You can have it, Father. I know you've not had any coin for mead for three whole months now, with the healer and the elixirs and the coin for my apprenticeship. But soon I won't be such a burden," Rion said, trying desperately hard not to cry, as fear of the future clutched his heart.

ANORION sighed. He'd so feared Alarion might have gotten hurt or even killed on the streets alone. And with a gold piece! But at least he'd been careful.

"Come inside, but quietly. Your mother's still sleeping. She's not slept so well in weeks. If the smell of the kakla brewing doesn't waken her, we'll let her sleep," Anorion said, and tousled his son's hair.

RION nodded, relieved his father no longer seemed angry nor afraid for him. He so wished he might be bigger and stronger, like his friends, so Father need not worry about him so much.

"Alarion, there must be five pounds of kakla here," his Father said in surprise.

"There is. And they're good beans too, not the stale ones the merchant first tried to sell me, before he found I knew the difference," Rion said, grinning in pride.

His father shook his head and smiled. "I can't see why you're worried about the test, with skills such as you already possess," Anorion said, admiringly.

Rion beamed.

A short while later his mother walked into the kitchen. "Is that kakla I smell?"

"It is, thanks to Alarion. He and his friends went to the Market this morning. There are also sweet buns for breakfast and bread for lunch and dinner, and even citrons for your tea. But I'll let Alarion show you the special surprise he got for you," Anorion said, eyes twinkling.

Alissa grinned, seeing her husband look so happy, as he always had before she'd taken ill.

"Close your eyes," Rion said.

Rion could see she was reluctant to do so. She stole one last look at Anorion's smiling face, then did as Rion requested. Rion took the flowering plant out of the cupboard where he had hidden it. "All right, Mother, you may open them now."

She did so and her eyes widened. "Oh, Rion! It's so beautiful!" she said, stroking the silken ribbon with her finger and breathing in the scent of the blossoms. Then she hugged him and kissed him and told him how much she loved him.

Rion squirmed happily at the fuss she made over him. It was one of the most wonderful moments of his life, the three of them, so happy together. He knew he'd cherish it always.

THE next morning Rion awoke at first light, surprised to smell the kakla already brewing, His father was up early, or perhaps he'd not gone to sleep. Today was the big day: Rion would be meeting Oberas, along with the other potential apprentices, and Oberas would be testing all of them.

Rion pulled on his new shirt with trembling hands. It was blue, like his eyes, and it had buttons, real brass buttons down the front, instead of a lace at the neck. Mother and Father had noticed Oberas wore shirts with buttons himself, and they'd wanted him to appear presentable, so they'd bought it especially for the test. He'd be able to use it as an apprentice, too, of course.

Rion carefully tucked his shirt into his pants as his father had shown him; he was used to tunics. He pulled on his socks and slipped on his boots. The soles and heels of his boots were getting fearfully worn, but his parents hadn't the coin to go to the cobbler to mend them; they'd thought a new shirt more important. Rion felt their decision was a good one. He was certain his growth spurt would hit any time now, and he'd need to replace the boots anyway. So he'd polished his worn boots to an extra sheen to mask their age.

Rion combed his hair carefully, using his parent's mirror, the one of polished silver, to make sure it looked just right. Then he went downstairs. He met his father at the bottom of the steps.

"Ready already? And here I was just coming to wake you. Let me take a look at you. My, don't you look fine. I hate to waken your mother, but she'd never forgive me if she didn't get to see you looking so grown up and to have a chance to give you a good-luck kiss," Anorion said. "Why don't you eat breakfast first, and then I'll wake her."

"Oh Father, please don't make me eat! I'm afraid I'll throw up if I eat anything. I've bats in my stomach, you know, the big scary looking ones that hang under the bridge in that story Mother's always telling me. I'll eat twice as big a lunch after the test, I promise," Rion pleaded.

"All right. I can't say I blame you. I felt the same way myself, when I was interviewed and tested for the City Guard, which is pretty ridiculous, considering your Uncle Farion was already a Guardsman. The only difference is, I forced myself to eat and I did throw up, all over the boots of the Captain who tested me," Anorion said, grimacing at the memory.

"You did? Really? You never told me that story!" Rion said, amazed his father had revealed it now.

Anorion laughed. "Of course I never told you! It's not something I'm proud of, but I figured now would be a good time to confess to it. Lucky for me Captain Mitchell liked my brother Farion so much. He still hired me, though the first job he gave me was to clean and polish his boots!" Rion's father said, shaking his head at the memory.

"And those of half a dozen others in the garrison for good measure! It was years before I found out that last part was Farion's doing, though I'd wondered at the time why all the men chosen happened to be friends of his!" he added, laughing, and Rion laughed with him, some of his anxiety lessening for it. He realized that was probably his father's intent in telling him the tale.

"Now let's go wake your mother."

They both crept into the family room. Alissa was sleeping soundly for a change, her breathing sounding smooth and easy for sitting in her rocking chair. Anorion stroked her hair and kissed her brow, then gently shook her. "Alissa, honey, it's time for Rion's test. You can go back to sleep in a few moments, after you give him his good-luck kiss."

Alissa awoke, yawning and stretching. She smiled at Anorion and Rion, and then her eyes widened in surprise. "Goodness! You're already dressed. Anorion, you should have awakened me earlier! I could have helped him get ready," she said, scolding her husband gently, still smiling at him fondly.

His mother was so lovely, and her smile was almost magical. She'd smiled too seldom lately. But she'd apparently slept well last night. Rion hoped it might continue and that perhaps with the coming of the rains, the illness might be less severe for a time and give her a chance to regain her strength.

"He's a big boy, now, Alissa. He can dress himself, even in fancy clothes such as these," Anorion said.

"Look at my boots, Mother! I spent the longest time yesterday shining them. Do I really look all right?" Rion asked.

She grinned. "More handsome than ever, Rion. Although I'm sure you don't need me to tell you that. One day soon all the girls will be saying so, if they're not already."

He blushed and impulsively went to her. "If I'm handsome, Mother, it's because I got my looks from you. You're the most beautiful woman in the City, and the most wonderful mother anywhere," he said, hugging her.

"And you are the most wonderful son a mother could hope for, Rion," she said, returning the hug and kissing him.

"I see. So your looks had nothing to do with mine, is that it?" Anorion teased his son.

Alissa laughed and Rion blushed and then laughed as well. "Don't be silly, Father! I've your looks as well. I've mother's smile, but I've your eyes. I've the best of both of you," Rion said.

"That's my little silver-tongued merchant," Alissa teased, and Rion laughed. "Now give me another hug and a kiss, and then off with both of you. I don't want you to be late." Rion hugged and kissed her and then left with his father.

They walked down street after street, his father confidently turning this way and that. Rion's father knew every street in Ardock, and Ardock was a sizable city.

"Anorion! My, my! Doesn't Alarion look fancy today?" Justin said with a smile as he came upon them. Justin was Uncle Farion's best friend and roommate; the two men had been as close as brothers since before Rion was born, like Father and Cedric. Justin was dressed in his City Guard uniform but walking alone, so Rion realized he must either be heading to the Tower or coming from it and not on patrol. The City Guard always only ever patrolled in pairs: it was safer that way.

"Justin!" Anorion said, greeting him with a hearty shoulder clasp. "That he does indeed. I'm taking Alarion for his test this morning."

"Oh, has Oberas come back then?" Justin asked, looking surprised.

"What do you mean come back?" Anorion asked.

"You mean you hadn't heard? It's the talk of the Market. Oberas is seven days overdue as of yesterday. Oberas is never late; if anything, he usually returns early. Some folks are starting to say he's not coming back this time," Justin said.

"We'd best still go to his shop and see what we can learn. Perhaps he arrived last night. Thanks, Justin," Anorion said, looking troubled.

"Good luck," Justin said and continued on his way.

"Father? What do we do, if Oberas isn't back?" Rion asked.

"We'll worry about that if we've a need to," Anorion replied.

They reached Oberas's shop, and sure enough, there was a sign on the door with the symbol for "closed" and the word below it. Anorion couldn't read more than a handful of words, but he'd seen that one often enough to know what it said even without the symbol. He scowled at the door and pounded upon it.

"Who's there?" a voice asked from inside.

"Lieutenant Anorion of the City Guard. My son is supposed to test with Master Trader Oberas today," Anorion said. He was already wearing his uniform, though he had the afternoon shift today; he'd traded with Farion for it.

The door opened, and a man wearing the uniform of Oberas's guards said, "I'm sorry, sir, but Oberas has yet to return. We're worried about him. He's never late. He's always ever only back early. We've filed a report with the City Guard about it, in case he makes it into the City but just not back to us, somehow, or in case someone reports seeing something north of here. But we have a list he left of all the apprentice candidates. We're asking the folks who come to write their names on it, those who can, or make their marks, so he knows who came by. If you'd care to come in for that, you're welcome to," the guard said.

"All right. Alarion, you write your name and mine, and that we were here and when," Anorion said.

The guard led them inside and showed them to the list, which was set out on a table, along with a pen, ink, and drying sand. Rion wrote beside his name on the paper, taking extra care with his letters to be sure they were neat. He was discouraged to see so many names. There were twelve boys altogether, six listed for yesterday and six for today. But he was encouraged that only four of the six had shown up yesterday, and of those only one of the boys who had signed had written his name. The other three had each only left their marks at the bottom of the column, not knowing which name was theirs. He was the first boy on the list for today. He wondered how many others might come for their tests later in the day. Even if they all did, he was still confident he might be the one chosen, if only he could be tested. He knew his letters and numbers and prices of goods in the market, and he'd done well buying the flowering plant and other things for his mother.

"We'll see that Oberas sends someone along, either to reschedule the boy's test, or to refund your coin," the guard said. "My name is Devrik, in case you've need of it." He looked at Rion and smiled. "Don't worry, son. Oberas has a habit of living through things that by all rights he shouldn't. I wouldn't be surprised if he comes through whatever trouble he's had this time as well. He's a survivor. You can do far worse than work for a man such as him."

Rion smiled back at him. Then Devrik turned to Anorion. "You've a fine lad, there. Between you and me, I hope he gets it."

Anorion looked at Devrik in surprise, and the guard smiled and explained. "You should have seen some of the spoiled young upstarts that came by here yesterday, strutting in, acting like they owned the place: second son of a carpenter, third son of a blacksmith, and fourth son of a potter. Each with older brothers to inherit their fathers' businesses, looking down their noses at us 'mere guards,' even though we was so much taller than the lot of 'em, they had to look up to look down at us!" he said laughing.

"Meanwhile, Curtis and I have been doing them a favor by answering the door while Oberas is away. We're not supposed to. Oberas is afraid thieves might trick us or force their way in." He smiled ruefully. "Like as not Oberas will yell at us for it when he comes back. I already told Curtis I'll take the blame. He's a sister and her son he helps feed; her husband was killed last year, just after the baby was born. Whereas me, I'm on my own."

"It eases my heart, speaking with you," Anorion said. "No offense, but Master Oberas does have quite a reputation for harshness. I've had some doubts about apprenticing Alarion to him, I'll admit. It's nice to know that he has such fine and caring men working under him."

Devrik eyed Rion again, this time thoughtfully. "Tell me, is your son of a sensitive nature? He seems quiet and he's got a pleasant disposition and a slim build," he said hesitantly.

Anorion smiled. "And you're tactful as well! I know, Alarion's small for his age—he's the first to admit it—and it's true he's sensitive, but in a good way. He's also tough. He doesn't cave to criticism and start crying. He works twice as hard to do better. And he's seldom quiet!" Anorion added with a laugh.

Devrik nodded. "Ah. Well, if I don't have to mince words… Oberas yells, frequently and loudly. He can make even a grown man feel the size of a gnat or as worthy as a worm with little effort. We've had four apprentices in the last six months. Two of them quit—he drove them off—and the other two he sent packing. Each lost half his apprentice fee, as per the contract he'll have you sign, twenty-five gold apiece.

"The work's tough. Oberas will have him doing writing and figuring with numbers, but also some lifting. He'll expect your boy to load and unload cargo, to pack and unpack things. Do you think he can? If not, you're better off losing the five gold you already invested than risking twenty-five more. Actually, he can't hold you to the five, either, since he was the one who didn't show for the test, not you, so you'll be getting that returned as well."

"Are you saying he never means to have an apprentice at all? That he just tricks people and seizes half their fee?" Anorion asked quietly. Rion swallowed. He could tell his father was enraged for the soft tone of his voice.

"No, not at all. Perhaps I've said too much," Devrik said, mollifying him. "Oberas has had three apprentices in the past twenty years that all did their seven years and became Master Traders themselves. Each of the other times he overlapped contracts, though it's not a common practice. He'd tried to do so this time as well. It helps to have the older ones teach the younger ones the ropes for the first six months or so. But Kenneth was eager to be off on his own, now that his contract was done.

"He and the other two have each done quite well for themselves. Without exception they've settled in cities outside of Ardock; that's in the contract, too. It's just that Oberas chewed up and spat out eighteen others to get those three.

"You should hear how much worse he is on guards! I've been here four years now. It's the only reason Oberas felt comfortable enough leaving the shop at all, without a seasoned apprentice to watch it. Most guards last three months under him, some as much as six. Few go longer, and the ones that do stay do it for the most part because he pays so high. I'll say that for him: his guard, food, wine, clothes, only the best will do.

"Your son dressed and groomed well today. The farmer's son yesterday was filthy and stank of manure and horses. It must have been months since he's had a bath. And the blacksmith's son was nearly as dirty, still smelling of the forge and hair every which way. Oberas cares about things like that. Those two would have been hard pressed after an impression like that to get the spot. Meanwhile, your son is dressed so fine, and smells clean, and his hair is all neat. And he writes, too, when most can't.

"Oberas likes it when his apprentices can already write. It's one thing less he has to teach them. He tries to have at least one of his four guards write, too. Logan's the one who does, now, of the four of us. I hope he's all right. He's getting old, now, to be a guard: he's twenty-four. He and Willis went with Oberas this trip, with two other men he hired a few months before the journey, Gregory and Temris. He usually brings four and returns with eight, then keeps the best two left alive, to add to the two already here.

"That's the other reason I've stayed so long. For most merchants, if a guard dies, it means lost time and coin for training him. With Oberas, if ever he loses a man, it hurts him. It hits him hard, even when it's one you'd have sworn he never really liked. Especially those. The ones he yells at the most, especially the young ones, are the ones that seem to hurt him the most.

"For all his faults, and he has many, he's a good man. He eats too much, he's been getting fatter, he drinks too much sometimes, though not often, and he yells to excess. Oh, and he hits, too, sometimes," Devrik added, and Rion swallowed, listening intently and wide-eyed.

Devrik smiled at Rion. "Never his apprentices, though, only his guard, if ever they do something foolish that endangers someone. Especially if they endanger themselves, strangely enough. He says the ground is full enough of stupid and careless men and others who were put there by them, that he'll not help Elmoth claim another. Oh, and about Elmoth. As you're a Guard's son, you probably follow Elmoth at home," he said, looking at Rion. "Be sure never to swear by him in Oberas's presence, not unless you want to see Oberas truly enraged. Oberas isn't a religious man. He doesn't worship Mereth as he should, for being a merchant. It isn't that he's intolerant. It's just that he hates Elmoth for some reason, may Elmoth forgive him for it."

"I'm almost glad Oberas wasn't here today," Anorion said. "You've given us a lot of information we'd lacked before. I hope your friends make it back safely. I guess we'd better be heading home now. Come along, Alarion."

Rion smiled at Devrik. "Thank you, Devrik. I hope to see you again soon," Rion said, the wish heartfelt.

They left the shop and began walking. Rion liked Devrik, and nothing he'd said about Oberas was too frightening, except…. "Father? He said that if I apprentice, I have to sign a contract saying I'll leave the City. But I don't want to leave! How can I leave you and Mother?" he asked forlornly.

"You'd be surprised what a man of seventeen wants to do that a boy of ten might never think he would. You can't let your love of us hold you back, Alarion. Besides, you can still visit. There's no contract that can keep you from doing that.

"Come, let's stop by the Market and pick up something special for your mother. She's bound to be upset about the test being postponed. I want to be sure we bring her something that might cheer her. But we mustn't take too long at it."

Rion nodded eagerly. They entered the Market and began looking. Rion stopped between two stalls, cocking his head and listening. Such odd but beautiful music was coming from down a row of stalls. He followed the sound to a stall filled with gleaming metal and intricately carved stone.

"Come, see the treasures of the Dwarven Lands! From the far Lost Kingdoms, brought to you at tremendous risk to life and limb, treasures no Man has ever seen," a voice proclaimed.

Rion looked about, puzzled. The music had stopped.

"And what might a fine lord's son such as yourself be in the Market for today? A gift for your noble father, perhaps? I have here…." the merchant began.

"The music. Excuse me, sir, for interrupting, but the music has stopped. I know it came from here," Rion said, looking about for the source of it.

The hawker grinned. "Ah, what a keen ear you have, lad! I do indeed have music here, of a kind few Men have ever heard." He held out an ornately carved box of stone. Rion looked at it, perplexed. Then the man lifted the lid, and suddenly the same magical tune began again, exactly as he had heard it before.

A grin of delight lit Rion's face. "May I hold it?"

"Of course," the man said. Rion realized with some guilt that the merchant thought him far richer than he was, for how he was dressed, that he'd never let a ten-year-old son of a City Guard hold such a fine piece, but he had to see the box.

"The Dwarves call them music boxes. It's a wonder of their craftsmanship that they can make an instrument so small and craft it so it can play itself."

Rion listened, enraptured, caressing the carving along the side, holding it carefully. Then he put it down and thanked the man. He would give anything to be able to buy it for his mother, but he knew without asking he could never afford it.

"Young sir, surely you cannot part with it, having held it? You are a gentle of means, I can see that. For a mere one hundred fifty gold it can be yours," he said.

Rion swallowed. One hundred fifty gold? Even though he knew that was probably at least a third above what the merchant hoped to get for it, it was still so much! He had actually held it in his hands? What if he had dropped it, if he had broken it? "No, but thank you, sir," he said, turning away firmly, ignoring the man's enticements.

He looked up at his father, who had been watching but hadn't approached. "It was so beautiful, Father. For Mother to always have music!"

Anorion shook his head. "She'd not have wanted it, Alarion. Those things that man is selling are all pillaged from the Lost Kingdoms. It's like robbing a tomb. No good can come of it. Your mother's music was always so warm, so alive. No cold thing of stone can replace it."

Rion's eyes welled with tears. "But... she can't sing anymore. She can't even play."

Anorion hugged him. "Then you and I will sing for her, today. We'll buy her a new ribbon for her hair so she feels pretty, and buy a meat pie and bread, so she doesn't have to cook lunch for us, and we'll sing to her. We can all eat lunch together, too, remember. Farion has my shift and I his. You and she can split the rest of the pie for dinner. You be sure to see that she eats. And I'll get some sweet cider for after."

Rion nodded. "Can I be the one to bargain, Father?"

Anorion smiled. "Dressed like that? I'm not nearly as good as you are at it, but I think this time you'd best leave the haggling to me, son."

Rion agreed. A short while later they headed for home.

"Father, what will we tell Mother?" Rion asked on the way.

"Don't you worry, you leave everything to me," his Father said, hugging him. "I know it's a big disappointment, son. I'm only thankful if Oberas was going to disappear, that he did so before you began working for him and not after."

Rion wondered what might have happened to Oberas. His imagination was more than up to the task. He came up with a number of theories, each more gruesome than the last, on his way home: bandits, wild beasts, ogres, or illness. He was relieved when they reached home. Lunch and singing would surely lighten his mood. They entered quietly, but immediately realized they needn't have, when they heard the mandolin.

"Anorion! Rion! You can't be finished already!" Alissa said, laying down her instrument. Then she eyed the sacks from the Market and smelled the meat and bread. "Especially not having gone to the Market as well. Surely Rion couldn't have done so poorly!"

"Oberas wasn't there, Alissa. His guard, Devrik, let us in and had us sign that we'd come. Justin told us before we got there that Oberas is a week late coming back from a journey. But Devrik thinks he might yet come," Anorion explained.

"It's all right, Mother. We got to speak to Devrik and learned much more about Oberas. And besides, we'd have missed your playing, if we came later. Please play more, Mother!" Rion urged.

"I really shouldn't have been," Alissa said wistfully. "I've the cooking and washing to do."

"But we've brought enough for lunch and dinner both. I'll do the wash later, Mother. It won't be the first time. I'm good at it now. Please play, Mother?"

She grinned. "How can I resist your heart as well as my own?"

Rion put the food in the kitchen and the ribbon. He'd give it to her later, when the music was done, and she started to cough, or worry, when she needed something to cheer her.

"What shall I play?" Alissa asked when he returned.

"'A Summer's Faire'!" Rion said, enthusiastically. It was his favorite. His Mother began to play and he and his father began to sing. This time Rion didn't even care that his voice still sounded like a girl's.

After the first song, she played three more. Then she began to sing; she couldn't help herself. Rion stopped singing. He held his breath and listened, cherishing each note. He willed her to finish without coughing. She finished the song without a cough, but he could see her smile was strained. It had cost her terrible effort to sing.

"That was beautiful, Mother. But could we eat lunch now and perhaps have more music later?" Rion asked, so she wouldn't dwell upon it. "I'm so hungry."

"Lunch? Rion, it's scarcely past breakfast!" she said, the smile genuine this time.

"I didn't eat breakfast," Rion admitted, blushing.

"What? Anorion! How could you let him go off to be tested without eating," she scolded.

Anorion smiled. "Blame the bats, not me." She looked at him as if he were daft and he laughed. "The ones from that story you tell him. He said they were in his stomach, that he was afraid he'd get sick if he ate, like I did on my Guardsman's test."

"Ah. Well then, I must confess, I am also hungry, since I also skipped breakfast," Alissa said.

The smile left Anorion's face. "Alissa, you have to eat, to keep your strength up."

"I know. I do usually. It's just… I felt so well, I thought I could play. It's been so long since I have. But I said I was hungry now, and I am, and I promise I'll eat, how could I not? What you've brought smells so good. I'll just heat it."

"You'll do nothing of the kind," Anorion said. "I'll build the fire in the oven. You'll either rest or play or listen to Alarion talk. He's as good at it as you are. You need not strain your own voice."

"I can tell you all we found out about Oberas," Rion said, eagerly.

ANORION went into the kitchen and built the fire, then rejoined them. It would take a while for the oven to heat. When he came into the family room, Alarion was talking animatedly about the music box he'd seen and heard. He stopped and looked up at his father.

"You've still time. The oven's not hot yet. Don't stop on my account." He listened to his son enthusiastically describe the music box and the other Dwarven wares he'd seen. Alarion had such an eye for detail. He'd always excelled at the memory games he and his friends played. Anorion had always done well in those same games when he was a child, but nowhere near as well as Alarion.

When the pie was heated, they ate. Anorion was pleased to see Alissa ate with some of her old appetite.

When they were done and he asked what she'd like to do, she said, "I'd like to go out for a walk. They'll be preparing the City for Feast Day. I'm sure they must have at least some of the decorations up. I want to go to the Square and hear the minstrels play."

Anorion looked at her. She looked better than she had in weeks and sounded it. But walking such a distance would put a terrible strain upon her. He had no idea how he could tell her so without crushing her spirit.

"BUT Mother, I was hoping you could play more here. Do I really have to share you with the City? None of the other minstrels are half as good as you. I hoped I could have you all to myself today," Rion argued.

Alissa laughed. "My, my! Well of course, then. I mustn't disappoint my loyal followers."

Rion was relieved his idea had worked. He knew the walk would have been bad for her. It was so hard keeping her safe without her realizing. They spent the rest of the morning and early afternoon singing and playing.

"It's time for my shift," Anorion said, reluctantly.

"Don't look so dejected. I should take a little nap, anyway," Alissa said. "Besides, Rion has the wash to do."

"It's time to pay the minstrel, eh?" Rion said, grinning.

"Honestly, Rion! How can you smile even about doing the wash?" Alissa asked, laughing. The laugh turned into a cough, but a mild one.

Rion fought to keep the smile upon his face as his father kissed her good-bye. "Remember, I'll be late. You mustn't wait up for me."

One look at her face and Rion knew she would. She disliked his father having the later shift. It was more dangerous after dark. She'd need to see his father come home, to be sure he was safe.

Once Anorion was gone, Alissa sat back in her chair, rocking it gently, with her shawl over her and her eyes closed, humming to herself. Rion was relieved when his mother fell asleep. Her breathing had been becoming more labored. She'd been over-exerting herself.

He went into the kitchen. Fortunately they still had four buckets of water. He could do the wash like he'd promised, without having to leave his mother alone while he went to fetch water from the well. The one nearest them was only ten blocks away, but he still didn't like leaving her, even for a little while. He worked hard the rest of the day.

RION woke his mother for supper. He'd built the fire in the oven to warm the leftover pie himself, and managed to only burn himself a little on one arm. Fortunately, he'd had the sense to change his clothes when he did the wash, so he might wear his good shirt for the test, once Oberas returned. He had gotten ash all over his everyday shirt instead.

"Goodness, don't tell me I've slept the day away again," his mother said, dismayed, when he woke her.

"Of course not. You were up for at least half of it, playing and talking and singing. Or did you think it a dream?" Rion teased.

"You are as bad as Anorion," she said, smiling.

They spent a quiet, pleasant evening together, waiting for Anorion to come home. It was after Rion had poured the water for his mother's third cup of tea that he realized his father was late. "I know it's late, but remember, the City is preparing for Feast Day next week. The City always has twice as many folk in it the week before. Many of them are unruly, many will be drinking. Father just has his hands full, that's all," Rion reasoned, hoping to reassure his mother.

Alissa nodded, wordlessly, but she was eyeing the door anxiously.

When there was a knock upon it a short while later, they both jumped. Rion leapt to his feet and ran to the door, his hand upon the sliding bolt. "Who's there?" he asked, eager to hear his father's voice.

"It's Cedric, Alarion," a deep voice said.

Rion's heart started pounding when he recognized the voice of his friend Ric's father. His mother had risen from her rocking chair. Rion could hear her labored breathing as the panic started to rise in her as well. They both knew what it meant when another City Guardsman came to your house instead of whom you were expecting.

Rion slid the bolt free and flung open the door, expecting to see that terrible look of sympathy upon Cedric's face, the one he'd seen far too often when people were trying to console Drew for the loss of his mother.

"Alarion, Alissa, no! It's not what you fear," Cedric said, seeing the terror in their faces, sweeping into the room, going to Alissa and after a moment's hesitation, putting his arm about her.

"Alissa, you have to calm yourself, you have to sit. Anorion's fine, I swear it. He sent me over to you so you'd not worry about him, and so I might stay with you until he comes home. He was worried to leave you alone for so long."

Alissa was gasping for breath, trying to force herself to calm so she could speak.

"But why didn't he come home himself?" Rion asked, voicing her question.

"There was trouble tonight. Some folks new to town for Feast Day were at the Gilded Stein, drinking. Some real troublemakers, apparently. You know the reputation that place has, even during a normal week. A fight broke out and escalated. There must have been at least twenty of us there, trying to pull it apart. It got really ugly. It ended with three dead, ten wounded, and another fifteen arrested, with seven City Guard wounded as well, though none of us seriously, praise Elmoth. Your father's a lieutenant. It's his job to sort through a mess like that, to see that they all get jailed, or tended to by healers, and to arrange for burials. He's still at it, that's all. He knew you'd be starting to worry and would be frantic by the time he finally came."

"I thought...," Alissa said, and began coughing.

"I know, Alissa, hush. You mustn't try to talk. Here, sit," Cedric said, guiding her to her rocking chair.

"Anorion's told me drinking something helps you, but I see you already have tea. Please, Alarion, what can I do for her?"

Rion knew Father rubbed her back, but it wouldn't be appropriate for Cedric to. "Nothing, sir. She'll be fine, once she catches her breath, now that she knows Father's all right." He walked behind his mother's chair and began rubbing her back as he'd seen Father do so many times before. But she turned in the chair and pulled him toward her, and he realized she meant to hug him.

He blushed to have his mother hug him in front of his friend's father, but he realized she needed someone to hold to calm herself, and he certainly preferred her holding him rather than Cedric. He let her hold him and patted her back gently while she did so. He realized she was trembling. Slowly she stopped and the gasping eased and she began to breathe more naturally.

"I've never been so frightened," she whispered and started coughing.

"Mother, please don't speak," Rion begged. "Think how Father would feel, seeing you like this, when you were so much better today," he reasoned.

She nodded mutely.

"Perhaps she should lie down?" Cedric suggested.

"No, sir, she can't. She breathes best sitting. She sleeps in her chair here on the worst days of it. That's it, Mother," Rion soothed.

"See, she's calmer now, she'll be fine," Rion told Cedric, relieved to see she was breathing more easily. Then he asked Cedric if he'd like some kakla or tea.

"I wouldn't mind making some," Cedric said.

"No sir, I can do it. I've done so lots of times. Which do you prefer? We've honey and citron for the tea, and sweet cream and honey for the kakla. They're good beans, I bought them myself in the Market, and we've plenty, honest." Rion had noticed that Cedric seldom came by now for kakla and cake as he used to before Mother was sick and coin became so scarce. Cedric still came by, but always politely refused what they offered, or instead came bearing baked goods for them that his wife, Katlina, had made.

Cedric smiled at Rion. "Then the kakla would be fine. You wouldn't happen to have a bit of bread or something to go with it, would you? Just a little something to hold me until your father comes and I can head home for supper," he asked, looking sheepish, his voice sounding apologetic for asking.

"Oh! I'm glad you said something. We've meat pie and bread. Neither Mother nor I ate much of it. There's still plenty left for Father. It will take a while to heat, though." It would mean building another fire in the oven, but he was happy to do it. If Cedric was hungry, that meant Father truly couldn't be in danger or injured. Fortunately the stove was still lit from the tea, for the kakla.

"If you're sure you've enough for me, you need not heat it, lad. As long as the kakla is hot, the pie need not be. I certainly appreciate it. Let me come into the kitchen and help you."

"No, sir. You're our guest. It's my job. But if you feel in need of something to do, while I see to your stomach, you might tell Mother about the preparations for Feast Day. I was very selfish before and didn't let her get out to see them, and I'm sure she'd love to hear about them."

Cedric grinned at Rion. "Selfish indeed! That's a terrible child you and Anorion have raised there, Alissa, right terrible," he teased. "To make up for the pie being cold, Alarion, how about a little bit of honey with the bread to go with it? Katlina's hidden the honey jar on me again and the ants have yet to lead me to it."

Ric's father was known for his sweet tooth. He favored honey the way most of the City Guard favored mead or oushka. "Of course. Perhaps then you'd also care for a slice of cake? We've two slices left, and Father will only want the one. For after dinner, of course," Rion said, then grinned at the eager look changing to one of disappointment. Cedric looked chagrined when Alissa laughed. Rion held his breath hearing her and was relieved when this time she didn't cough because of it.

Cedric did his part to keep Alissa's mind off both her absent husband and her illness, telling her all about what was happening in the City. Then he ate, and he and Rion talked the whole time in an effort to continue to distract her.

Finally, a long while after Cedric came, there was a knock on the door. Rion jumped up to get it. "Who's there?" he called.

"It's me, Alarion," his father said tiredly.

Rion opened the door eagerly. "Father!" he said in relief, but then he saw his father had a bandage wrapped about the bicep of his sword arm. "You're hurt! What happened? Cedric didn't tell us you'd been injured," Rion said, looking at Cedric accusingly. Cedric looked at him and Alissa guiltily.

"That's because I told him not to. I knew you and Alissa would be upset about it, I didn't want you to know until you saw me, so you could see at the same time I was all right." Anorion turned to his friend. "Thanks for seeing to them, Cedric. That's one I owe you."

"Your son fed me dinner, so we'll call it even," Cedric said. "I'd best be getting back to my own house. I stopped by to tell Katlina I'd be back late and why, but she'll still be wanting me home, especially now that I've already eaten and she'll not have to cook for me! Thanks again for dinner, especially the cake and honey," he said, grinning. Then he left.

"What happened?" Alissa asked.

"Cedric told you about the trouble at the Gilded Stein? Well, I was one of the seven who were injured. It's a sword wound, not deep nor serious, not even as bad as the knife wound I received rescuing you the day we met. Some dinner and some rest and I'll be good as new. Now, about that meat pie."

"I'll heat it, Father. I just need to build up the fire first," Rion said.

"You'll do nothing of the kind. It's fine the way it is. But I do smell kakla. I'd certainly welcome a cup."

Rion got supper for his father while he and Mother talked softly. His father ate with a healthy appetite, and when it was time to go to bed, Mother went upstairs with him, for the first time in weeks. Rion pretended to go to sleep quickly. When his parents came in and kissed him a short while later, he didn't let them know he was still awake, but his mind was busy with the events of the day. He was still awake a short while later when he heard his parents' passion through the thin wall that separated their rooms. He blushed darkly and squirmed, but it was good to know they were together and safe.

Chapter 3
Trappers

ELADAR and Lunahr were talking animatedly. It had only been two days since they had met, yet it sounded as if they had known each other always. Talon smiled to see them together. His own kin were all older than Lunahr; they had all already been through a lifetime of hardship, through more than a lifetime. The Amontir lived to be two hundred and fifty, when injury or illness did not claim them, not sixty as other Men. Few of his people were younger than sixty and none nearly as young of heart as Lunahr. Elves lived to be one thousand and only came of age at forty-nine. Eladar was still as much of a child as Lunahr was. He had also led a sheltered life, from what he knew of Elven children in general and this prince in particular. Friendship with him would be good for Lunahr, if Eladar could keep his innate passion for mischief and his other passions in check.

"DON'T you ever tire of being watched all the time?" Eladar asked softly, sighing.

Lunahr grinned. "Ah, you've noticed that, have you? Laren can't help it. He means well by it, really, they all do. They are more than a little overprotective, I'll admit. But they have reason to be. I'm last of my House, and I've Power besides, as strong as Laren's, they say, perhaps even stronger. None of them could help him when...." He trailed off, realizing he was revealing far too much. It was hard to keep things from Eladar. He liked him so much already. He seemed such a kindred spirit.

"Do you sing?" Lunahr asked, changing the topic. "I can't believe I didn't think to ask until now! I hadn't heard you, but you might only be protecting me. I've heard Elven songs are strong with magic, that Men who listen can lose their hearts forever."

Eladar laughed. "Your own songs were magic enough. Those Men weren't the only ones entranced by them, Beryl." Two days ago, even yesterday he might have stroked Beryl's face as he'd said so. But he'd seen enough of Beryl's tender heart to know that it would be perilously easy for Beryl to fall hopelessly in love with him, and he'd not so injure a friend. If

Beryl was to be staying with his people for any length of time, he might instead have a friend he could treasure.

"Oh, but I didn't! I mean I didn't use the King's Voice upon them. I'd never do that," Lunahr said.

"King's voice? You might be Heir to the Throne, Beryl, but you're no more a king than I am," Eladar said.

Lunahr grew silent for a moment, then excused himself and went to where Laren was walking, twenty paces ahead of them. "Laren, the Elves are our allies now, aren't they? They know about our Power, don't they?" he asked his cousin in Amontirin.

"No, Lunahr," Talon said. "There is much we haven't told them, much we can't. Arcanus has advised me against revealing our Power to them. Elves can be difficult to deal with. They are suspicious of Men and are quite prideful. They possess true magic, though few of them can do more than walk without being seen and the other tricks for which Elves are infamous. The rest of it is not something they wield lightly. Though few of our people have Power to any great degree, still, we can do things that they cannot. They might become jealous of us, or fear us if they realized the true extent of my abilities or yours. That's not something we can risk.

"I thought I'd made that clear to you, before, or hadn't you been listening? This isn't the first time this has happened lately, Lunahr. Sometimes your head is so full of music you don't seem to hear what anyone is saying to you. You haven't been speaking to Eladar of our Power, have you? I've stopped listening to everything you've been saying, now that Eladar seems to have stopped flirting with you. Perhaps I stopped too soon."

Lunahr felt suddenly angry. "Why is it every one of you cherishes his privacy so greatly, yet feels I'm entitled to none? What gives you the right to listen in on everything I say? How am I to ever come-of-age if you never let me do anything on my own, even talk to a friend?"

TALON felt Lunahr's anger burning across the bond they shared. Lunahr was always so happy and cheerful. He was new to such dark and powerful emotions. He mustn't allow it to continue, when Lunahr was so new to his Power as well. Lunahr had not had years of practice, years of restraint, mastering either his anger or his Power. He could easily lose control if he grew enraged, with devastating results.

"Lunahr, that's enough. You can't allow yourself to get angry. You know how dangerous it would be. You need to calm down. Come, we'd best rest for a while. We'll run through the meditations…," Talon began.

LUNAHR'S temper flared. "I will not! I've no need to meditate to keep my Power in check. I'm not like you, Talon: I'm stable. I'm not about to go mad and try to kill everyone like you...." Lunahr stopped, stunned, both by what he had said and by the look on Laren's face for it and the sharp lance of pain that lashed across the bond from him. And he'd called him Talon. He never called him that! What was wrong with him?

He fled into the woods, wishing he could also flee from the bond. He went only a short distance, where he could still be seen, then turned his back and pulled out his flute and began to play it: a harsh, discordant melody. Not appropriate for a flute at all. He wished again he had his other instruments with him.

He started to sing instead, a Thenalonese war song that Farad had taught him, something that suited his mood.

ELADAR had been watching the two of them intently. He wished he knew what they'd been saying to each other. It was probably about him, he realized. Talon didn't much like him, he knew. He thought him a child, a troublemaker, no doubt a bad influence upon Beryl.

He knew that Talon had expected to be met by Elavar, not him. Elavar, who was so silent and guarded, like enough to Talon to be a brother to him. Eladar sighed. He'd never been able to get that close to his older brother, for all he'd tried. Elavar saw him as an annoyance, someone to be tolerated, watched over, endured. At least Elanara almost seemed to understand him sometimes, though far from often.

What in the world was Talon doing now? He looked like he was gathering firewood; he was picking up pieces of dry wood, but it was still half a day until dusk and dinner. Yet Talon gathered an armful of wood and kindling and set about lighting it. Then he sat down cross-legged in front of it. Eladar approached silently, to just within earshot. Odder still. He was chanting in that odd language of theirs, a singsong rhythm.

He headed for Beryl, lest Talon realize he was watching. Beryl noticed Eladar approaching and stopped singing. Eladar continued his approach when Beryl looked like he might want the company.

"I SHOULDN'T have yelled at him," Lunahr said mournfully. "I especially shouldn't have said what I did. I know better than to upset him like that but...

Eladar, what's wrong with me? I've never been so angry in my life! I've seldom been angry at all. Fa... Hunter says it's not in my nature to be. He says it's one of the things he loves about me, that I only hold love in my heart, when so many of our kin...." He trailed off, sensing he was telling Eladar things he shouldn't. He'd almost spoken Farad's given name, too, the most crucial part of his true name.

"You are a boy, Beryl, who has been given the responsibility of being a man, by being told you must keep secrets even from those you consider your friends and by being made Lord of your House and Heir to the Throne of a king. Then you have been made to leave the very people whom you will one day rule and enter the world they have kept you sheltered from. You are hurt and frightened and confused. You desperately want to show them you are worthy of the responsibilities they have entrusted to you, but you are still boy enough you also want even more to fall to your knees and beg Talon to take you back home. There's nothing wrong with you at all, Beryl. You are merely growing up. It can be a painful process, as I well know, but you will live through it, as we all do."

Eladar grinned. "Although he-who-is-my-brother and she-who-is-my-sister might argue that they might not live through my own coming-of-age. I am quite a trial to them! They won't hesitate to tell you so, at length, when you finally meet them. The burden of being related to me has become their favorite topic of conversation of late," Eladar said, eyes twinkling.

Lunahr stared at Eladar, astonished. "That's it exactly. Only I'd not understood it so clearly until I heard you say it. I sit for half the day, sometimes, singing, trying to work it all out through the music and here you've brought me back to myself with a few simple sentences," Lunahr said, worship in his eyes.

ELADAR smiled at him. "I felt the same way, before. I was so angry when Oberas insulted me. I went into the River to find peace. Normally it takes a long time for the calm of the water to fill me. Yet hearing your songs, you brought me to peace so quickly and thoroughly that I was amazed.

"I think it is a very fortunate thing for me that your people have found reason to send you to my parents for sanctuary. You are already becoming as a brother to me. And I think that what I need most right now is a brother. Perhaps it is a good thing neither of us is of age, yet, much as a part of me regrets it. More than one part, actually," he said, eyeing Beryl wistfully for a moment, then grinning as Beryl blushed darkly but eyed him coyly as well.

"I suppose it is fortunate for me Talon is so busy staring into his fire that he missed that look. Beryl, what's wrong?" Eladar asked, seeing the sudden alarm in his eyes.

"Fire? Idare, is he chanting? I'd not realized I'd upset him so much!" Beryl said, rising and looking about for Talon. "Wait here, Eladar. I must go to him," he said, as soon as he spotted him.

Eladar was surprised. There had been such a wealth of compassion in his voice, but also fear. Was he afraid for Talon, or was there reason to be afraid of him?

LUNAHR approached Laren cautiously. Laren was indeed chanting; Lunahr recognized it instantly. He shivered. He'd not thought Laren might need to meditate like that ever again, or at least, not for years, perhaps, or at the very least, months. Laren was newly healed, stable again. He shouldn't need the fire so soon.

"Laren? Laren, I'm sorry. I didn't mean to hurt you. Please forgive me for it? Please, talk to me. Don't seek refuge in the fire, not so soon," Lunahr pleaded.

Laren was ignoring him, if he even heard him at all. Perhaps words weren't enough. Lunahr had felt pain come across his bond to Laren from him. He was sure Laren had not meant to send it. But he'd heard you could also send emotions and even thoughts and sensations across intentionally.

Carefully Lunahr thought of how much he loved his cousin, of how like a father to him Laren had been since Lunahr's own parents were taken so suddenly from him, by illness, when he was but twelve. Of the warmth and security he felt when Laren hugged him. He sent a wave of love and warmth coursing down his bond to Laren, certain that it was the right thing to do, that even if it did not help him, it could not cause him further harm.

TALON stopped the meditation suddenly, in surprise. How could he feel such warmth? He'd not felt this way since before his father had died. He basked in it, as if it were the sun. He'd dared not gaze at the sun before. He would have blinded himself before it helped him, nor could he lie naked under its rays; it was too low in the sky for such comfort. He'd felt so cold, he'd hoped the flame might help. But he was no longer cold. Lunahr! Of course, the warmth came from him, across their newly forged bond. He opened his heart and his core to his cousin and sent an answering wave across.

LUNAHR gasped in surprise. He felt so wonderful! It was as if his mother were holding him. And to his joy, he saw Laren rise and head for him, looking at him, eyes lit with love.

Lunahr ran to him and embraced him. "Oh, Laren, please forgive me! What I said before! I'm so ashamed."

"NO, LUNAHR. I'm the one who should apologize. We've been asking so much of you. Sometimes we forget how young you are. It's hard to remember, when you are already a man in so many ways. I don't mean to encumber you; I'm only trying to protect you.

"We can't ever risk you coming to harm, Lunahr, and you're in such terrible danger, now more than ever. I know how hard it is to go, but this is the only way to see you safe. If ever we were to lose you I don't think we could survive it. You and Rowena and Fenris... there are so few of us now," Talon said, despair rising in his voice.

"Laren, stop," Lunahr said, hugging him again. "You mustn't dwell upon it. Come, let's put the fire out and continue our journey. Surely we must be nearly at Ardock by now? It will do you good to be in a real city again, especially since after Arcanus's last visit you actually have some coin to spend there."

TALON nodded and put out the fire, carefully and thoroughly. He wondered what Eladar might be thinking about them. He saw him watching. He hoped he'd not say anything to his father, King Laranela, about this.

He forced the worry aside, concentrating upon the continual stream of warmth now flowing across the bond from his young cousin. Talon could not so easily succumb to the darkness of despair with his cousin always with him.

He had not expected their bond to be like this. His bond to Farad was so different, so closed, so guarded compared to this one. Even his bond to his father had not been as warm and open as this.

And when he had needed him most, two weeks ago, when he'd again fallen to the King's Madness, Farad had not come. Farad had not saved him as he had done once before, six years earlier, the time he'd nearly killed those he tried so desperately to protect. Talon feared for his cousin, that he had not come.

Lunahr began to sing, softly and sweetly. Talon's fears for Farad faded with the song. For a moment he wondered if Lunahr might be weaving his Power into his song again, as he had when he saved him from the Madness, but then he ceased to care as the song lifted the heaviness from his heart.

ELADAR eyed the two Men before him. Talon was far different this journey than he had seemed the last time he had met him. He had been so cold, aloof, self-assured, and then he had seemed dangerous, deadly. There had been no sign of such love and warmth, but also, of such vulnerability. Eladar now suspected Talon was far more complex than he had before guessed.

And Beryl was quite remarkable. He looked forward to spending time with him. Riviera would not seem nearly such a prison, with him for company. He sighed. Riviera was wonderful, beautiful; he loved his home. How could it also feel like a prison to him?

A TERRIBLE bellowing roar cut the air and echoed all around them. Lunahr shivered and stopped singing, the hairs on the back of his neck rising. His hand instinctively went to his sword hilt, and he drew Loruthanar. Talon drew Kathalanar, scanning the trees about them, expecting to see a lumbering behemoth charge out of the woods at them.

Eladar had nocked an arrow. "It's coming from the left, about four hundred paces, I'd say." The three of them moved toward the sound, rather than away from it.

"Beryl, you're to stay behind me," Talon commanded.

"Yes, Laren."

"That's not right. It shouldn't be bellowing like that, giving itself away. And it's not moving closer. It doesn't sound like it's fighting. It sounds like it's in pain," Talon said.

ELADAR looked at him in surprise, that a Man might be able to tell so much from an animal's cry, then cursed himself for a fool. Of course! It was an obearn's bellow they heard. He'd recognized it instantly, but he'd forgotten for a moment that Talon was Lord of House of Obearn. And it did sound like it was in pain. It sounded like it was trapped. Eladar shivered as memory washed over him, of the last time he'd heard a trapped obearn cry.

"ELADAR!" Lunahr said in concern. Eladar looked suddenly ill.

"Ignore me. Concentrate on the obearn. I think it's caught in a trap," Eladar said.

Talon looked at Eladar sharply. Sure enough, a few moments later when they entered a clearing, that was what they found. There was a fallen tree, with honey dripping from it, though there was no sign of bees. And there was an obearn, a small one, a scant six feet long. She was clawing at her right hind leg, tearing horrible gashes in it with her six-inch black claws. Crying piteously in distress by her side were two cubs. They couldn't have been more than six months old, for their size.

"Fur trappers," Eladar said in loathing. Talon started to approach the trapped obearn. "Talon, what do you mean to do? Symbol of your House or not, hurt or not, she'll tear your throat out if you get within her reach."

"I'm going to free her," Talon declared.

"No. Talon, you must not. I'll relieve her of her pain," Eladar said, raising his bow.

"No! Eladar, how can you? Can't you see she's a mother?" Lunahr asked, horrified.

"I see that all too clearly. She is already injured. I doubt she will be able to survive for long. Perhaps just long enough to kill the Men who set this trap for her. Chances are, those men are fathers and they hope to sell her pelt to care for their own young. We can bring the cubs with us to Riviera. My people will care for them until they are grown. We will bypass Ardock."

"The Men who set this trap are more monsters than this poor beast," Talon said. "I'd hardly have thought you might side with them, Eladar."

"Perhaps this time I speak from experience, whereas you speak from your heart. You cannot interfere with the work of trappers, Talon, not so close to Riviera. As Prince, I cannot allow it, not after what happened last time," Eladar commanded imperiously.

"I do not answer to you, Eladar," Talon said loftily.

"No, but you do seek sanctuary amongst my people for Beryl," Eladar countered.

Talon glared at him and for a moment, Eladar thought he saw his eyes change, that the blue of them was replaced with golden flame, and his heart raced, as he sensed he was in terrible danger.

But Talon looked away from him, back toward the obearn. When he looked up again, his eyes were blue, cold and hard as ice. "Never attempt to use the safety of my kin against me," Talon threatened him.

"Laren, Eladar, please!" Lunahr said, looking from one to the other, agonized. "You have to help her. You can't let her suffer," he said, begging Eladar.

"Beryl, you do not know what you ask of me. If we rescue her, I fear much ill will come of it. Men may well die. And she would not live, in any case," Eladar reasoned, a note of true fear in his voice.

"I WILL tend to her," Talon said, his tone brooking no further argument. Then he turned to the obearn, sheathed his sword and began speaking to it in Amontirin, weaving his Power into his words. "**Mother of my House, hear me. I will not harm you. I seek only to aid you, to reunite you with your cubs. Do not attack me, when I come to help you. You must sleep now. Sleep and when you awaken, you will be free. You will be tended to, if not healed, and your children will be beside you. Cease your struggles. You only injure yourself by them. Find peace here, with me, now, so you and they might live.**"

The obearn shook her head, as if a bee had flown in her ear. Her roars lessened to a rumbling growl. Then gradually she sank to the ground, looking for all the world as if she were asleep.

Talon approached the great beast. The cubs cried piteously, backing away from him in fear. He knelt beside the beast and studied her leg. He was confused. He'd expected the trap to be one of those he'd seen before, with great metal teeth made to rend and tear flesh and snap bone. But this trap was far more intricate than that. It was constructed to confine, without causing great injury. The obearn had instead injured herself, by tearing at her leg with her claws. Talon studied the trap and found the release mechanism and triggered it. Then he took out his healer's kit and began tending to her.

ELADAR watched the woods around them warily. "Keep an eye out for the trappers. If you see them, hide. You look too much like one of our people. You would be in great danger from them were they to find you here, interfering with one of their traps."

"Where are you going?" Lunahr asked, surprised.

"Hunting," Eladar said, and he shuddered. "Do not let Talon wake her until I return."

Lunahr looked at him in confusion, but Eladar slipped quickly through the trees. Lunahr watched the trees nervously and watched Laren as well. He knew if the obearn awoke, she could easily kill his cousin; she would not hesitate to do so.

Laren finished tending to the wounded obearn and rose and backed away from her.

"Don't waken her yet, Laren. Eladar said to wait until he returned to do so," Lunahr said.

"Returned? Where has he gone?" Talon asked, annoyed. "How like what Elavar had told me of him, that Eladar might go off to get into mischief at such a time."

Lunahr swallowed. "He said he was going hunting. But Laren, Elves don't hunt, ever. The way he said it…. You don't think he was going after the trappers, do you?"

"I have no idea. He isn't acting as I expected. I thought before he was himself from how he sounded; I didn't test him as I should have. I should have forced him to let me touch him. I cannot believe I was so careless. I fear he might be a Resemblant after all."

Lunahr could hear how upset Talon was with himself over it, and sought to reassure him. "He's not, Laren. I know he's not. I tested him. When he pinned me before and then I pinned him, when I caressed his face. I had to be sure. I tested him and he wasn't."

"Lunahr! You might perhaps have the Power to shield yourself from the Enemy, but you've hardly the skill! Don't ever try something like that again, without my knowledge and consent, do you understand?" Talon commanded sharply.

"Yes, Laren," Lunahr said meekly.

TALON spun about as a movement caught the corner of his eye and stared in surprise as Eladar emerged from the woods. There was a limp fox in his hands. The hands that held it were shaking violently. Eladar's face was streaked with tears. He walked over to Talon and held it out to him.

"What's this? You found another trap?" Talon asked, and took the fox from him. "There's nothing I can do for him, Eladar, he's dead," Talon said, examining the fox briefly.

"Of course he's dead," Eladar said. He looked like he might collapse. "Put him into the trap. Spring it, so it looks like the fox sprang it himself. Then take the obearn's forepaw and claw the body, mangle it, be sure to bloody it fully. Then erase any tracks you might have left, though from what

I've seen, I doubt you've left any that might be discernible. There's nothing we can do about the fox not having left any, but hopefully the trappers will believe the evidence their eyes do see. Then waken the obearn and let's leave this foul place.

"I can ill afford to be sick here. I need the River. You'll have to camp by it tonight. I'll need to lie in it for at least that long for what I've done." Eladar fell to his knees, clutching his stomach. "Hurry," he said, then pressed his hand tightly to his mouth.

Lunahr was staring at Eladar, horrified. "He killed it. Laren, he's the one who killed the fox!"

ELADAR stumbled to his feet and ran for the River. He managed to travel only a hundred yards through the trees before he fell to his knees, retching. He disgorged the entire contents of his stomach, but his body was wracked with dry heaves, until, unable to catch his breath for them, he finally passed out.

TALON stood looking at the dead fox in his hands and studied it carefully. Lunahr was right. There, in the chest at its heart, was the mark of an arrow. It had died almost instantly. It was an old animal. Its fur was the same color as Aramis's hair, red frosted with gray. Talon thought of his older cousin painfully. Aramis was Lord of House of Foxes. He might meet a similar fate all too easily, all too soon; they all might, now that Caramore was lost.

What could have possessed Eladar to kill this fox? But he was not possessed. Lunahr would have sensed it, when he touched him. Lunahr was yet pure; he could feel it across the bond they shared.

He carried the fox's body to the trap and did as Eladar had instructed him to. Talon told Lunahr to climb the large oak at the edge of the clearing, and he followed him into it. Talon stretched his Power to its limit by maintaining his hold upon the obearn from such a distance. Then he released it, confident that Eladar was far from the awakening beast.

The obearn awoke and stood. The terrified cubs ran eagerly to their mother and began nuzzling her. She stared in confusion at the fox in the trap and growled, then lifted her injured leg, licking at the sticky substance upon her fur, then drawing her head quickly away and growling her displeasure.

Talon smiled grimly. The *lashar* and *resan* he had used upon her wound must have tasted terrible to her. He was relieved. He knew otherwise she would have torn at any bandages he wrapped about her leg. Hopefully she might leave the medicine alone long enough that she might begin to heal. She lumbered, limping, into the woods, her cubs trailing behind, her interest in the honey within the tree gone.

Fortunately, the obearn was heading away from the River and from the route Eladar had taken. When Talon felt it safe enough, he and Lunahr climbed down and began following Eladar's trail. Talon was relieved to see it was barely detectable amidst the leaves. But he was deeply disturbed to find Eladar unconscious, still so close by, where he might easily have been mauled to death by the angry obearn, had she come this way.

Talon tested Eladar's core while he was unconscious. He had to be certain this truly was King Laranela's son and not a monster in his form or a puppet under the Enemy's thrall. Talon was relieved beyond measure to find Eladar's core was clear of taint, but was astonished to discover it was remarkably bright, like that of a kinsman. None of the Elves he had tested and negotiated with in Erenia had cores so strong. He resisted the urge to probe more deeply. Eladar's core was in terrible turmoil, for him to be in such a sorry physical state. He had done enough damage today, may Elavar forgive him for causing his younger brother to come to harm.He lifted Eladar carefully, astonished at how heavy he was, even though he had known he would be heavier than a Man of comparable build. Elven bones were far more dense than those of Men. Eladar would not be pleased at all to find he was being carried, if he awoke. But he did not awaken.

Talon carried him all the way to the River. "Make camp, Lunahr. I must stay with Eladar."

Lunahr nodded and began doing as he'd been told, his gaze going to the two of them more than once, as Talon brought Eladar to the water's edge and stripped him completely of his clothes. Then Talon took off his own clothes and walked into the River with Eladar.

ELADAR awoke to the feeling of strong arms holding him and for a moment thought they were Elavar's. Why would Elavar be holding him in the River? Had he been ill or injured again?

Memory slammed into him as hard as Hardred's tree had. He saw the intent black eyes staring curiously back at him, as he let loose the arrow that pierced the fox's heart. He saw the light leave the fox's eyes.

He convulsed as he began heaving again, and the arms kept his head from going under. He fought against them, thrashing. Eladar opened his eyes. It was Talon holding him, Talon's fault he'd killed the fox. "Release me!" he commanded, his voice as cold as a mountain stream in spring thaw.

TALON instantly let him go. Eladar was conscious; he was lucid. What he did now was his choice.

Eladar disappeared into the water. Talon walked back onto the bank and watched the water as he dressed. He knew Elves could stay submerged far longer than Men, but when Eladar did not emerge, he realized Eladar might be anywhere within the River. He apparently no longer wished to be seen.

LUNAHR had gathered wood for a fire but not lit it yet. There was a pot full of water and a small pile of greens beside it. Lunahr looked up at Laren and spoke to him in Amontirin, likely because he knew an Elf's hearing was keen, and he didn't want Eladar to possibly overhear and understand. "Laren? What's wrong with Eladar? Is he… has he gone mad? How could he have… hunted?" Lunahr asked, his voice low and fearful. Lunahr looked almost as ill as Eladar had.

Talon sighed. Lunahr belonged with the Elves. Their gentle cousin had no business staying with them. He was ill-equipped to deal with the horrors he would face if he stayed, trained though he was to face them. Seeing the dead fox, knowing Eladar had killed it, had upset him terribly. He was hardly ready to confront the Enemy and his minions, to do what would need to be done to defend himself and his kin.

"I've no idea what possessed him to do what he did, but I do not think he is mad. You saw how it affected him. If he were mad, he would have reveled in the taking of a life. I would not let him slay the obearn, but I did as he told me to do when he returned with the fox. I am hoping he'll be able to explain it to us, when he leaves the refuge of the water. If he leaves. Lunahr, he might not return. I refused to do what he asked of me. He is an Elf, a prince. He is prideful, his people are. I fear I may have jeopardized your one hope for safety, for the life of an obearn."

"I don't care! You couldn't let her die, Laren, how could you? You saw those cubs. You did the right thing. I'm sure Eladar will see that. I'm going to play for him. On the bank, as I did before. It helped him, that time. He told me how much. Perhaps I can help him again," Lunahr said hopefully.

Talon nodded. "I'll start dinner. You play." He doubted it would truly help soothe Eladar, but at least the music would ease Lunahr's own troubled spirit.

"Nothing for me, Laren. I can't eat, having seen the obearn's blood, the fox's," Lunahr said.

Talon sighed. Ill-equipped indeed. He must shield his cousin from ever viewing his core too deeply, lest Lunahr see some of the things he had been forced to do over the years, those he had been forced to kill and to destroy, Resemblants and Revenants, all the grim mockeries of life he had faced. There had been women and children, as well as what once had been men. The Enemy delighted in the destruction of innocence, the corruption of it. The Enemy had turned more than one child into a monster. He had turned many.

LUNAHR shivered as Laren's thoughts and fears slipped across their bond from his core. Laren thought him so weak. But he'd be able to face the Enemy's servants in combat. He knew he would. He'd turned the tables on Eladar when he'd flirted too forcefully before, hadn't he?

He shouldn't have let Laren see how much the dead fox upset him. He should have pretended to have an appetite. Only, as much as he knew he'd have to learn deception to live, he'd hoped he'd not have to deceive his own people. Certainly not his cousin, his king.

Lunahr took a few deep breaths and focused upon his flute. Then he began to play, a haunting, soulful melody of death and despair. As before, he then picked something lighter, still tragic, but tragedy mixed with hope. He waited eagerly after the fifth and final song for Eladar, but he did not emerge. He played other songs, then, ones of life, of hope, even of love, his heart sinking further with each piece as Eladar failed to appear.

"Lunahr, come. You must eat. He'll return when he's ready. Or he'll leave and we'll proceed to Riviera on our own and hope our words might sway the King more strongly than his own might influence him against us. Elavar might stand with me against him, and King Laranela values his elder son's counsel."

"But Laren, we can't! We can't just abandon Eladar! We can't leave him out here like this. What would his people say? I wish… I wish you'd listened, now, Laren, that you'd let him kill the obearn. Eladar's afraid of those trappers. They terrify him. I could feel it. He tried to make it right again, somehow, by killing the fox and setting it in the trap, but still, he's afraid. Something happened, Laren, something terrible. Remember what he said. He said, 'Men may well die,' that much ill might come of our rescuing the obearn," Lunahr said, his voice warm with concern.

Talon frowned. Eladar had said that; he remembered hearing it, now that Lunahr repeated his words. At the time, he had been too wrapped up in the obearn's pain to listen fully to what Eladar was saying.

He did not take Eladar seriously, he realized. If Elavar had told him the same thing, he'd have done as he asked: he'd have slain the mother as a mercy and taken the cubs to Riviera.

"It is too late now for second thoughts. What's done is done. You should get some sleep. I will wake you for your watch or if there is trouble."

Lunahr looked longingly toward the River, then nodded and lay down.

TALON was relieved to see Lunahr had fallen asleep almost instantly upon laying down. He had been ready to help Lunahr sleep, but he'd not needed to use his Power. Lunahr was tired from their journey. He had not had decades of such travels to harden him, to increase his endurance. Even Rowena was a seasoned traveler. The smile left his face, replaced by a frown. A seasoned killer. She still looked so soft, so gentle, and sounded it, but though she had the body and grace of a dancer, she had never learned the art. But she could kill—swiftly, efficiently, purposefully—as they all could.

Only twenty of his people survived. Twenty! So few children born; so few women to bear them. They were dying as a people. *The Ring, please Idare, let us find the Ring, so we might end these centuries of madness and live.*

Someone was in the trees! There, to the left, more than one, and too loud to be Eladar.

Talon swept the large mound of dirt he'd put beside the small fire for that purpose over it, plunging their campsite instantly into darkness, waking Lunahr by lashing him sharply across their bond a moment before he yanked him along the ground toward the cover of the trees, in case arrows came. The moon betrayed them with its brightness.

Talon could feel Lunahr's terror across the bond at being wakened so violently, but then he felt Lunahr master his fear as he stood and silently drew Loruthanar. They reached the safety of the trees and then, moving in perfect synchronization, started creeping toward the sounds Talon had heard, until they could make out frantic whispering in Common.

"… told you we shouldn't risk it! They're bandits, river pirates. Who else would be out here by the river instead of the road? You saw how fast they moved. It's a trap, that fire, but they panicked and moved too soon. There must be dozens of them out here with us."

"Then be quiet, fool! Do you want to lead them to us?" another voice hissed.

The voices stilled, but Talon could still hear the men, the rustle of the leaves they stepped upon, their heavy, fearful breathing, the crack of a twig, and a sound of moaning, all of which had first alerted him to their presence. They'd been surprisingly silent at first; they'd gotten dangerously close to their camp before they'd betrayed themselves.

He'd thought them bandits for it, but perhaps they were hunters; from their words, they didn't sound like brigands. He could not kill them one by one from the safety of the trees, as he'd first thought to do, if they were hunters, if they were innocents.

Talon could see them now, by moonlight. There were three men standing and a fourth upon the ground, moaning. The three standing had bows drawn, aiming into the trees around them.

One of the men knelt. "Raymond, please, you must try to be silent," he pleaded softly. He sounded young and afraid, for all he had the height and build of a man. This one was a boy, not a man. He would be Talon's target. His being endangered would affect the others the most. He signaled to Lunahr to circle twenty paces around them, to make a small noise to attract their attention and then flee, to keep to the cover of the trees, lest their arrows find him.

Talon waited a few moments, positioning himself as closely as possible to his target. Then to his left he heard a noise, and the two standing men spun toward it and fired their arrows at the sound. At that same moment, Talon leapt forward, lunging for the boy, taking him completely by surprise. Talon grabbed him and held him, his sword to the boy's throat.

"Tan!" the boy screamed in terror, dropping his bow.

The other two spun about, desperately reaching into their quivers for arrows.

"Drop your bows, now, or he dies," Talon said, voice cold, deadly, holding the trembling boy.

"Tan, don't! He'll kill you!" the boy in his arms sobbed, and to Talon's astonishment, the boy kicked backward sharply, into Talon's shin, even with his blade against his throat, thinking he'd die for it. But at the same moment a hand closed about Talon's other ankle from nowhere like a vise and yanked, hard.

Talon cursed as he half spun and toppled sideways, keeping his hold upon the boy but forced to drop Kathalanar, lest they both be injured by his sword. He would not harm an innocent, a child, not even to save his own life, though he'd slay him along with every man here with a single thought to save Lunahr, even knowing it would drive him to madness. Talon had thought the man on the ground who'd grabbed him helpless, but he had the strength of a Revenant. He prayed silently to Idare that he might not be one even as an arrow imbedded itself in the ground by Talon's head.

"**No, don't hurt him!**" Lunahr cried out, betraying his position, but his voice, though full of fear, also vibrated with Power. "Please, we thought you bandits. We were only defending ourselves. Talon won't harm your friend; he was only trying to force you to disarm without injuring you. He'd never harm an innocent. He dropped his sword so he wouldn't, when he fell; he'd never have released his hold upon it otherwise. I'm sheathing my own sword and there's only the two of us; we're no threat to you. **Please, lower your weapons as well, that's it, we'll talk instead, talking is better,**" Lunahr said, his final words as laced with Power as were his first.

Talon wondered if Lunahr was fully aware of the risk of what he was doing, whether that was why he was using his Power so sparingly. Men's cores were so small and brittle, so easily shattered. Lunahr was taking a tremendous chance, using the King's Voice upon those they had once, in their arrogance, called Lesser Men. A single misstep and they would be turned into drooling husks. But the two men before him returned their arrows to their quivers and shouldered their strung bows.

"Tan? What are you doing? It's a trick! He's an Elf. He's entranced you. He's using his magic on you. Forget about me! Kill him! He'll kill you, like they killed grandfather, like they killed everyone," the boy Talon held said, terror in his voice as he kept struggling.

Talon wondered at his terror, his words. Elves did not kill Men.

"No. I am not an Elf and we will not harm you, I swear it," Lunahr said, flicking his hair back and revealing his ears. They were pale but rounded; these men could see even by moonlight they were the ears of Man.

"We are travelers, on our way to Ardock. We heard you approaching our camp, attempting to be silent, and we feared you were bandits. We were merely defending ourselves. My name is Beryl. This is my cousin, Talon."

"It's not a trick," Talon said to the boy, not daring to take the same risk Lunahr had, of weaving his Power into his voice. "We won't harm you. I'll release you, now, to prove it." He was watching all of them carefully. Lunahr had exposed himself to them. He was in terrible danger if what he was attempting did not work. Talon would kill the others instantly if Lunahr was endangered by it, all at once; he'd not need Kathalanar, despite what it would do to his core to misuse his Power so terribly.

He released the boy he held, and in turn the restraining hand let go of his ankle. Talon retrieved his sword as he stood and sheathed it, eyeing the boy warily, lest he attack Lunahr.

Lunahr took a deep breath, and Talon suspected he broke his hold upon the two men he had been controlling, from the increased tension in them. The two groups viewed each other suspiciously.

"Why were you sneaking up on us? Who are you?" Talon asked, needing to cement the tenuous bonds of truce Lunahr had forged as quickly as possible.

"I'm Tanran. This is my friend, Dustin. The man you were threatening is my brother, Sevran. That's his friend, Raymond, on the ground, there. We saw the smoke and hoped you might be men from a caravan fetching water, or from a boat, tied ashore for the night, that you might have a healer with you. Raymond's been injured. An obearn's mauled him. He won't live to make it even to Ardock, let alone home," he said, his voice filled with pain.

"Then it's fortunate your arrow missed. I've some skill in healing," Talon said, then walked slowly and nonthreateningly to the downed man. He knelt beside him, removed his glove, and felt his chest, underneath his torn and bloody shirt. His heart was still beating; he was still alive, not a monster in Man's form, praise Idare. He also still had all his limbs, and his injuries, though grave, might not yet prove mortal. "I can tend to Raymond, if you'll carry him the rest of the way to our camp. My medicines are there," Talon said, rising.

"Why would you help us, after all this?" Tanran asked suspiciously.

"Because I can," Talon said, simply. "Come, Beryl, we'll need to gather a little more wood on the way. You restart the fire and then fetch some fresh water from the River. We'll speak later about the chances you took, tonight," he added critically.

"YES, Talon," Lunahr said, unable to keep the dismay at his cousin's tone from his voice.

What was he supposed to have done? They could have killed Laren, or more likely, made him kill all of them. Lunahr knew it was a risk to use the King's Voice upon men without the Power, but he'd had to take the chance. He would do anything to save Laren's life, but also, to keep Laren from falling to the King's Madness again. And it had worked, hadn't it? Lunahr sighed heavily and began picking up pieces of dry wood.

TALON rearranged the stones about the fire pit, his magic-laced gloves shielding him from their heat, and began laying new wood and kindling.

Lunahr hadn't remained hidden in the trees as Talon had ordered him to; he'd exposed himself dangerously. And he'd used his Power on these men, despite the danger to them by him doing so. But it had worked. He'd not had to slay them. And Lunahr had remembered to call him Talon, at least, in front of the strangers.

He hoped Lunahr might spot Eladar and warn him to stay away from their camp. These men hated and feared the Elves. He had to learn why. He was entrusting Lunahr to the Elves of Riviera. If they had a darker history with Men than their western cousins, he had need to hear of it.

The strangers laid Raymond down beside the growing fire. Talon sighed, looking at him. He wasn't a man, either, he was a boy, but unlike his friend Sevran, he still had the look and build of one. His arm and chest were swathed in bloody cloth beneath the shirt. Talon removed his gloves and began unwrapping the wounds. "How did it happen?" he asked Tanran.

"We're fur trappers. We don't usually range so far north, but we're here trapping an obearn for Feast Day, a live one. It's dangerous work, but worth a fortune in coin to those who manage it. We almost had one today, too, only a fox sprang the trap first and then the obearn came. It had cubs. We could have made a fortune selling the cubs to the Governor of Sarna instead, for his menagerie," he said bitterly. "We followed the tracks, hoping to catch up to it, to kill the mother and capture the cubs. We'd have forgotten about trying to get an obearn for the pit fight if we could have gotten those cubs."

Talon was glad neither Lunahr nor Eladar were there to hear them. "Pit fight? Obearn against dogs?"

Tanran scoffed. "Dogs! Hah! Maybe where you're from, stranger, but not in Ardock. In Ardock they do it better than that: obearn against wolven, wolven against pumar. Those cats are rare now; the Thenalonese exterminated every last one of them from their mountains, after what they and the ogres done to them in the War. Oh, and ogres too, sometimes, in the pits I mean. My father told me about those, how in the old days, they'd even have ogres. Never an Elf, though. I'd give much to see a pit fight with an obearn against an Elf. We'd see how well their magic works against something like that."

Talon felt a chill, hearing him say so. Pit fights were brutal and vicious and deadly, often with hundreds of spectators screaming encouragements and betting upon the outcome. It was a scene from a nightmare, picturing Eladar or one of his kin in such a vicious, obscene display as that.

Lunahr laid a pot of water beside him. The hand holding it was trembling.

Talon cursed silently. Lunahr had heard that much at least and possibly the rest.

"How can you hate the Elves so much that you might wish something so terrible upon one of them?" Lunahr asked softly.

Tanran's eyes narrowed. "One of 'em? I wish it on all of 'em! I'd pay any price to see it, after what they done to us. They killed my grandfather. They killed most of the men in our village and then drowned the village under the cursed river. It was twenty-two years ago. Terleth's but a memory, a painful one, but we'll never forget. I'll never forget. I lived through it.

"We're from Lethos now, the four of us. Half the town resettled there, after they flooded us out. Our elders went to Alridge, even to Ardock when those in Alridge wouldn't listen, to try to get them to retaliate against the Elves for what they done. But those cowards wanted no part of it.

"They sent emissaries instead of warriors. They and the Elves all talked about how they wouldn't let it happen again, about how it was 'justified,' what they'd done. Justified! Killing twenty-three men for trying to protect their livelihood!

"We lost fifteen children and nine women that winter, starved and frozen—my brother was one of 'em—for want of men to cut the wood and coin to feed us. The Elves done that, too. Drove off the animals so's we have nothing to hunt, let alone trap. Made the snows last twice as long as we thought they would, made the winter twice as hard."

Talon stayed silent and listened. Had the Elves done even half of what he'd said? Elves might have some magic, but not enough to control the weather: only wizards could do that. Had Arcanus done so, for some reason? Could even he wield such magic? Talon knew Arcanus had conjured more than one thunderstorm; he perhaps could conjure a blizzard, but a series of them?

Had the Elves truly destroyed a village, killed twenty-three men? From what Tanran said, the Elves hadn't denied doing it. He'd best have a talk with Eladar to see what he knew about this. He must know something.

He felt a sudden chill, remembering what Eladar had said to him, before, when he'd not listened. Something about not allowing him to interfere with the work of trappers, so close to Riviera. That he couldn't, after what had happened last time.

Last time? Had he meant Terleth? Had he somehow endangered not only Lunahr's sanctuary, but Eladar's very people, by saving the obearn?

Then why had Eladar not tried to stop him more forcefully? He realized that, when Eladar had slipped into the trees earlier, to go "hunting" Eladar might just as easily have driven his arrow into his heart as the fox's. But Eladar's plan had worked. These men did not suspect the fox in the trap was anything other than miserable luck.

Talon finished cleaning and treating the wound and then turned to Lunahr. "Beryl, why don't you lie down? I'll take first watch."

Lunahr nodded mutely. His eyes were wide and haunted looking, but he said nothing and lay down.

Talon looked up at Sevran. "I've done what I can for your friend. He's still very weak, but I've stopped the bleeding and cleaned the wounds so hopefully they won't fester. If you keep him here, camped, and feed him meat broth for a few days and then more solid foods, once his strength begins to return, he should live.

"He'll need at least five days here. I'll also leave medicine with you to treat fever, in case he develops one despite my efforts. That often happens with such wounds. I'll show you how to prepare it and instruct you how much to give him. My cousin and I will be leaving in the morning for Ardock. We've urgent business there," Talon said, slipping his gloves back on.

"Five days! We can't spend five days here! We'll miss Feast Day!" Tanran said in dismay.

Sevran said, "You and Dusty can still hunt. I'll stay here with Ray. I'll tend to him."

"No, Sev. We'll not leave you here like that. It's too dangerous," Dustin argued.

"You can camp here at night and then go out during the day, setting and checking the traps. Please, I'm old enough to do it. You've seen I am, haven't you? I kept my wits when the obearn attacked, didn't I?" Sevran asked.

"That ya did," Tanran admitted reluctantly. "We have to, Dusty. It's the only way."

"You'd risk your brother's life for coin?" Dustin asked Tanran in dismay. "You've changed, Tan. I'd never have thought you might, but the things I've seen on this trip.... We'll tend to Ray here and then we'll head home. I'll not face his mother with a handful of cold coin when she's wanting her son back."

"Fine. Then you stay here with Ray while Sev and I go hunting," Tanran said.

"Sure," Sevran agreed.

Dustin shook his head. "I hope you're more careful about it this time. I still say you're mad, the two of you, trying for a full-grown obearn, especially without a cart to haul it in. You think you can just tie a rope around its neck and lead it like a dog?"

Tanran glared at him and motioned to Sevran, and the two of them went to the rim of camp and started talking.

Dustin sighed. "I'm sorry we've gotten you in the middle of this, Talon. You're a good man for helping us.

"I still can't believe Tan didn't kill your cousin the instant he revealed himself, looking like an Elf as he does. If you plan on going to Ardock and on to Alridge or beyond, you'd best have him cut his hair, or tie it back, at least," he said, looking at Lunahr. Then he looked over at Sevran and Tanran.

"Tan was five when the Elves came, when they attacked. Old enough to be terrified; old enough to remember watching it. He remembers his brother, too and his grandfather. It's a shame he's taught Sevran how to hate, too, when he wasn't even born then."

"I know something of Elves," Talon said carefully. His father had studied them extensively and had written an entire book on them: *Understanding Elves: One Man's Perspective.* Talon had read it; he'd studied it intensively. He knew more about Elves than anyone.

Yet still, they'd only learned of Nalea a scant few years ago. His father had never suspected the Elves might have more than the seven known kingdoms, that there was an eighth, although not a kingdom, exactly: Nalea was the city that contained the Army and Navy of the other seven, when none of them had ever suspected that the Elves might have soldiers, or a need for them. The Elves had never known war; at least, not in the three millennia they had lived amongst Men.

"I cannot believe any Elves might attack a village of Men, that they might destroy one, unprovoked. Surely they must have had some reason to do so?"

Dustin looked cautiously at Sevran and Tanran, and then at Lunahr, who appeared asleep, and back at Talon. His eyes bore into Talon's, and he nodded, then spoke, his voice scarcely above a whisper. "It's not something we usually speak of to those outside the village. It's one thing to tell folks how wronged we were, to encourage others to live in hate and fear of the Elves as we do. It's another to admit there might have been a reason for it. Not reason enough to kill twenty-three to atone for one, nor to drown the entire town, I'd have thought. Although I've suspected there must be more to it than I know, for them to do what they did. Certainly the Elves had reason for wanting some revenge."

Talon looked at him in surprise. "Twenty-three to atone for one? You can't mean... you killed an Elf?" he asked, appalled at the idea.

Dustin's face darkened in shame. "We caught one of them. He'd cut our snares, smashed our traps, freed what we'd caught, the animals that still lived. We caught him doing it. The trappers did, I mean. They dragged him back to the village.

"They'd beaten him, but that wasn't enough for what he'd done. It was going to take weeks to fix all the traps and they knew we'd lose at least a month of furs. They were enraged over it. They went mad, for a time, I think.

"They whipped him. They tied him to one of the drying racks, where we cure the furs, one of the big ones we use for obearn pelts. They stripped off his clothes and they whipped him to death for it.

"My mother still remembers it. She's told me about it. She still wakes up crying some nights, about how beautiful he was, how like a child, such terror in his blue eyes, how he looked at her, begging. He couldn't beg any other way: they'd broken his jaw when they beat him.

"She tried to stop them. She ran to grab for the whip—the man's name was Harold, the one who'd done it—but my father dragged her back. She never forgave Father for that, not till the day he died, that he stopped her from helping the Elf.

"After ten lashes Harold called out for the others to get a few lashes in as well. He was laughing. He said we'd take his hide, for the ones he'd cost us, that we'd skin him alive for it. And they did. The others helped whip him. They flayed him alive.

"Anyway, some traders came and we sold them the body for twice what we'd lost. Aralyn only knows what they might have wanted with it," he said, shuddering.

Talon felt ill. The Enemy must have engineered it all, somehow, to set Men against the Elves and Elves against Men, and then taken the body to turn into a Revenant. He listened as Dustin continued.

"The village had a feast that night, a tremendous celebration. All the men in the village got so drunk they couldn't walk. But a few days later the Elves came. They attacked without warning. They surrounded the village and disarmed everyone before we had a chance to resist. They called out Harold's name and he came forward; he was too arrogant to be afraid of them. And they dragged him off. We never saw him again.

"But the Elves came back, the ones of them who had left, and they called out other names and dragged them off, then others still. Twenty-three in all, including Harold: every single man who'd raised the whip to the Elf, even those who'd given him a single lash, pressured into it by the others.

"Then the Elves told everyone left in the village that they were going to flood it, destroy it. They could take only what they could carry on their backs, only what they could gather quickly. No one believed it at first, but then they saw their eyes. A terrifying thing, an Elf's eyes, or so I've heard.

"Our people started gathering things quickly after that: children and food and clothes, everything they could carry. The women whose husbands had gone and the children whose fathers were missing had begged the Elves to tell them where their men were. But they remained silent.

"Then our people were all escorted out of the village, dozens of Elves with bows to either side of them. We were told not to look toward the river. But some of us did, of course. Then there were screams and everyone looked and then there was chaos. The men were there, the missing ones. They were tied to the drying racks. They were dead, all of them, a single arrow to the heart.

"The Elves dragged everyone off after that, no matter how they struggled to go to the bodies. They carried them, even the grown men, the ones they'd not slain. They were so strong! Then there was this roaring sound. And then the Elves were gone. They just disappeared into the trees. And everyone ran back to the village. Only there was no village. There was only the Methris River, where the village had stood.

"The village was gone and the bodies were gone. We couldn't bury them. Their spirits were doomed to the river and our homes were gone. The entire village was lost. So we left.

"Our people settled far from the river, in what's now called Teris, only the hunting was miserable there. After the first winter, when so many starved, many of them went to the other side of the Methris; they formed Lethos. The others in Teris became farmers, instead. We've had nothing more to do with them.

"Anyway, that's it, that's the story. My mother's talked about Teris a lot, now, since Father's died. She says she'd like to live there.

"Trapping's all I know. It's what my father taught me. But I've not the stomach for it anymore, nor for life in Lethos. Living in constant hate and fear like that does something to a people. It turns your heart to ice. You can see it in the eyes of those who live like that."

He looked intently at Talon. "I wonder what it is that you hate and fear that your eyes look as they do? Your cousin's eyes aren't like that yet, Talon, not by far. I hope you're going to Ardock to live, that you're fleeing your own dark past, so Beryl might have a better life by it. Don't tell me if I'm right. I'd rather think I am than know the truth."

Talon eyed him in surprise. He pulled off his glove and clasped Dustin's shoulder, careful to touch part of the exposed skin at the neck of his shirt. "You're a good man, from what you've told me and what you've said now to me. May you find the peace you seek," he said, taking advantage of the contact to probe outward with his core.

Remarkable! No Power at all, not a trace, yet this man had read so much from his eyes. He'd described them as he'd heard other's speak of Farad's eyes, cold and hard and dead, to those that did not know him well enough to see past the surface. It chilled him to know that his own eyes might now betray so much.

Talon was glad they'd be parting company on the morrow. Men such as Dustin were valuable and rare; it would not do to put him in danger by associating with him.

Dustin rose and headed toward the trees, no doubt to relieve himself before bed.

Talon winced at the pain coming across his bond from Lunahr. He knew Lunahr was only pretending to sleep, that he'd heard. He realized Lunahr had been silently crying and hadn't wanted him to know. He was torn as to whether he should say anything to him, but Lunahr solved the dilemma for him. Lunahr came to him, his face streaked with tears.

Talon held out his arms, and Lunahr dove into them and began sobbing against him. Talon hugged his young cousin tightly and did his best to calm him.

"Laren, it can't be true, can it? The Elves wouldn't really do something so terrible, even if those horrible Men did something so cruel. How could they have done what he said?" Lunahr asked in Amontirin.

"We have yet to know the truth, Lunahr. We cannot, until we hear the Elves' side of it. The truth most likely lies somewhere in between, though from what I've seen, as a rule, Elves are more honest and less biased in their history than Man is in his. I will ask Eladar, when he returns. If he does. I cannot risk leaving you with his people until I learn as much as I can about what happened. If even some of Eladar's people truly have learned to hate Men, then I'll not leave you there with them. Now get some sleep, Lunahr. It's going to be a long night," Talon urged.

Eladar did not return that night. Talon kept careful watch for him, lest Tanran see him first. He awoke Lunahr for his watch and did his best to rest, but he would not sleep, not here.

When morning came, they readied themselves to leave. Tanran and Sevran left, to check their traps. Talon checked upon Raymond and changed his bandages, showing Dustin how to do so and making sure he understood how to correctly administer the medicines he left with him. "Now, I would ask a boon of you, for the aid I have given your friend."

"Name it," Dustin said, intrigued.

"We have a friend who has been traveling with us. If he appears here looking for us, I would ask that you tell him we have gone on to Ardock and that you warn him of Tanran, so he might be on his guard. He is a River Elf. His traveling name is Fisher," Talon said solemnly.

Dustin's eyes widened. "An Elf? You are friends of the Elves? And after what Tanran has said and what I revealed to you, you still aid us?"

"Should I punish Raymond for the words or deeds of one he travels with, or for the actions his people took before he was even born? I trust you with what I have told you, because you also are a different man than Tanran is. I know that you will not set Tanran upon my friend Fisher's trail, from your own words and deeds. Now we must go. Farewell."

"Farewell, Talon, Beryl. And thank you," Dustin said.

TALON and Lunahr began heading again toward Ardock. They traveled for a while in silence. Lunahr was looking terribly forlorn. "Laren? Will Eladar be safe? What if those Men find him?" Lunahr asked in Common.

"I doubt they might see him, even if he was standing before them, or catch him, if he was, or be able to injure him with their arrows. Not even the Horsemen of Aralon can outshoot an Elf at the bow and Elavar once spoke highly of Eladar's bow work in my presence." Talon laughed. "Though that single compliment was so enmeshed in a string of complaints it is a small miracle I heard it. I remember it distinctly, though, for that reason," Talon said, hoping to lighten Lunahr's mood, to reassure him Eladar would be safe, although he was more than a little worried about Eladar as well.

"How like my dear brother," Eladar said, coming out from behind a tree to their right. Talon and Lunahr both jumped, startled, hands instinctively going to their swords, then stopped.

"Ha! So I did manage to sneak up on you this time. You'd wounded my pride, terribly, you know, my not being able to before. Despite what my brother might think about it, I am as good as he is in the woods arts, or I would be, had I five hundred or so more years of practice at it.

"I take it you are referring to those Men who are now in what was your camp? I was concerned, at first, that they were bandits and had somehow managed to overcome you, until I found your trail, hard though you've made it to follow. I can see I was wise not to enter the camp. So, they are Elf-hunters. Not a safe nor profitable pursuit for anyone," Eladar said, apparently amused.

"Sneaking up on an Amontir is also not a safe nor profitable sport for anyone either, Eladar," Talon scolded. "You're lucky I am a swordsman, not a bowman. Were you to pull that little stunt upon my cousin Hunter, you would not now be laughing about it." Talon felt his bond to Farad again, gently, just to reassure himself it still existed. No warmth nor light came from it, little seldom did, but he valued it as keenly as he valued his bond to Lunahr.

Eladar looked at Lunahr. "Why is it older relations feel so compelled to chastise younger ones, even when they are someone else's relation?"

LUNAHR eyed Eladar critically. Eladar's cheerfulness seemed forced, to his ear. "Eladar, you had to kill that fox. You were right to. Those men in our camp, they were the ones who set that trap. They believed the fox sprang it, as you'd hoped they would. They set off after the mother, to kill her and steal her cubs, but she instead wounded the one man. Talon used his skills to aid him."

"Ah, I see. And did you find out what those *kethshalathu* wanted with a live obearn and why they might instead kill her and steal her cubs?" he asked, his voice suddenly soft.

Lunahr wondered at the unfamiliar Elvish word, but he'd ask Laren later what it meant. "They wanted to catch a full-grown obearn to pit fight in Ardock. I can guess what pit fighting is, from what they said. I've not wanted to ask Laren about it. They have a celebration coming up called Feast Day. They said they'd have sold the cubs to the Governor of Sarna, for his menagerie. I hope the obearn are already far from here. I wouldn't want to see them or the trappers hurt."

"Then it is a good thing I was not there. I might have been hard pressed to restrain myself, hearing what you've just told me. I flattered them, by calling them what I did. I'm afraid my vocabulary is not yet up to describing them adequately," Eladar said darkly.

"It's a good thing you weren't there, Eladar, for you as well as them. They might have harmed you. They certainly would have tried to. The one, Tanran, said... he said some terrible things. But then Dustin told us why. I still can't believe it's true, Eladar, that your people might have done something so terrible. Did they really kill twenty-three Men? Did they really drive the rest from their homes and divert the Methris to destroy their village?"

Eladar stopped walking suddenly. Lunahr turned to him in surprise. There was a look of terrible pain upon his face; Lunahr recognized guilt, but also terror and more that he could not name. Lunahr reached out his hands and clasped Eladar's shoulders. "Eladar, never mind! Forget I asked. I wouldn't have said anything if I knew how much it might upset you. Forgive me."

Eladar was trembling. Elves never trembled. Eladar's reaction was frightening him. Lunahr embraced Eladar, as Laren would have embraced him, were he the one in such distress. To his surprise, Eladar didn't draw back from him, but held him. Lunahr felt the trembling ease.

"Forgive me," Eladar said. "You have caught me at a time when I am too vulnerable. I still cannot forgive myself for the fox. I doubt I ever will be able to." He shuddered. "I saw his eyes when the light left them. Even though it was necessary, even though, from what you have told me, my worst fears might have been realized, had I not done what I did. Although Ardock was not drawn into the morass as much as Alridge was...

"I should not have let you free the obearn, Talon, but I had seen I couldn't stop you, short of killing you, and at the time I had thought taking such action extreme. But I have endangered my people again, by allowing you to do what you did. Tell me what they told you of Terleth, who they are to know of it. I must know everything you do," Eladar commanded of Beryl, as if he were his prince.

Lunahr looked at Laren for permission to do so, and he nodded. Lunahr told Eladar everything he had heard Tanran and Dustin say.

Eladar nodded, and then signed heavily and looked at him intently. "Never make a mistake, Beryl. Never, in your youth or ignorance or arrogance, do something that might endanger your people, that might cause others harm. You will, I know you will. My mother has told me we all do. I wondered what her mistake might have been, that she had such pain and compassion in her eyes when she told me. I wondered whether anyone might have died for her mistake. I wondered, and then she told me."

Eladar took a deep breath. "I am babbling, I know. You must be content to hear me babble for a time. No, I have nothing further to say. You must instead be content to hear only silence from me. You might think that a blessing, having known me even for so short a time, until you hear it. Hearing silence from me is like listening to you when you are not singing, Lunahr. It is wrong, somehow, unnerving. You doubt me, now, yet you will see." True to his words he grew silent.

They walked in silence for a time, and Talon looked at Eladar in surprise as if it was indeed unnerving for him as well. Lunahr was eyeing Eladar in compassion, in concern. He began singing softly; he couldn't bear the silence. He doubted his music might help, this time. It apparently hadn't last night. He was discouraged to know it hadn't.

"We should be seeing the City walls by mid-afternoon, from what I remember," Talon said, into the stillness.

"Tell me again what you remember about the City, Talon?" Lunahr asked carefully in Common, using Laren's traveling name. It felt wrong, doing so. Like it felt wrong hearing only silence from Eladar. Lunahr listened intently as Laren began telling him about Ardock.

"ARDOCK is a walled city, the last of the southern cities before reaching the Velmar Mountains, which we've just crossed. They keep their gate open during the day, as most cities do, so we should have no trouble entering. They're not one that charges a toll to enter, or at least they weren't last time I entered, but it's been four years. It's a sizeable city. They've a governor, not a king."

He looked at Eladar. He couldn't stand him being so silent. "Eladar, what do you mean to do, while we are in the City? Where should we meet you once we are done?" Talon asked, not sure he would answer.

"Meet me? What do you mean? I intend to come with you, of course," Eladar said.

Lunahr looked at Laren in surprise. "Of course he's coming with us. Why wouldn't he?"

Talon looked from one to the other. "Because he's an Elf: Elves despise cities, at least, Cities of Men. They are smelly, noisy, dirty, squalid, and overcrowded to their sensibilities, and severely lack the trees and waters which they need to survive. Ardock's relatively clean, for a city, and it's got the Methris River running alongside it. But the Men he would see there would become quite distressed upon seeing him, especially considering what we now know. You must know Elves are not well loved, Beryl, not just by those Men we met, but by everyone. They are far too misunderstood to be. Most Men fear them and some even hate them, only for them being different from us. They might either flee from him in panic or attack him out of hand."

"PLEASE, Laren, he has to come! It won't be nearly as much fun without him there," Lunahr said. Lunahr was in desperate need of fun. It was as if he was forgetting how to smile. He loved Laren, fiercely, but traveling with him had not been at all what he had suspected it might be. Laren was so guarded out in the world, so very different from the Man he knew. He missed the cousin he loved.

TALON sighed. He could imagine the "fun" Eladar might have, unleashed upon a City of Man.

Eladar saw the look Talon was giving him. "Again, you do not give me enough credit, Talon. I have been in City of Man before, many years ago. As much as I am loath to admit it, an Elf, when cloaked, is indistinguishable from a Man to all but the most discerning eye. I can be discreet when I have need to be."

Every instinct Talon had was screaming at him that this was a bad idea, but one look at Lunahr's face and all the arguments against it melted to nothingness. "All right. Discreet. Lunahr, you already swore no music, neither singing nor playing. Eladar, you must now swear as well: no tricks, no pranks, nothing that might lead anyone to suspect who you truly are, and nothing to bring undue attention to Beryl or to me."

"Believe me, Talon, drawing attention to myself is the furthest thing from my mind. I swear I shall do nothing to do so," Eladar said, seriously. Then he removed his cloak from his pack and donned it, carefully tucking his long silver hair fully under the hood. And suddenly his posture and gait changed as well. He slouched and shortened his stride and made it choppy, so he no longer glided along the ground as if water flowing over smooth river rock. He appeared an ordinary traveler, cloaked against the cold.

"Laren! He's wonderful! He does exactly as you do! I'd no idea!" Lunahr said, grinning in delight. He slipped on his own cloak and bound his own long hair in a ponytail, the way some woodsmen wore theirs, long but confined. He tried to mimic Eladar's stride, but stumbled. Then he tried to slouch, but quickly straightened. "How can your back bear it?"

Eladar said grimly, "Far more easily than it can bear the lash, as it did the last time I was revealed to Man's eyes. Although as you have heard, those who harmed me were punished for it far worse than I."

Lunahr's eyes widened in horror. "You? That was you? But... but it couldn't have been! I mean, you're not dead. They said...."

"No, I am not dead," Eladar said softly. "I was not quite killed. Almost. It was a close thing, so very close. But not quite.

"I was truly still a child, then. I'd only just turned twenty-one. I so wanted to see the world the others spoke of, the world outside Riviera, the world of Men. So one night, I snuck away. I'd prepared well for my journey: I'd learned Common, I had food, even a purse full of coin.

"I went to Alridge first, but I traveled through without stopping. I knew they'd look for me in Ardock and Alridge when they noticed me gone, that they'd scour those areas closest to Riviera and Loatia first, once they'd searched everywhere within them for me. So I went to Sarna. I stayed there for a number days; it was truly wonderful. I learned so much. No one suspected who I truly was. I kept carefully cloaked.

"But then I made the mistake that almost cost me my life and cost others theirs. I wanted to see more. I left, heading for Kalten to the south. I didn't know about Terleth, that little village they told you of that used to lie between Sarna and Kalten, by the River. It was a village of fur trappers. They'd go into the forests on both sides of the River, for miles in all directions, and lay their traps. Terrible traps. I found a dead fox in one and a fawn in another that died soon after I freed it. And I found worse.

"I found skinned animals beside the traps, their bodies left to rot, and to attract more predators, to be caught in the reset traps. There were foxes and beaver and raccoon and wolven, even an obearn cub. I found more traps as well: empty ones that hadn't caught anyone yet, baited with animal flesh and other enticements. I knew that Men hunted, that Men ate the flesh of animals, but many animals hunt to eat, to survive. This was different. This was terrible, monstrous, cruel, barbaric.

"So I destroyed the traps. All of them. I routed them out and slashed the snares and smashed the others. I waged systematic war against the callous murderers who had placed them there.

"I had destroyed many dozens by the time I came upon the wounded obearn cub. It was crying and howling so piteously. I was so intent upon freeing it, that I didn't hear them come up behind me, even with my ears. I didn't realize I'd been seen.

"I awoke in terrible pain, outside their village, where they'd dragged me. Amongst other things, my jaw was broken, I think from the blow that felled me. But they'd not just hit me once, to knock me out, they'd hit and kicked me everywhere, while I was unconscious. I could feel it upon awakening. Once I was conscious, they did more of the same, cursing me for costing them a fortune in pelts. They yelled they'd have nothing to sell to the boats heading upriver, how when their children were starving that winter, it would be my fault.

"Then they strung me up by the drying skins of the animals they'd slaughtered on one of the racks. They tore off my shirt and pants and began whipping me. They said they'd take my skin in trade for the ones they'd lost.

"Of all of them, there was only one woman who tried to stop them. Her eyes… it was her eyes that kept me alive, after a while. From what you said, it was Dustin's mother. I wish I'd been there when he told you. I'd have asked him her name," he said softly and then continued more strongly. "That's when Oberas came with his friends. They were on a boat that had just docked. They'd wondered where everyone was, why no one came to the dock to meet them, so they went looking. They found the villagers and they saw me.

"Terhannon was the youngest of them, just a boy, though an adult by Man's law; he was only sixteen. He had no business being with them with what they were planning: they were heading for the Dwarven Lands, for the Lost Kingdoms. Oberas was the one who'd brought him. Terhannon was a minstrel and Oberas wanted someone to write ballads of their adventure who'd been there to see them. Terhannon worshipped Oberas like a God. In retrospect I realize it was love I was seeing, but at the time—anyway, when Terhannon saw what they were doing, saw what I was, he begged them to stop. He cried for me. He had the most amazing blue eyes, that boy," Eladar said, wistfully.

"But those men told them what I'd done and why they wouldn't free me. Vargas tried to get them to stop as well. Lonas, Harnel, and Loessen thought it best not to get involved. I learned all their names, Terhannon's age, and their motivations later, of course.

"Finally, it was Oberas who succeeded. He offered them coin in exchange for my life. He asked them how much loss I'd cost them and then offered them double that amount, in coin, if they'd release me to them. The villagers must have thought Oberas mad, if they truly thought me already dead, as you said, but Oberas talked them into it, though he hates me for it to this day, for what came of it.

"It was such a paltry sum: only two hundred gold. Although afterward, you should have heard them bicker over it, how they'd not be able to make it all the way to the Dwarven Lands because of it. But Oberas knew. He said my people would pay any price to see one of their own returned safely to them.

"That's why he'd done it, for the reward, of course. He didn't care about me. He had no idea who I was, none of them did, and I could not speak to tell them.

"They took me onto their boat. They left Terleth right away, lest the trappers change their minds about releasing me. They bound my wounds, tended to me as best as they could, and laid me upon my stomach on the deck. Terhannon held my hand and spoke and sang to me almost the entire journey.

"I kept trying to rise, to go over the side, into the River, so the waters might help me but they would not let me: they thought me delirious. They sailed straight through, past Sarna without stopping, heading for Alridge. They'd heard the Elves lived just past there. Even Men knew that much at least.

"They never made it to Alridge. My father had discovered me gone and he'd sent men everywhere to look for me. They'd searched Alridge and Ardock in secret, cloaked. But they also searched every boat upon the River, and they were far less subtle about it. Oberas and the others didn't even see them coming. One moment the River was empty and the next there were a dozen armed Elves swarming up and over the sides of the boat. My father's Guard would have killed all of them, then and there, finding me like that, except they knew such justice was my father's. So they disarmed them and bound them and then they pulled me over the side.

"I was barely conscious, barely alive. They'd kept me for days out of the water, not realizing how dangerous that was for me, especially so injured. I still remember the sound of Terhannon's voice begging them to stop. He thought I'd drown, that the water would cause my wounds to fester. He thought they were mad.

"They swam me home, while the others followed on the boat. I truly would have drowned without them aiding me, of course; the current would have claimed me. I was far too weak to swim or even stay afloat.

"When I saw my father and mother, and brother and sister, I cried. I'd thought I'd never see them again. And they cried for me, also, even he-who-is-my-brother wept seeing me so injured, but also, there was such anger upon their faces. Even my sweet, gentle sister was enraged. Then my mother touched my face and I slept.

"It was Mother who healed me, though it took many days, as my injuries were so severe. My back was far too damaged to heal quickly as it otherwise would have, but also, my jaw and shoulder and ribs had all been broken and they'd damaged my insides as well. Mother almost died saving me.

"While I slept and healed, they interrogated Oberas and the others. You've heard something of our methods, I'm sure, Talon. They were far from merciful or gentle with those Men. But my people learned they were not the ones who had harmed me: to the contrary, they had instead actually saved me. They learned who was guilty, who had harmed me." Eladar stopped, lost deeply in memory.

"You've said Oberas hated you. For the interrogation? Or did they lose the two hundred gold after all?" Lunahr asked cautiously.

"No. Terhannon's love of me spared them much pain. And once my people learned the truth, they received far more than the two hundred gold, though they received that amount first. They received other gifts, as well, that aided them on their quest. Oberas had made a sound investment, as he'd known it would be. No, Oberas hates me for Terleth," Eladar said softly.

"My people took most terrible revenge upon them, for what they had done. They had tortured an Elven prince nearly to death, but far worse, an Elven child. As crimes against our people go, that one is unforgivable.

"My father led the attack upon Terleth personally, to ensure that only those who were guilty were punished, that there be mercy for the rest. My people would have torn every adult male in the village to pieces.

"They found the Man who had first whipped me and interrogated him to learn the names of the others. Then they questioned those Men, until they had the names of all those who had helped him harm me.

"They slew every Man responsible. They evacuated the remaining adult males and all the women and the children. Then they obliterated the village. They changed the course of the River and washed that cursed scar upon the lands away. Those who survived the flood rebuilt far from the River, in what are now the towns Teris and Lethos.

"Oberas still blames me for it. He won't blame himself, of course. He won't acknowledge that it was his greed that led him to free me, to return me. He never considered what the consequences to those people might have been. His eyes were filled only with an image of the reward he might claim.

"He got his reward. He's had to live with it, both what he gained in Riviera, and what he lost by it in the Dwarven Lands. Terhannon died there and Vargas lost his arm. Oberas and the others barely lived, all of them. It was my mother who healed them, who saved them. But I tell you too much. That was two years later," he said softly.

"You blame yourself for it, too," Lunahr said in wonder. "For Terleth, even after what they did to you. You still feel guilty for it."

"Of course. Though I was unconscious at the time Terleth was destroyed and unaware of what my people did, and unable to stop them, it was all my fault.

"I hadn't understood about the trapping, at first, why they might do such a thing. I thought them cruel, evil. I had thought they killed without reason, until they screamed at me about the coin they lost, about their children starving in the winter for the lack of it. They were cruel, but their actions and their anger were at least understandable, then.

"I learned that the world is a cruel place, that perhaps one must become just as cruel to survive in it. Isn't that what we try to protect children from? From losing their innocence, from becoming the very people we despise? And there was Dustin's mother, also, who had tried to save me, to stop them. They held her back, when if they hadn't, they all might have been spared.

"Also, I'd seen a City of Man. It was filthy, but there was beauty there as well. There were terrible Men there doing evil deeds, but there were good ones as well, doing kindnesses. As I had suspected, the world was so much more complicated than I had known it to be from living my sheltered life.

"I longed to return, to learn all I could. But I was forbidden. I was watched, how I was watched! My people had acted against Man.

"We were confronted for it by emissaries from Alridge and Ardock both. They were afraid we'd gone mad, that we might attack their cities next. We explained why we had acted as we had, that the one they'd attacked had been a child, for all he appeared a man to their eyes, that I was their prince.

"We came to agreement with them. We withdrew to the shelter of our River and Woods, careful not to set foot outside them for a long time thereafter. We could not risk a full-scale confrontation between our peoples. My brother was allowed to leave, of course, and some of the others, on missions of diplomatic necessity, but not me.

"I begged my father to let me go on this mission to meet you, Talon. My father, my sister, and especially my brother were all against it. But my mother… she convinced them to let me go. I could see the fear in her eyes, but still, she knew I had to be allowed to go. I had hoped I might get to see Ardock. I've never been there before, but I hoped it might be like Sarna. I've heard much about it.

"I truly appreciate your faith in me, Talon, that you allow me to do this, that you act so against your instinct, even though I can see you are doing it for Beryl's sake, not mine," Eladar said somberly.

Talon was silent. He'd judged Eladar too quickly before, that much was certain. There was far more to Eladar than met the eye. He found he liked him much more than he had at first thought he might.

ELADAR sighed. He'd told them too much. He should have kept silent as he had first intended to. He had revealed more of himself than he felt comfortable about. But it was as if he needed to let Beryl hear his darkest secrets, to see whether he might draw away from him, or still wish to befriend him as intently as he already seemed to want to.

It was astonishing that a Man might have such an effect upon him. But Beryl was also still a child, twice a child, for not having come-of-age yet, but also, for being a Man. All Men were children, or so his people thought. Except, perhaps, for the Amontir.

Perhaps they seemed more adult, not merely for their longer lifespans, but for all they had endured. They had survived such a terrible war, a war they yet fought. Eladar knew his own people had once survived such a war, long ago, though they never spoke of it, even amongst themselves, and certainly no Man would ever learn of it. Even he only knew as much as he did of it for being the son of a king.

"We will reach the City this afternoon. We will stay there exploring the City for one day. We will spend the night in an inn and then leave the following afternoon, agreed?" Talon asked.

"Agreed," Lunahr said eagerly, and Eladar echoed softly. Then Lunahr began singing again, happier songs.

IT WAS afternoon when they first saw the City. Talon said, "This is Ardock. You can see the wall, from here, and some few of the rooftops beyond it."

Lunahr looked at it in excitement. "It's so big! Oh, Laren, it's wonderful!"

Eladar gave a lopsided smile, a shadow of his usual grin. "You only say so because you can't yet smell it from here," he teased.

Lunahr shook his head at Eladar, smiling, and they continued onward.

"Remember, let me do the talking if we run into any trouble entering the City," Talon instructed. "Although a walled City, Ardock's gate has always been an open one, but sometimes they question travelers. If they insist upon you removing your hood, do so, Eladar. Elves are not barred from the City.

They should allow you entry anyway. There's no reason to make them nervous. We've nothing to hide."

Eladar nodded. He wished now he hadn't insisted Beryl be allowed to come here, for being so late and all that had happened. He wanted desperately to be home, to be within the safe confines of his kingdom. He shook his head at his folly. After such a trip, he might not be allowed to leave again for some time.

He hoped his parents wouldn't be too angry with him, too disappointed, and that Elavar wouldn't be. And he hoped his parents would welcome Beryl, that they would let him stay. He knew that sheltering Beryl would put their kingdom in danger, were the Enemy ever to discover it. Perhaps most of all, he longed to see Elanara's scowling face, longed even more for her to smile at him, for her to just once, perhaps, be proud of him. He sighed. He asked too much.

Then he cocked his head and listened. What a remarkable song. He forgot his troubles for the moment, and let Beryl's song soothe him.

LUNAHR smiled at Eladar as he saw the expression upon his face change, from one of sadness to one of contentment, and his heart swelled in pride, knowing he was helping his friend.

Chapter 4
Journey's End

OBERAS stretched and yawned and walked over to Hardred, who was turning the newly carved rudder this way and that in his hands. Hardred obviously had been hard at work while Oberas and most of the others had slept. "It's ready then?" Oberas asked.

"Aye, it should be. I'm just about to try it on her." Hardred roused Sadrin and Alnas. "You told me to wake you when I was going to put it on her. I'm ready."

Sadrin sighed. "Not even a cup of kakla for me, eh, just a dunk in the River, first thing upon waking?"

Hardred grinned. "You'd never make a seaman, Sadrin."

ALNAS stared at him. Hardred had smiled. He'd done more; he'd grinned. It must be the boat, the water that was affecting him so, or perhaps the knowledge that he yet lived when he should be dead. Alnas walked over to the River's edge with them.

"We're ready, Tebras," Hardred said. He handed him the rudder to inspect.

Tebras whistled. "That's fine work, Hardred."

"How much would a rudder cost you, Tebras, if you'd had to get it replaced in a City?" Oberas asked him.

"At least twenty gold for the rudder. They have to craft them carefully, you know, and there's often a wait. And at least five gold to raise her from the water, plus dry-dock fees. I probably couldn't have done it for under forty gold and it might have cost much more," Tebras said.

Oberas nodded, his expression thoughtful.

HARDRED took the rudder from Tebras and slipped into the water. It was cold. It felt good. He was tired. It had been a long night. It wasn't easy, carving by firelight. He slipped the rudder on, and clipped the end cap on to fasten it as Sadrin watched intently. He bobbed to the surface. "Give the tiller a try," he told Tebras. Tebras boarded his boat and did so. "Does it feel right?" Hardred asked.

"Near as I can tell, from being docked. The true test will be once we get underway, but I'd say you've done it, Hardred. I'm much obliged. You've saved my boat," Tebras said, relief strong in his voice.

"I'm pleased I could help. Good voyage," Hardred said. "May the water be calm and the wind at your back," he added by rote.

"LOGAN, rouse the rest of the guards, tell them we're pushing off shortly," Oberas said. Oberas headed for his bedroll, as if to pack it, and then took out his purse from beneath his shirt, stood where no one could see it, and counted out a handful of coin. He never let anyone see how full his purse was. Loyalty only ran so far. He rose, his hand clenched into a fist, and approached Hardred. "Hold out your hand, Hardred. I've something for you."

Hardred did so, obviously puzzled. Oberas opened his fist and let four ten-gold pieces drop into his palm. "That's for you. Payment for services rendered."

Hardred stared at the coins in surprise. "I didn't help you for coin."

"I know. But I'm paying you for it anyway. The Code doesn't prevent me from doing so. It's the least of what it would have cost us, were we in a City with the facilities to help us. You've earned it.

"Tell me, once you're in Ardock, you'll be staying, won't you? When you've spent all the coin you've made on this trip, I'd be pleased if you'd seek me out. I always have need of good guards, and you're one of the finest I've met. You'd be valuable to me, on trips such as this, though I won't be making any for a while, with a new apprentice to train; I never take them from the City so young.

"It's easy pay; just ask any of my guards, especially Logan or Devrik, they'll tell you. They'll tell you an earful, I'm sure. Logan's been with me two years and Devrik four. I understand I'm no joy to work for. But still, few would take the risk of trying to rob me, so as I say, it's easy work. Just think about it. I've a shop on Market Street, near Tailor. Just about anyone in the City can tell you where to find it. It'll be well worth your time to come by."

Then Oberas turned to Tebras and in a far more harsh tone said, "Well, come on, Tebras. What are you hanging about for? We've a City to get to."

HARDRED watched him board the boat, intrigued by both the man and the offer.

Alnas approached Hardred, shaking his head. "Forty gold!" he said, then lowered his voice. "Forty more. Forgive me, Hardred, but I saw your purse in the bottom of your pack, when we thought you lost. You must have had at least one hundred fifty gold in it. I stopped counting it when I got to one hundred."

Hardred looked at him and sighed. "One hundred sixty-five, not counting what's in the second purse at my side, or this. I estimate about two hundred thirty all told. I've made more in nine months as a guard than I might have made in three years at sea," he said, frowning. "I only wish I had a safe way of sending it back home to Riana."

ALNAS decided to risk asking. This was the first time Hardred had mentioned home at all and the first time he'd mentioned Riana while awake. So Riana, at least, yet lived. "Is Riana your wife?" Alnas asked, hoping he sounded casual enough that Hardred might answer before thinking not to. There was no way Hardred could know how important the answer was to him.

Hardred looked at him in surprise. "No," he said simply.

Alnas had just resigned himself to having to settle for that much, for hoping to learn more some other time, when unexpectedly Hardred volunteered more.

"She's my sister," he said, softly. "She only just turned sixteen two months before I left. She's a little over a year and a half younger than me. Mother died of illness when she was three and the sea took Father when she was only twelve. When Father died I'd just turned fourteen. I was too young to sign onto a ship as anything but a cabin boy, and that's not an easy berth to find. Julian was fifteen, but nearly sixteen. He was able to sign on as crew to a merchant ship: the *Silver Gull*," Hardred said, eyes distant with memory.

Alnas held his breath. Julian. Hardred had mentioned Julian as well! He prayed silently to Elmoth that Beltris wouldn't call him now, that nothing would interrupt them. It might be months before Hardred opened up like this again. It might be never.

Hardred continued. "He took a terrible risk. We both did. He snuck me aboard the *Gull* as a stowaway. We hoped that once I was found, they'd be too far out to sea to do anything about it, that they'd make me work for my passage, maybe earn something, too—that I might be able to earn enough so Riana and I wouldn't starve. We're lucky they didn't keelhaul us instead."

"Keelhaul?" Alnas asked and then bit his tongue. He'd not meant to risk causing Hardred to slip back to silence.

But Hardred apparently wanted to talk, or maybe needed to. "Keelhauling is when you tie a man to a rope and throw him overboard from the bow, that's the front of the ship, so he's dragged along under the length of the boat. Few survive it."

Alnas stared at him, wide-eyed. "What happened?"

Hardred said grimly, "The plan worked. Jesred, our neighbor Kessel's older brother, knew me. He stood up for me, said that I'd be able to pull my weight. And I did. Two months later, when we returned to port, I had a handful of coin, and I was offered a job as cabin boy on the *Gull*, when theirs was made a full seaman.

"Fortunately, while I was gone, Riana had been able to sing for her supper enough to eat, in the Market, and we'd the shack still, so she had a roof over her head. I gave her what I'd earned and I shipped out again, the next time the *Gull* sailed. Two month voyages, with two weeks off in between, over and over again, until I became a seaman as well, after a time. I stayed with the *Gull*, always with her and with Julian, right up until her final voyage."

He looked up at Alnas, and there were tears in his eyes. It chilled Alnas to see it, a man as strong as Hardred, in tears.

"We came back to port a ghost ship. We missed the docks and almost ran aground on the rocks, but they boarded us in time to save us, what there was left to save.

"Riana came. She was there. She shouldn't have come aboard. It's bad luck for a woman to be aboard. She's so jealous, the Goddess. She takes revenge for it, but She'd already taken almost all She could off that cursed ship.

"Only three of us survived of the forty who had crewed her: me and Remis and Toby. She took the rest. Jesred and Derek and… everyone, even little Randy… I thought I'd go mad, from the wailing of the women as they mourned, but it was the nightmares that were claiming me.

"We'd been best friends since I was old enough to walk: our mothers were like sisters. Even as a baby, Riana loved him. She crawled around after him as if she were a puppy and he held the leash. There was no question. Everyone always knew that they were to have been wed, but it was before that voyage that he asked her. Julian." He spoke the name in a whisper, and the tears that had been held so perilously in check in his eyes fell. They rolled down his cheeks.

"I still hear the roar of the storm. I still feel his hands, dragging me to the wheel when I couldn't walk, the rope tightening about me. I see his eyes, blue like the sky should have been.

"It was late in the season for such a storm; there never should have been one. It was Her doing.

"I still hear Julian's voice, telling me I'm safe, that he'll be beside me, and that we were almost to port, almost home. How I had to live, to come home to Riana. I see him start to lash himself beside me. Then the terror in his eyes as the wave crests behind me and he grabs me. And I feel the wave, it hits like a hammer and it tears him away from me and washes him into the sea, into Her cold embrace."

Hardred wiped angrily at the tears. "I shouldn't have told you. It's bad luck to speak of it. I must be mad telling you. No, not mad. Not yet. I thought I could flee from Her, that I could get far enough inland that I'd no longer hear Her calling to me.

"She's been calling us to Her, the three of us She missed. Remis found his refuge in a flask. He's drunk himself safe, but what kind of a life is that? Toby... poor Toby... he was so afraid of Her taking him he made sure he'd be safe from Her. A week before I left, he took his own life, safely on land. He cut his wrists and watched his life's blood flow freely. They said he had such a smile upon his face when they found him: a look of calm and peace and joy. We buried him on the hillside, on the side away from the shore, where you can't even see the water," Hardred said, wistfully.

Alnas feared for his friend. Hardred had sounded so envious of Toby, when he'd spoken of him.

Hardred continued. "I used to climb the cliffs and look out over the sea, hear the pounding of the surf on the rocks below. I'd see Her image floating in the first mists of the morning. She'd be waving Her arms, beckoning me to Her, urging me to embrace Her, to take one step forward, just a simple step. And I heard Her with every wave that hit the rock.

"I never should have told Riana what I saw, what I heard, not after them finding Toby. Riana was so frightened I'd jump she wouldn't let me leave the house, after a while. None of them would. They watched me, night and day. But it didn't matter.

"The walls couldn't keep the sound of the sea at bay. Nothing could. There's not a building in Meria you can't hear the sound of the surf from. So I left. I had to, to be safe from Her.

"But it's hopeless. She's in the River, too, they've told me She is, though I haven't heard Her here, nor seen Her. Still, I can't escape Her. I'll never be free," he said softly.

He turned to Alnas, his face haunted. "I have to keep moving, Alnas. Don't you see? I didn't know She swam the rivers as well. I have to keep moving, or She'll find me."

Alnas argued, "But She already tried to take you, didn't She? Only the Elf stopped Her. Maybe the Elves' magic is stronger than Her power, so far from the sea. Maybe you're safe from Her here."

Hardred looked at Alnas. "I've known you for two weeks now, Alnas, but I've never before known you to spout blasphemy before breakfast."

Alnas's face flushed. "That's because you don't talk to Elmoth, Hardred. If you did, he'd tell you I've done so on a number of occasions, though I usually have the sense to insult the God I worship, not someone else's. Forgive me, Hardred. I won't ask Her to. I don't think She might. From what I've heard these past two days, She doesn't seem to be the forgiving sort.

"Come, let's get some kakla. We'll be mounting up soon, and you'll need something to sustain you until you can get some sleep." It was unnerving hearing Hardred talk calmly about hearing and seeing the Goddess, about contemplating taking his own life.

Alnas had known something terrible haunted Hardred, but he had never guessed how horrible. To lose all his shipmates and his best friend! No wonder Hardred kept apart from the others, kept his heart so carefully guarded.

HARDRED looked at his friend's worried face. He was tired, so very tired, or he'd never have spoken to Alnas about Julian and especially not about the Goddess. He thought it would hurt worse, speaking about Riana, about Julian, like saltwater upon an open wound. But it had helped somehow instead. The pain had dulled, not sharpened.

He looked at Alnas thoughtfully. Could he truly stop running? Could he perhaps settle in Ardock? Could he live so near the Methris? He hadn't heard Her here. Perhaps Alnas was partially right. Perhaps Her power was weak here. Perhaps he might be safe. He'd have to see.

"Are you coming, Hardred?" Alnas asked, eyeing him carefully.

Hardred nodded wearily and headed for the pot of kakla.

"WE'VE only one more day and we're safely in Ardock," Velson said eagerly.

Beltris glared at him, "Quiet, you fool! A trip's not over until you're safely in the city, the coin in your hand, the wagons gone, and you've been discharged from service. My last trip ended with only three guards surviving, though we'd had seven of the fifteen with us the night before our journey ended."

"I know there's often attacks nearer the cities, since many of the bandits live in them. But surely with so many travelers coming for Feast Day the bandits would pick those more poorly defended? We've still too many guards for such ill to happen to us," Velson argued.

"Too many indeed," Leeson the cloth merchant said. "When we hired you as captain for this trip, Beltris, you told us you'd not take the job with less than thirty men for the ten wagons, and you tried to argue for forty. We all thought that extreme, but you came highly recommended having survived two other caravan trips, though you'd never captained before. I'm sure the cost in coin to us never entered your mind. Well, I for one consider our coin poorly spent! We ran into little trouble along the way and have not lost a single guard. It is obvious now we could have made the journey with half the guards we had, had we chosen a different captain."

"Is that so?" Beltris asked softly. "And how many bandits didn't attack us, for us being too well armed and too well guarded? Did you figure that into your calculations as well, merchant?" He said the word as if it were an insult, using Leeson's occupation instead of his name in his anger.

"We saw the remains of more than one caravan on our way, and not all were old and weathered. Or do you so easily forget the men I made you stop the caravan to bury, when you would have left them for the carrion birds to eat, out of fear it was a trap to lure us to our deaths as well? How many axles might have broken if we'd not had the men we needed to properly push the loaded wagons from the mud when the Methris rose so high in the storm that it flooded the Road? Might we have had to unload all your cloth into the mud otherwise? I've earned my pay, as has every one of these men, men who may yet die to see you safely to Ardock."

"Pay him no mind, Beltris," Roberthan the carpenter said. "The craftsmen amongst us, at least, recognize what a fine job you and the others have done, even if the merchants are too stupid to see it. Merchants ever only think in terms of coin earned and coin spent. A man who crafts things with his hands thinks differently than that."

"That's why you have so little coin to protect," Garrett the jewelry merchant scoffed. "Men only work with their hands when they don't have the wits to do better."

"It takes just as much skill to work with your hands as with your tongue," Willeth the tinker said.

"Leave it to a tinker to think so! You don't do either, do you? You merely patch what others have crafted poorly enough so it needs mending," Leeson scoffed. "Or things so old and worn they should be replaced."

"Not many can buy new all they need for a home. When I mend their things for a fraction of what they'd have to pay, they have more coin to buy things they don't truly need, like fine jewelry and fancy clothes. Name me the man who says he lives well who hasn't a pot to cook in or a bucket to haul his water in," Willeth said angrily.

Hardred spoke up softly. "What about farmers? Those who till the soil for their livelihood? A man might argue their labor requires neither skill nor wit. Yet who of those amongst you would not starve without their grain to make the flour for your bread, or die of thirst for lack of the mead you drink, when the water might kill you?"

"Well spoken, Hardred! More than half our men are second and third sons of farmers," Beltris said loudly. "The other half are second and third sons of craftsmen and merchants both. Would you start a battle now, amongst those men, who would be better served guarding you?"

He'd seen more than a few of his men around him taking insult to what was being said. "Look sharp, men, and pay them no mind! Keep an eye out for bowmen. The rocks up ahead are a perfect spot for ambush. Velson and Ledrus, it's your turn to scout. We'll wait here until we hear it's safe. Anders and Jenson, you best go with them; that's a lot of rock to cover."

"Thanks, Captain! I was about ready to lose me breakfast listening to these varging idiots," Velson said.

Beltris sighed. Now that they were so close to Ardock, discipline amongst the men was becoming lax. It might have broken down altogether, were it not for the end-of-trip bonus. More than a few men would ride off to the City leaving the caravan behind were it not for that. Men sometimes did anyway, those who didn't own the horses they rode, like Hardred. Except Hardred would never do something so dishonorable.

Beltris hoped Hardred might find reason to stay in Ardock. This was Hardred's fifth caravan, and his third. It was a miracle they'd both survived. So far. He'd not tempt Elmoth with such confidence, not when he was so close to the City.

The Southern Road was ancient, this portion of it made of solid rock, worn smooth long ago by hundreds of thousands of hooves, feet, and wagon wheels, dating all the way back to when Thenalon was the capital of the Thenalonese Empire, long before the once-great Empire withered and shrank to a single city.

Beltris eyed the scrub around him suspiciously as he waited for the men he'd sent out to report back, though he doubted the trouble, when it came, might come from here. The land was too open for ambush. There weren't any trees, just what few scraggly bushes and succulents managed to find purchase in cracks in the windswept bare rock. There were steep cliffs on all sides, but the walls of the pass were far from the road here. This portion of the Methris was narrow and deep, having carved a great swath into the rock many ages ago.

The rock ahead was where the trouble likely lay. The pass narrowed considerably, and the cliffs up ahead were unstable. There was the evidence of countless rockslides, enormous chunks of the cliff which had sheared off and thundered down onto the floor of the pass below. Some of the rock was all harsh planes while others were tremendous rounded boulders, the edges worn away long ago. The jumbled piles of rocks on both sides could easily hide an entire army, with none the wiser, until they attacked.

Beltris scowled in disgust as all too soon Velson, Ledrus, Anders, and Jenson rode back. "Nothing there, Captain," Velson reported.

"Of course not," Leeson scoffed disdainfully, beginning to urge his horses forward.

"Wait!" Beltris commanded, riding in front of them. "You're back too quickly. You couldn't have checked all that rock carefully enough. I'll not risk our lives for you being too impatient to have a woman and a mug of mead to do your jobs properly. Hardred, Alnas, Sadrin, Kard, go see what they missed!"

"You're wasting our time, trying to find trouble that's not there, to justify your own inflated wages," Garrett said. "I say we go on now."

"Well, then, it's lucky for the lot of us that I'm Captain and not you. You'll stay here," Beltris ordered.

"Who are you to order me? You forget who it is who's paying your wages! And your bonus! You'd do well to remember that," Garrett said imperiously.

"As you'd do well to remember that you're surrounded by armed men who are loyal to me and who have had enough of your arrogance," Beltris snapped.

Garrett's face darkened in outrage. "Are you threatening us? Is that why you wanted so many guards? So that once we got close to the City you could kill us and take our goods, and make it look like it was brigands?"

"What I meant was, you'd do well not to threaten a man's bonus after he's earned it. You're stupider than I thought, suggesting something even worse, to men who are already angered against you.

"But they're honorable men, all of them, and they'd not do something so despicable, not for fear of what Elmoth might do—though you can bet He'd take his vengeance for such treachery and betrayal of an oath—but for what their own conscience dictates," Beltris added loudly, to be sure all the men heard.

The few hands that had quietly gone to sword hilts just as quietly moved away from them at his words. None would risk calling Elmoth's vengeance down upon himself.

"Now go, the four of you," Beltris commanded.

"AYE, Captain," Hardred said, seeing Beltris had the men in control. He'd seen the remains of more than one ship where the men had mutinied close to shore and ended up running the ship aground when they might just as easily have reached port safely.

Now to the task at hand. Beltris was right. The others couldn't possibly have checked the rock thoroughly in so short a time. Such sloppiness had cost the life of three guards his last trip. He'd not see it happen again.

It was Sadrin who found the first of the hidden men. He managed to dispatch him with his sword a scant moment before an arrow caught him in the throat and felled him.

Hardred drew his sword, turning to Alnas. "Warn the caravan it's a trap and that they've got bowmen!" he yelled, slapping the flat of his sword against the rump of Alnas's horse. It leapt forward just in time to avoid an arrow.

Hardred's own mount wasn't so fortunate. His horse was felled out from under him. He barely sprang free of it, then ducked behind it for what scant cover it offered. "Kard! Are you still with me?"

There was no answer. Either Kard was trying not to betray his position, or he was already dead. If the latter, Hardred was alone here.

He heard the sound of several horses galloping off after Alnas and cursed. The caravan hadn't come to the bandits, so they were going to the caravan.

He took the risk and ran for the cover of the rock. He'd search the rocks for men who might still be hidden; maybe he'd find a horse he might use to get back to the caravan. Kard's might yet live, even if he did not.

Hardred came across a swordsman, his leg bloodied, but not nearly as bloodied as Kard's body, which lay at his feet. Hardred thought he might dispatch him quickly, so injured, and avenge Kard, but it soon became apparent that the man was a far better swordsman than he was, even injured. Hardred cursed as he snapped inches off the top of his blade when it hit neither flesh nor sword, but the rock beside the man.

Hardred fled into the rock, glad the merchants weren't here to see it, for what they'd think of him. Then he dropped his sword and pulled the knife from the sheath on his leg. He'd survived more than one pirate boarding of the *Gull*; he'd learned to fight as they did. Blade held securely in his teeth, so both hands were free, he began climbing the rock as if it were the ship's rigging.

He came up behind the unsuspecting swordsman silently, and leapt down from the rocks upon him. It was over in moments.

He wiped the bloodied blade on the body and re-entered the rocks, looking for other prey. Not all the brigands might have had horses. Some others might yet be here amongst the rocks, lying in wait for those of the caravan who might try to flee this way.

ALNAS galloped back to the wagons. "Brigands! Circle the wagons!" he yelled. He could hear the sound of galloping horses coming up behind him, though still at a distance, too many to be their own men.

Hardred! He couldn't be dead, not a day from the City! It wouldn't be fair.

BELTRIS cursed. The merchants had brought this down upon them, for their arrogance, and the men, for their overconfidence. He'd no wish to die here, not when he'd finally have the gold he needed with this trip to build his inn.

"Faster, you fools! They'll be here in a moment. Now get into the circle, stay down. Bowmen, first volley at them!" Beltris called. Six of his men let their arrows fly.

"Second volley!" he shouted, and the other five shot while the first six nocked new arrows. They'd practiced this maneuver a number of times since first leaving Logareth, circling the wagons and alternating bowmen; it was a trick he'd learned on his first caravan. It had served them well then and served them well now. A number of the brigands fell before ever reaching them. But then they were upon them, and it became swordsman's work.

ALNAS fought desperately. The men that attacked were vicious, their eyes gleaming with lust for the treasures all around them. Alnas wished Hardred was fighting beside him.

He saw Jenson fall soundlessly. He'd paid for his earlier mistake in not searching carefully enough. It was impossible to tell who was winning; all Alnas's concentration was merely upon staying alive.

He was astonished when only a short while later, after felling his current opponent and looking in vain for another, he heard Beltris's voice calling for a head count and he realized their foes were defeated. The battle was won.

Of the twenty-seven guards who'd been there, including Beltris, nineteen yet lived, eleven of whom were wounded. Of the eighteen brigands who'd attacked them, none lived; the wounded thieves had been quickly dispatched. Antris the tanner and Willeth the tinker, both of whom had joined in defense of the wagons, were dead. The other four craftsmen and the four merchants were alive, although Roberthan, who had also fought, was wounded.

Leeson and Garrett, of course, the two who most deserved to be dead, had cowered in their wagons and were unharmed. But they'd not thank Beltris for it. They'd blame him, for the danger they'd been in, he was sure.

Hardred! He had to find Hardred! "Captain, please, I want to go to the rocks. Hardred and Kard might yet live," Alnas begged.

"What about Sadrin?" Beltris asked.

"Sadrin's dead. He's the one who found the first of the hidden men. A second man's arrow claimed him just after he slew the first. Then Hardred sent me to warn you."

"I'm sorry Alnas, but I can't risk it, not yet. There may be more of them in the rocks. We need every man to guard the wagons," Beltris said.

"But Hardred might be injured! He might die if I don't go to him now," Alnas argued.

"I know. But we all might yet die. None of us are safe, not yet. Not until we reach Ardock. You signed on for the full journey, Alnas. Hardred wouldn't have wanted you to leave it unfinished, nor to risk the lives of others for him. Here, help me with these bodies."

Alnas swallowed hard. Beltris spoke of Hardred as if he were already dead. Alnas nodded reluctantly and bent to the grisly task.

They lined up their own dead and the brigands as well. The thieves were searched for coin and other valuables, all of which was collected in a pile, to be evenly divided amongst the surviving guards, as was custom. The valuables of the fallen men went to their closest friends amongst the guards.

Hardred's pack was on his horse. Alnas hoped there hadn't been other brigands within the rocks who might have taken it. Not as much for the loss of the gold, though Alnas was certain Hardred's sister could have put it to good use, but for the loss of the statue and the letters to Riana and his flute. Those things should go to Hardred's sister. He'd take them himself, to Meria. He'd risk a second caravan downriver to do it and the sea voyage to Meria. He'd be more likely to survive that than by trying to repeat Hardred's feat of five caravan trips.

He'd feared Hardred couldn't survive a fifth. How could Hardred be dead? Now, after he'd survived drowning, after he'd just remembered how to smile again, after Alnas had finally even heard him laugh?

"Horseman," Anders called. "Just one, coming slowly."

"Ready your bows. This may be a trick of some sort," Beltris said.

The men strained to see more detail. "Elmoth! It's Hardred, leading a horse," Alnas said, mounting his own and spurring it into a gallop toward him. He reached him quickly.

"Alnas! You're all right! I was worried for you," Hardred said.

"Worried for me! We thought we'd lost you! I wanted to come but Beltris wouldn't let me."

Alnas looked at the horse. It was Kard's. There were two bodies over the saddle, face down, their heads on the other side. "Sadrin and Kard? Both dead?" he asked, and Hardred nodded.

"You're lucky there weren't more men in the rocks. What took you so long to come?"

"Because there were more men in the rocks. I had to make sure I got all of them, that there wouldn't be any left to cause trouble for the caravan. There were five, none of whom will be troubling anyone ever again. I have their things. I found their camp as well and checked it for men. There's things there we'll want to scavenge. How many did we lose?" he asked softly.

"Eight guards here, ten with Sadrin and Kard. We've also eleven wounded, but none seriously. But Antris and Willeth died as well. They fought bravely beside us. Roberthan did too, but the Gods smiled upon him and he was only wounded."

HARDRED nodded. He didn't ask the names of the dead; he'd find out soon enough. He mounted up behind Alnas on his horse at his urging, and the two proceeded to camp.

Chapter 5
Ardock

TALON, Eladar, and Lunahr entered Ardock without the Guard at the gate stopping them or asking them any questions. They were part of a continuous long trail of people entering the City. At first Talon was surprised, until he remembered the trappers telling them about Feast Day. He'd not realized it was a holiday of some apparent import. The streets were remarkably crowded.

Lunahr was staring at the throngs in wide-eyed amazement. "I didn't know there could be so many people!" he said, astonished.

Talon smiled at him. "Just remember what I told you. Stick close to me, keep an eye on your purse, and be ready for anything, but don't draw your sword within the City unless you're in danger. We certainly don't need any of us getting arrested."

Talon glanced at Eladar. Eladar was blending in remarkably well. He'd unstrung his bow and wrapped it in a long, thin bag he'd carried with him for that purpose. An Elven bow was quite distinctive. It would draw too much attention, otherwise.

Talon turned back to Lunahr and cursed. He'd only looked away from him for an instant, but Lunahr was gone. He looked about, fighting his panic. It might take days to find him if he wandered far enough. There was a sea of unfamiliar faces.

Then he stopped searching with his eyes and used his ears instead. There, to the right: singing! Eladar heard it at the same moment, and they headed for it. Then Talon realized what a fool he'd been: the bond, he could trace Lunahr through the bond. And there was Lunahr, standing under an open window, a beatific smile upon his face, head cocked, eyes closed, listening.

Talon thought he'd both test his young cousin and teach him a lesson. He approached Lunahr from behind, silently, part of the crowd, and casually reached for his purse. He promptly found himself grabbed by the wrist, his arm painfully twisted behind his back, and his face slammed into the wall in front of him. He heard Eladar laughing behind him as Lunahr stammered an apology.

"Lar... I mean, Talon, forgive me! I thought you a thief," Lunahr said, letting him go. He blushed. "I can feel you, now. I was distracted. I was listening to the music and—oh no! I wandered off, didn't I? I didn't mean to. I just needed to get closer to it, so I could hear it better. It's so noisy here," he said, looking at him, eyes bright.

Talon sighed. "Beryl, I'll take you to all the music you might ever want to hear: minstrels congregate in the Square in this City. But you must promise to stay close. Even bonded, I'd have a hard time finding you in such a crowd."

Talon felt a strong hand clamp on his sword arm from behind. He twisted and struck out for the Man's face, barely pulling his hand back from connecting the blow in time when he saw the uniform, cursing his luck: it was a City Guardsman. No, two; there was another Man at his back, hand on his sword hilt. They must have seen what he'd done and thought he was truly trying to rob Lunahr.

The Man pulled back from the blow that didn't connect, ready for a fight, and was surprised and suspicious when Talon became suddenly docile.

"Guardsman, please, this isn't what it looks like," Talon began.

"That's better. You almost earned yourself sixty days in jail for striking me, instead of the twenty you'll get for purse cutting," he said, glowering at him, his hand still firmly clamped on Talon's arm.

Then he turned to Lunahr, and his expression softened. "Are you all right, lad? He didn't hurt you?" he asked solicitously.

Lunahr looked from the Guards to Talon in dismay. "Wait, please! He's telling the truth. He's my cousin, he wasn't really trying to rob me, he...."

The man's look of concern turned to a scowl. "Oh, so you were just roughhousing, is that it? Well you picked the wrong week for it. Fighting on the street the week of Feast Day will get you both ten days. Surrender your swords. You're coming with us."

"Surely not?" Talon asked. His purse was heavy with coin from Arcanus; he actually might find another way out of this. And he'd not keep any of his coin if he landed in jail. City Guards were not by their nature an honest lot. "There must be a fine we could pay instead, for disturbing the peace?" Talon suggested hopefully.

The man's eyes narrowed. "You're not trying to bribe me are you?" he asked glacially.

Wonderful. Of all the City Guard in a city the size of Ardock, he had to get caught by an honorable one. Talon looked around quickly for Eladar. Talon saw Eladar standing a distance away, and he caught a glimpse of Eladar's face under the hood of his cloak. He was still laughing.

"Of course he wasn't," Lunahr said earnestly. "Please! It's all my fault. I wandered off to listen to the singing. I couldn't help it. It was so beautiful! And my cousin just thought to teach me a lesson for it, about how dangerous that was. Or maybe he was testing me, to see whether he really could rob me. He does that sometimes. He's very protective and...."

There was a laugh from above. "So this is all because of my singing? I truly almost brought the house down this time, then, didn't I? At least it felt like you were trying to knock the house down, when I felt the wall shake. It's good to know I haven't lost my touch."

Lunahr looked up. There was a beautiful woman looking down at him, fine boned, but thin to the point of gauntness, pale as an Elf, with shadows beneath her laughing brown eyes and a mischievous smile.

"That was you? What was that you were singing? What's it called? I've never heard it before," Lunahr asked eagerly.

The woman leaned out the window further. "Never heard it? Then you must never have been to Ardock for Feast Day before. It's called 'The Revelry of Rialto.' Rialto's the one the Feast is for, of course, or didn't you know? He was the Governor, about, oh, at least fifty years ago and...," she began.

"Excuse me, Alissa, I know you don't get a chance to get out much, now, and how you love to talk, but we're trying to arrest these two. Surely Katlina or one of the others will be stopping by to stay with you today and...," the Guard began.

ALISSA grinned and said, "Nonsense, Farion! You can't arrest this sweet young man and his cousin for listening to me sing, can you? Why then, you'd have to arrest me too, wouldn't you, for singing in the first place and causing such chaos?

"I have a better idea. I'm already dressed, and I was only trying to work up my nerve to go out by myself. I wanted to go to the Square, but I knew I'd get a terrible scolding if your brother found out about it. Now I can have you escort me. I'm sure I'll know enough of the people there that any number of them can escort me home, afterward."

She looked at the beautiful boy with the bright-green eyes and long blond ponytail. "If you like music, the Square is where you should go. All the minstrels gather there, for Feast Day and the days before and after. We should call it Feast Weeks, really, for the week before and after, the way it's grown these years. A day just isn't long enough to contain it anymore. I hear people travel upriver all the way from Seaview on the coast to the south for it and cross the Velmar Mountains from as far north as Fenemal. I'll be right out," she said, and her head disappeared from the window and she closed the shutters.

FARION studied the pair before him intently. The younger one—a boy, really—looked back at him openly and the other guardedly. "What are your names?" he asked reluctantly, caving in to the inevitable. He hadn't seen Alissa so animated and lively in weeks. He'd cut off his own arm before he'd deny her something she wanted so fiercely. He only hoped he wouldn't regret it later and that Anorion wouldn't be upset by it.

"I'm called Talon. This is my cousin, Beryl," the older one said.

"All right then, Talon, Beryl. You listen carefully now to what I'm going to say. Alissa's a good judge of character; I've never known her to be wrong about anyone. She's my brother's wife besides, and I'm not wanting to sadden her or you'd not be getting off so easily. She's plenty of friends in the Square, both Guard and minstrels, as well, or I still wouldn't risk it. I'm going to take you there with her, like she's asked me to. You'd best be certain nothing happens to her after that or I'll know who to come after, and every man in the Guard loves her as much as I do. Is that understood?"

"Perfectly, sir," Talon said, acknowledging the warning.

"We'll guard her as if she were kin to us," Beryl swore solemnly.

"Guard her? You're a good lad after all, aren't you? I liked you before, when first I saw you, taking on a man bigger than you. You remind me of my nephew," Farion said fondly.

ALISSA came out, mandolin in hand, grinning broadly, her eyes bright, a shawl over her shoulders.

"Now, Alissa, are you sure about this? It's quite a walk to the Square. And are you certain you'll be warm enough?" Farion asked.

She looked at him and then at the green-eyed boy conspiratorially. "What is it about older male relations that make them so overprotective?" she asked, grinning. Then she turned to Farion.

"I'm fine, Farion, really. I've been feeling much better since the rains started. I promise I won't stay out so late that I might need to be carried home, all right?" she said as she began walking. Then she grew more serious. "I can't miss Feast Day. I haven't once in the eleven years since I came to Ardock. I have to sing and play at least once."

"Might I see your mandolin?" the boy asked eagerly. "Hold it, just for a moment? Perhaps you might even honor me by letting me run my fingers across the strings just once? I know how to play. I had to leave my own behind, you see. I've only my flute and it's been almost two weeks now since I've been able to hold or play anything else and... oh. No, never mind, I forgot. I promised I wouldn't play here," he said forlornly.

"Promised you wouldn't play?" Alissa said, looking over at him in surprise as they walked. "Surely you can't be as terrible as that, that someone would have you make such a promise," Alissa said, smiling.

"No, no, of course not, just the opposite actually, I...." He looked from his older cousin to her and grew silent.

She eyed the stranger thoughtfully. "Aha. So you're the one who made him promise. Shame on you, making someone who loves music enough he'd wander off to a stranger's window to hear it promise such a thing. Whyever shouldn't he play?" she asked, looking at him intently.

TALON looked at her in surprise, hesitating for only a moment, trying to think of something. He couldn't very well say so they'd not draw attention to themselves, especially not after he'd nearly gotten them arrested.

"Never mind, then. If you wouldn't be answering with the truth, I'd not want to hear," she said, scowling.

Talon was concerned to see a look of strain upon her face, and he realized her slow pace, which they had matched to begin with, was slowing further. He was flummoxed by her. He'd seldom met someone so perceptive. It was unnerving for him, shrouded as he was in secrets, to suddenly appear so transparent to someone he did not know. But he realized she also seemed to be in increasing distress. Her breathing had rapidly become ragged and rasping. He debated saying something when Lunahr spoke.

"I'm content to listen for today, really I am," Lunahr said. "I hoped I'd hear new songs, so I might write them down and remember them always. I brought my pen and ink with me. I brought my music of course, just one book, though, is all I could carry. I copied some of my favorite songs into it, but also I've a number of blank pages, for the ones I learn while I'm away. Do you think you might sing 'The Revelry of Rialto', for me?" he asked eagerly.

"OF COURSE," Alissa said, but began coughing on the word. She stopped walking entirely as a fit of coughing seized her. She gasped for breath as Farion held her. She'd have fallen to her knees, were it not for his strong arm around her.

Farion put his hand to her back and started rubbing it. "That's it, Alissa. I knew this was a bad idea. I'm taking you home."

Her face showed her dismay, but she nodded, unable to speak. She truly thought she might be well enough to sing and play in the Square, but the dust from the street had entered her throat and now she couldn't catch her breath.

"To get to the Square, you just continue on Wright Street the way we were walking, past sixteen more streets, some to your right, some to your left, then turn left on the sixteenth: that will be Carter Street. Go three more and turn right at the herbalist's shop on the corner. You can't miss it. You'll hear the minstrels before you see it," Farion said.

"WAIT! I've some skill at healing. Perhaps I can help?" Talon offered.

Farion shook his head, "I wish you could, but it's the wasting sickness. She's had it these four months past," he said softly. He needn't say more. She'd not live past six months; no one ever did, and she was already terribly thin.

"Isn't there anything we can do?" Lunahr asked.

"Not unless you can conjure an Elf for her. More than anything in the world, she'd hoped to see one again before she dies," Farion said, mouthing the last three words silently, so she'd not hear them. Farion scooped her up into his arms as if she were a child; she looked light enough to be one. He began carrying her home, the second Guard carrying her mandolin.

Lunahr's eyes filled with tears. "Laren, can't you help her?" he asked in Amontirin, forgetting himself for a moment in his distress, watching her go.

Talon put his arm across his shoulder. "I wish I could, Lunahr," he answered in the same language.

Eladar approached. He'd been following them stealthily. He was no longer laughing.

"Can't you do something, Eladar?" Lunahr asked in dismay.

ELADAR shook his head. "Not even my mother would be able to help her," he said, speaking only part of the truth. She would be able to cure her, but only at the cost of her own life. Even his people feared the wasting sickness.

"But I can grant her wish, for her aid of you. I will wait until the Guard leaves her, then I will go to her. I can find my way back to her house. I will meet you in the Square afterward. I heard him tell you how to get to there."

Talon nodded. "Come, Beryl. You've need of music."

LUNAHR nodded mutely and began walking with his cousin to the Square, all the joy drained from him as Eladar began walking back the way they had come. When he and Talon got to the Square, however, he could not remain melancholy for long, not with such music all around him. He sat eagerly before one minstrel and then another, at first merely listening. Then he took out his book and pen and ink and began transcribing what he heard.

Talon meanwhile, although he kept a careful eye on Lunahr, listened eagerly to the chatter that was going on around the minstrels, listening as always for signs of the Enemy. He was relieved to hear nothing of interest. He suspected Incuban and his minions had yet to penetrate into the Lands of Men. He was still wreaking havoc upon the Dwarven Lands, sending kingdom after kingdom into oblivion.

Thoughts of the danger in the Dwarven Lands inevitably led him to thoughts of Farad. He wished his oldest cousin would come home. He wished there were still a home for him to come to.

Talon fidgeted. He might hear more in the Market or in one of the many taverns. He wished Eladar were here; he might trust the two of them together to avoid mischief. Eladar, so far, was little like he had expected. "Beryl, it's about time for lunch, don't you think?" Talon asked hopefully.

"I'm not hungry. I could sit and listen here for weeks. Who needs to eat, when surrounded by such music?" Lunahr asked joyfully. "Besides, what if El… Fisher returns, while we are gone? Why don't you go eat and bring me back something?" he suggested. "There's Guards all around, here. I'm safer here than anywhere."

Talon eyed the Square carefully. There were indeed a number of City Guards, with so many travelers stopping to listen, and so much coin at the minstrels' feet a tempting target for thieves. Talon suspected a minstrel might make enough here on a day like this to equal what he might normally receive in a week if not two.

"All right. But you're to stay here, in sight of the City Guard. I shan't be long," Talon averred. He'd go to the Market and get food from the stalls there, while listening to the merchants' tales and those of their customers.

He left the Square, glancing back more than once at Lunahr's back as he did so. It felt wrong, leaving his young cousin. He had so little time left with him. The thought of leaving Lunahr with the Elves still cut like a knife. Yet it did feel good to be on his own again. He was not used to traveling with someone, especially someone he had to watch over.

He slipped into the crowd, finding his way to the Market with practiced ease. He had a mental map of much of this city already, as he did of most of the cities of these lands. Most of them had changed little within the decades since he had visited them.

Talon reached the Market without incident and pretended to eye the wares while he listened in on the conversations all around him. Then he was drawn to one of the stalls as he heard the hawker extol the virtues of his stock, which he claimed came from the Dwarven Lands, from one of the Lost Kingdoms.

"Which one?" Talon asked the man levelly.

"Which one what, sir?" the man asked politely.

"Which kingdom? If I'm to view your wares, I would be assured of the authenticity of your merchandise," Talon said.

"The name will mean nothing to you, unless you have traveled the Dwarven Lands yourself. And if you had, then I'd not want to reveal where my treasures come from, now, would I?" the man reasoned.

"**But I must know, so you will tell me anyway**," Talon said, weaving his Power into his words.

"Of course. These are from Armsguard," the merchant said.

"Armsguard fell some thirty years ago. It is deep in the Dwarven Lands. Why go so far?" Talon asked.

"It's safer, sir. It's truly a dead kingdom. Many of the nearer ones have far greater treasures, entire treasure vaults of gold and silver and gems that have yet to be plundered, from what I've heard. This is just what others have overlooked or left behind as not worth the trouble. Those others, the ones with the real treasure, also have terrible creatures guarding them, things that were once Dwarves, I've heard, though I can't believe that part of it. Taveras swore to me they were the dead, come back to life, but of course, he might say something like that. Who ever heard of such a thing?"

Talon asked him a few more questions and then released him from his thrall. The man knew little of the Revenants guarding the kingdoms; he did not even believe they were truly the walking dead, as Talon knew them to be. He knew nothing of the Enemy, nothing of which kingdoms yet stood.

Talon sighed. His bond to Farad was so weak. He feared his cousin might be shielding him, trying to protect him. Farad knew how fragile his core was, how close to madness he had been, how it might again claim him. Talon would give anything, pay any price, to see his cousin safely returned to him.

He sighed again. He should return to Lunahr, to the Square. But he could not shake the feeling that there was something of importance to find in this City. The longer he stayed, the stronger the feeling grew. His intuition had never misled him before.

Surely he should at least check the rest of the Market? And the weapons stores and jewelry stores, of course, as each of his kin did upon entering a city or town of any size. He doubted he might find the lost King's Knife or King's Ring, but it was possible, and more than one House sword and even a few bands had been reclaimed that way, to be passed on to an heir who yet lived, or more often to be buried, in the case of the many Houses that no longer had living heirs. After he checked, he would return to the Square and Lunahr.

He was confident Eladar must have already joined Lunahr there by now. The two of them would keep each other safe in case of trouble. But he also reassured himself that in view of the numerous City Guards there should be none.

Later tonight, when Lunahr and Eladar were safely in bed, he would go to the taverns and see what information he might find. He began checking the rest of the Market.

LUNAHR stretched, working a cramp out of his leg. He had sat here for some time, transcribing all he heard. His stomach rumbled. He realized he was hungry. He looked at the sun, which was now low in the sky, then around him, expecting to see a familiar face. It was far later than he had realized. Surely Laren should be back by now? And Eladar should have returned long ago as well, Lunahr realized nervously.

He began packing up his book and ink, feeling along the bond for his cousin. Was it that way? Or this way? He kept getting distracted by the loud crowd of people milling everywhere. Perhaps he should retrace his steps to Alissa's house, instead, and look for Eladar first?

He hesitated. He had told Laren he would wait here. But surely Laren had not expected to take so long, nor expected Eladar not to reappear? What if some ill had befallen Eladar? What if someone had discovered he was an Elf, someone dangerous, like those trappers, someone who hated Elves? He remembered what that horrible Man had said, about wanting to see an Elf in a pit fight with an obearn or some other vicious creature. He must find him; he must ensure Eladar was safe.

Lunahr left the Square, carefully reversing the directions that had brought them there. As he walked, he began humming some of the music he'd heard. He especially liked that piece, the one where—wait. How many streets had it been so far? Seven or eight or perhaps even nine? He'd lost track. He must concentrate. These streets were very confusing; they turned every which way. Not a one was in a straight line.

He counted the rest carefully: sixteen. Only this didn't look right. He'd try two more. He did so and looked about him in dismay. This wasn't right, either. He'd best return to the Square and start again, this time paying closer attention.

He tried retracing his steps. No, none of this looked familiar.

"You look lost, friend. Can I aid you?" a boy slightly younger looking than him asked.

Lunahr smiled at him gratefully. "I'm looking for the Square. I'm supposed to meet some friends there, but I seem to have gotten turned around."

The boy smiled. "New to the City, eh? Don't feel bad: everyone says it's like a maze. I was actually going that way myself. You can just follow me. I know a few shortcuts. We'll be able to avoid most of this crowd. The City gets so crowded near Feast Day."

He led Lunahr down a narrow street which was indeed less traveled, and then another and a third and then toward the mouth of an alley. "This will put us right on Carter Street."

Lunahr smiled in relief at the familiar street name. He was fortunate to have found someone so helpful.

He was halfway down the alley when he heard a strange noise behind him and turned. Two men were coming up behind him. One of them was holding a knife, looking like he meant to use it, and the other some sort of club.

Lunahr called out a warning to the boy and drew his sword, confident he could protect the boy and himself. The two men stopped advancing and began slowly backing away from him.

Lunahr was relieved. Perhaps he need not hurt them; he was scaring them away just by holding his sword. They could see that he knew how to use it, that he meant business.

Then something heavy and hard cracked into his head from behind, and blackness claimed him.

ELADAR stood unmoving, cloaked in the shadow of the alleyway where he had been for half the day or more. A Man might have gone mad long ago, waiting. Eladar sighed. He had hoped to investigate this City of Man, but the day was rapidly slipping away from him. It would most probably be years before he might get such a chance again. But he had a duty to perform, a responsibility. He would carry it out.

He exhaled in frustration. Instead of the woman leaving, three children were now knocking upon Alissa's door. He would endure. He would wait. If Talon and Beryl grew concerned, this is the first place they would look for him. If it was Elavar, he would wait. He would sacrifice his own happiness to aid someone who had aided his friend. He would prove to Talon he was an adult by his patience; Talon might praise him in front of Elavar. Not that it would help. Nothing he did ever helped.

What was this? The door was opening again, so soon. "... sure you'll be all right?" the other woman was asking.

"Yes, I told you, he'll be home soon. He's never late. He's such a responsible boy, and you've children of your own to tend to. Besides, it's been hours since I last coughed. Go, Emma, and give my regards to Darhew," Alissa said firmly.

"All right. Come along then, children, and we'll see what we can do to clean it up before your father gets home. Although if you think you'll avoid a scolding for it, you've not considered how upset I am...," Emma said and then faded from earshot.

Eladar waited five heartbeats and then went to the door, just long enough so Alissa might think it was still her friend, so she might open the door without asking who it was. He knocked, exactly as he had heard the children do it, in case they used some special pattern to identify each other. He'd heard Men sometimes did so. Men were so odd. Odd, but wonderful.

"Who's there?" Alissa called.

Eladar sighed softly. This might not be so easy. "Fisher. I am here at Farion's bidding," he said, speaking truthfully.

The Guard's name worked, as he hoped it might. The door swung open.

"THAT'S sweet of him, but I told him...." Alissa gasped in sudden fear and began trying to close the door when she saw the cloaked figure before her, face in shadow, when she had expected to see a City Guardsman.

The intruder slipped past her effortlessly, entering the house as Alissa opened her mouth to scream, praying she might have breath enough to, that someone might hear. How could he have moved so fast?

She saw a moment later, and closed her mouth, her scream dying stillborn, as he swept off his hood, revealing his ethereally beautiful face, his long silver hair, his upswept ears.

"I did not lie to you, Alissa. I am truly here at Farion's bidding and at your own. I heard him say that you wished to see an Elf. I grant you your wish."

Alissa's eyes widened in sudden recognition. "You! It's you! The one from Father's book!" she said, staring at him in astonishment.

ELADAR looked at her, amused. "Because I am an Elf, you think me the exact Elf from a picture in a storybook your father read you as a child?"

She looked at him as if he were a backward child. "Of course not. You're the Elf from the book Father started to write, until he got stuck, trying to get the picture of your face just right. He drew you twenty-two times and—but he couldn't have been as wrong as that! Your forehead should be higher, your nose thinner, your cheekbones more pronounced. It's as if he drew you older than you are, and it was years ago."

Eladar stared at her in astonishment. "Your father was Alistair?"

Alissa looked at him in sudden suspicion. "How can you know that? How can you know his name?" She drew back from him. "I've heard about Elves and names, how you never tell us yours and how foolish we are to tell you ours, how dangerous it is for you to know them."

"You need not fear me. I would never harm you," Eladar said, looking her in the eye.

Alissa gasped and drew forward again, as if she were made of iron and he a lodestone. "No. No, you wouldn't, I can see that. But how do you know Father's name?" she asked and then answered her own question. "What a fool I am! Of course, from the book! I knew it must have been one of your people who took it, for the flower you left. Who else could make a flower bloom overnight upon a grave? It was your magic."

Eladar laughed. "It was indeed one of us who took your book. It was he-who-is-my-brother. But he used no magic. He gifted a flower in exchange for the book, after he saw what was inside. He carefully uprooted a lily from further upriver and planted it on the grave, in honor of the one who had gifted it to him, who had left it where he might find it. Though he had no idea why a Man might draw so many pictures of him, and leave him such a gift upon his death. He was pleased by the likeness, by the love and artistry that had gone into each line. He gifted the book to our mother. He thought she might like to have it, for her love of him, but also, for her love of Man."

"Your brother? It was your brother that Father saw? It was his face that haunted him? I never understood the wistfulness inside of him, until the day I stood by the river on the way to Ardock and caught a glimpse, the tiniest hint of a cloaked face as it turned from me, as it disappeared into the woods. I always hoped to meet one of you again, to truly see you. I hardly thought I might get the chance to speak to you, let alone that you would knock upon my door!" she said, eyes alight with joy.

"I am pleased I am the one who was able to fulfill your wish," Eladar said sincerely.

She looked at him, hope in her eyes. "Seeing you was only part of my wish," she admitted. "What I want most of all, what I've ever wanted, is to hear you sing. One of your people, I mean. I've heard my whole life about Elven songs. If I might hear one, just once?"

"You wish me to sing?" Eladar asked in surprise. "I do not sing often. It is not that my voice is not pleasing. I have heard even my own people say that it is. I flatter myself to think that it might not merely be those seeking to curry favor with my parents who have said so," he said, with a self-deprecating smile. "It is just... certain voices were never meant to be heard alone, but only in harmony. I sing best when I sing with another, most often with she-who-is-my-sister, for few others wish to have much to do with me."

Alissa laughed. "You sound like me!" she said in delight.

At the look he gave her, she grinned. "I'd not meant that as a slight, comparing you to a Man, well, a woman of Men. It's just you don't ever quite get to the point, do you? You talk in circles, spirals really, always arcing further and further away from what it is you are truly trying to say."

Eladar sighed. "I try not to, you know. I pride myself upon my brevity of phrase. If you think I am longwinded, you should hear he-who-is-my-brother. He might speak from midday to dusk, trying to convey the most simple of points. Most often, it is when he is scolding me. I try very hard not to disappoint him, if only to spare myself from hearing him lecture me afterward."

She laughed again. "You are wonderful! I wish my son was home, and my husband, so they might speak with you."

He shook his head. "I specifically waited until you were alone. I thought that woman—Emma was it—might never leave."

She looked surprised.

"I am here for you, Alissa. As a gift to you. And as you have requested it of me, I shall sing for you. An Elven ballad, in Elvish, as you might wish to hear it, though it was first written in Common in honor of the Man it was written for. It is a threnody. It is called 'River's Ballad of Walker'."

"You don't mean 'The Ballad of Riverwalker'? The song about the Man who sees the Elven maiden bathing, how cruelly she uses him, how she takes him into the riverbank for a single night of passion and then leaves him the Elfstone, and he wastes away trying to find her?"

Elavar scowled. "I see you are familiar with it, although you misspoke the title, and I find your interpretation of the motivations of River highly insulting."

"I meant no insult to you. But that song's not Elven at all! How could it be, a song that teaches Man the folly of ever loving an Elf? Oh, and of course, an allegory for why there are echoes," she added.

Eladar said, vexed, "It is Elven, because an Elf wrote it. She is known as River to your people, as the Man whose given name she protects was known as Walker. The song is often misunderstood by my own people to be a warning of the folly of ever loving a Man, though that is not why River wrote it at all. She wrote it in her despair, to ease the pain of her heart, when she lost her love so soon, so suddenly, to death's cold embrace.

"She gifted Walker the Elfstone to protect him while she returned to our kingdom, while she sought permission to leave it forever. When she came seeking him, when she tracked him through the Elfstone she had gifted to him, she was astonished to find him so far downriver.

"She knew fear as she traveled, as she heard those of the villages and towns he had passed speaking of him in such pity. Then finally she knew despair, when she saw they had spoken truly, that her gift would have protected him from all external danger, but not from his own heart.

"He had died for his love of her, after she had sworn to him they would be together always. He had not understood, had not waited, had not believed. Two months is the blink of an eye to our people, to the older ones of us, at any rate. I often find two days interminable. Walker perceived their time apart quite differently. To him it was as if a lifetime, and so it became a lifetime—his lifetime."

"But that's terrible!" Alissa cried. "It's a double tragedy, then, both for River and for Walker. How could her heart ever heal after something so terrible? Please, you speak as if you know her. Tell me, I must know, when a heart is so broken, when someone loved so fiercely is lost to death, can that heart ever heal? Did she ever find joy again? Did she learn again how to smile, to laugh, perhaps even to love again?" Alissa asked, her eyes intent upon his own.

"I have already said too much. I never meant to tell you so much; it is remarkable that I have done so…," Eladar began.

"Please, I must know. I am dying, you see. It will be soon, I think. And when I go I will leave behind me a husband, but also a son. I need to know they might still truly live when I am gone. It would break my heart were they to never again smile, or laugh, or love another. It is my hope that my husband will marry again, when I am gone, though he will not hear me speak of it. And my son is at such a tender age to lose his mother. Also, he is entering an apprenticeship and they will be without even each other. They will be all alone, and it breaks my heart to know I will be breaking theirs," she said, as her tears began to fall.

"Remarkable. You speak of your own death and you do not weep, until you speak in terms of how it might harm those you love.

"You need not further burden your heart. They might again know love, as my mother, River, learned to love again, when her heart opened to my father. Father loved her, though he risked his station, for a time his very life, in so doing, for at the time, my mother was quite infamous for her love of Man, and the politics of the Elven kingdoms are not so different from those of Man's world, I think.

"But also, and I am a fool for saying so, but I feel you must know, there was another, a Man, not so very long ago, for whom, had she not loved my father so deeply or her children, she might have left her people. My father knows of him, she would not keep such a thing from him; she could not, had she tried. It is the measure of his bottomless heart that he hated neither her nor him for it. He should not have, for they both subsumed their desire to their duty, never acting upon it, yet still, we Elves are known for our jealousies as well as our passions, and there, at least, we are not so maligned.

"Again, I say too much. Suffice it to say, you must know that love crosses all boundaries—of age, of station, of heart—that even death cannot stay love. Be comforted, knowing so.

"Now, I will sing to you, in Common, first, as it was written, so you may hear how the song you know differs from the original and then in Elvish, for Common is not a language of music as my own tongue is," Eladar said. Then, without further spoken word, he began to sing.

ALISSA listened, spellbound, as the familiar song unfolded anew, and the tears streamed from her eyes. Then she listened to it in Elvish.

"Please," Alissa begged. "Do not leave me beside the river. One more song, only one, I beg you. I fear I will never see the sun again, that I will spend my last days under the shroud of her tears."

"Forgive me. I forgot how deeply our music affects you. It affects us just as deeply, but we know how to cherish even the pain of it. But I will sing another. Something soothing, something healing. In its simplest form, it is a child's lullaby. In its most complex, it is something far more. I will sing it only as well as I am able," the Elf said.

Alissa listened with her ears, her heart, her very spirit, and knew such warmth and comfort and joy that she knew she would never again feel fear. She might never sing nor play again, but she need not. She would be content to die, knowing Anorion and Rion would live and love and having this Elf's music be the last she ever heard. She drifted off to sleep on that comforting thought.

ELADAR gazed fondly at the sleeping woman. He had given her what peace he could. He left her home, no longer discouraged that he had not had more time to spend in this City of Man. He felt as fulfilled as she to whom he had gifted his song.

What bright lights, these Men! He was as drawn to them as a moth to a flame. Last time he had been terribly burned. Perhaps this time he would be fortunate enough to merely bask in their radiance.

TALON looked about in frustration. Where were they? He had traversed the entire length and breadth of the Square. It was impossible to see from one end to the other; it was thronged with people. They must be here! They certainly shouldn't have left it, not after what he'd told Lunahr. Had Eladar somehow convinced him to leave, to go off exploring with him?

"There you are," a familiar voice said, in relief and annoyance. "I've been looking everywhere for you. Where's Beryl?" Eladar asked, looking around Talon for him, his face showing his puzzlement.

"You mean he's not with you?" Talon said, his own relief kindling suddenly to fear.

"With me? He was with you. Surely you don't mean you've lost him? That he slipped away again without you seeing?" Eladar asked in disbelief.

"No. I left him here, in the Square. He swore he'd stay here, in sight of the City Guards. I went to check the Market, the shops. You should have been back long ago! I thought you'd be here with him," Talon accused.

Eladar scowled at him. "I had to wait most of the day for Alissa to be alone. I can't very well go around revealing myself to everyone in the City, can I? Don't blame me for this, Talon. How could you have left Beryl alone here? You know how dangerous a city can be far more than I, and he's even more naïve than I am. Besides, placing blame won't help. We have to find him."

"Forgive me, Eladar! You're right. The fault is mine. If anything's happened to him...." Talon grew silent as his eyes focused inward upon his bond to Lunahr. He extended his consciousness, feeling along the coppery strand, and to his horror was met by a wall of pain and lack of conscious thought. He vaguely heard Eladar's voice calling to him and forced his focus outward once more.

"Talon? Talon, are you all right?" Eladar asked, eyeing him in concern.

"This way," Talon said in sudden conviction. "He's hurt, unconscious." Talon began cutting his way expertly through the crowd, no longer caring whether Eladar followed or not. Lunahr! He had to save him!

ELADAR kept pace with Talon easily. He dared not lose sight of him. Talon was not looking back to see if he followed; all his attention was upon finding Beryl.

How could Talon know he was hurt, or which way to go? Whatever would have possessed Beryl to go this way in the first place? He must have wandered off with one of the minstrels, or followed a person singing after hearing them.

Talon stood at the intersection of two streets, hesitating, his eyes casting to the left and right and then down the other street. Then they again glazed over, then focused, and he turned left and moved quickly down the street.

TALON came to another intersection and felt along the bond. Which way? This was madness, trying to find him using the bond! What if he couldn't?

Talon was fighting panic, trying to force himself to calm. He was hurt! Lunahr was hurt! He'd abandoned him, instead of protecting him. Lunahr could have been killed! He might yet die, before Talon could reach him. He couldn't die, not Lunahr. *Idare, please save him,* he silently prayed.

He wished Farad were here. Farad could find a single boy in a city of thousands far easier than he. Farad would never forgive him for allowing harm to come to their gentle cousin.

What if Lunahr lived, but was terribly maimed? What if his throat had been cut, his voice taken from him? Or his hand? Self-recrimination and terror began to override rational thought. The sun, where was the sun? So low in the sky, too low; it could not help him. It could not burn away his fear.

Two strong hands grasped his shoulders. Instinctively he yanked back, but the hands were like vises upon him; they did not release. "Talon, stop! You have to stop. You have to focus. You're not helping Beryl this way," Eladar said.

Talon focused upon the voice, dragging himself toward it.

"You know which way to go. I don't understand how, but I can see that you know. You must find him," Eladar said intently.

To Eladar's relief, Talon's eyes focused upon him, and Eladar let go.

"Thank you, Eladar. I have been unwell. I thought myself cured of the ills that have plagued me. I am glad you are here," Talon said and then headed to the right.

Eladar stared at Talon in surprise, shocked at his words of praise, then quickly followed, lest he lose sight of him.

They were in a narrow street now. Lunahr was to the left, so near. In one of the buildings? No, there was an alleyway. Talon entered it. There, upon the ground! So still.

"Lunahr! Lunahr, can you hear me?" he asked in Amontirin, eyeing him critically, stripping off his gloves, touching him, relieved by the warmth of his skin. But he was pale, and his golden hair was stained sticky brown with drying blood.

Talon's fingers gently probed the injury, parting the matted hair. Lunahr's scalp was badly swollen. He did not feel the terrible softness of shattered bone, but it was hard to feel anything through such swelling. He looked for further signs of injury.

His arm! The band of his House no longer graced it; his shirt was torn where the band had been hidden. Someone had taken it.

He forced the thought aside, continuing to check Lunahr. His throat was undamaged, his hands as well, Talon's worst fears not realized. The only injury appeared to be the blow to his head that had felled him. Still, it might yet prove devastating, even if not fatal. Talon well knew the harm such injuries could cause.

He would not have thought Lunahr might be overcome so easily, although he had apparently been struck from behind. What had happened?

Talon saw his sword was gone and his pack as well. They'd taken his knife. He spied his own gloves lying forgotten upon the ground. He quickly put them on. He might have left them here and been without their magic. What would Arcanus have said?

He turned his thoughts again to Lunahr. Lunahr's purse was gone, of course. Talon remembered how excited Lunahr had been, how proud, when he'd given him the five gold. Coin was painfully scarce for his people these days. Even five gold was a minor fortune until Arcanus had come with so much. But the band, the sword! Both symbols of his House gone! He must find them. But first he would see to Lunahr. He lifted him gently.

"The bleeding has stopped. He is not in immediate danger. There is an inn, five blocks from here; I saw it as we passed. We will take him there. I will tend to him there."

ELADAR nodded, face grim. He would give much to have the people who had harmed Beryl before him. He would give more to see him whole again.

THEY began walking to the inn, Talon carrying Lunahr as if he were but a child, his head propped carefully against his shoulder. Talon studied the inn, The Fatted Pig, carefully before he entered, then again once inside. It looked in decent repair, surprisingly, for this part of the City. Whyever had Lunahr come here?

Talon spied the innkeeper and headed for him. "I need a room for three, preferably with two beds. My cousin's been injured."

"We've no rooms for the likes of you," the innkeeper said sternly, eyeing the injured boy, the hard, angry-looking man with the sword at his side who held him, and the cloaked figured with his face in shadow behind them, obviously not liking what he saw.

"Maybe he's your cousin, maybe he's not. More likely you're the ones who harmed him. I want no part of you ransoming him nor abusing him, not in my beds. I don't want no trouble here. My three sons are in the kitchen, and the eldest is bigger 'n you, so git, now, before I call them or set the Guard upon ya."

Talon forced his anger down. The man was only protecting himself, his family, and his customers. He might sway him, were he not so upset, or force him to change his mind. But he could not risk using the King's Voice, not with his core in such turmoil; he could easily kill him.

"Please, we are truly his friend and his family. We will not harm him here. Far from it. We have saved him. We seek only to aid him. I swear upon my River that I speak truly to you," Eladar said, pulling back his hood slightly, exposing the fine-boned beauty of his pale face, his silver hair, and elegant ears. Eladar obviously hoped the Man might be swayed by his plea. Few Men could resist anything an Elf asked of them.

The Man's eyes widened, and his face softened upon seeing him. "Of course. Forgive me. This time of year, this part of the City, we often see such trouble. The City Guard are all in the Square and Market and at the Theatre, though we call it the Arena for Feast Day. There's not enough of the City Guard to comb every street, and the bad ones know where to go to cause trouble without fear of reprisal.

"The room's a gold. I know you'll think that high, but I usually charge three for it just before, during, and after Feast Day. You're lucky I still have one of the two. It's only got a single bed, but I'll have my son bring you a second set of bedding. Considering who you are, I'd not ask you to share a bed. If the boy needs a healer, I know of one," he offered.

Eladar pulled his hood forward again. "The room is all we require. And dinner, later. Although a bath would be welcome. For now, this is for the room," Eladar said, handing him three gold. "I would not have you lose coin for your kindness."

The Man flushed darkly. "I'll take it, but you'll not pay extra for the bath nor the meal, and you'll get our best meal, and mead as well. Let me know when you want it, so it'll be hot. Meanwhile, let me show you upstairs to it. Alroy will be by with the bedding."

He led them up a single flight of wooden stairs to one of four doors. "It's got a lock," he said, showing them the bolt.

Talon viewed the room critically. It seemed clean enough. He hoped the bed was free of vermin. It seemed to be, when he laid Lunahr down upon it.

"Alroy will bring up some water as well, so's you can wash the travel dirt off if you've a wish to," the innkeeper said, and then he left them to their privacy.

"Thank you," Talon said to Eladar. Then he removed his gloves, unpacked his healer's kit, and began preparing different powders, using the water from his skin, which he knew was fresh. He carefully cleaned Lunahr's wound, spread ointment upon it, and bandaged it.

The bedding and water were brought while he did so. He glanced up at the man who brought them and then returned to his work. Lunahr did not waken while he tended to him. Talon knew it might be a while until he did. He knew he might never waken. He forced the thought aside.

He sat upon the bed beside Lunahr and held his hand. Lunahr's fingers were so long, so narrow, so delicate. So fragile. Last of his House. His band! His sword! Talon had to recover them.

He would visit the shops he'd gone to before. But the thieves might well sell them elsewhere. There were so many travelers in the City. They might sell them on the street to passersby. Any of them might have need of a sword, and the armband was made of solid pallenteum, a metal so rare most Men lived and died without ever seeing it. The thieves would probably think it merely silver.

At least the band was not jeweled, as was his own, that the gem might be pried out and forever lost. He wore only the King's Band, which they now called the band of the House of Obearn, though it did not bear the symbol of the beast. The true band of his House had been lost long ago. So had the original King's Band, which had been made of pyrenteum, the same metal as Kathalanar, the King's Sword, which he yet wore at his side. Lost, so much lost: bands, swords, Houses, people, history, art, music—gone, all gone. Dying, they were dying!

Idare, no! He must not dwell upon such things, not with Lunahr unable to aid him. He could all too easily fall again to the Madness sitting here, waiting for Lunahr to waken. But he should be here for it; he must be, for what he might find.

Although Eladar was here. Eladar could tend to Lunahr, protect him. Talon turned to Eladar and caught him eyeing him in concern.

"I must find the band and sword of his House, now, or they might never be recovered. The men who have taken them will sell them. You must stay with Lunahr for me. If... when he wakes, you must test him. His reason may be lost, or his speech. He might be dizzy and unable to stand. Head injuries can be terrible. You must ask him who he is, who you are, what happened. He might not remember what happened, not yet, perhaps never, but if he can remember the rest, if he can still move, still speak...." Talon's voice broke. Still sing. Still play. What if he could do neither? How would he live?

"I will care for him. Go. I will not leave his side," Eladar swore.

Talon nodded gratefully. "I have prepared something for the pain, in that cup there. I was careful not to make it too strong, or too much. He may drink all of it." Then he left, leaving his pack in the room, taking only his sword and purse and cloak.

Before leaving the inn, Talon spoke to the innkeeper. "My cousin was robbed as well as injured. I must find the things that were taken. It happened in an alleyway, five blocks from here. Is there a place nearby where thieves might take what they have stolen? A sword and jewelry?"

The innkeeper said, "Nothing that I'd know of. I'm sorry, sir."

Talon nodded and left, but had only gone twenty paces when he heard the sound of footsteps coming up quickly behind him.

He spun, hand on the hilt of his sword, but did not draw, as he felt the naked leather of the hilt upon his bare hand. His gloves! They were still in the room. He would draw only as a last resort. Without the masking spell upon the gloves, once unsheathed, the true nature of his sword would be revealed. After so many decades of secrecy, he could not risk an agent of the Enemy seeing that he held the King's Sword.

Talon recognized the Man coming up behind him. It was the innkeeper's son, Alroy, the one who'd brought the bedding.

He eyed Talon warily from a distance and then approached once he saw his hand relax upon the hilt of his sword. "Forgive me for startling you," he said, casually looking about him. Then he approached closer and spoke more softly. "I have a message from my father. He dared not say so in front of the other patrons. Many of those drinking inside are from here. It would be dangerous. But he knows the place you're looking for. We've helped recover lost items for guests before, though it costs plenty to do so.

"There's a shop that buys and sells used wares, both valuable and not: the Copper Hand. It's on this street, seven blocks from here in the direction you're facing, about halfway down the block, on your right. There's a sign of a hand holding copper coins over the door. They know half or more of what they get is stolen. You won't be able to talk them out of it, but if you pay enough, you should be able to recover it. Just don't tell them we sent you there. We don't need the trouble."

"Thank you," Talon said gratefully. "I'm much obliged." He reached for his purse.

Alroy said, "Save your coin. We didn't do it for that. Father imagined all too vividly it being Fenroy, my youngest brother. We hope your cousin will be all right. We did it for him."

Alroy turned and went back to the inn, and Talon proceeded to the shop with the sign Alroy had described. He was cautious, of course. The man had seemed sincere enough, but it could well be a trap. He approached the door, eyeing his surroundings carefully, then entered.

It was well lit inside, and there was the shine of metal here and there, different objects for sale. He began looking at the stock. The band would be behind the counter, if it was here at all. The sword might be here, and the flute, perhaps even the book and writing materials, but not the fine clothes that Lunahr was to have worn before the Elves. There were no other clothes here. They'd have sold them elsewhere. The shirt had been the green of Lunahr's eyes.

He had been a fool, chasing after signs of the Enemy when other evil had been so near! Seeking bands and swords of lost Houses only to lose those of one of the few extant Houses. Now Lunahr might die, and his House with him.

He forced the thought away as he looked about, hiding his growing desperation. Nothing. They were not here.

He was being carefully watched by the proprietor. He approached him. "Is this all the stock you have? I am in the market for a sword for my nephew, but I'd not wanted to get him a new one. The two you have here are not long enough. He's got the length of arm I do."

"You're lucky I've the two. Most of those I get in I sell off right away to Seth's Swords on Tanner Street. If you tell him I sent you, you'll get a discount. We have an arrangement, he and I," the smooth-talking shopkeeper said. "Also, I may yet get something. This time of year, I get plenty. So many sell what they own to have coin to spend for the Feast. You'd be surprised how much turnover I see."

Talon nodded. Of course. With so many in the City for Feast Day, many unwary travelers might be separated from their goods. He'd been to Seth's Swords earlier in the day. It was almost twenty blocks from here. But if he had an arrangement with this man, it was possible Lunahr's sword, Loruthanar, might be there now. He had to find it. He pictured despair replacing the laughter in Lunahr's eyes, knowing he'd lost both his band and sword.

"Is there anything else you're looking for?" the man asked.

"No. Not unless you've a mandolin, or lute, or some other instrument for my niece. She loves music, you see, and I can't very well bring her brother something and nothing for her. My sister might never let me hear the end of it," he said, casually. He couldn't specify a flute. The Man might become suspicious, if he'd seen the sword.

"You're in luck. I usually sell what I get to Melanie's Melodies. I've not the room here to store them, or the clientele, usually, to buy them. But I got in a dulcimer yesterday and a flute only late this afternoon, and I've not had chance to take them there yet. I'll be but a moment," he said and disappeared into a back room. Another man came out, big, silent, to watch the shop while he was inside. Then he reappeared with the instruments and laid them upon the counter, and the other man disappeared again into the back.

Talon looked at what he held out to him, trying not to appear too eager. The flute was Lunahr's! He recognized it instantly. He had to question this man, but he had to be careful, lest the other was listening and became suspicious. "How much are you asking for the dulcimer?" he asked.

"Thirty gold. It's of fine workmanship. They've used three different woods crafting it," he said.

"And the flute?"

"Fifteen gold. That's pure silver there."

Talon wove his Power into his words as he began questioning the shopkeeper. "**Were there other things brought to you at the same time as this flute?**"

"Why yes, there were. But nothing I'd planned to sell."

"Do you have them? **I'd like to see them,**" Talon said.

"Of course, let me get them," the man said, completely in the thrall of his Power. He returned with Lunahr's music book and writing supplies. "I thought I'd tear out what's written there and use the blank pages myself, but if you're interested in buying it as well, it's for sale."

"**This is all? There weren't any weapons, or jewelry?**" Talon asked, disheartened. The sword of House of Eagles, Lunahr's dagger, and the band of his House weren't here, nor his clothes, pack or, of course, his purse.

"No, nothing like that. This was all," the man said, and Talon knew he spoke the truth. He could not do otherwise.

Talon spoke softly now, so the man in the back couldn't overhear. "**Do you know the men who sold these to you? Did they tell you where and how they got them? Tell me all you know about it. Whisper to me.**"

The man did as he commanded. "Oh yes. Mik and Drake and Martin, they're regular customers. Mik came in laughing about how easy it was, luring that lost boy down the alley, pretending to help him. Drake said how stupid he was, warning Mik about him and Martin and then turning his back on Mik to try to protect him, facing the two of them with his sword, how Mik just came up behind him and hit him from behind."

Talon listened, enraged, but forced himself to stay outwardly calm. "I need to find them. **Describe them to me and tell me where to look.**"

"Of course," the shopkeeper said, and did so.

"**Here's twenty gold for the flute and book and pen and ink,**" Talon said more loudly, giving the man two copper pieces instead.

"Thank you, sir. Come again," the proprietor said, pocketing the copper coins happily, still under the thrall of Talon's Power, believing the coin was what Talon had told him it was.

Talon left, hurrying down the street. He had to find those three thieves. If he couldn't, he'd still check the sword shop again. He might at least recover Loruthanar.

ELADAR began singing softly to Beryl, the same healing song he'd sung to Alissa. If only he had his mother's magic, the song would actually help him.

After the one song was done, he began another. Beryl was so absorbed in music; somehow it wasn't right that there be silence about him.

Eladar was not sure how long he had sung when there was a knock and the innkeeper was asking him if he wanted dinner brought, or a bath. He'd not realized it was so late. He had certainly not felt hungry. But Beryl might be unconscious for a long while yet. He should eat. He told the innkeeper what to bring him, greens and wine and bread. He'd not eat cake, not here, in Man's world; they'd make it with eggs. The thought made him nauseous.

When the innkeeper returned, his appetite did as well. He discovered he was hungry after all, although the wine was quite vile, barely drinkable, to his palate. Perhaps he should have asked for water, but the water here would probably be far worse than the wine, even with the River so near. Elavar had warned him about the water in the Cities of Men.

After he'd eaten, Eladar began to sing again, wondering whether Talon was having any luck finding Beryl's things. He couldn't imagine he might in a city this size. And it was late. It might already be dark, or soon would be; there was no window to see the sky by. The City would be more dangerous after dark. Eladar knew Talon was well equipped to deal with such dangers; he was sure he'd faced them many times. Yet still, Talon was worried about Beryl and might be distracted at a crucial moment because of it. That might prove dangerous, perhaps even fatal.

There was a moan from the bed. "Beryl? Beryl, can you hear me?" Eladar asked hopefully.

But he was answered only by a louder moan. He took Beryl's hand in his own and began rubbing it, wondering again how he did not mind Beryl's touch. Beryl had embraced him before, when he'd had need of it, and he had welcomed it. Elves did not usually like to be touched by Men, and he was certainly no exception. Men were often hairy and smelly, sweaty and dirty.

But Beryl was not at all like that. He had the grace of an Elf. Beryl had such beautiful hands. He had looked forward to hearing Beryl play. Now he might never be able to. The thought troubled him deeply.

Talon was right. He was partially to blame for Beryl being so injured. He had spent too long waiting for Alissa. He should have returned to them far earlier. But he'd thought Talon would be with him; he could not imagine him having left Beryl. He still didn't understand why Talon had.

Beryl's hand squeezed his own weakly, for a moment.

"Beryl? Beryl, can you feel my hand? Can you hear me?" he asked eagerly, squeezing his hand gently. "Please, Beryl, open your eyes, speak to me."

Beryl's hand squeezed his again, and his eyes fluttered open and then closed again.

"Beryl, open your eyes again. Look at me. Can you see me? Can you hear me?" Eladar asked.

Beryl moaned, his brow creased in pain, and he lifted his other hand, trembling, to his head. His eyes opened again, and this time, they stayed open.

"Beryl, can you speak? Say something, Beryl. Do you know who I am? Do you know my name?"

"LAREN?" Lunahr whispered. "My head, Idare, my head," he moaned in Amontirin, and a tear rolled down his cheek from the pain.

BERYL had spoken, but not his name and not in a language he understood. He might be delirious or confused. "It's Eladar, Beryl. Do you remember me?" Eladar asked in Elvish this time. He'd been speaking Common before, but he suspected before this journey Beryl had seldom spoken it.

Beryl said "Yes," in Elvish, at the same time he made the mistake of nodding. He cried out, clutching his head.

"Talon left something for you to drink, for the pain. If I help you sit, can you drink?" Eladar asked.

"I'll try," Beryl whispered.

Eladar put his arm behind him and lifted him, propping the pillow behind his back.

Beryl suddenly tensed and then jerked his head to the side and, body wracked with spasms, began heaving onto the floor.

Eladar was terrified. Talon had said nothing about this! How was Beryl supposed to drink the medicine he'd left for him if he was vomiting like this? Beryl would have fallen out of the bed if Eladar had not held him. Finally, it was done, and Beryl fell against him, sobbing.

"It's all right, Beryl. You must calm yourself. I am here. I will take care of you," Eladar swore.

"What's happened to me?" Beryl asked between sobs. "I was in the Square. Where's Laren? Why isn't he here?" he asked, panic rising. "I'm dying!" he sobbed.

"Hush. You are not dying, Beryl. You will not. You are only injured," Eladar assured him, desperately hoping that it was true. He did not tell Beryl he had been robbed as well. He would learn of that later.

"Talon will be back soon. Please, Beryl, you must lie back down, you must be calm. I'll sing to you again. Perhaps that will help. I sang to you before, but you were unconscious. This time you will be able to hear." He sang the song he'd sung before, the healing melody, then other soothing songs, gently stroking Beryl's face, his arms, his chest as he did so.

The panic and the tension gradually left Beryl. Beryl still held him, but he no longer clung to him so desperately. Then his breathing slowed and calmed further still, and Eladar realized he was asleep.

Eladar waited awhile until he was sure Beryl would not soon waken, and then he unbolted the door and left the room, heading downstairs. The common room was quiet, now; two dozen men lay out upon the floor on their bedrolls. He spied the innkeeper, to his relief, coming from the kitchen, and spoke softly so as not to disturb the other guests.

"My friend has been ill upon the floor. Might someone come to clean it? Fortunately, he managed to use the side of the bed the spare bedding was not on. Also, I am in desperate need of that bath you promised me. You need not heat the water. Cold would be fine. Cold would be better. I can help you carry the buckets up the stairs. I know it is late."

"That it is. When you said bath, I'd not looked forward to heating so much water. I'd have tried to have talked you into waiting until morning. But as cold will work, my sons will bring it, and I'll send my wife up to clean the mess," the innkeeper said.

"Thank you," Eladar said, truly grateful, and returned quickly to the room. Beryl was still asleep.

A short while later, the mess was cleaned and the tub brought and filled while Beryl still slept. Eladar eyed the metal tub. It was smaller than he wished, than he needed, but he would make do. He stripped off his clothes and folded himself into it.

After a while, he got out and knelt beside it, and lowered his head into it, feeling his long hair flowing about his face, imagining he was in his River. More at ease, he toweled off using the coarse towel they'd left him and dressed again.

Talon had yet to return. He was either still searching for the lost sword and band, or he had met with some danger that had overwhelmed him. If Talon was not back by morning, Eladar would have the innkeeper summon that healer he had told them of, to aid Beryl. He had coin, a purse full, more than he might be able to spend.

He could not imagine Talon would not return within another day. If he did not, then he would entrust Beryl to the innkeeper for care, leaving enough coin and sufficient promise of more that he might do so. Then he would go to the City Guard and see whether he might find Talon there: either his body, if he had met with more trouble than he could handle, or in jail, if he had been caught seeking his revenge upon those who had harmed his cousin. He would see Talon buried or freed. Then, once Beryl was well enough, he would take Beryl to his parents for sanctuary.

He spent the rest of the night sitting upon the chair beside the bed, watching Beryl sleep. Talon did not return.

NOTHING. Talon had scoured the weapons shops, the jewelry shops, the Market, the Square, the streets, all to no avail. It was well past dark now. The shops were all closed, and the inns would be locked for the night as well. Only some of the taverns were still open. Talon had spent time and coin in a number of them, listening and looking while sipping at mugs of mead. He'd been sure to dump one upon himself at the last place he drank, careful not to spill any of it on the side of his shirt under which he'd tucked Beryl's book. He left weaving as if intoxicated; he certainly smelled as if he were, which was the point.

He headed toward the alleyway where they'd found Lunahr, then past others, so many others, up one street, down another. Trouble found him, as he'd hoped it might. Only it wasn't the men he'd been looking for. He wiped the blood from his sword on their bodies and continued onward. Again he was found. Three men this time, again the wrong ones, but hardened men, killers and thieves. He slew them as well.

He had despaired of finding the ones he sought when he saw a lone boy walking up the street, looking about furtively. A boy shouldn't be out alone, so late; it was dangerous here. Talon headed for him, remembering to reel drunkenly, in case it was a ruse of some sort, though he doubted it might be. Still, some others may have seen the boy, might be ready to prey upon him, perhaps those he was looking for. The boy didn't run when he saw him coming.

"Please help me, sir? I'd not meant to stay out so late, and I'm frightened to go home by myself," he said, fear in his voice. "You shouldn't be out alone either, even with a sword. Excuse me for saying so, but you've had a bit much to drink. We can walk together."

"Sure. Where do you live?" Talon said, slurring his speech as if drunk.

"Thank you, sir! I live just off of River Street, about five blocks from here if we take the shortcuts. You looked like an honest man. I'd hoped you were, but I figured I could run faster than you if you weren't." He began leading Talon, looking about fearfully as he went.

He reminded Talon painfully of Lunahr, young and vulnerable. His parents should take better care of him than this.

The boy led Talon down four narrow, deserted streets, then toward the mouth of an alleyway. "It's just on the other side of here," he said eagerly, heading into the alley.

The light of the moon didn't illuminate it well at all. Talon couldn't make out the street on the other side and could see little within the alley itself; much of it was completely in shadow. "Wait! We should go around. It might not be safe. Come back," he commanded, hesitating at the entrance, but the boy had already penetrated more deeply than he could see.

Talon heard a yelp of fear and a scuffle and a thud. He drew his sword, the hilt still feeling odd in his naked hand, even after having used it tonight twice before. He plunged into the blackness of the alley after the boy, letting his Power flow into Kathalanar. The pyrenteum blade, which had gleamed the color of blood-dipped copper when freed from the masking spell of the sheath and without the spelled gloves to conceal its true nature, flared red with light, illuminating all around it.

There was a yelp of fear and a cry of "He's a wizard!" Two men stood on either side of the alley, one with a knife, another with a club, and Talon saw to his surprise the boy stood in front of them, also with a knife raised.

His eyes narrowed. He'd been tricked: the boy was one of them. He realized with a start that these might well be the three he had been looking for. The three of them ran from him, but the boy tripped and the knife flew from his hand. Talon recognized it: it was Lunahr's! Talon let the others escape, grabbing the boy and putting his sword to his throat.

"Please don't hurt me! It's not what you think. I was just defending myself from them," the boy pleaded convincingly, but Talon would not be so easily fooled this time.

He dragged the boy back into the street, where there was more moonlight to see by, letting the glow of his sword fade. Thankfully, the street was still deserted. "I'm not the first person you tried to rob today, am I? **Tell me about the boy you attacked, the one with the long blond hair, tied back, the one you took the knife from,**" Talon commanded, weaving his Power into his words.

"That one? He was lost, trying to find the Square. I told him I'd guide him and he believed me. I brought him into the alley Drake and Martin were watching. I thought he'd be easy prey, but he heard them somehow. He turned and drew his sword on them, turning his back on me. He even tried to warn me, to protect me. He was such a fool!" the boy said scornfully. "I hit him from behind. Then we took his purse and his sword and knife and pack and searched him. It's a good thing we did. We almost missed his armband."

"The things you stole from him. Where are they?" Talon demanded, seething at the boy's callous recounting of his attack upon Lunahr while he had been trying to protect him.

"Martin kept the clothes and Drake wanted the pack. I took his knife; I didn't have one before and they let me, since I was the one who felled him. We sold the flute and the book and the writing things to the Copper Hand. We sold the sword to Seth's Swords. Martin still has the armband. We've not quite figured out what to do with it yet. It's far fancier than anything we usually get."

"You're lying," Talon said, astonished the boy could while he used his Power upon him. **"The sword wasn't at Seth's. I checked. Where is it?"**

"Well of course you'd not see it there yet," the boy scoffed. "Seth always waits at least a week to put out anything we sell to him, in case the owner comes by looking at the shops for it. He only puts it out once he's sure they'd have given up."

Talon was torn. He was a boy. But he spoke of the attack so coldly— worse, as if he reveled in the cruelty of it. He'd hit Lunahr and might easily have killed him, he'd struck him so hard. Lunahr might yet die, or wish for death if he was permanently impaired. The boy had seen the Sword, unmasked. Worse, he'd seen it lit with Power. He should not let the boy live. He was not an innocent, but still, he was a child. **"How many people have you robbed, harmed, killed?"** Talon asked.

"Robbed? Hundreds, I suppose. I'm not usually the one to hit or stab them: Martin and Drake do that. But I've helped them before sometimes, like in the alley. I don't know how many have died. Who cares? Why bother to count them? It's their things we want. The people don't matter."

Talon's heart hardened. **"You will tell me where Martin and Drake live,"** he said, and the boy did so.

"I'LL get it," Rion called out eagerly, answering the door. "Cedric? Cedric, what's wrong? I've seldom seen you look so grim."

Cedric tousled Rion's hair. "Nothing for you to worry about, lad. Is your father ready?"

"He's in the kitchen with Mother, finishing breakfast. It's still early; we'd not expected you yet. Cedric, you'll never guess! An Elf came by the house yesterday! A real live Elf! He spoke to Mother. He even sang to her! And I missed it! When I came home, she was asleep and when she woke up she told me…. Cedric, what's happened? It must be something bad for you to not even react at all to what I just said. You're as Elf-happy as we are," Rion said, his face creased with concern.

"I'm sorry, Alarion. It's just... Feast Day is always trouble, but this year... good morning, Alissa, Anorion. Anorion, if you're ready, we'd best go. They want us in as early this morning as we can make it," Cedric said.

"Cedric? Is it something dangerous?" Alissa asked.

"Now, Alissa, I don't want you to worry. It might be nothing. Even if it is true," Cedric hedged.

"Anorion, you're not leaving this house until I hear," Alissa said.

"Now, Alissa," Anorion began.

"No. I mean it. You scared me nearly to death with what happened at the Gilded Stein. Now what is it, Cedric?"

Cedric looked from Alissa to Anorion. Anorion nodded slightly. Cedric sighed. "It's a wizard. One's been seen in the City, working magic. Not by drunks or foreigners, either, but by respectable folk, in their homes. Justin came by my house at the crack of dawn. He was up half the night over it. He said we got four separate reports of it.

"And that's not all. There were killings, right around there, in the same area. Nothing magical about it, at least not that we could tell: sword wounds, all of them. None that didn't deserve death, mind you, thieves and scoundrels, the lot of them, each who have spent more than a few nights in our jails. We had a total of twelve dead last night, all over the City.

"We usually get dead around Feast Day, only this was different. Eight of them were within twenty blocks of each other, east of River Street, right near where those folks say they saw the red light of the wizard's staff: two in one alley, three in another, then three in a house near Baker Street. One of them was Mik, that bad apple you kept trying to turn around last year, before you gave up on him, Anorion. He and his friends Martin and Drake were all killed.

"I'd say somebody managed to rob the wrong man, that maybe he was trying to punish those who did it or maybe get back what they stole. They might even have stolen from the wizard, or maybe the wizard is after whatever it was too. The swordsman might either be working for him or against him. In any case, the Governor's up in arms about it, as you can imagine, with what looks to be an angry wizard loose in the City so near Feast Day."

"Anorion, I don't want you guarding today. Tell them you can't, tell them I'm worse, tell them whatever you have to," Alissa said, the fear naked on her face.

"Alissa, I can't. Enough men will be doing so today, you can well imagine. They'll need me even more. It's not that I'm not afraid of wizards,

Alissa. I'd be a fool not to be, though I've never seen one myself before. I've heard enough to know how dangerous they can be. But someone has to protect the City from him, if what's been said is true. I'll be careful. You know I'll be.

"Alarion, I don't want you leaving the house today. You're to stay with your mother, do you understand? Practice your writing and your sums for your test. You'll be plenty busy enough doing that. If Oberas doesn't return, we'll find you another apprenticeship."

"Yes, Father," Rion said, trying to hide his disappointment. A wizard! An Elf yesterday that he'd missed, and now a wizard! He was sure Ric and the others would be going to River Street to try to find him. But he'd not disobey Father. He'd stay here, as Father had told him to.

ELADAR could tell from the sounds downstairs that it was morning. Talon had not returned. He'd have the innkeeper fetch the healer for Beryl. When he rose to go, the chair creaked. Beryl stirred on the bed. He couldn't leave the room if Beryl was waking. He might panic if he found himself hurt and alone.

Beryl opened his eyes, his hand immediately going to his head.

"Beryl? How do you feel?" Eladar asked in Elvish.

"Terrible. My head's coming off. What happened?"

Eladar sighed. "You still don't remember? We don't know all of it. But we found you in an alleyway. You'd been attacked."

"Attacked? Why? You mean robbed? My purse, they took the gold?" Beryl asked in dismay. Then, realizing the implications, he said, "They didn't take my pack? My music? My flute?"

Eladar didn't answer. Then a look of fear filled Beryl's face. "My band!" he said, as he reached with his left hand for his right bicep, his hand closing over the torn sleeve of his shirt. "Idare! Not my band!" he said in despair.

"They took everything, Beryl. Your sword as well," Eladar said reluctantly.

"No! No, they can't have! I can't have lost them, not my band, my sword!" he said, sitting up suddenly. Then he cried out and fell back onto the bed, clutching his head. But he didn't vomit.

"Beryl, please, calm yourself. Talon's out looking for them. If anyone can find them, he can," Eladar said, sounding far more confident than he was. "He left you medicine to drink. If you think you can keep it down, now, I'll give it to you, to ease the pain."

"No. I won't drink it. I deserve to be in pain. How can I have lost my band, my sword? Laren will never forgive me for it. He'll be so angry with me. Where was Laren? Why didn't he protect me?

"Where were you, Eladar? I waited so long for you in the Square and... and I left... I... I went looking for you, I think. Only I can't remember exactly and I can't remember anything after that, until I woke up and... you were singing. Before, I woke before, too, and you were singing to me then," he said, brow creased in concentration. "It hurts, it hurts! I can't even think for the pain."

Eladar raised the cup to him. "Please drink it, Beryl. I can't stand to see you in pain. Now I know how my brother must have felt when they found me and brought me home so injured, how helpless, how terrible it was for him, for my sister, for all of them. Please drink this," he urged, his voice agonized.

"For you, Eladar. I'll do it for you. Forgive me, I didn't realize I was hurting you," Beryl said. And he drank, slowly, what was offered. After he was done, he lowered himself back onto the bed, hand to his head. "I feel so dizzy. It makes me sick even to sit. How am I to walk to Riviera tomorrow, like I promised?"

"It is tomorrow, Beryl. I mean, it's the day we were supposed to have gone. It was yesterday you were attacked," Eladar clarified.

"Yesterday? But... but Laren's not back? He can't have been gone the whole night!" Beryl cried in concern, sitting up again, then grabbing his head and then his stomach. He began retching, spitting back up the medicine he had drunk onto the floor.

"That's it, Beryl! I'm getting the healer," Eladar said, holding him. "I don't know what else to do. Talon should be here. I don't care if the band and sword are symbols of your House. You're more important! Talon should be here for you, not chasing across the City for pieces of metal!" Eladar said angrily.

Beryl fought for breath, for his voice. "You don't understand! You're not one of us; you can't know what they mean to us. They're all we have left! They're all that's left of the Houses, of our home, of our ancestry, our history, our people: just the bands and the swords. How could I have lost them? Laren entrusted them to me. Even though I'd not come-of-age, he made me Lord of my House. I swore I could do it. I swore I'd protect them with my life. How can I live yet they be gone?" he asked in despair, tears welling in his eyes.

"Beryl, you mustn't say such things; you mustn't even think them."

"You don't understand," Beryl repeated, burying his face in the pillow, sobbing.

Eladar looked at him helplessly. Then he began to sing. He didn't know what else to do, how else to calm him. Gradually Beryl's sobs lessened as he listened.

When the song was finished, he said, "That was so beautiful. I have to write it down, or I might forget...." His face fell as he remembered his ink and pen and book were gone. "The songs! The new songs I heard! They took my music," he said, anguished. "They took my flute! It was the only instrument I could bring, and now I don't have anything!" Beryl sobbed anew.

Eladar hugged him. "Beryl, please, stop! I cannot bear to see you sad. I'll buy you a new flute, a dulcimer, whatever you wish. I've yet to hear you play one, or a lute, when I'd so wanted to. And there are many songs for you to hear, new ones, old ones, songs are everywhere. I'll get you a new book to write them in and I'll teach you the ones I know, until you are well, until you can leave here, and then you can hear more," Eladar said soothingly.

Beryl looked calmer again. Eladar breathed deeply. "Beryl, I'm going to go downstairs. I need to have the innkeeper get the healer for you, all right? And you should have some breakfast, if the healer says it's all right. You need to stay strong."

"All right. I'm sorry I'm such a burden, Eladar. I'll try not to be," Beryl said sadly.

"I'm just glad you're alive, Beryl. We almost lost you. I've only once before ever been so frightened. When I saw you lying in that alley.... I'll see you well again, I swear it. I'll be back shortly."

He went downstairs and told the innkeeper to get the healer, and that he needed another mess cleaned up. Then he went back upstairs.

He wasn't there for more than a moment when there was a knock. He was surprised at how fast they were being to clean the mess. He unbolted and opened the door.

Talon stood there, scowling at him. "What's the use of locking it, if you don't ask who's there before opening it?"

"Talon! What's happened? You look terrible!" Eladar said. Talon's clothes were torn and dirty, liberally splattered with dried blood, and he stank of mead.

"Laren!" a concerned voice said from the bed.

THE scowl left Talon's face. "Beryl!" he said in relief, heading for the bed. Then his face creased in concern. There was a pool of vomit on the floor, and

Lunahr hadn't gotten up; he hadn't moved at all, other than turning his head to him. He was propped up in a sitting position in the bed. And Talon could see from his face he was in terrible pain.

"You're hurt," Lunahr said in concern.

"No. The blood's not mine, but I couldn't very well go through the City looking like this, now that it's daylight. I need to bathe and change and go out again, Beryl. I've yet to recover your sword, but I know where it is, now. I'll not risk losing it."

Lunahr looked down, ashamed. "I'm sorry, Laren. I won't ask you to forgive me; I know you never can. I don't even remember what happened, but Eladar told me I was robbed, that they took everything. I never meant to lose them, the band and the sword. I'm sure I tried to fight them. I must have," he said mournfully in Amontirin, eyes tearing.

"Forgive you?" Talon asked in Amontirin. "Lunahr, it is not you who needs me to grant forgiveness! How can you ever forgive me, for leaving you alone and letting you come to such harm? You could have been killed! You came so close to it I'm still terrified by it. You've been terribly hurt. I can feel the pain of it, though I blocked it away before so I could concentrate upon what I had to do. And that boy who tricked you tricked me as well, even though I knew to be on my guard. None of this is your fault.

"You couldn't drink what I left for you, I can see that. I'll make you something else, for your stomach. I'd not realized you'd be so nauseous. Are you dizzy, as well?"

"Terribly. I can't even sit on my own. I will recover, won't I? I mean, this is just temporary, for the pain in my head, isn't it?" Lunahr asked, sounding young and afraid.

Talon couldn't lie to him; Lunahr would know he was, for the bond they shared. "I think so. I hope so. I'll do all I can to help. You know I will."

"Eladar's had the innkeeper summon the healer for me. We… we weren't sure when you'd be back," Lunahr said.

Laren could tell he meant if he'd be back, not when. "The healer shouldn't see you, Lunahr. He'd mean well—they all do—but so many healers in these lands don't really know as much as they think they do. Many times they hurt you rather than help." Talon had learned as much as he could of the art of healing from the Dwarves and the Elves, after the last of their healers had died in the plague. Their people could ill afford to be without a trained healer.

Talon turned to Eladar and said in Common, "I'll tend to him. He shouldn't see their healer. Pay him whatever you need to, to have him go."

ELADAR nodded. He'd been listening to the two of them, frustrated. He'd have to learn Amontirin somehow. Perhaps Beryl would teach it to him.

"TELL me how you feel," Talon asked Lunahr, still in Common.

"My head hurts terribly. And I get dizzy and sick when I try to move," Lunahr said.

"But you can move easily? Wiggle your fingers for me," Talon commanded and was relieved when Lunahr did so without difficulty. "Now squeeze my hand, as hard as you can." Lunahr did, and he sighed in relief. His fingers were still agile, his grip still strong.

"Laren! Your gloves! Where are your gloves?" Lunahr asked in concern. "You said the blood's not yours, but it can't be from your sword, not without your gloves!"

Eladar eyed them, obviously baffled by Lunahr's concern.

Talon looked about the bed and found them. "I did what I had to do, Beryl. And I wasn't entirely unsuccessful." He pulled Lunahr's band off his own bicep, from where he'd tucked it under the sleeve of his loose shirt.

Lunahr cried out in surprise and joy upon seeing it and took it, hands trembling.

"Put it on your other arm, under your shirt, until I come back with a new shirt for you," he said. "And I was able to get these back as well," he said and handed him the flute and music book, still holding the small sack containing his writing implements in his other hand. Tears filled Lunahr's eyes upon seeing them. "I didn't expect you to even think to look for them, with what else I'd lost."

His words cut Talon deeply.

THERE was a knock upon the door. "Who's there?" Eladar said, mindful of Talon's words before.

"Janice, sir. The innkeeper's wife. Royden's said you've a bit of a mess again. I've come to clean it."

Eladar opened the door for her. She had a bucket and rag.

SHE smiled at Lunahr. "How are you? I've made some meat broth, special for you, to ease your stomach," she said.

"That's very kind of you," Talon said, knowing Lunahr wouldn't drink it. He had an Elf's palate: he never ate meat. He couldn't bear the thought of the animals slain for it. "Might we also trouble you for a hot bath?"

She eyed him in concern. "Whatever's happened to you? You was out all night, wasn't you? Royden saw you come in this morning and slip so quick up the stairs. It's a miracle you're alive, what with all that happened." Then she knelt by the puddle and began cleaning it.

"What happened?" Lunahr asked, his voice small.

"Why the killings! And the wizard! All sorts of evil been going on last night round abouts here. Makes me glad I was safe in me bed."

Lunahr and Eladar looked at Talon. "There was a wizard?" Talon asked cautiously.

"Was there! They say this red glow came out of his staff, what lit up the night like it was day, Areth watch over me."

Talon swallowed. He'd not thought anyone had seen the Sword alight with Power, other than the three in the alley, and they'd not be speaking to anyone about it. This was bad. If the Enemy heard of it.... They had to leave here, as soon as they could. But he still had to retrieve Lunahr's sword, and Lunahr couldn't even stand, let alone walk.

"Alroy will bring the water for your bath. The buckets is too heavy for me, nowadays. I ain't so young no more. And I'll bring the broth, too," she said.

"And a plate of fruit and vegetables, bread and some wine, for our friend," Talon requested.

"No wine, thank you. Clear water, if you have any, fresh from the well," Eladar said hopefully.

"O' course. You sure you don't want some meat pie as well? I was up before sunup and skinned the rabbits meself and baked it fresh this morning," she said proudly.

"That sounds delicious. I'll be down for some later," Talon said quickly. Lunahr and Eladar were both beginning to look a little green.

She smiled and nodded and left.

"Laren? Laren, what did you do?" Lunahr asked in Amontirin.

"What I had to," Talon said. He sighed. It wasn't just the Enemy he had to worry about. If Arcanus heard about this, he'd be none too pleased. And

Arcanus would know; he always knew. People were skittish enough about wizards without him adding to their fear. Well, he couldn't undo what had happened. He hoped no ill would come of it. "I'm going to make you some medicine and bathe, then retrieve your sword. And as soon as you're able, Lunahr, we have to go. But I don't want you straining yourself, hurting yourself worse."

Lunahr nodded, wincing. Talon pulled out his healer's kit and began mixing more medicine for Lunahr, something to calm his stomach mixed with the medicine for pain, and had him drink. Once the tub was filled, he bathed and changed into his good clothes, the ones he'd brought to wear in Riviera. He'd have to pick up some new things for himself as well as Lunahr, after he retrieved the sword.

He received more than a few glances when he came downstairs, dressed in his burgundy silk shirt and black pants. They were far too fine for this part of the City, for an inn like this. He hated attracting attention. At least on the street there would be others finely dressed as well. Of course, the clothes meant he'd be able to bargain the price of the sword down less easily. He'd appear too wealthy. But by the same token, he was well dressed enough that the proprietor might be convinced to show it to him without him having to resort to using his Power right away.

Chapter 6

Oberas

OBERAS looked at the City in relief. Soon he'd be docked, his goods would be unloaded, and he need never see Tebras or his worthless new guards again. But as they approached the pier, he scowled at the unfamiliar boat that was docked in his berth. "You tether yours to her. I'll go see the Dock Master to get this craft towed. They've no business being here," he said to Tebras. He heaved his bulk into the other boat and climbed the ladder up the dock, his guards trailing after him.

A short while later he was bellowing at Granger, the Dock Master. "Rented it! What do you mean, rented it? That's my pier, my berth! My boats dock there, mine alone! We've a contract!"

The man before him was sweating. "Well of course, Master Oberas, we did have one, but when you didn't return, we thought…."

"Thought! You didn't think! If you had, you'd never have risked losing my business to East Dock. They've been begging me for years to go there. Well, they need beg no longer! You couldn't get me to use this sorry facility again if you gave it to me free of charge for half a year!" Oberas bellowed.

"But Master Oberas, surely…. How about if we were to give it to you free of charge for a full year?" Granger asked hopefully.

Oberas grinned evilly, the kind of look a cat might give a mouse before he starts toying with it, knowing he'll get to swallow it in the end. "Well now, perhaps if you were to offer a year and no unloading fees," he said, rising to the challenge.

By the time Oberas strode down Market Street, his mood had greatly improved. With the docking fees he'd be saving, he'd made up a considerable amount of the losses he'd suffered on this trip so far, assuming he could keep the business of the four buyers he was in danger of losing. Now, if only his shop was still there with its contents intact, and his two guards still watching over it.

He glared at the "closed" sign on his door. Ridiculous! Two days before Feast Day, and he was closed! Inexcusable. He tried the door and was somewhat relieved to find it locked. He'd lost his key, though, early on in the trip. He pounded upon the door. "Open up, Devrik! You'd better be in there, you and Curtis both, or…." He stopped pounding as the door opened.

Devrik grinned at him. "Master Oberas! I knew you'd be back! I told them all you would be!" He looked in relief at Logan and Willis, and Mevan and Temris, obviously pleased to see they'd survived the journey and appeared uninjured.

"Don't just stand there grinning at your friends, you lazy oaf! Get to work! Brew me some kakla. And get that list of apprentices!" Oberas ordered.

Devrik set to brewing the kakla and got the list. Oberas glared at it and then looked at it in surprise. "What's all this?" he asked, pointing at the writing in consternation.

"Well, Master Oberas, that's my fault. I know we weren't supposed to open the door for anyone but you, but I couldn't very well let the boys and their fathers knock without an answer; they might have gotten all kinds of wrong ideas about what happened to their fees. So I had them come in and sign, those that could. I memorized the names of the others to go with their marks, since they couldn't read their names nor could I. I wished Logan was here, let me tell you! I told them all that you'd send for them when you returned, that I was hopeful you'd arrive soon. I hope you're not too angry with me for it," Devrik said contritely.

"Angry? You've done well, Devrik. It was a relief to me, knowing you were here while I was away. I'll tell you all about the trip later. First, tell me the names that go with the marks. I'll be sending you around to their houses. I have their addresses here. Logan will go with you to read it. I'll need to reschedule the ones that came, but for next week. I'll need time to get things in order, what with Feast Day so near and the mess my affairs are in from the week's delay."

RION rushed to the front door at the unexpected sound of the loud, forceful knock. His mother was asleep in her chair; he hoped she'd not waken. "Who's there?" he called through the crack between the door and frame, trying to keep his voice low but loud enough to be heard.

"It's Devrik, with Logan, from Master Trader Oberas's shop. We met when you came by with your father."

Oberas had returned! Both nervous and excited, Rion released the bolt and opened the door. "Please come in," he said politely. "But please, speak softly. My mother's been ill, and she's asleep in the family room."

"Is your father home? We were hoping to reschedule your appointment with Master Oberas. He's returned," Devrik said far more softly, confirming Rion's hope.

Rion grinned. "I guessed as much, from your stopping by, but also because you said Logan was with you, and you'd told us he was with Oberas. I'm glad you made it back safely," Rion said, smiling at the other guard.

Logan grinned back at him. "I'm glad too. It was touch and go for a while there. We had quite a journey."

"I'd love to hear it!" Rion said enthusiastically. "Oh, but I suppose we should reschedule me. That's why you're here, after all."

Devrik smiled at him as Logan held out the new schedule. "If you have somewhere I might sit?"

Rion realized he'd need room to write. He took them to the kitchen, so they'd not disturb Mother, and Logan took out his pen and ink and drying sand.

"Oh! I'm being remiss. I almost forgot. Can I offer you some kakla? And we've some honey cake, as well." Rion opened the cupboard door and eyed the thin slice in dismay. "Well, we've a little. Cedric came by last night and had a few slices. He's a friend of Father's; everyone says he likes honey even more than the obearn do and—oh, but I'm being too chatty! Forgive me, I do that. Would you care for some?"

Logan smiled. "No, we'd better not tarry. We've a number of houses to go to still. Master Oberas has a list here, with the two days he's testing, like before. Devrik tells me you can read. Can you make any of the slots on the second day?" he asked, showing Rion the list.

Rion snuck a look at the list for the first day, trying to quickly tell as much as he could about the other boys from what they'd written and how they had, and their locations in the City, without looking indecisive. "Certainly. I'll take the first slot again on the second day." It was for a week after Feast Day. "Would you like me to sign my name again?"

"Sure. Right there. You'll remember to tell your parents?" Logan asked.

Rion grinned. "Of course!" Then he signed, careful not to smudge, and he dried the ink.

"Well, we'd best be going," Devrik said.

"Thank you so much for stopping by. I'll be sure to tell Mother as soon as she wakens," Rion said.

Both men smiled at him, and he let them out.

Rion began jumping up and down in excitement, careful to land softly, as soon as they left, but resisted the urge to wake his mother. She needed the sleep. She'd had a rough night again last night, after a number of good ones. Perhaps now she'd sleep better.

He'd heard his parents discussing other apprenticeships for him last night before they went to bed. He'd heard how concerned they were. He was sure that was part of what had kept mother from having a restful night. Now he still had a chance at this apprenticeship. If he got it, she'd need not worry so about him.

OBERAS looked at the list Logan handed him and grunted. Only seven of the twelve boys had signed it. He'd lost almost half of those he'd had before. But three of the boys who were left could actually write, which was encouraging, at least. Last time there hadn't been any.

He scowled. The most urgent business he'd needed to take care of was done. He'd docked, seen to the unloading of the boat, and contacted his buyers and the potential apprentices. Of course, there was still plenty of work to be done—the stock to be brought from the dock warehouse to the shop, the inventories, the rescheduling of all his business—but nothing that couldn't wait. He couldn't delay it any longer. The sun would be setting soon.

"Logan, Curtis, we're going out," he said, fastening his cloak about him.

THE three of them left the shop. Logan was surprised at the pace Oberas set. He seldom moved so quickly. He was further surprised when they didn't stop at any of the inns Oberas usually ate at. Even more so when he continued onward, passed the Market without a glance, and headed westward. The only things out this way were residences and the temples.

Logan glanced in surprise at Oberas when he turned onto Temple Way. He stared in openmouthed astonishment when Oberas began climbing the steps of the Temple of Elmoth, but then quickly hid his reaction.

"WAIT here," Oberas said to his men.

Oberas entered the massive stone edifice alone. He strode up to the offering altar. He pulled the dagger from its concealed sheath about his ample waist. The hilt no longer fit quite as comfortably in his hand as it should; his fingers were fatter than they'd been.

What need had he for a dagger, anyway? He had guards of his own now to protect him. He'd had them for years. It had been years since he'd drawn the dagger in his defense. So why should surrendering it to Elmoth hurt almost as much as if he were taking his arm instead, like he'd taken Vargas's?

"Take it, curse you, you insatiable bastard," he said, flinging it upon the altar. Then he turned and exited the Temple, stalking toward his guards and passing them without slowing his stride. Then he tore down the steps, as if they were on fire beneath his feet. His guards formed about him as he reached the street. He strode purposefully past the Market, headed for the Painted Pony.

The tavern was packed. There wasn't an empty table. He glared, looking about him. "Meris! I need a table," he demanded, spying the owner.

"OF COURSE," Meris said, quickly masking his surprise at seeing Oberas. He cleared a table for him by offering a free round to those there if they'd surrender their table. Then he came up with a bottle of Thenalonese wine from the stock he kept specifically for Oberas and his business associates, and a real crystal goblet, one of the ones hand-blown in Thenalon that Oberas had brought to him years ago. Oberas imported the wine himself as well, to be sure he always had the finest on hand. They had a rather complicated but profitable arrangement.

He'd not expected to see Oberas here so late. Or alone, save for his ever-present guards. He'd not thought to see him at all. He was pleased the rumors were unfounded and Oberas had returned safely after all. Oberas was an excellent customer.

"No, not wine," Oberas bellowed as he sat. "Oushka, aged, the older the better. A glass bottle, if you've any so fine, a flask if you haven't. And two glasses. Not those pathetic thimbles, either! I want real drinking glasses!"

Meris raised a brow at the order. So there was a business associate on his way. Still, the oushka was a surprise. Fortunately, he'd bought two cases of twenty-year-old oushka for his son's wedding and still had half a case left. He'd been saving it to celebrate their first child, but his son had been married six years now and his wife was still barren. It was a shame. She was a fine wife in all other regards.

He went into his private rooms and got one of the bottles, along with two of the glasses Oberas normally used for the rare instances he drank mead, instead of two of the smaller ones it was customary to drink oushka from.

OBERAS opened the bottle and breathed deeply of the oushka inside and then poured a glass for himself and a second glass. He looked up at Logan. "Sit," he ordered.

Logan looked at him in surprise. "Sir?"

"Sit your arse down. You're drinking with me," Oberas commanded, glaring at him.

Logan looked at Curtis uncertainly.

Oberas glared at them both. "You keep telling me what a fine guard he is. So let him guard me and you, too, if you feel a need to be guarded. Now drink or you're released from my service," Oberas threatened.

LOGAN sat and lifted the glass reluctantly. Oushka was usually only drunk from tiny metal cups and never in such quantity as this. And to be holding real glass! The glass he held must be worth at least a month's salary, quite possibly two or more.

He drank and was amazed. Oushka usually burned like fire going down. But this was far different. He savored the taste of it.

Oberas put down his empty glass and poured another. He glared at Logan's glass, which was still nearly full, and topped it off. "You're a follower of Elmoth, aren't you, Logan?" he accused.

Logan eyed him warily. "I never speak His name in your presence," he said, stepping cautiously around the question.

"Of course not! I didn't call you a fool; I called you a worshipper of Elmoth. Although, I suppose, I'm calling you a fool then, at that," Oberas said, with a harsh laugh, downing the second glass of oushka.

Logan looked about cautiously. Fortunately, it appeared no one else had heard Oberas speak such blasphemy. "Yes, I follow him. I'm a guard, who else am I to follow?"

"Why not Ragnar? He's good enough for the Dwarves and for Men. Plenty of warriors and guards follow him instead, though this City doesn't have a temple to him."

Logan sipped his drink. "You're not trying to tell me who to worship, are you?" he asked softly.

"Who, me? No of course not. I just asked you a simple question," Oberas said, voice slurring, as he downed the dregs of his second glass and poured a third.

"Sir, you've not eaten lunch," Logan said to Oberas in concern.

"What does my eating lunch have to do with you worshiping Ragnar?" Oberas asked, his voice surly as he drank deeply from his third glass of oushka.

"Not a thing. It's just, you've not eaten dinner either, and I've never seen you drink oushka before at all and never seen anyone drink it in such a large quantity as quickly as you've been."

"Imbecile! I was drinking oushka before you were born. I've drunk Dwarven warriors under the table!" Oberas shouted, slamming the glass down for emphasis. It shattered against the hard wood surface, sending a small wave of oushka mixed with blood across the table. Oberas stared at his hand stupidly, at the blood welling up from three of his fingers.

Logan stood. "Curtis, tell Meris we need some bandages."

Oberas reached for the bottle with his good hand and was bringing it to his lips when Logan yanked it away.

"What are you doing? Give that back!" Oberas yelled.

"No sir. You've had enough. You've had too much. You're hurt. I'm bringing you home. We'll stop at the healer on the way."

"What, this little thing," Oberas said, flinging out his hand. Drops of blood spattered the table and Logan's uniform. "You call this hurt? Working for me has made you soft if the sight of so little blood upsets you. You should see what Elmoth took from me and my friends the last time, the greedy bastard! As blood offerings go, this is a pittance," Oberas stated loudly.

Sudden quiet enshrouded the six tables around them, and then there was a screech of wood as chair legs scraped against the floor. "Did that fat pig just blaspheme Elmoth?" a hard-looking man growled.

Logan stepped in front of Oberas. "He's drunk. He doesn't know what he's saying," he apologized, arms out to mollify the irate man. "You have my apologies for it now, and I'll make an offering tomorrow, in the Temple, on his behalf."

Meris came up with the bandages, but there was no sign of Curtis.

"Sirs, please, this is all a misunderstanding," Meris said. He turned to Oberas and back again quickly. "There, he's apologized for it," he said, as if Oberas had spoken to him, "And to show there's no hard feelings, he's offering to buy a round for each of you," Meris added.

Oberas opened his mouth in denial, but the excited roar of voices calling for serving wenches drowned out the sound.

"Come on, Oberas, quickly, while we yet can," Logan said, yanking upon his good hand. "Now, you arrogant whoreson! I've no wish to die because of your stupidity."

OBERAS had pulled his hand away, but as Logan's words sank in, he rose, stumbling from the table. Logan had never before raised his voice to him, nor insulted him. It was a shock to hear. But Logan's words of dying because of Oberas were what got him moving. Never again: he'd die before he'd see another man come to harm because of his stupidity and arrogance.

They exited as quickly as they could. But they'd only made it twenty paces past the entrance when five men came out and began running toward them.

LOGAN cursed and drew his sword. Where was Curtis? He'd not expected him to abandon them like that. "We don't want any trouble," Logan said, trying to appease them, holding his blade in a defensive position across his body, rather than moving toward them.

"You should've thought about that before bringing him here, then. We're going to take him to the Temple steps and make sure he makes a proper blood offering to Elmoth," the biggest man said, drawing his own sword, and the four others with him followed suit. "This is your one chance to live. We've no argument with you. Sheathe your blade and let us take him. Who's to know? You can say you did your best to defend him, say we overpowered you."

OBERAS eyed them blearily and reached for his dagger, his hand closing on emptiness. He cursed. This was all Elmoth's doing, him needing the dagger and not having it. He could hear Elmoth laughing at him. And he was putting Logan in danger, just as they both had feared. Logan wasn't lowering his sword. They'd kill him, five against one. No, they'd not hurt him, he'd see to that. "Give me your sword, and get out of here," Oberas ordered Logan.

"No, sir. It's my job to defend you. Like you said, I've had an easy time of it until now. Here's where I pay for it. Do your best to run inside. I'll try to stay between them and the door so you can."

"Sheathe your blades, all of you, or you're under arrest!" a voice barked from their left.

The men turned and cursed, lowering their blades, and Logan dared look. Two City Guardsmen had just arrived, hands on their sword hilts, with Curtis, who was gasping for breath.

Logan lowered his own blade, but waited to sheathe it.

"He blasphemed Elmoth. We was just going to teach him some respect," the spokesman for the others said.

"Why don't you leave that for the God to do? Or the Temple Acolytes? Now go back inside, or go home. We've had a long day and we'd just as soon not have to walk all the way to the jail with you, or drag your bodies to the morgue," one of the City Guard said.

The men grumbled, sheathed their blades, and went back inside, as Curtis went over to Logan. "Are you all right?" he asked between breaths. "Meris sent me to get the City Guard. He could see trouble was brewing, and he was afraid he'd end up with a full-scale riot on his hands, like they had at the Gilded Stein. They all but destroyed the place, and there were more than a few dead there."

Logan exhaled and sheathed his sword. "I'd wondered what happened to you. I couldn't believe you'd just left us there like that, but I was afraid you might have taken offense yourself at what he said about Elmoth."

Logan turned to the Guardsmen. "Thanks for the rescue. Sorry for the trouble. We should be able to get him home safely now, I think. We can bandage his hand there rather than go to a healer. It's not serious."

"Curtis tells me that this is Master Trader Oberas. We'll walk you home anyway. We're just about to go off shift and our homes are near enough to there. I've got a vested interest in seeing you get there safely. My friend's son is applying for an apprenticeship with him next week. Though his father will be hearing about this, you can be sure. I'd not want my son apprenticing under a drunkard and blasphemer," the City Guardsman added, glaring at Oberas in loathing.

OBERAS'S face darkened, but he held his tongue. He wondered which boy. The man hadn't said, probably because he didn't want him taking out his frustrations on the lad.

The walk back to the shop was a long one. Devrik was anxious when he opened the door and saw the City Guard, until he saw they were all right. The City Guard left.

LOGAN bandaged Oberas's hand. Oberas sat silently the whole time. Logan was worried about him. Oberas was seldom silent and never when so angry. But Oberas went to bed without further word. Then he and Curtis filled Devrik and Willis in on what had happened.

OBERAS awoke the next morning to the feeling of Dwarves wielding war axes upon his head. He rolled from the bed and looked at himself in disgust in his large mirror of silvered glass. He'd slept in his clothes last night. He'd only taken his boots off. He always took his clothes off and folded them neatly and slept in a nightshirt, never his clothes. He cursed. There was dried blood upon his shirt. The shirt was yellow Thenalonese silk. The stain would never come out; the shirt was ruined.

His hand hurt like a wolven was chewing on it. He scowled at the bandages. He should go to a healer today. It was his writing hand; he couldn't risk losing use of it. And he needed something for the pain in his head. But he needed a bath first. He stank of oushka. He'd maintain what dignity he could, after last night. "Logan!" he roared and then cursed, clutching his head.

"Sir? Logan is off shift. Can I aid you?" Devrik asked from the doorway.

Oberas began cursing, a long string of colorful expletives, slipping into Dwarvish ones for a moment. He stopped and glared. He'd not used those in decades. "I need a bath. I need a lot more than that, but I'll have to settle for a bath, as it's not in your power to hand me Elmoth's head on a plate."

DEVRIK winced. "It will take a while for the water to heat," he said cautiously.

"As if I've somewhere to be, looking and smelling as I do? Get to work!" Oberas bellowed.

Devrik disappeared quickly. Oberas on a regular day was no joy to work for. Oberas injured and hungover was a new experience in unpleasantness.

Devrik began heating the kettles of water for Oberas's bath. Oberas had a special bathing room he used, with a large tub sunken into the floor that he could actually lay his considerable bulk down in.

It took over an hour to fill. Oberas liked his baths deep and hot.

OBERAS was bathed, dressed, and about to exit the shop with Devrik when Curtis approached him.

"What are you doing here, Curtis? This isn't your shift," Oberas said, anxious to be on his way to the healer. "And what's that you're carrying?" he asked, eyeing the package in Curtis's hands suspiciously.

"As you said, sir, it's not my shift. Although it wouldn't matter now if it was. What I mean to say, sir, is I'm sorry, but I can't work for you any longer. Not after last night. I saw you safely home, but I stayed up all night thinking about it and I did some praying and… I'm resigning my position, sir. These are my two uniforms."

Oberas glared at him. "Elmoth told you to do this, did he? Curse Him! Where am I supposed to find another guard, the day before Feast Day? You had to wait until I'd already released Mevan and Temris and those others from my service, didn't you? Fine, go, get out!" he roared.

Curtis left the package on the table and left.

Oberas began cursing again, long and loudly, and this time most of his curses were directed specifically at the God. Willis watched from a distance, lest any of them be directed at him.

"Well, what are you waiting for?" Oberas growled at Devrik.

"For you to stop, sir. I'll not go onto the street with you cursing the God like that," Devrik said.

Oberas glared at him but quieted.

HARDRED scowled at the innkeeper. This was the seventeenth inn they'd tried. "You can't all be full. Someone must have a room," he said sourly.

"Not the day before Feast Day we don't. Folks have been in the City for a week now, some for two. Next year, come earlier," the man snapped, obviously having no patience for taking surliness from someone who wasn't staying there.

"Why don't we go to Oberas's shop, the one he told us of? Maybe he'd be able to guide us to an inn," Alnas said hopefully.

"If we can find it. I've never seen a city so crowded. Can you at least tell us how to get to Market Street, near Tailor?" Hardred asked the innkeeper.

"You're already on Market Street. Leave here and turn left and go about fifteen blocks, there's Tailor," the harried innkeeper said, then turned to help a customer.

They headed down the crowded street. "At least we're on foot now and not on horseback any longer," Hardred said.

Alnas laughed. "I was just about to say, I wish we still had our mounts! It's madness trying to push through the crowd on foot. Be wary of cutpurses, Hardred. There will be many in a crowd like this."

Hardred said sarcastically, "Thank you, Mother, I'd never have guessed."

Alnas laughed again. They finally made it to what they took to be the right place. "Can this truly be it? It takes up half the block!" Alnas said, admiringly.

"Well of course, what did you expect? He'd have to store his goods somewhere, wouldn't he? A man like Oberas would want them where he can see them. And you don't expect him to have a single room to live in, do you?"

They entered the shop. A uniformed guard greeted them, and Hardred recognized him immediately. "Willis! We won't need to bother Master Oberas at all, if you're here. We didn't know we'd see you or Logan or Mevan or Temris. You told us Oberas had more guards here," Hardred said in relief.

"Hardred! Glad to see you made it. You never know with caravans. The trip's not over until you're safely within the City walls," Willis said.

"That was all too true this trip. We lost a number of men yesterday, a day's journey from the City, but Alnas and I were fortunate," Hardred agreed.

"How might I aid you?"

"We're in need of a place to stay. We've tried seventeen different inns, and there's not so much as a spot of floor in any of them, and we were hoping for a room; we've certainly earned it. Can you recommend a place?"

"The day before Feast Day? You won't find a room left in the City, on your own. You've come to the right place. Master Oberas has arrangements with more than one inn in this City, in case of important clients he needs to house. When he returns, I'll tell him you've asked. I'm sure he'll be happy to help." He smiled, ruefully. "Even more so if you're considering that job he offered. Curtis quit this morning. Oberas wasn't expecting it. He's in quite a state, what with that and what happened last night. We've not had a dull time of it, I can assure you. Why don't you go out and enjoy the City? You can leave your packs here if you wish. I can watch them for you, if you'd like."

"Thanks just the same, but we'll take them with us. We'll be back this evening, after dinner," Hardred said.

"Why not make it before? If I'm right, Oberas will feed you, and you need not spend your hard-earned coin. If not, you'll but eat later," Willis suggested.

Alnas laughed. "I can tell you work for a merchant! You haggle like one! Sure, we'll come back for dinner. As you say, at worst we'll only be out some time; at best we'll be fed."

"So, where would you suggest we go?" Hardred asked.

"I know where I'd go, were I not working: to the Arena. It's where the Amphitheater is, the rest of the year. They remove all the planking of the stage and down below are all kinds of specially designed areas. The events don't officially begin until Feast Day, of course, and the trials are nearly over, but they've plenty of practice sessions there now, and others who aren't skilled enough to be in the actual Games, challenging each other to all sorts of feats. There's wrestling and archery contests and dueling, even swimming and diving: they flood a whole section of it and make a big tank just for that.

"I hear this year they've something special planned; they've got some sort of terrible creatures in the diving tank for the divers to get past. But the one who does and dives all the way to the bottom can find and claim a bag of one hundred pearls!

"And there's the pit, of course, for the pit fights on Feast Day. Sometimes you get to see one or more of the beasts that will be fighting. They like to show them off ahead of time to entice the crowd and raise the wagering. There's lots of coin to be made and lost, let me tell you. They bet on everything," Willis said, sighing wistfully.

"This is the first year I'm liable to miss it. You'd think a man like Oberas would rent his own private box. Many of the merchants do. But Oberas despises the Games. He says that real men don't fight in them, only boys trying to prove they are, that men prove themselves in other ways."

He laughed. "I guess by making more coin than they can ever spend! Anyway, the Arena's at the end of Market, just past Temple Way. Oh, and you'll be wanting to visit the Temple, too, of course, to thank Elmoth for surviving your journey." He gave them detailed directions for doing both.

"Thank you, we appreciate all this," Alnas said. "Oh, one last thing. Do you know of a weapons shop near here, where we might buy a blade for the God? Also, Hardred needs to replace his sword. He managed to break his yesterday. Fortunately for him, he also managed to single-handedly slay five brigands while doing it, and get the coin from all of them, so he's actually better off than if he hadn't broken it, even with what it will cost to replace," Alnas said, grinning.

"Where you want is Seth's Swords. That's where I'd go, if it was me," Willis said, telling them how to get there as well.

The two friends followed the directions to the sword shop, keeping careful track of each other. It would be easy enough to get separated from each other or from their purses in such a crowd. It was a relief to be in the shop and off the crowded street. Hardred began looking at swords and Alnas at daggers. Alnas quickly found one that would make a suitable sacrifice to Elmoth, but Hardred was having worse luck.

Hardred approached the proprietor. "Excuse me, but do you by chance have other blades than these on display? I just arrived in town this morning with a broken blade and I've need of a replacement, but you don't have any long enough for me."

"LET me see the one you're carrying now," Seth said, eyeing the customer. He'd not reveal the blade he was thinking of if there was any chance this was the man it had been stolen from.

He'd purchased the sword from those petty street thieves for a pittance compared to what it was truly worth. He was almost certain it was Thenalonese, what with the exotic look of it and the strange writing on the blade, though not enough remained of the latter to tell. From the age and wear of it, he suspected it had been stolen from a noble's tomb. A man might see a blade such as this once in a lifetime. If this man was a tomb robber, it would be dangerous to anger him.

He'd originally thought to search for the perfect buyer for the blade, knowing he could make hundreds of gold in profit. But now he was eager to be rid of it quickly. He'd heard about what had happened to Mik and Drake and Martin. He wanted no part of a blade a vengeful killer, or especially a wizard, might be after.

He could talk his way out of most any trouble and take most men in a fight, fair or otherwise, when that failed, but he'd have no possible hope of surviving a battle with a wizard. He'd have already thrown the blade in the river because of it, but he'd been afraid to leave the shop with it, knowing he might run into the wizard on the way there. He might talk his way out of certain death if it was in his shop, but not if it was upon his person. Now perhaps he could still make a decent profit, though nowhere near what he'd originally hoped to, of course.

The man drew a battered and broken blade from the sheath at his side. "I kept the piece as well," the man said, sliding it out and placing it against the jagged end to show him how long the blade was before it was broken.

Seth smiled. This couldn't be the man the sword he had was stolen from. "Sure, I've a blade in the back that should suit you perfectly. I won't be but a moment."

THE shopkeeper went into the back and came out again with a sword and scabbard in his hands. The scabbard was of worn leather, old and travel stained, but etched with an eagle in remarkable detail.

Hardred drew the blade. It was slightly longer than his own sword. The blade was thin. There was what appeared to be etching upon the blade, but it was illegible, worn away by time and use. For all its great age, though, the blade looked surprisingly sharp. The leather of the hilt was black with age, and also looked as if it once had some sort of etching upon it. The sword guard was in the shape of encircling wings, formed so fine it was as if real wings had been dipped in gold and then outlined in black, although they were not quite perfect. The right one curved up a little, and the left was chipped near the blade's edge. It was a beautiful blade, old and proud, one that had been lovingly cared for. Not a hint of rust marred it. Once it might have been wielded by a lord or perhaps even a king.

"It's old," Hardred said uncertainly.

"Old indeed, but made by a master. This blade would never fail you by breaking as your own did. Look at that metal! And see how well it cuts," the shopkeeper said, pulling a hair from his head and slowly lowered it upon the blade. It fell in two parts to the counter.

"The blade is worn thin, though," Hardred said, pointing to the worn etching. "It might break."

"NOT this sword. The technique used to make this is something I've heard of yet not seen before. It's Dwarven, you can tell by the metalwork and the age of it. Look at that blade. See how the metal looks as if it were ripples of water? No Man forged this sword, that's for certain," the proprietor said confidently.

"How much are you asking?" Hardred asked cautiously, concealing his true interest, confident he'd hidden his reaction to the man's words about the ripple marks. Dwarven! That was even worse than he'd feared. A Dwarven blade would certainly cost far more than he was willing to pay. But the moment the man had brought his attention to the watermarks upon the blade, he knew he was lost. He had to have it. Regardless of the cost, he couldn't leave here without it. He knew that the cost in doing so, whatever it might be, would be far more than he was willing to pay.

"For a blade as fine as this? Dwarven forged, with true gold leaf upon the handguard, sharp enough to cut a hair? A mere ninety gold."

"Ninety? Ninety! I make my living as a guard, not a prince! What makes you think I might ever pay so much for a sword?" Hardred asked, feigning astonishment.

"Because I've seen your eyes; it was the ripple marks that did it. It was when I showed you those that you were lost to it. You can't leave here without it. You'll not rest until you own it. It was made for you," the shopkeeper said smugly.

Hardred silently cursed. The man was remarkably perceptive. "If it was new," he began, knowing he was already at a terrible disadvantage in the haggle for having somehow betrayed his interest.

The man laughed. "If it was new I'd sell it to the Governor, or to a noble, for ten times what I'm asking you for it. It would hang upon the wall of a Great Hall and be admired by fine ladies and their men. It's a shame it has been so well used. But the fact that it has been shows how valuable it would be to a guard."

"Not valuable enough, or its last owner would still have it," Hardred argued.

"Not at all; the man who sold it to me did so because he had earned enough with it that he was able to open a tavern and give up guarding for good," the shopkeeper replied.

Hardred picked the sword up by the hilt and weighed it in his hand. It was surprisingly light. The hilt fit his hand as if it had been crafted just for him. He knew he was not swordsman enough to wield such a blade, in spite of all he had learned these past nine months.

He looked again at the ripple marks upon the blade and the handguard. The eagle was a fierce, proud, lonely bird. He was such a man. The ripples showed his ties to the sea. He knew he dared not ignore such an omen. He was fated to buy this blade, though he had no idea why.

He was careful to keep his need concealed this time and tried to appear casual as he set it down, but it would not be released so lightly, even for a moment. This blade did not belong here; it belonged at the side of a man worthy to wield it. He shook his head at the fanciful thought. Yet still.... Reluctantly, he continued the haggle. He would need to utilize all his skills for it.

Sometime later, he left the shop, the sword at his side in the sheath that was made for it, his own protruding from his pack, with the broken blade still inside.

Alnas shook his head. "Seventy-five gold! Seventy-five gold for a used sword! A new one of fine quality should only have cost you thirty!"

"I'd not make sport of me, were I you. Or do you forget I got him to bring the price of your knife for Elmoth down from fifteen gold to ten?" Hardred said, knowing he'd haggled well in that, at least.

"No, I'd not forgotten. Forgive me Hardred, but... you're not much of a swordsman, for all you're a fine guard. Whatever made you buy it?" Alnas asked.

Hardred sighed. "I know I've not the skill to wield it properly, but still... it spoke to me, Alnas." At the look he received, he laughed. "No, I didn't mean like that. You need not fear I'm hearing voices! I mean... I couldn't leave it there, to gather dust, or to be bought by someone who might put it over his mantle and never use it.

"It was the ripple marks that did it. I was destined to buy it, although I've no idea why. We mariners believe strongly in omens, signs from the sea and sky that others might ignore." He quieted. He'd referred to himself as a mariner. He was a fool. He was rapidly becoming a lander. If he stayed here, in Ardock, he'd become one for sure. He scowled at the thought.

ALNAS sighed, frustrated. The armor was back, the one Hardred had worn since he first met him. It had cracked and shed piece by piece this past week, but now suddenly it was in place again, as if it had never gone.

"Come. I'm curious as to what sea creatures they have in that tank of water Curtis described to us. Many deadly things live in the sea, but I can't imagine them bringing any of them so far inland, so far upriver," Hardred said.

Alnas was relieved. The armor was cracking already. He'd feared it might be weeks until Hardred warmed to him again, that he'd have to endure days more of total silence from him, as he had the first few days he'd known him. "First I need to make my offering to Elmoth," Alnas said. "It wouldn't do to appear to Him that I'd forgotten Him, not after He saved you so many times for me."

Hardred stopped walking and looked at him, baffled. "After He what?"

Alnas's face flushed. "After He saved you for me. I asked Him to. I certainly couldn't save you on my own, though not for lack of wishing to. I've been kicking myself for never learning the art of swimming. Hasn't anyone ever prayed for you before, Hardred?"

"No. I mean, not to someone else's God. I don't worship Elmoth, Alnas, you know that. I've offered to Mereth a few times, for His aid of my ship. She was a merchant vessel after all. And I used to worship Her, of course. I'll not speak Her name. But though I've guarded for nine months now, five caravans, I've not once offered to Elmoth. It touches me deeply that you've prayed on my behalf, that you now make an offering on my behalf."

"What are friends for?" Alnas asked. He plunged boldly ahead. "I've never had a friend like you before, Hardred. I feel I could spend a lifetime knowing you and still be surprised by you."

Hardred would certainly be surprised by him, as well, if Hardred knew his true desires, if he learned it wasn't only his friendship he sought. Alnas had hoped when he'd left home to travel the land that he might somehow find another man who shared his unusual predilection, but he'd not even known for certain anyone else truly could, until the Priest and the Acolytes in the Temple of Elmoth in Logareth had enlightened him.

Since then he'd heard rumor of sailors on long voyages and what they did to slake their base lusts while at sea. Had Hardred and Julian been lovers as well as friends? Part of him wished they had been, so the same might be possible between the two of them, but that same part fought jealousy over the thought of another man touching Hardred the way he wished to, or Hardred touching someone else like that. Elmoth help him, he was becoming more enamored by the day with his taciturn friend, and he was yet unsure whether his growing feelings would remain forever unrequited.

HARDRED smiled. "Julian always said that...." He stopped speaking abruptly. Julian had always said he was the most vexing person he knew, that he'd not have loved him half as much were he not so difficult.

Hardred knew that Julian had truly loved him, but only ever as a brother, never the way Hardred had longed for him to. Not once in all their many long voyages together had Julian ever touched him in anything but friendship. Others aboard ship found release with one another, but it was always quick, discreet, hidden; a necessary evil, tolerated, accepted, but never sought after nor desired. Certainly none would ever think to engage in such a pairing if there was a woman available instead. At least Julian had never known, never realized his shameful hidden desires.

Hardred could well imagine how Alnas might react, were he ever to confess the forbidden longings he'd had for his friend. Alnas must never learn of it. He could not lose Alnas too. He'd not survive it. Alnas had done much even in the short time they'd known one another to fill the terrible, aching void left by Julian's death. It frightened him how much Alnas was coming to mean to him.

THEY proceeded the rest of the way to the Arena silently, each lost in his own thoughts. They found the Arena without difficulty, for the size of the building and the throngs of people around it and the hawkers.

"Roast rabbit, seven coppers a skewer!" a man called out.

"Mead, seven coppers a skin!" a second man enticed.

"Seven? They must be mad! Who would pay such prices?" Alnas asked, shocked but relieved for the excuse to break the awkward silence that had shrouded them.

"Everyone, it seems," Hardred replied dryly, pointing to the throngs of people about each man, swapping coin for wares. He shook his head at their folly. "For the mead, you're at least paying for the skin it's in as well, but the skewers are only wood."

They entered the building and immediately began to hear more hawkers. "Come, try your skill at archery! Only two copper to compete and winner takes a silver!"

"Come, wrestle against those who competed for a place in tomorrow's games! Only two copper to compete, the winner's purse is a silver! Or view it for free. The bet's five to one against Marcus, even odds on Delson."

The bowels of the enormous building below the raised stands of the open-air Amphitheater were just as Willis had described. Area after area was specifically designed and engineered to house whatever contest was taking place, with room for spectators to stand, sit, or both around them. You could compete for coin, or view for free in most of the areas, but many of those watching were also betting on the outcomes.

Alnas was eager to watch the wrestling, but he soon saw Hardred's mind was elsewhere. Hardred looked at him. "I have to go see the water. They've saltwater here, I can smell it. I have to see what they've brought."

"All right," Alnas said, curious to see some of the things his friend was so familiar with. They headed deeper into the building.

"Come, see the denizens of the deep, the mysterious creatures of the sea! Only two copper apiece, well worth the price! You there, keep back from that tank, I said! That thing'll lunge out of there and take your arm off before you could sneeze. Don't say I haven't warned you! You'll see them soon enough. We're going to hang some fish over the tank, as soon as we've enough people inside. Come see the creatures the divers will challenge tomorrow! Would you risk your life against these beasts for one hundred pearls?"

"What's in there? What have you got?" Hardred asked.

"For that, my friend, you need to pay a mere two copper. But it's well worth the price," he said with a wink.

Hardred paid four copper. "For me and my friend."

"Hardred, I could have paid my own," Alnas complained. But Hardred was ignoring him, pushing forward into the viewing area.

There were bleachers set up all about a tremendous tank that was sunken into the floor, ending a scant few feet from it, and there was a board suspended over the tank. The bleachers were three-quarters full. The water looked perfectly still, murky and opaque. There was no sign of whatever lay within. The smell of salt and rotting fish was overpowering.

It was Meria all over again. Hardred all but heard the Goddess whispering to him. It had been a mistake to come. But he'd not disappoint Alnas. They'd see what the tank had to offer, then go elsewhere, away from the smell and the memories they dredged up.

The crowd was getting restless, and there was more than one man drinking here. They'd have to show the creatures soon, or there would be trouble.

RION answered the door at the gentle knock. "Matt! I scarcely heard you, you knocked so softly."

"I was afraid your mother might be sleeping. I didn't wish to wake her," Matt said. Ric and Drew were with him.

"No, she's up. Annabelle's here. She's Josef's wife, he's one of Father's friends we don't know. They've a daughter," Rion explained.

"Great! Then since she's not alone, you can come with us!" Drew said eagerly.

Rion looked wistful. "I can't. Father doesn't want me hunting after the wizard with you. I figured you'd already be on River Street."

"Are you daft? I'm not chasing after a wizard," Drew said loudly, for his mother's benefit, Rion guessed. "At least, not after the tanning my father gave me when he caught me there in the wee hours of the morning," he said softer. "Just my luck he switched shifts and didn't tell me. I could've used your silver tongue, Rion. It hurts to walk."

"We're going to the Arena," Matt said. "We've still the whole day ahead of us, it's nowhere near lunchtime yet, and we've each a few copper. We plan to see some of the bouts. Someday we'll be old enough to enter them. You can come, can't you?"

"Father told me not to leave the house. He said I should study…," Rion said forlornly.

"Let me take care of it," Ric said confidently, entering the family room where Alissa and Annabelle were sitting, sewing and talking.

Ric waited for a pause in the women's conversation and then spoke. "Excuse me, Alissa. We were wondering if Rion might come to the Arena with us. We've only got a few more days to be with him. We're sure he's going to pass the test and get the apprenticeship. Couldn't he please come with us?" Ric entreated. "We promise we'll take good care of him. I swear to Elmoth we're not going anywhere near where the wizard was. We'll keep him safe from harm."

Rion fought to keep from laughing. Ric was using the same big brown soulful puppy-eyed look Cedric always used when he was begging for honey cake or other sweets from them.

Alissa laughed and grinned. "You've more than a little of your father in you, Ric."

Rion was always surprised how his mother called him and his friends by their nicknames, whereas their fathers and all their mothers only used their full names. He'd asked her about it once, and she'd said conspiratorially, "I was young once, too. So were their parents, of course. The only difference is, they grew up!" Then she'd laughed. He loved his mother's laugh. It was good hearing it again; she laughed so seldom now.

"Rion's father told him to stay home and study," Alissa said, and Ric's face fell. "But, since you're not heading off to River Street to look for the wizard, you can borrow him for the afternoon. I'll take full responsibility for it. You can tell Anorion that too, if he happens to catch you in the street, Rion. He'll beat me terribly for it, but I'll just have to suffer," she said, laughing.

The boys laughed too. Rion remembered how shocked his friends had been at some of the things his mother would say, until they realized she was only teasing. They loved his mother. They'd told him so often. She was more often a co-conspirator than an authority figure.

Annabelle shook her head in disapproval. "You spoil the boy, Alissa."

"That I do," Alissa admitted with a smile, hugging Rion and kissing his cheek.

Rion's face flushed hotly that she'd done so in front of his friends. "Have a wonderful time, Rion. Just be back before dinner," his mother said.

"Thank you, Mother!" Rion said, suddenly not caring what his friends thought as he hugged her fiercely. Then he let out a whoop and headed for the door.

"Rion!" she called.

"Yes, Mother?" he asked, heading back to her, hoping she hadn't changed her mind.

"You'll be needing this," she said, holding out her hand. He held out his own hand, curiously. His eyes widened as she dropped the silver piece she was holding onto his palm. "What, you can spend fourteen silver on me and give one to your father, when you only had fifteen in all the world, and I can't give a silver to you? I know you'll spend it frugally, son. But you're to spend it on yourself, not me, this time."

Rion grinned. "Most of it, but don't be surprised if I come home with something for you anyway."

Alissa shook her head, laughing. "You see, Annabelle? For all I spoil him, he spoils me right back."

THE boys left, heading for the Arena. "A whole silver," Ric said, enviously. "I wish I had your mother, Rion, instead of my own. My father wishes it, too. For all my mother's a wonderful baker, your mother's a better cook by far, and never hides the honey from him," he added, laughing.

"You shouldn't say such a thing, even in jest," Drew said solemnly. "The Gods might hear you and think you mean it."

Ric suddenly looked nervous, and Rion realized he must be remembering how Drew's mother had been taken from him. "You don't really think so, do you? I love my mother. Of course I wouldn't want another," he said, loudly.

"Elmoth knows what you meant," Matt said.

Rion didn't say anything. He never did, when the others talked about the Gods. His own parents were an oddity in the Gods they followed. Neither of them was very religious. Mother was a bit fond of Meloneth, the God of Music, but she said he was best worshiped by giving him beautiful music to listen to, not by entering a stone building. And his father followed Ragnar, not Elmoth, as his father and mother before him had, but he didn't do so avidly, although Uncle Farion did.

Uncle Farion and his best friend and roommate, Justin, had a shrine to Ragnar in their house. Rion had heard his grandmother had brought the flame all the way to Ardock from the Temple in Logareth decades ago. The two men were careful to replace the candle nightly to keep the sacred flame always lit, because there was no Temple to Ragnar in Ardock. Because of that, Rion had not once been to temple, any temple. Sometimes he felt he was missing something important by not worshipping the Gods like his friends did.

"That's enough of that, you three!" Matt said, obviously thinking they'd all gotten too quiet. "We're supposed to be having fun, remember! Come, I'll race you to the Arena!"

"No, Matt, not in this crowd. We'd spend the rest of the day looking for each other," Rion said. "I promise I'll not be somber, all right?"

The four friends hurried to the Arena, careful to stay together. They listened to the hawkers for the Games intently and just as eagerly to those selling food. "Candied sweet apples, only five copper apiece!"

"Roasted rabbit, seven copper a stick!"

"Seven! You can buy a full lunch at any inn for that!" Ric said indignantly.

Rion laughed. "Not the week before and during Feast Day you can't! Honestly, Ric, you complain about the same thing every year. You'd think you'd accept it by now." Matt and Drew laughed.

They wandered excitedly here and there, watching the archery first, and then some wrestling.

"Come see the mysterious creatures of the deep! Caught live in the sea and brought upriver, see these saltwater monsters today, before they become guardians of the pearls in the dive tomorrow!" a hawker called. The boys were drawn irresistibly to him. "Only two copper apiece, boys. You'll not be sorry! See the creature men call the wolven of the deep!" the hawker enticed.

"Sea-wolven? That I must see!" Drew said. "Remember the wolven that fought the obearn last year in the pit fight? What would a sea-wolven look like? Here, I'll pay."

"But I've only two copper for the whole day," Matt bemoaned.

"Don't worry, Matt. It will be my treat. Two please, sir," Rion said, producing the silver and carefully counting his change.

Matt cheered up instantly. Then Ric paid his way, and the four went inside.

"Hey, there's room enough for four right in the front row if we're friendly enough," Drew said, excitedly.

Matt hesitated. "I don't know. I don't know that I want to be that close to sea-wolven."

"It's not like it can jump out of the water and get you," Drew reasoned. "Come on, it'll be great!"

"We won't let any harm come to you, Matt," Rion assured him, and Matt let them coax him into going.

A short while later the boys were getting fidgety. "I don't think there's anything even in there," Ric said in disgust. "At least nothing we can see."

They weren't the only ones to think so. The crowd was restless, and there were annoyed mutters from all around the tank. A few men who'd been drinking loudly demanded their coin back.

"Now sirs, I told you before, we'll be dangling a fish in the tank any moment, and it'll come lunging up out of the tank at it. You'll get your coins' worth, mark my words," the hawker said.

"That's what you been saying since I got here. I'll make it come to the surface," one of the men with a flask in his hand said. He set the flask down and headed angrily for the tank, pushing past Rion and his friends.

The man taking the coin had turned from him for a moment to accept another entry fee. He turned back and paled. "Hey, you! Are you mad! Get away from there!" he called out in a panic as he saw the man looking over the side. "Dirk, quick! Get him outta there!" he yelled.

A large man on the other side of the tank turned and saw the man leaning over the tank and started heading for him at a run, yelling.

"Sir, I think you'd better sit back down," Rion said in concern, seeing the fear on their faces. He stood and pulled on the man's sleeve. But the man was oblivious to him as he reached his other hand over the edge of the tank and started slapping the water, shattering the still surface.

Suddenly, a tremendous gray mouth full of teeth thrust up from the water. The man screamed in terror and pain as the jaws closed about his arm, engulfing it. He grabbed desperately with his remaining hand as his blood began dying the water red, clutching Rion, the only thing within his reach to hold. Rion fell forward, terrified, as the creature pulled the man into the tank and the man pulled him.

Rion grabbed futilely at the rough wood of the edge of the tank as he was yanked up and over, and he felt the desperately clutching hands of his friends' slip away from him. He heard his friends screaming his name as the water closed above his head. Then all sound was oddly muted, replaced by strange hisses and pops as he was dragged down.

Salt. The water tasted of salt, he thought, as he struggled futilely, terrified, as he drank it, as he breathed it, as the darkness of the water grew to a greater darkness and all thought ceased.

HARDRED stared in horrified disbelief as the shark lunged up from the water and took the man's arm. Not sharks! Surely they hadn't done something as mad as to bring sharks here! But he saw the churning water stained red as the man was dragged under, as his grasping hand grabbed a boy and dragged him under with him, though the boy's friends desperately tried to save him.

"Rion! Help us! Someone, help him!" they screamed.

Hardred's pack was already on the bench beside him. He sprang to his feet and shed his sheathed sword, stripped off his boots, and then ran for the edge of the tank as a burly man with a fishing spear reached the part of the side where the two had disappeared, scanning the water desperately.

Hardred leapt from the bench the boys had been sitting on beside the edge of the tank, ten feet from the man with the spear, up and over, diving into the reddened waters. The drunken man was lost, but he might still save the boy, if he was fast enough, if there was only a single shark, or even two, although the hope was a slim one. He'd fought sharks before, he knew how to, but the blood would have driven them into a frenzy. But he couldn't leave a boy to die like that. The lad couldn't have been more than nine years old.

Hardred pulled his knife from the sheath on his leg and put it in his teeth to keep both hands free as he swam downward into the murkiness with fast strong strokes until there were shadows before him. He reached out, hoping he'd not feel jaws close about his hand. But instead he felt clothes; he had no idea if it was the boy or the man.

He pulled and the figure floated toward him and then he closed his arm around him. The boy! It was the boy! But he wasn't struggling. He wasn't moving at all.

Hardred started swimming upward with him, afraid of what he would see when he reached the surface with his burden. The boy was small enough the shark could have easily cut him in half with a single bite of its jaws. He felt at least one leg bang against him, but couldn't tell if the boy still had both.

Then he felt something hard and sharp rake against his own leg and with his free hand punched hard. His hand connected with something soft and slippery, and he struck it again and a third time, then kicked toward the surface, the knife still in his teeth, fighting the urge to feel for his own leg. He felt it kicking and was relatively certain he still had it. But that was what poor Francis had thought also, only to find the shark had severed his leg at the knee, that it was the shock that made it feel only a gentle tug, when it had been bitten cleanly off. He'd bled to death within minutes of them pulling him back aboard.

Hardred forced the thought aside as he broke the surface. There was screaming and chaos, the sound of utter pandemonium all around him.

"Hardred! Praise Elmoth! Take my hand!" he heard Alnas yell over the rest of the noise, as soon as he surfaced. He saw Alnas reaching his hand bravely over the side, eyeing the water as he did so.

Hardred swam toward him and hoisted the limp boy out of the water as high as he was able, the effort pushing him downward. Alnas grabbed the boy and fought to lift him without going over the side himself. He got him up and over the edge of the tank as a pole was thrust toward Hardred. Hardred recognized the big man who'd held the spear before.

He grabbed for it as he saw the terrifyingly familiar shape of a fin break the surface of the water at the opposite edge of the tank and begin heading for him, likely drawn by his blood. He pulled himself along the pole with his arms as he kicked strongly, as hands grabbed for him. Alnas and the man pulled him up and over as the shark thrust into the air, its jaws snapping shut on nothing, and it slipped back into the bloody waters.

Alnas was pale and shaking violently. "Are you all right?" he asked, looking Hardred over frantically. "Your leg!"

Hardred looked down fearfully, felt along his leg, and sighed in relief. The shark's teeth had raked across him, but his leg was whole; it hadn't cut bone nor taken a mouthful of flesh and muscle off the bone. He sheathed his knife. "I'm fine. The boy. How is he?"

"You tried, Hardred. You did more than anyone could have asked of you. I'm sorry. He's dead," Alnas said, hand upon his shoulder to comfort him. "But at least his parents will have a body to bury."

Hardred could hear the sound of sobbing. A boy was holding the dead boy by the shoulders, shaking him, the dead boy's head lolling limply as he did so. "Rion! Rion, wake up!" he was calling. A second, smaller boy, though not as small as the dead one was the one crying. Hardred remembered seeing them reaching for the boy as he was dragged in. He'd thought there had been three of them, but he only saw the two.

Hardred rose and went to them, looking critically at the dead boy. He had all his limbs, he didn't see any blood upon him. So the water had claimed him, not the shark.

A sudden wild hope seized him. "Here, let go of him. I can help him," Hardred said firmly.

Alnas went to him and looked at Hardred, eyes pained. "Hardred, you can't. He's dead. He's not breathing. He's drowned."

"Your friend's right He's dead. Seneth's taken him, the poor lad," the big man with the pole said.

"No! No, he's not dead! He can't be dead!" the bigger boy screamed, his voice nearly hysterical. "I promised his mother we'd keep him safe! I promised!" He shook him again. "Wake up, Rion! Please wake up!" he begged, tears streaming down his face.

Hardred grabbed the boy by the shoulders and looked him in the eye. "Listen to me. I swear I can help him. But you have to let me." He released the boy and straightened the dead one so he was laying upon his back on the wet floor, checked his mouth to make sure his tongue wasn't blocking the way, then lowered his mouth over the boy's and began breathing into it, as the Elf, Fisher, had taught him.

"Hey, now, what do you think you're doing?" the big man asked, outraged. "You let his body be!"

"Alnas, don't let him stop me. I swear I can help him," Hardred said, between breaths, hoping his friend would intervene if the man tried to stop him.

When the boy didn't start breathing on his own, he began using the chest compressions as he'd been taught, and then began breathing into his mouth again, as he heard Alnas and the big man scuffling and angry voices.

"Get off of him!" a different voice yelled, as water spewed from the boy's mouth and he began coughing and gasping, just as rough hands grabbed Hardred, yanking him off the boy.

The hands dropped away. Hardred saw it was a City Guard who'd been holding him; the man was looking in amazement at the boy, whose eyes were open. He was breathing on his own now, still coughing, but breathing. He'd done it!

"That's not possible! He was dead! I swear to you he was dead!" the big man said. "It's wizardry! He's a wizard! No wonder he survived the tank, the sharks," he said, backing away from Hardred in fear.

Alnas was looking at Hardred, dazed as well.

"Rion? Rion!" the older boy said, hugging the revived one, who was still coughing, but breathing on his own steadily now.

"RIC? You've been crying!" Rion said, his voice warm with concern.

Farion fell to his knees beside him in awe. "Alarion! Praise Ragnar!" Farion said piously, thanking the God for his miraculous intervention on his nephew's behalf.

"Uncle Farion? What's going on? Why is everyone standing around me, why am I on the ground, why am I all wet? I… that man… the tank! That thing with the teeth!" Alarion said, horrified as memory apparently flooded him.

"It's all right, Alarion, you're safe now," Farion assured him, hugging his nephew tightly, shaking.

When he and Douglas had heard a young voice coming toward them, screaming for the City Guard, they'd come running. When he'd seen it was Drewan, he'd been afraid one of Alarion's other friends, Matthew or Adric, might have been hurt. He knew Alarion was safely home. Anorion had told him so.

When Drewan told them Alarion was here and what had happened as they ran toward the tank, he had been sure his nephew was dead. Then to see him lying pale and limp and that man on top of him had enraged him. But somehow he'd saved Alarion. He must truly be the wizard to have saved him, when others swore he was already dead, that he'd drowned. They'd been told to bring the wizard in, for the murders by River Street. But he was Ragnar's instrument and he'd saved his brother's son.

Farion turned and looked carefully at the man who had saved Alarion's life. Or brought him back from the dead. He was dark-haired, his hair longer than usual for a man, like a hunter might wear it, one who'd been in the wilds for too long, although he was beardless, when such a man wouldn't be. He was blue-eyed, his eyes darker than Farion's own or Anorion's or Alarion's. He was tall, with long limbs, and leanly muscled. He was bleeding, Farion realized in surprise; his leg was injured. He hadn't thought wizards could bleed.

"I didn't hurt the boy. You can ask his friends. I dove into the tank after him when that other man dragged him in. I found him, pulled him to the surface, got him out, but he'd breathed the water. He'd drowned. If it was a week ago, I'd have given him up for lost as well. But I drowned myself, in the River, and an Elf saved me. His name was Fisher. He taught me how to do what he did, to save others," the man explained.

"An Elf? Fisher? You can't mean the one Alissa said came to sing to her? We all thought she'd dreamt him!" Farion said in shock.

"I didn't," Alarion said, sounding surprised. "I believed her. You mean you and Father didn't?" Then he turned to the man who'd saved him. "You dove in after me? With those terrible things in the water? And I'd drowned? You mean I truly wasn't breathing? I remember the salt, tasting it, the feeling of it as...." He shivered.

"It's all right, Alarion. You're safe now," Farion reassured him.

"You, there. You're under arrest. We're taking you in. No sudden moves, now," Douglas piped up.

"Arrest!" the pale young swordsman hovering protectively beside Alarion's savior cried indignantly. "For saving a boy's life?"

"For wizardry. We all heard him. He admits to rising from the dead and raising another from the dead. And to consorting with Elves," Douglas said sourly, as if doing so was even worse. "He's the one who killed them men near River Street."

"Now hold on, Douglas," Farion argued.

"It's him! It's true! He's a wizard! There ain't no way that thing wouldn't ha' eaten him otherwise!" a man yelled. There were other Guard, too, now around them, but none Farion knew well.

"And the boy! Why'd the wizard save him? I'll tell you," the friend of the man who'd fallen into the water said. "He's taken his spirit! He only looks alive! I seen it happen, in the Dwarven Lands. We was there, me and the others. We seen the walking dead! They call us drunks and madmen for it, but I tell you it's Elmoth's own truth, I swear to you what we seen! You let that boy go home now, he'll kill both his parents in their beds. He'll do worse!"

Alarion was looking wide-eyed at the man. Farion put his arm around him protectively. The crowd was getting ugly.

"ENOUGH!" Hardred yelled over the crowd, with a voice that had roared over more than one gale. The chaos dissolved into uneasy murmuring. "I'll surrender myself to the City Guard. I don't want any trouble. I certainly don't want any of you harming the boy after all I did to save him."

"I'm coming with you," Alnas said. He was holding Hardred's pack as well as his own, and his sword and boots.

Hardred took the boots from Alnas and slipped them on, grunting as the boot pressed against the gash in his leg. He'd need to get his leg seen to; it was still bleeding, but the pressure of the boot against it might help.

"No, Alnas. Go to Oberas instead. He might have influence enough to help me. He might feel obliged enough to me for the aid I gave him to want to." He didn't really believe it, but he saw the crowd. They were afraid. Frightened people often do terrible things. He knew his life was in danger. This way Alnas would be safe at least. Otherwise he might be in danger for knowing him. And if Alnas left him, the statue would be safe, and the letters for Riana, and the gold. He knew Alnas would see Riana got them.

He'd not tried to take his sword back from Alnas. The Guard wouldn't have let him have it in any case, and Alnas could better use such a blade. He was by far a better swordsman. And Hardred wasn't unarmed. He still had his knife, sheathed under his boot now.

"Where's your sword?" Douglas said, eyeing the sheathed one in Alnas's hand. "That's it, isn't it? It looks like a wizard's blade," the man said, reaching for Hardred's new sword.

"It's not. It's my friend's. He bought it as tribute for Elmoth," Hardred lied. "Mine is in my pack," he said, reaching for his broken blade, the hilt of which protruded from the pack.

"Oh no, you don't!" Douglas said, yanking him back.

ALNAS took the sheathed sword from the pack. It was broken and useless, not of fine enough quality to pay to reforge it. Alnas could see Hardred was trying to protect his new blade, and he'd had no special fondness for his old one. Alnas held the sheathed broken blade out to the City Guardsman. "Here, take it."

Douglas eyed the blade warily, and none of the other City Guard moved to take it. No one wanted to risk touching a wizard's blade, especially not one that had already slain so many.

FARION reached out and took it gingerly, and the others tensed. Then they breathed a sigh of relief as no ill befell Farion.

"Let's go," Farion said. "Alarion, you stay close to me." He'd be able to reason with the watch Captain, but these men were too frightened for reason, and he knew frightened men sometimes can become like a pack of ravenous wolven.

"We'll all go," Drewan said, and he and Adric and Matthew went to form up around Alarion.

"No, boys," Farion said intently, softly. "Get Justin, Anorion, your fathers, and as many of our other friends as you can find. We may well have need of them."

"Yes, sir!" Drewan said. He and the others ducked quickly away.

More and more people gathered around them as word spread, and they began calling out all kinds of wild claims.

"The wizard! They caught the wizard! He tried to kill a boy!" one yelled.

"He fed a man to his monsters!" another yelled.

"He killed four children!" another cried.

"He brought a boy back to life by feeding him his blood!" a fourth yelled.

Finally they were out on the street, trailed by dozens of fearful men, yelling all kinds of things.

"Don't worry, we'll soon sort this out," Farion told Hardred. "I'll not let them harm you, sir. I'm grateful to you. This is my nephew you've saved. I'm Farion, this is Alarion. It would have killed my brother and his wife had he— were anything to have happened to him. What's your name?"

"Hardred."

Hundreds of curious onlookers watched the mob's progress down the crowded street, as they headed to the Guardhouse and the Tower.

TALON entered Seth's Swords. He saw Seth, the proprietor whom he'd spoken with only the day before, behind the counter and went to him immediately. "Pardon me. I've been told you have some new blades since the last time I was here. **I would see them. I'm looking for one in particular, an unusually long blade, in a sheath of tooled leather with the image of an eagle. The handguard is black and gold, shaped in the form of a pair of wings,**" he said, directly, focusing his Power upon the man, in spite of his earlier thoughts to the contrary. He'd not waste time with games, nor could he afford to pay what the Man might ask for Lunahr's blade.

"Sure, I had a blade like that. Sold it only a short time ago," Seth said.

Talon cursed. "**Sold it? To whom? Describe him to me; tell me his name, if you know it.**"

Seth described the man to him. He didn't know his name. He had no distinguishing features. It could have been anyone. Hundreds of men fit the description he'd given.

"**Do you know where he lives, where he was going?**" Talon asked.

"He and his friend only just came to town. They were talking about going to the Arena to see the Games," Seth said.

Wonderful. Them and thousands of others. He shouldn't have taken the time out to bathe, to change. He should have risked coming as he'd been.

No, he couldn't have. Word of the wizard and the men he'd killed had spread. He'd heard it. The Guard would have suspected him instantly had they seen him in that part of the City, in clothes bloodied as they had been.

But he'd lost the Sword of Eagles, after he'd told Lunahr he'd bring it back to him. How was he ever to find Loruthanar now?

He left Seth's and headed for the Arena, knowing his quest was now a hopeless one. But still, he had to try.

As he neared the Arena, a huge crowd was surging from it. There was fear in the air. He could taste it. "What is it, what's happened?" he asked one of the men who passed.

"It's the wizard! They caught him! They're saying that he killed a man and used his blood to bring a boy back to life, one the sharks killed! And he's bragged that he rose from the dead himself!" the man said.

The hairs on the back of Talon's head stood on end. The Enemy! The Enemy was here, in Ardock, or at least one of his minions: Resemblants or Revenants, one or the other. And a child! Not again! Not another child-turned-monster that he'd have to lay to rest. It had been over six years since it happened, but the boy's face still haunted his dreams. Beheading the monster he'd become was what had damaged his core enough to send him to madness the first time he fell to it.

Lunahr! If there was one agent of the Enemy in the City, there might be more. He must be protected from them!

But Eladar was with him. No evil would touch Lunahr while Eladar yet lived. Lunahr had touched his heart as deeply as he'd touched his kin's. Eladar was already devoted to him. No one could meet Lunahr and not love him.

No, that wasn't true. Those men in the alley hadn't; they'd harmed him terribly. And it was his fault. Talon felt himself falling to indecision, to self-criticism and doubt, always the worst of the demons that plagued him.

Should he follow the crowd, try to locate the Enemy's minion and destroy him, or protect Lunahr? If he attacked the undead creature, he risked revealing himself to the Enemy. But he couldn't let one of the Enemy's monsters loose in this City. The Guard had no idea what they were dealing with.

The crowd was quickly pulling away from him. He followed the crowd, which was swelling as it went. Eladar would keep Lunahr safe; he would have to. Talon was needed here. Once the crowd turned into a mob, chaos would soon follow. He'd seen it happen many times, in many cities.

"DON'T bring him to the jail! Hang him before he kills us all!" a voice cried out.

"No, let him go! He might yet spare us!" another begged.

"Hang him! Hang the wizard and the boy!" a third called.

"No! You can't hurt the boy!" a fourth insisted.

Rion was looking about him, afraid. They all sounded so angry, the men surrounding them. His father had warned him of things like this, where reasonable people, even friends and neighbors, became vicious. He couldn't believe it was him they were screaming about, him and the man who'd saved him.

Fighting began at the back edge of the crowd. There were screams and shouts as the frightened, angry men surged against the Guard, fighting them and those others who stood in their way.

Rion was fearful they'd not make it to the Guardhouse, but they did. Rion was never so relieved in all his life as he was to see the Tower, to be brought inside, to have the thick iron-wrapped wood doors close behind him.

"Farion, whatever's going on?" a familiar voice asked.

"Cedric! Am I glad to see you! Have you seen Anorion? I need you to bring him, Justin, Darhew, everyone, as many of our friends as you can quickly find. Alarion's in terrible danger," Farion said. There were angry shouts from outside, and someone began pounding upon the door as Cedric left through the other door.

"What's all this?" Captain Willsley said, entering just after Cedric left, scowling at the group. Farion was relieved that it was Willsley who was on duty. He'd not soon let a man be hanged without just cause and especially not let harm come to a boy.

"We caught the wizard, the one who killed those people near River Street," Douglas said. "He was at the Arena. He brought a dead boy back to life; he bragged he'd died as well. We've the sword he used to kill those men."

"You caught the wizard?" the Captain asked skeptically. "Let's see him."

The Guard parted, revealing Hardred. The Captain eyed Hardred up and down. "He's not even bound! You idiot, everyone knows you have to chain a wizard in cold iron so his magic won't work! If you haven't, then the only reason he's here is because he wants to be. Which means you've either just put all of us in terrible danger from him, or this man's no more a wizard than I am. Since I'm still standing here talking, I'd guess he's not who you thought he was. So tell me why you think he's a wizard, and be quick about it. That mob outside sounds ready to knock the Tower down."

Douglas said defensively, "He was in the Arena. A man fell into the shark tank and pulled that boy in with him. This man dove in after the both of them and pulled the boy out. The boy was dead, he was drowned, he wasn't breathing. We all seen it. Then he done something to him, the wizard, and the boy come to life again. And he bragged he'd been dead before, too, and the Elves had brought him back. That's magic—it has to be—and he's no Elf. That makes him a wizard."

"I see. Then did it ever occur to you there might be two wizards loose in this City? That saving a boy's life makes him a good wizard, not an evil one? That maybe he's here to catch the other one?" Willsley asked. "Let me see the boy he saved."

"It's Alarion, sir," Farion said, revealing him. "He's my nephew, Anorion's son."

"Anorion's son? Why don't you tell me what happened, lad," the Captain said in a kindly voice. "One of you, get him a blanket. He's soaked to the skin and his teeth are chattering."

Rion spoke, his voice betraying his fear. "My friends and I were in the Arena, at the tank, where the sea-wolven were. The sharks, I guess. I heard some men call them that, only we didn't know that's what they were, at first.

"There was a man who'd been drinking. He was upset he couldn't see anything. He thought he was being cheated. He came up to the edge of the tank and started hitting the water, and the men, the one he'd paid the coin to and the other with the spear, they were afraid. They told him to sit back down, but he wasn't listening.

"I stood and told him to sit too; I could see they thought he'd get hurt. Then that thing came up out of the tank, all mouth and teeth, and it grabbed his arm and dragged him in, and he grabbed me and dragged me in with him," Rion said, shivering.

"I can't swim, sir, and even if I could, he didn't let go of me, and the shark was pulling him down to the bottom. I… I breathed the water… and that's all I remember, until I saw Ric. He's my friend, Adric, Cedric's son. I saw him crying over me."

"Have you ever seen this man before? Is there a reason he might have saved your life at the risk of his own?" the Captain asked.

"No sir, I've never met him. He's incredibly brave. He must be a wonderful man, to have done what he did. I'm very grateful to him for it. I still can't believe it, what they said, him jumping into the tank with those things, finding me, pulling me out and… and making me breathe again," Rion said, looking at Hardred, hero worship in his eyes.

Captain Willsley turned to Hardred. "Are you a wizard, sir?"

"No, Captain. My name is Hardred. I'm a guardsman; I was part of a merchant caravan coming from Logareth. I can give you the names of the men we guarded, the names of the other guards; you might be able to find some of them to vouch for me. But even if you can't, Master Trader Oberas can vouch for me, sir. He was on the river, two days out from the City. His boat had fouled on a sunken tree. I freed it for him, but got hit in the head by it, and the tree dragged me downriver.

"An Elf named Fisher found me under the water. He saved my life. I'd already drowned, but he saved me anyway. He breathed for me until I could breathe on my own. Then he showed me how to do the same when I asked him to. I've seen many men drown, sir, I'm a mariner, or was one. I'd never known of a way to save them before. Master Trader Oberas knows the Elf too, sir. What he taught me wasn't magic, much as it seems like it must have been.

"In the Arena, the shark had that man by the arm. The water was red with his blood; I knew it was too late for him. But I thought I might be able to save the boy. I had to try. So I dove in and brought him to the surface. When I saw he'd drowned, I did as the Elf taught me, so he might live again," Hardred said.

"And you didn't kill any men in the City last night?" the Captain asked.

"No, sir. I only arrived in the City this morning. I've not killed any men within the City, I swear it. I killed a number of men a day's ride outside of the City, but they were bandits. We were set upon by a large group of them. They'd ambushed a number of other caravans before us. We found their remains in their camp, after we defeated them."

"There's more I need to hear before I can free you, but I've heard enough for now. Douglas, I need you and twenty men to back me. I've got to try to convince the crowd they've nothing to fear here and disperse them before we have a full-scale riot on our hands. They'll not hang an innocent man while I'm the Captain on duty.

"Farion, I want you to bring Hardred and Alarion to my office. It'll be safe up there, in case any of the crowd surges past us when we open the doors. They'll still have two more sets of doors to breech to get to them. Bring as many men as you need."

"Yes, sir!" Farion pointed to ten men and said, "You, come with me," and started to lead them upstairs. Then he said, "You see, Alarion, I told you you'd be safe."

Rion nodded, hugging the blanket he'd been given tightly around him.

Hardred, who was limping noticeably, stumbled. Farion put out his hand and steadied him. "Kevan, get the healer. Have him meet us up there. Hardred's injured, bleeding. He needs to have his leg seen to," Farion said.

Rion looked at Hardred, wide-eyed, "You mean it bit you after all?"

Hardred smiled at him reassuringly. "Don't worry, Alarion, I'll be fine. As shark bites go, the one I've got isn't a bad one. I've still got the leg, after all."

When they got upstairs and the healer came, though, he was not nearly so unconcerned. "I'm going to have to cut your boot off, the swelling's already so bad." He proceeded to do so.

The healer, who worked for the City and was a uniformed Guardsman as well, started swearing as he cut the leg of Hardred's pants off at the knee, revealing the wound and the sheathed knife, which he handed to Hardred, as he'd been told he wasn't a prisoner.

"They might at least have wrapped something about it, even if they didn't know how to bandage you properly!" he said indignantly as he began cleaning the wound.

"Doesn't it hurt?" Rion asked, amazed, seeing Hardred watching the healer with interest.

Hardred smiled at him. "Oh yes, the pain is as sharp as the beast's teeth."

"You're not to walk on this leg," the healer said, bandaging it tightly. "I'll get a pair of crutches from the infirmary to give you only to get you home. You're to keep your leg up, propped on pillows on a second chair, preferably, when you sit and on pillows in bed as well. I've cleaned it as well as I could, but it might fester still. It should have been taken care of immediately. Teeth leave unclean wounds. I'll give you something for the pain."

"You can, but I'll not take it here. Those folk might yet storm the Tower to get me," Hardred said.

Farion smiled. "You need not fear that. Though I admit, I was concerned before I saw it was Captain Willsley who was on duty. He's a talent for cutting to the heart of a matter and for calming people. If anyone can turn that mob, he can."

"Would they really have hanged me?" Rion asked his uncle in a small voice.

"They might have tried to, Alarion. But they'd have had to kill me first, as well as a number of others. Now tell me, why were you in the Arena in the first place? Anorion told me you were staying home with your mother today," Farion scolded.

"I planned to. But Ric and the others came by and convinced Mother to let me go with them. They were hoping to spend some more time with me before my apprenticeship starts. I wouldn't have gone if I'd known what would happen," Rion said forlornly.

"Apprenticeship? What trade will you be learning?" Hardred asked, curious.

"Trading," Rion said. "Master Oberas is the one I'll be apprenticed to, actually, if I pass the test next week. Logan, one of his guards, said they had a tough trip. I guess part of it was getting his boat stuck like that. He was late returning. He was supposed to have tested me already. Will you be joining the City Guard, now that you're in Ardock? They can always use good men. I'm sure Uncle Farion would put in a good word for you, for all of this. Working for the City Guard's what I would do, if Father would let me," Rion said wistfully.

"Alarion!" a voice said from the door, and Rion turned as his father came in with Cedric and Darhew and some of his other friends.

"Father!" Rion cried and leapt up and into his father's arms, shedding the blanket, hugging him tightly.

"What's happened? Is your mother all right? Cedric only knew you were here, that Farion told him you were in danger."

"It's all right, Anorion, he's safe now," Farion said, telling his younger brother all that had happened.

Anorion turned to Hardred. "Thank you for saving my son's life," Anorion said, his voice shaking with emotion.

"I am glad I was able to do so. You've a fine son, sir. Did you come from outside? Do you know if the crowd's been dispersed safely?" Hardred asked in concern.

"Yes, I did and they have been, most of them, though it took a while. They'd worked themselves into quite a frenzy. We've a dozen or more jailed from that mob, and others healers are tending to. But things are settling down again. Of course, everyone's edgy now that this means we've not yet caught the wizard, but we'll find him, if he can be found, if he's still even in the City. If we don't hear of any more killings, I'd suspect he's found whatever it was he was looking for and has left us," Anorion said.

TALON listened to the Captain speaking to the crowd. He told them the man they'd captured wasn't a wizard at all, that he'd been falsely accused, that he'd done no wrong. He'd instead saved a boy from drowning and been injured doing it. He told them they were in no danger from the man and certainly none from the boy. He said they were going to release him, as soon as he was recovered enough. After a few minutes of answering questions from agitated men, the bulk of the crowd was reassured and dispersed, many of them muttering that they still weren't safe now, with the wizard still on the loose.

Talon wasn't so easily convinced. The rumors he'd heard, of the boy and the man rising from the dead, had been too worrisome. He was debating how best to enter the Tower when to his surprise, he heard his traveling name called. He turned. It was Alnas, and he looked nearly frantic.

"You've no idea how good it is to see a friendly face!" Alnas said, sounding breathless. "I went to Oberas's to try to get his help, but he's not there and there was only a single guard of his, one I didn't know. I left a message with him about what's happened but thought I'd best hurry here to see if I could do anything to help. Have you been watching? What's been going on? Is Hardred still all right?" Alnas asked, his voice shaking.

"Hardred? You can't mean Hardred's the one they thought was the wizard?" Talon asked, amazed.

"I never should have left him, but he sounded so sure Oberas could save him."

"Don't worry. From what the Captain said, it sounds like they plan to release him," Talon soothed. "But tell me what happened."

Alnas explained it to him, and Talon shook his head. He'd been so sure it was one of the Enemy's minions! He was quite relieved to hear it hadn't been, and that Hardred was all right after such a feat. And he'd saved a boy's life with what Eladar had taught him. Eladar would be surprised and pleased to hear.

"This is the third time I've almost inherited Hardred's pack, but the first time I've been forced to carry it for so long. It's more than a little heavy, when carried with my own," Alnas said, shifting the strap about his shoulder. "And we've yet to find an inn. Who knows where we'll be spending the night, now that Oberas wasn't there to help us find a room?"

Talon looked at his burden sympathetically, and then stared in disbelief, astonished he had not seen it immediately, that he had been so preoccupied with thoughts of the Enemy he might have missed seeing it had Alnas not spoken. It couldn't possibly be Loruthanar! But the hilt of a sword was poking up from the pack, an unmistakable hilt.

"That sword you are carrying. It is my cousin Beryl's blade. He was attacked and it was stolen from him. I spent the night scouring the City for it. I learned where it was, but I was too late to recover it, yet still I have been looking for the men who bought it. Hardred is the one who purchased it this morning from Seth's Swords?" Talon asked, still scarcely daring to believe it might be true.

ALNAS looked at him in surprise. "How can you tell so easily it's the same blade?" he asked, suspiciously. Hardred did not know Talon and those he traveled with well, though he owed the Elf his life. He had paid quite a sum for the sword. But what if it truly was the same blade? How else had he known where and when Hardred had bought it?

"I know Beryl's blade as well as I know my own sword," Talon said, eyes intense. "The name is inscribed on the blade, but the letters are worn too low to read, now, and they are in a language few speak any longer. The leather of the hilt once bore the image of eagles. The handguard is in the shape of encircling wings, formed so fine you'd swear real wings had been dipped in black and gold. The right part curves up a little, and the left is chipped near the blade's edge. And the sheath bears the image of an eagle as well."

"That's it, all right. Stolen! And you said your cousin was attacked? Was he injured?" Alnas asked in concern, pulling the sheathed blade from the pack.

"Yes, terribly, although he is recovering now. He was heartbroken that they took it from him. Seeing it again will help him. Please, I must recover it for him. Name your price and I will pay it," Talon said.

"Hardred paid seventy-five gold for it. But I can't ask you to pay for it when it is already Beryl's," Alnas said, handing it to Talon.

"No. I cannot see Hardred lose so much coin when he did nothing wrong," Talon said, reaching into his purse, counting out, and handing him the coin. Seventy-five gold was almost half of the coin he had, and he had not held so much in a very long time, but he would pay it gladly; he would have paid far more to recover Loruthanar. The men he had killed had certainly paid a far greater price. It did not help much that Drake was the one who had slain Mik, the boy, for betraying them to him. The boy would not have died, were it not for him. But he had deserved death: he had slain others and would have continued to.

"Talon? Are you all right? Here, take the coin back," Alnas said in concern.

"No, it is not the coin. I was thinking of Beryl," Talon lied. "Please, the least I could do for this is to give you a roof over your head for the night. We have a room at The Fatted Pig, near River Street. You may share it with us. I will tell the innkeeper to expect you so that he knows it is safe to let you up."

"Really? I'm very grateful!" Alnas said.

Talon smiled. "It is not the best of inns, but it is not the worst, by far. The innkeeper is a good man. The food is edible and there are no bedbugs. I must bring this to Beryl now; I had not expected to be gone so long. Farewell, I will see you later." He turned and quickly headed down the street, the sheathed blade clutched tightly in his hand.

Chapter 7
Brother-of-my-Heart

"PLEASE, Beryl, try to eat something. You might feel better. You'll not get stronger if you don't eat," Eladar coaxed. "I had the innkeeper send his son to the Market. I even gave him the coin to spend. The fruit and vegetables are all fresh now, not like those withered things he gave you before. Surely Talon's medicine has helped?"

"It has," Lunahr said. "My head no longer feels as if it were coming off, as if I wished it did come off. And I don't feel nauseous now. I suppose I could keep something down, only I'm scared to try. I've never been injured or sick like this before. It frightens me, seeing how easy it would be to succumb to it.

"My parents died from illness, both of them, within a day of each other. It happened so suddenly. I was only twelve. The others raised me. Laren's been like a father to me. He was devastated when Father and Mother died. They were Lord and Lady of House of Eagles. They were so well loved, but also, Laren's mother had been House of Eagles and... oh, but I shouldn't have told you that! Talon, I meant Talon! I must remember not to call him Laren amongst your people. His identity is such a secret, you see.

"We lost so many all at once in such a short time to illness, not only my parents. La... Talon thought it was a plague sent by the Enemy, but Arcanus denies it. He knows the Enemy better than any of us. He's been fighting him far longer, and he says he'd never waste us like that I overheard him telling Talon."

He blushed. "I do that, sometimes. Hear things I'm not supposed to. People tell me more than they should, but also... they keep so much from me, to protect me, but surely I'd be safer knowing? So sometimes I listen on purpose. I'll try not to in your kingdom, Eladar. Honest I'll try."

Lunahr looked at Eladar and sighed. "I've said too much. I know I have. Forgive me. It's just that I feel so alone. There are so few of us now, but the others have always been there for me. I suppose you think I'm foolish, being so afraid of dying. Elves know Men die so easily, it's Men who have a hard time accepting it."

"Beryl, stop! Please," Eladar pleaded. "When you talk about dying it… it upsets me. It shouldn't, I know. You're right. It never has before, not with other Men, but… it's different with you, somehow.

"You're special, Beryl. What you just told me. You are such a kindred spirit to me. You have no idea what it is like to be only forty-three and to be an Elf, the second son of a King. No one takes me seriously, especially when I most try to be serious, to be responsible. Is it any wonder I find refuge in mischief-making, in driving my sister and especially my brother to distraction?

"But also, there is more. The music you make, and when you sing…. It's some small comfort the Amontir live to be two hundred and fifty, not merely sixty as other Men do. At least, when illness or injury doesn't claim you. That woman, Alissa; it bothers me that she's dying, that her music will die with her."

"It bothers me too," Lunahr said softly. "You are so special also, Eladar. I wish your family could see it as I do. You even understand about the music, about how important it is, how music should never die. They laugh at me, sometimes, the others. They tease me about it, about how much I value songs, how easily I am distracted by them, even though they love me for it.

"I've felt so lost, knowing I had to leave them, to be exiled to live amongst your people. No, not exiled. I'm sorry, that's not the right word. I love your people, Eladar, I've always ever only most wanted in the world to live amongst you. It's only that—not alone. I never thought I might be so terribly alone. But now it doesn't seem so terrible, knowing you'll be there with me.

"You already seem as a cousin to me, Eladar, only one I'd never met. It's so amazing, getting to know you, a stranger. I've only ever known my own kin. I've never even seen others before, except for the Dwarves, of course, but my kin were so protective of me then, and I'm even more of a child to Dwarven eyes and…. And now, to be in a city! But I'm stuck here, in this room. I can't even walk, let alone stand," Lunahr said in despair. "To be surrounded by music, and hear none of it. I… I can't bear it, Eladar."

ELADAR looked at Beryl in dismay. He didn't know what to say, how to comfort his young friend. Friend? Yes, already he was truly a friend; he was more. He could be as a brother to him, the bond between them was already so strong. Even now he felt closer to him than he'd ever been to Elavar. Beryl could be far more than a brother. Were they both older, Beryl could be his *lythenia*, his heart's mate. The potential was already there.

Beryl was so warm, so alive; music seemed to flow from him, as joy had, when first he'd met him. So many of his people, everyone in his kingdom it sometimes seemed, were so staid, so sedate. It was like being a stream in spring flood, racing down the mountains only to meet a ponderous slow-moving river, to be overwhelmed by it, to vanish into it. Beryl was alive like that as well, or he had been, before those terrible Men had harmed him, had taken what meant so much from him. Now all the joy, the life, the energy was gone. It was like standing upon dried, cracked mud that had once been a river bottom. A terrible feeling of loss overwhelmed him.

"I'M SORRY, Eladar. I don't mean to upset you," Lunahr said, seeing Eladar's distress. "I'll try to eat. But... what if Laren can't find Loruthanar? What if he can't recover my sword?" Lunahr said in despair.

"I'll see that a new sword is forged for you. An Elven blade, finer than anything you have ever before seen. I never looked closely at your own blade. I know the mark of House of Eagles was upon it. I saw the handguard, although I did not see it in detail, but... anything you desire, Beryl, it will be yours," Eladar promised. "Now please eat? For me?"

Lunahr smiled at Eladar shyly. "I'll try." He took a deep breath and began to hesitantly eat what the innkeeper had prepared for him. He was surprised. It tasted good. He had no trouble keeping it down, when he'd been so afraid he might vomit again. He'd been feeling so weak and helpless.

"Share it with me? It truly tastes good and you've not yet eaten, and this is far more than I might be able to eat," he coaxed.

Eladar smiled at him. "I cannot resist you, when you look at me like that. You have such amazing green eyes, Beryl. You are aptly named. Your eyes shine as Elfstones might, were they ever so warm and liquid and perfect."

Lunahr's face flushed, and his heart quickened at Eladar's words, at the look he gave him.

Eladar saw and sighed. "Forgive me. I did not do that intentionally, this time. I will admit, I was flirting with you rather shamelessly before. It is a hobby of mine, at times. Normally, I take particular delight in being able to fluster those who think themselves immune to my charms. I would never try such a thing upon Talon, of course. He is made of ice, I think: he is so cold he burns."

"But he's not cold at all!" Lunahr argued, coming immediately to his cousin's defense. "I mean... he's so passionate and compassionate. Our people would be lost without him to guide us. They all love him as fiercely as I do.

"It is so hard to protect him, when he always seeks to protect us instead. Outwardly, he appears so strong, as if no danger might ever harm him. Yet he is so terribly fragile. Only Fa… Hunter and I know him so well, of course, but even the others know he is not made of ice. You just do not know him yet. Although I admit, he is hard to get to know, but it is not by choice. He has to be so cautious, you see, lest the Enemy find him. Also, so many have died and each loss pains him terribly. He is like a father, a brother to each of us.

"He was born to be a king. He has the heart for it. A king should suffer when his subjects do. Only no other king in all the history of the world, except for his father and his grandfather before him, has had to watch his people die, first by the thousands, then by the hundreds, then by the dozens and now one by one.

"There are only twenty of us left. Twenty, in all the world! Sometimes… sometimes I fear we are the last. But then Laren comforts me. He swears he will lead us to victory, that we will find the Ring in time to use it, that the Enemy will finally be defeated."

"Beryl, you have stopped eating. You must eat now. You may talk later," Eladar urged.

"Sing to me? I get so afraid, when I think of such things, when he is not beside me. If you sing, I won't try to talk to you. I'll be silent so I can hear, but I promise I'll still chew and swallow," Lunahr said hopefully.

Eladar sighed. "Very well, I shall sing for you. But my voice sounds best in harmony. It was never meant to sing alone."

Eladar began to sing, and Lunahr grinned in delight. It was an Elven song, one he'd never heard before. He listened eagerly and remembered to eat.

When he was done, Lunahr said. "You must sing that for me again, later, so I can be sure I heard all the words and remembered them correctly. Perhaps I might sing it with you?"

Eladar smiled. "Only if you continue to eat," he threatened gently.

Lunahr grinned and ate with renewed enthusiasm. Eladar seemed tremendously relieved to see it. He ate as well. When they were done, Lunahr said. "I think I might be able to stand. I'd like to try. I feel like such an invalid."

"I don't know that that's such a good idea, Beryl. You don't want to lose your lunch," Eladar said, though he was obviously reluctant to curb his enthusiasm.

"I'll take it slowly, I promise," Lunahr said. Lunahr sat up, and then lowered his legs over the edge of the bed. Slowly he stood. He smiled. He took a step forward but swayed and fell against Eladar. Eladar had wrapped his strong arms about him, so he didn't fall far. Eladar helped him back onto the bed. The smile was gone from Lunahr's face. "I can't even walk two steps from the bed! How am I to finish walking to Riviera?" he said, discouraged.

"Beryl, you must give yourself time to heal. You were terribly injured. You nearly died. You will walk again; you will even run. If you cannot of your own accord, my mother will be able to heal you so you might. I'm sure of it," Eladar assured him.

The frown left Lunahr's face. "Laren has told me of her. He said she is a healer, that she has true magic when the others or your people no longer do; or so very few of you. That you all can walk without being seen of course. You still wield little magicks and you keep your kingdoms concealed because all your magic pools together somehow. I can't pretend to understand it all. But he said she uses her music to heal, that she sings and the magic somehow flows from her through the song. I would give anything to hear a song like that! All music heals, to some degree, of course, but a song made especially for healing is the most wondrous thing I can imagine." To be able to heal a body the same way he had healed Laren's core!

"THEN I will sing one for you. I have already sung it within this City. It is what we call 'Theela Siafana Mytheria'," Eladar said.

"*Life's Eternal Promise*?" Beryl asked, translating the Elvish title into what he thought was the Common equivalent.

"Not exactly. I might be driven to madness, trying to translate Elvish to Common. Common is such a clumsy language, a conglomeration of so many tongues of Man. Although it is amusing, really, that I should feel that way, when you think about it, considering what you call Elvish is really a synthesis in itself, of two languages."

He grew silent. That was not a commonly known fact; he should never have spoken it to Beryl. At least he had not revealed why the language was formed or when. Such knowledge was carefully guarded, even amongst his own people. It was forbidden to speak of it to any but the kings' families. He was one of the few who had been taught that there had once been four races of those Men called Elves: Oceana, Aerta, Faeren, and Aerie. The remnants of the two surviving races, the Oceana, those Men now called the River Elves, and the Aerta, those Men called the Wood Elves, had merged their languages as they yet seldom merged their peoples. The other two races had become extinct during the Night of Fire, the final terrible battle of the War of Flame that they had ignited and that had obliterated their shared Homeland.

"Now I know what it's like. It's terrible, isn't it, when someone hides so much from you? You are our allies now, Eladar. I wish it was in my power to tell you all I wish I might. It is only fair, I suppose, that you have terrible secrets of your own that you must keep," Beryl said softly.

"You could see so much?" Eladar asked, astonished. "Men are usually so baffled by us. Men are easy to befuddle. They usually do not even notice when our sudden silences come. They expect us to be mysterious, incomprehensible, vexing. But I was thinking of things that are not lightly spoken, Beryl. Things even few of our people know. It can be a tremendous burden to be the son of a king. Yet because of it, I am privy to knowledge so few have, and I prize knowledge above all else."

Eladar laughed, his eyes twinkling with sudden mischief. "Though he-who-is-my-brother and she-who-is-my-sister would be surprised to hear me say so and might well doubt me were I to enlighten them! They are as perplexed by me as a Man might be, I think. It is my favorite pastime, you know, driving them to distraction. They will tell you how terrible I am, at length and often. You must prepare to be lectured endlessly if you live amongst us. You will be quite surprised by how determined they all are to take even the most minute fragment of joy from you. Although perhaps not from you.

"I might like them, the two of them, I think, were they not my brother and sister. Our people think quite highly of them both, not merely because they are Prince and Princess, either. They think little enough of me, despite my royal blood!" Eladar said, laughing. But there was such sorrow and loneliness and wistfulness in his words, though he had tried so hard to conceal it, that Beryl cried out and impulsively hugged him.

Eladar held Beryl for a moment in his surprise. He was strong for one so fragile, and his scent was enticing, neither the familiar scents of earth, nor wood, nor water, nor mist, yet somehow wonderful. He felt Beryl's heart quicken as they held one another and Beryl's scent intensified remarkably, until it was almost intoxicating. Now he could identify the different elements: the rich loam of an unknown wood, the clean fresh scent of new leaves, and a fascinating and somehow miraculously not frightening scent of woodsmoke. His own heart quickened, and he felt himself stiffen with completely inappropriate and forbidden desire. Abruptly and reluctantly, he let Beryl go.

"I must begin instructing you in our customs, if you are to live amongst us. You must not do that with the others you will meet. Elves do not like to be touched by Man, Beryl," Eladar gently scolded.

At the look on dismay on Beryl's face, Eladar smiled. "I did not mind; far from it. You must not touch me like that again for a far different reason," he admitted, and Beryl's eyes widened in understanding and he blushed.

"I did know that, actually, about not touching you," Beryl said sheepishly. "Laren has taught me much more than your language. I won't be disruptive or an embarrassment or any of the things I might have been otherwise. But you looked like you so desperately needed a hug, and I hugged you before and… and I must adapt, that is all. I am so used to touching and being touched, to hugging and being hugged. I knew the hardest part of this would be that I no longer could be, amongst your people," he said sadly.

"Please, Beryl, I cannot bear to see you sad. I will sing to you. I promised I would, remember? The song I named is many things. In its simplest form, it is a lullaby we sing to our children. But it is first and foremost a healing song. Its uses, its power, are as numerous and as varied as the voices which might sing it." Eladar began the song, his voice clear and sweet.

Beryl listened, enraptured, the fear and sadness upon his face transformed to joy. When he was done, Lunahr said. "Never have I heard such a song! Please, might I sing it with you?"

"Of course; I will teach it to you," Eladar said.

"No, I meant now. I have a talent for learning songs, both the music and the lyrics, usually upon one hearing. But that one… I will try, but I can see what you meant. There are so many layers to it! Perhaps I should try upon my flute, first," he said in inspiration. He took it out and then looked at it in sudden dismay. "But I can't, not here. I promised Laren I wouldn't play or sing in the City," he said sadly.

"No, Beryl, you did nothing of the kind. You tried to promise you wouldn't play or sing while you are here, that is true. But I distinctly recall Talon gently chiding you, saying 'You go for an entire day without singing or playing? That I find impossible to believe.' And you swearing you wouldn't for that one day. That day was yesterday, Beryl, not today. You have fulfilled your promise.

"Also, if you need further convincing—I see your face, you are about to argue with me—but you swore, 'I won't sing or play, nothing that might draw attention to me.'" Eladar grinned. "But how can it draw attention when we are the only two in the room? You may sing and play without fear of breaking your word, Beryl," Eladar said smugly. "Do not even try, Beryl. You cannot out-reason an Elf. That much about us, at least, is true."

Beryl laughed. "I surrender! You have a devious mind, Eladar. I am glad you are my friend, and not my enemy! I fear I would fall all too easily before you," he said, laughing again. "I can see I will have to watch myself carefully around you! Every word I speak might be later turned against me." Then he lifted the flute to his lips and began to play.

Eladar looked at him in surprise, as he not only played the piece flawlessly, but with such feeling that he felt the same warmth he had when his mother sang it to him. "You already knew it," he said in surprise.

Beryl laughed. "No, not until you sang it. I told you, I have a talent for learning music."

"But to know it so well after a single hearing? Surely not! I have never known anyone to possess such a gift! Be careful, Beryl. We Elves are known for our jealousies. My mother will envy you your gift. And you do not want an Elven queen amongst your enemies," he said, and then he laughed at Beryl's knowing expression. "Good, you could tell I was joking. So many cannot, and I certainly would not wish you to think ill of my mother. She would never harm anyone. She cannot. She is by her very nature a healer. Come, you must sing with me, now, I must share my voice with yours."

They began to sing, in perfect harmony. First the single song, then others, Eladar teaching some to Beryl, Beryl teaching some to Eladar, though Eladar realized he learned far less quickly.

There was a heavy knock on the door. Eladar approached it, hand upon the hilt of his dagger. "Who is there?"

"It's Fenroy," a breathless voice said. "I'm the innkeeper's son. He sent me to speak with you. Let me in."

Eladar opened the door warily, and the boy slipped inside. He looked at Eladar in wide-eyed reverence. "You said you were sent to speak with us. Yet I do not hear you," Eladar coaxed wryly.

"Oh! Forgive me! It's just... I've heard so much about you. Elves, I mean. I knew half of it couldn't possibly be true but... to be standing here beside you! I... how could they do such a terrible thing? They truly must be evil men," Fenroy said.

At Eladar's puzzled look, Fenroy said, "Father heard some customers talking, men who are here drinking, ones he doesn't like at all. The one was speaking about how he and his brother have something special planned for the Games, how they need the other man's help, smuggling a surprise for the beast pits into the Arena. He said he and his brother were trapping obearn, to the north, by the river, when they caught something better: they caught an Elf," Fenroy said, voice soft with the horror of it.

"They mean to push him into the pit, to feed him to the wolven, in front of everyone. The one man was laughing about it and the other looked so vicious. We don't know how they might have caught one of you—everyone knows of your magic. But Father remembers what happened the last time one of you was killed, how a whole village was destroyed for it. He's afraid your people will take revenge for this as well, that this time you'll destroy Ardock like you did Terleth, that you'll move the Methris to do it. He was hoping by warning you, you might spare us, the whole City, I mean, not just our family."

"These Men, they are still here?" Eladar asked, bracing himself for what he must do.

"They were when I came up. That's why Father didn't come himself," Fenroy said.

"You must show them to me, without exposing yourself to danger by it. I will be cloaked. I will not let them see my face. But also," he turned, his face pained. "My friend is still ill. He cannot walk. Our other friend is out. You must be sure no harm comes to him. I am entrusting his safety to you." He reached into his purse and handed the boy five ten-gold pieces. "This is for your father, for the care he will take of my friend while I am gone."

The boy's eyes widened in amazement at the coin in his hands.

"El... Fisher, you can't! It's too dangerous. You can't go alone," Beryl said in distress.

"I will be fine, Beryl. I am considerably harder to harm now than I was those many years ago. You must explain to Talon why I have gone. He would never forgive me leaving your side otherwise, but he would do the same, were one of his own people in such danger," Eladar said.

"Please be careful! Please, be safe," Beryl entreated.

Eladar smiled. "I shall certainly try to be. Farewell, my friend. Talon should be back soon. I am surprised he is not here already." He turned to the boy as he slipped on his quiver and his cloak over it, donning the hood, bringing his cloth-sheathed bow. "Come, lead me to these men," Eladar commanded and then followed Fenroy down the stairs.

"That one there, in the brown, he's the one who caught the Elf. The other man, the one he was talking to, I don't see him now," Fenroy whispered.

Eladar slipped silently away from the boy. He'd follow this man and hope he led him to the Elf they held captive. He would try to do this subtly. But if he did not lead him, Eladar would seize him, interrogate him, and force him to speak. The man finished his drink and rose, heading for the door. Eladar slipped out onto the street after him and promptly became his shadow, moving when he moved, stopping when he stopped, following him soundlessly through the City streets.

The man was headed for the docks. The smell of rotting fish was horrible. Eladar felt his gorge rise and forced it back down. He would endure. He must find and free the prisoner before he came to further harm.

The Man entered a large building. Eladar proceeded forward. He must not lose him. His eyes adjusted easily to the almost total blackness of the building, as if it were one of the tunnels in the rock below the buildings of home.

"Sev? Sev, where are you? I can't see a blasted thing," Tan called in frustration.

"Tan? Am I glad to see you!" Sev said, his voice thick with relief. "He's awake again. He's still tied tight and gagged, but he's been trying to talk to me and his eyes... are you sure we should do this?"

"You can ask me that, after what they did to us?" Tan asked acidly.

Sev looked at the bound and helpless Elf. He knew he should hate him, but he couldn't. How could anyone hate something so beautiful? At least, he should be beautiful. Sev could imagine how he must have once looked. But even when they had found him in their trap, he was already too injured to be.

He tried a different tack to try to convince his brother that what they were doing was wrong. "Won't they avenge him? Won't the City be put in terrible danger?"

ELADAR silently removed his cloak as well as the concealing cloth sheath from his bow and strung it and began creeping closer. He was cautious. These Men had been able to catch one Elf. He didn't want to give them the chance to catch a second.

"To Ragnar's fire with the City! Where were they when the Elves were drowning our home? Them and Alridge both? They talked to them! These fiends killed most of our men, drowned our village, sent women and children off to starve to death, and did Ardock come to rescue us? Even to aid us? All these City Guardsmen and did they send even one out to us? No! They talked. We died and they talked. Now they'll be doing the dying, them and this," he said.

There was a soft thud and a muffled cry of pain.

Eladar winced and fought the urge to run forward.

"Ah, you felt that, did you?" Tan said. "I surprised you, made you yelp that time. That's nothing, compared to what we're gonna do to you!"

There was another thud, louder, but no accompanying cry. "Sure, you just try to keep silent. You'll be screaming. You'll be begging for mercy, like the men you killed, like their wives and children were, when they begged you to spare them."

There was another thud.

"Tan! Stop! If you keep kicking him like that, you'll kill him!" Sev cried.

Tan ignored him, his voice cold with hate. "You won't feel so high and mighty, lordin' over all o' us once the wolven get through with you. They're gonna eat you alive and gnaw on your bones until there ain't nothin' left. Let your people think you was here. They ain't gonna find no body to bury, that's fer sure," Tan spat with another thud.

Eladar sprang from his hiding place, caution thrown to the winds, nocking an arrow as he came. He couldn't bear to hear the Elf being tortured any longer.

He took the scene in at a single glance. The Man he'd followed, Tan, was standing over a bound figure crumpled on the floor, long silver hair spilling everywhere. The other Man, Sev, was shaking the one he'd followed.

"Stand away from him," Eladar commanded, his voice iron.

The two Men jumped, startled, and turned.

"No! Don't hurt him!" Sev said, eyes wide with fear, springing in front of Tan, trying to shield him with his own body.

"Get out of my way, Sev!" Tan said, drawing his sword.

"Tan, no, he'll kill you," Sev begged, but Tan pushed him aside and lunged at Eladar.

Eladar let his arrow fly. Even as it neatly pierced the Man's wrist, and the Man yelped in pain and dropped his blade, Eladar nocked another arrow, "Don't make me kill you. No other of our people would let you live after what you've done, what you were planning to do. Don't be a fool. This is your final warning. Leave, now."

Tan roared in rage, drawing his knife, but before he could lunge for Eladar, before Eladar could let his arrow fly, Sev tackled Tan, knocking him to the ground. "Please, Tan! Let him go! Let him live!"

"He's entranced you, turned you against me!" Tan roared.

The two Men fought for control of the knife. There was a cry and Sev crumpled.

Tan stared in horror at his bloodied hand, holding the knife, and at the limp body. "Sev? No! No, no, Sev!

"You! You did this!" he screamed, lunging at Eladar, eyes mad with hate.

Eladar released his arrow, piercing the man's heart cleanly. Tan's eyes widened in disbelief, and he fell with a little gasp as his shirt began to redden. Eladar went cautiously to him, another arrow nocked. But the light had left the Man's eyes.

He turned to the other, feeling for the beat of his heart, but he was dead as well. No, he had not wanted this!

There was a moan from the floor. He couldn't think of those Men, their eyes, or he'd be paralyzed with the horror of what he had done. Killing the fox had been as nothing compared to slaying that Man, mad though he had been.

Eladar went to aid the Oceana they'd harmed, turning him over gently. It was horrible. He'd been severely beaten: his face was a swollen mass of bruises, both eyes blackened, his nose shattered, and his skin was terribly dry, so cracked and blistered he was bleeding from dozens of small lesions. He had not been in the water for days, to look like this. He was gagged, and his hands and feet were bound. His hands were swollen and purple, his circulation cut off by the rope. Eladar cut his bonds and carefully removed the gag from his mouth, his hands trembling.

The Elf was squinting through lowered, swollen lids. His eyes must hurt terribly for lack of water; he must be nearly blinded by it. Eladar remembered how that had felt. The freed prisoner's eyes, they looked so familiar, they were ice blue....

"Eladar?" the Elf whispered.

Eladar could barely hear or understand him, but his eyes widened in horror as he recognized him, from his eyes alone. He looked and sounded nothing like the Elf he knew and loved.

"Elavar?" he asked in disbelief. No, this could not be his elder brother! But he knew he was not mistaken. "Elavar!" he cried, hugging him gently. Then he released him, and, hand shaking worse than before, he brushed the hair from his brother's battered face. "Elavar, forgive me! I... I would have spared them before. I didn't realize it was you! I didn't know... what they have done to you!" Eladar said, horrified, his eyes welling with tears.

"Safe. You are safe. I was so afraid," Elavar whispered. Then he crumpled in Eladar's arms.

"Elavar!" Eladar cried, feeling desperately for the beat of his brother's heart. Alive, he was still alive! Water! Elavar needed the River.

He should not have waited; he should have attacked, slain them immediately. That horrible Man had hurt Elavar further. He remembered all too clearly the dull thuds he'd heard, as he kicked Elavar, while his brother lay bound and helpless, while he'd stayed hidden and listened.

Eladar lifted his brother into his arms. He had vague memories of Elavar holding him like this, after he had been nearly killed by those cruel Men in that awful village.

A boat! He needed a boat, to get Elavar to clear water, to get him home, to their mother. Their mother could save him.

He carried Elavar from the building, toward the River, not caring who might see. He was no longer hooded, his face no longer cloaked in shadow.

"Fisher, what are you up to this time?" a biting voice called out.

Eladar welcomed it as if it were the River. Turning, he spied the fat merchant who was watching him suspiciously and his two guards. "Oberas! I never thought I might be glad to see you. Your boat; I need your boat. He needs the River, but not here. We need a boat. He will die if I do not get him to Mother quickly. My purse is at my side—it is full, take it."

"WHAT are you babbling about, who is that you're holding? Beryl or... no... Elmoth!" Oberas said, forgetting himself completely and speaking the God's name in his shock as the young prince shifted his position to face him more fully and he saw it was another Elf he was holding, limp and battered. "Who is it?" Oberas asked, approaching.

"Sylvan," he said, speaking the name Oberas knew his brother by, the name a sob.

"No! Devrik, tell Granger I need a boat, a fast one, and a crew. I need it now. I'll pay whatever he asks for it," Oberas commanded. He could see from Devrik's expression that the guard was likely as astonished that Oberas might leave himself unescorted as he was by Oberas's offer to pay whatever was asked. "Now!" he barked in command, and without further hesitation, Devrik ran to do his bidding.

"Get your brother into the water. I'll get the boat, the crew, you keep him alive until I do," Oberas said.

"I CAN'T, not here. The River is full of waste from the City and of rotting fish. It is filthy. It would kill him. We'll take the boat to where it runs clear again, nearer our Wood. I'll go over the side with him there, you'll tow us."

Oberas nodded, and Eladar was amazed by how compliant he was being. Oberas seemed agitated, as if he were truly concerned for Elavar.

"Talon and Beryl, the Men you met, I need to get a message to them. I need to do more. Talon entrusted Beryl to my care after he was attacked on the street. He is injured. I need to send some of your guards to protect Beryl until Talon returns, but also to send a message to Beryl."

"When Devrik returns, he'll do it. He's smart, loyal. Tell him what you need and he'll do it. What happened?" Oberas asked.

"Men," Eladar said, as if it were a curse, then was silent.

Oberas did not ask more.

Devrik ran up. "There's a boat and a crew. Granger said you can have it for free. He's having it dock here."

"Here? Free? Whatever did you tell him?" Oberas asked, amazed.

"That you were helping an Elf and that another Elf would die if he didn't move fast enough," Devrik said.

"Devrik, you've done well. Now I've an important job for you. This is not just any Elf, he's a prince of the Elves, and that's his brother, the Crown Prince and Heir to the Throne he's holding. They've two friends here in the City, two men that Logan and Willis met on the road with me. They'll recognize them. I need you to go to the shop and fetch the both of them. You watch the shop. Highness, you tell him where they need to go, what they need to do," Oberas said deferentially.

ELADAR was stunned. Oberas had called him Highness and spoken respectfully to him. Oberas had never referred to him with anything but contempt before.

Eladar spoke to Devrik. "The men they are looking for are named Talon and Beryl. They're staying in a room at The Fatted Pig, near River Street. I paid the innkeeper fifty gold to protect Beryl. The innkeeper and his family are the ones who told me an Elf was captured. Logan and Willis will need to convince the innkeeper it's safe for them to speak to Talon and Beryl. The innkeeper is named Royden, his wife is Janice, the eldest son is Alroy, and the youngest Fenroy. Any of them might help. Logan and Willis need to stay and guard Beryl, if Talon isn't back yet. In any case, they need to give them both a message. Tell them, 'Sylvan lies near death. Fisher has taken him home to River so she might heal him. Do not delay. Carry Beryl to the docks and rent a boat. Go to Riviera. Fisher's people will meet you.' Can you remember that?"

Devrik nodded and repeated it.

"Excellent. Now go," Eladar said.

"You heard him," Oberas said. Devrik nodded and ran.

A boat pulled up to the pier beside them. It was small and sleek. The man at the helm said, "Granger said you need to get downriver in a hurry. Climb aboard; I'll get you as far as the Elves' Wood, at least. I'm the pilot and captain. My name's Nelson."

"You'll be taking us all the way to our City, Nelson," Eladar said, climbing aboard with Elavar. He sat, cradling Elavar in his arms. Oberas climbed aboard as well, settling upon a bench to the rear of Eladar.

Eladar began singing to Elavar, the healing song he had sung to Beryl. He wished he had his mother's Power, that it might truly heal him. He wished Beryl were here with him. He was worried about him. But he was more worried for his brother.

How had they caught him and harmed him so terribly? Why was he traveling alone and so far from home in the first place? He feared he knew the answer, from what Elavar had said. Father had sent Elavar to look for him when he did not return, when he was late because Talon was late. He'd not sent his men because it was Talon, and he was so skittish. Or maybe he had, maybe the water was even now thick with his father's Guard, farther north.

The four-man crew quickly cast off. The pilot hoisted the sails and the boat sped forward. Normally, boats only used their sails going upriver, against the current; it was fast enough going downriver without them, and less treacherous. Sails with the current added too much speed for most craft to safely steer around obstacles. But this captain apparently knew what he was doing, and his boat was built for it. It darted expertly along the water.

"What did Granger offer you, that you'd make such a trip on such short notice?" Oberas asked, curious.

"The chance to sail to the Elves' Wood and maybe into it," the captain said reverently. "I've wanted to enter there my whole life, and I doubt I'll ever have the chance again."

"If you get us there, fast and safely, we will grant you special permission to sail our waters twice a year, the same privilege Oberas and another man, Bertam, enjoy, though Oberas uses it less frequently than that," Eladar said.

The man's eyes widened, and he grinned and began humming.

Eladar kept a cautious eye upon the water. When it finally ran clear, he told Nelson, "I'm going over the side with my brother. I'll need a rope, tied to the stern. You'll be towing us for a while."

Nelson looked surprised. "I've a dingy we can tow, if you need to be closer to the water."

"No, we need to be in it, and it would create further drag and we'll slow you enough for a while." He went over the side and had them lower Elavar into his arms. The water was cold and clear and felt good. Eladar held on to the rope and to Elavar as well, careful to keep his brother's face above the water.

Elavar moaned and stirred as the cold water engulfed him. Then he began struggling with terrifying weakness, fighting to be free of Eladar's restraining arms.

"Elavar, stop! It's me, it's Eladar. You're safe now. You're in the River. Can you hear me? Do you understand me?" he asked in Elvish.

Elavar's eyes fluttered open. He squinted, peering through lowered lids.

"I know your eyes hurt from lack of water, and that it's hard to see because of it. I remember what that was like. I'll put your face under for a moment. Hold your breath and keep your eyes open," he said. Then he did so.

A short while later, he raised Elavar's head again. "Don't try to talk. Save your strength. Listen to my voice. Focus on my voice. That's what helped when I was injured, hearing you speak to me when I couldn't speak myself. I was singing to you before, do you remember? Did you hear?

"Elavar, why did you come looking for me? I was fine! I found Talon, but he was late, that is all. He's brought his cousin, Beryl. Caramore's fallen so they're bringing him to us for sanctuary. They've made him a Lord and Heir to the Throne besides.

"I did well. I told you I would. Why did Father send you? Why couldn't he have trusted me? Now you're hurt so badly. It's terrible seeing you like this, Elavar. Now I understand how you felt when I was injured. I'd rather it was me than to see you suffer so because of me. I'll sing to you now. I can't bear that you were hurt because of me. I can't dwell upon it; I'll go mad if I think about it."

"Not Father… forbade me to go…," Elavar whispered.

"Forbade you? You can't mean you went off on your own to find me, against Father's command?" Eladar asked, shocked. Elavar would never defy their father. He had no reason to: they thought so much alike they never disagreed on anything.

Elavar nodded, belying Eladar's thoughts, and then moaned in pain at the effort it cost him.

"Elavar, please, it doesn't matter. None of it matters. You mustn't try to talk. Don't try to swim. Don't move. I'm holding you; I'll not let you go under. You have to let me help you this time. Here, let me sing to you again," Eladar said and began to sing. He felt Elavar relax in his arms as the water gently caressed him.

Eladar felt the Power of the River flowing into him, but not the calm, not this time. His father would blame him for Elavar being hurt, for Elavar disobeying him. Elanara would as well. He could picture their faces, the looks they would give him. And it would harm his mother terribly to heal Elavar when he was so injured. Eladar remembered all too keenly her pain from healing him. Father would not forgive him for that either.

And Talon. He would never forgive him for leaving Beryl. What if Talon forbade him from seeing Beryl, from speaking to him? Beryl must be so worried about him; he knew Beryl had wished he could come with him. He hoped Talon was with Beryl now, or Oberas's guards, or both.

Oberas… he'd not expected such selfless aid from him. Oberas had made no move toward the purse he'd offered him; it was still tied to his waist. Could he truly be so concerned for Elavar?

OBERAS looked into the water. Seeing the elder Prince, Sylvan, so harmed after almost losing Hardred to the river, after losing his dagger to Elmoth, had brought it all crashing back to him. And now the younger one, Fisher, this time, was singing to his brother, holding him, the way Terhannon had held Fisher and sung to him. The fear, the despair, the love were the same.

He'd never had much use for Fisher before. Even his own people didn't seem to, from what he'd seen over the years. But somehow Fisher had rescued Sylvan, and Oberas could see his love for his brother. And the concern he was showing over Talon and Beryl… perhaps he was finally growing up. Oberas reminded himself that Fisher had been but a little boy when first he met him, for all he'd looked a man. Boys made mistakes, terrible ones. If they were fortunate, they learned from them and grew into fine men. Perhaps Fisher would as well.

Oberas breathed deeply. He was on his way back to Riviera. He'd not prepared himself for the trip this time. And he'd be seeing the royal family, not merely sailing past the falls. He'd be in the City again. He'd be seeing the Queen again, River, the only woman his friend Vargas would ever love.

Perhaps he shouldn't take another apprentice. Perhaps he should sell his shop and go to Athanark, like Vargas and Lonas and Harnel had pleaded for him to. They'd all forgiven him, for what happened, for Vargas's arm, for Terhannon. All but Loessen. He'd not forgiven any of them. And Oberas had never forgiven himself. He never would. It was his fault, all of it.

LUNAHR was playing his flute when there was a loud knock on the door. He looked at it anxiously. It was unlocked; he couldn't get to it to bolt it. He felt under the pillow. The dagger Talon had returned to him was there; he could grasp it easily. "Who's there?" he called.

"Royden, the innkeeper."

"Come in," Lunahr said in relief.

The man did and then looked at Lunahr in surprise. "You've not bolted the door."

"I couldn't. I can't yet walk. Have you seen my friend Talon, the one with the brown hair? Or Fisher, the Elf?" Laren should have been back long before this, and Eladar had been gone for longer than he liked.

"That's why I come to see you. There's two men here, looking for you. They knows you're here. They knows my name, too, and that Fisher paid me to keep you safe. They says they got a message from Fisher, that they's here to guard you if Talon ain't here. They's wearing guard uniforms, too. Not City Guard, other guards."

"Why would Fisher send them, instead of coming himself? I don't think he would have. Did they tell you their names, can you describe them?" What if the Enemy had sent them? He desperately wished Laren or Eladar was there.

"They calls themselves Logan and Willis. They says they met you, that they's the guards for someone called Oberas," Royden said.

"Oh! I did meet them, I do know them. Can… could you bring one of them here, but without his sword, and with you or Alroy to protect me, in case it's not truly who I think it is?" Lunahr asked.

"O' course! After the coin that Elf gave to Fenroy for me, I's not about to let harm come to you. Besides, I like you. I'm glad for the coin, mind you, powerful glad, but I'd have tried to keep you safe anyways," Royden said.

"Thank you, Royden, that's very kind of you," Lunahr said.

Royden left, and Lunahr fingered his dagger, putting it in his hand with the blanket about his shoulders, so he could fling it off and use the blade if it became necessary. But when Royden returned, he recognized the man with him. It truly was Logan, or looked like him. But the Enemy's minions could assume the appearance of anyone, by killing them, by taking their bodies for their own, by becoming a Resemblant. He'd be cautious.

"Logan? I was told you have a message for me, from Fisher? How did you come by it?" Lunahr asked warily, relieved Royden was in the room with him.

"Devrik was at the pier with Oberas when Fisher found them. Fisher had Devrik remember this message for you, and Devrik told it to me and Willis. Since you know us, I guess Fisher figured you might trust us easier for it. Fisher said, 'Sylvan lies near death. Fisher has taken him home to River so she might heal him. Do not delay. Carry Beryl to the docks and rent a boat. Go to Riviera. Fisher's people will meet you.' He said if Talon wasn't with you that we should guard you until he returns. Oberas left with Fisher, for Riviera I guess. Fisher was carrying another Elf. Devrik saw him. He said he looked terrible. He looked already dead."

"Sylvan? No, how could he be? And Fisher's left? And Talon's not yet returned? This is terrible! I have to find Talon!" Lunahr said. He tossed off the blanket and stood, then took a step forward and swayed dizzily, as before. Logan caught him as he crumpled.

"Here, now, you shouldn't do that. Fisher sent us to look after you, until your friend Talon returns. I'd do a better job of it, though, if my sword was returned to me. Royden here made me surrender it before seeing you. And Willis is waiting downstairs."

Logan was holding him. Lunahr extended his Power outward cautiously. He felt no taint of the Enemy, no deception. Praise Idare! He'd still been so afraid this was all some elaborate trap the Enemy had set for them. "Of course. Royden, please, this seems genuine enough. Give him back his sword and send his friend Willis up. Thank you for taking such good care of me."

"My pleasure, sir," Royden said. He left the room.

"Please, you must tell me everything you know about Fisher and what's happened," Lunahr said.

Logan did so, and Lunahr was even more concerned when he was done. Where was Laren? Why wasn't he back yet when he needed him to be?

Of course! The bond! He'd been such a fool not to think of it before. He knew that you could send more than feelings along such bonds, with practice. If you had Power enough, you could send messages. You could even send your strength to another through it. He focused upon the thin coppery strand that bound his core to Laren's.

Come! Hurry! he sent along the bond, or tried to. He hoped Laren might hear it, might understand, that whatever had delayed him wouldn't prevent him from coming.

TALON was halfway back to The Fatted Pig when he stopped walking so suddenly that the man behind him slammed into him. The man bristled and started to say something but then apparently thought better of it when he saw Talon had not only one sword, but two, and when he saw how hard his face looked.

Talon focused inward again when the man moved onward without confronting him. Lunahr! He had sensed something along their bond. There it was again. It was fear, but more, it sounded like Lunahr might be trying to call for help. Lunahr was in danger!

Talon ran, darting expertly in and out of the crowd around him, not caring for once that he was drawing attention to himself. Lunahr! He had to get to him!

Talon reached the inn. From outside he could see no danger. He entered slowly, carefully, darting to the stairs and up them. Their door was closed; he'd had visions of swarms of Revenants, of it being torn off its hinges, of finding Lunahr dead inside, or worse, of not finding him at all, of him having vanished. But he could feel Lunahr; he was alive, behind the door. He tried the handle and then knocked when he found the door locked.

"Who's there?" Lunahr called.

"It's me. Talon. Let me in, Fisher." The door opened, and Talon started to enter, then dove away from the door, dropped Beryl's sword, and drew his own. Strangers! There were strangers in the room with Beryl, one of them had opened the door, and there was no sign of Eladar. The two men started to draw in their own defense.

"Laren, no, wait! They're here to guard me!" Lunahr cried, springing from the bed but then crying out as he crashed to the floor.

Talon ran to Beryl, protecting him from the men, eyeing them warily. Why weren't they attacking? Their uniforms, their faces, he'd seen them before. "Oberas's guards? Forgive me, I didn't recognize you at first," Talon said, lowering his blade. The others warily lowered their swords as well. Then all three sheathed their swords.

"Beryl, are you all right? What are they doing here and where is Fisher?" Talon asked, lifting his cousin back onto the bed, eyeing him critically. If Eladar had gotten into another altercation with Oberas when he'd left him here to guard Beryl, Talon thought, fuming.

"Fisher sent them to guard me. He had to, Laren. His brother Sylvan is dying," Lunahr said, and his eyes filled with tears.

"Sylvan?" Talon asked, a wealth of anguish in the name. "No, he cannot be," he said in denial. His friend Elavar was still in his prime; he was not yet even six hundred, and Elves lived to be a thousand. What could have happened to him?

"Royden overheard some customers talking about an Elf they captured, about how they were going to throw him into the pit during the pit fights. Fisher paid Royden to guard me and went to free him and… he didn't come back. Devrik told Logan and Willis about it. He was there," Lunahr said and described what he'd heard, all about Sylvan's injuries and the message Eladar had sent.

"Please don't be angry with Fisher, Talon," Lunahr said, remembering to use both their traveling names this time. "Fisher had to leave me here, but he made sure I was guarded, first by Royden and then Logan and Willis. He kept me safe. Talon, we have to go to Riviera right away. Fisher needs us. You heard his message. That's why I called to you. I know I can't walk, but Fisher's right. I can make it by boat. I'll be all right that way," he pleaded.

"I'll carry you. Logan, Willis, forgive me again for almost attacking you. Please, if I am carrying him, I cannot defend us. Can you escort us to the docks?" Talon asked.

"Of course. We'll do more than bring you too. We'll help you rent a boat. We know where Oberas would go for one, and they'll recognize us, or our uniforms, at least. We'll tell them you're good customers of his that he needs seen safely downriver. In fact, we'd better come with you, to Riviera, to the Elves. Oberas wasn't thinking it through when he sent Devrik off. He never travels without his guards. This way we can guard him on the return trip," Logan said.

"He makes far too tempting a target, otherwise. He always carries a full purse and there are river pirates that he might have to face, especially this time of year. All sorts of bad folk come out of the woodwork to plague travelers to Ardock near Feast Day. Oberas might not be the most agreeable man to work for, but he's a fine man. I'll not see him come to harm, especially not for helping someone in need."

"You're a fine man as well, Logan. I hope he appreciates you half as much as you appreciate him. I'll tell Royden we're leaving," Talon said, heading for the door, then spied Lunahr's sword and picked it up, turning back to the bed. "Lest I forget, be sure to hold onto it this time, Beryl. It was a miracle I recovered it. It had already been sold when I got to the shop. Luckily for us, Hardred was the one who'd bought it."

"Loruthanar!" Lunahr cried joyfully, holding it reverently.

"That reminds me," Talon said. "I need to tell Royden about Alnas and Hardred as well, so he doesn't rent the room to another. I'd offered to share our room with them." Talon left to do so.

"I'VE never seen someone move so fast in my life as your friend did, Beryl," Logan said. "Thank you for saving us from him. I've no doubt I'd not have stood a chance against him in a fight, and I'm no mean swordsman. Are you all right, or were you injured from the fall?"

Lunahr rubbed his ankle. "Actually, I was, I just didn't want Talon to know. He blames himself for enough. I think I've sprained my ankle. But it's not as if I could walk before anyway," he said sadly.

Then he brightened. "But my sword, I've got my sword back!" he said, caressing the hilt. But then thinking about Eladar, about how his brother might die, nearly brought him to tears again.

TALON came back upstairs. "We're in luck. When Royden heard I planned to carry Beryl all the way to the docks, he told me his son Alroy can take him in their cart, instead—the one they use to haul food from the market. He'll drive it to the docks and the rest of us can walk beside it. He wouldn't even let me pay him to do so. He said Fisher paid him enough, and Alroy needs to pick up some fish in any case, that he's a supplier right at the pier for it."

A short while later they set out for the docks. Lunahr looked at the City wistfully as they passed street after street. He'd have liked to have stayed, to have gotten to hear more music, to see the City itself. He wondered when he might ever have the chance to. Soon he would be amongst the Elves and then Laren would leave and… he fought despair. Eladar would be with him, still. But Eladar's brother was dying. He couldn't die, he just couldn't!

"I CAN'T do it. If I bear right there, I'll run us aground," Nelson said stubbornly.

"No, you will not. I will guide you. Close your eyes if you must, if they prevent you from trying," Eladar said.

"I've heard of the tricks your kind plays on mine, but I can't imagine you doing so when the life of your brother hangs in the balance. All right, you guide me and I'll steer, despite what it looks like." He followed Eladar's commands and then tensed as his boat seemed doomed to slam at full speed into the bank. But there was no bank. They'd gone through it, somehow, entering another branch of the River.

"I'd not have believed it if I hadn't seen it. I'll know where it is for next time," Nelson said.

"No. The opening won't be there, next time. You don't think we keep it in the same place, do you?" Eladar asked. "Now remember, when we're confronted by the Guard, you mustn't make any hostile nor sudden moves, or they…." He didn't finish his sentence, as suddenly a dozen Elves with spears swarmed up from the water and over the side of the boat.

"Highness!" one of them said in Elvish, in surprise. "Why do you bring Men here?" he asked suspiciously.

"One of them is known to you: he is Oberas. This Man, Nelson, and his crew have aided me and are not to be harmed. I bring my brother home; he has been terribly injured. I have done all I can for him. We must bring him to my mother at once," he said, revealing Elavar to them. He was under a tarp, to shield him from the sun.

The Elven Guardsman's eyes widened upon seeing the Crown Prince so injured. "Of course, Highness!" At a signal from him, one of his men dove back over the side, disappearing into the River. Eladar knew he'd be alerting the King and Queen. Elavar was unconscious again. He had not wanted to face his parents alone. He desperately wished Beryl, or even Talon, was here. He knelt beside his brother and held his hand.

THE Elven Guard turned to the Men. "You cannot be allowed to see more," he said ominously in Common.

Nelson looked at him uneasily, but Oberas said, "Don't worry, they'll not harm you." He turned to the Guard. "The hold is large enough for all of us. Would that suffice?"

The Guard eyed him shrewdly. "Yes," he said.

Oberas followed the others inside, as the Elves took over steering the boat.

The boat sailed toward the falls that concealed their kingdom, past the many deadly hazards that guarded it, and through the falls safely. It was quiet on the other side of the roaring falls. There was a perfect, unearthly stillness. It should not be so quiet, Eladar knew. The whole kingdom must now know this boat bore both princes, and that the Crown Prince was gravely injured, for there to be such silence.

The boat docked flawlessly, and Eladar lifted his brother and carried him ashore. He saw his parents immediately and headed for them with his precious burden. He saw Elanara as well, but her eyes were upon Elavar in his arms, not him. She didn't even seem to see him.

"My son!" his mother said, eyes upon Elavar, her voice anguished.

His father held out his arms for Elavar wordlessly. Eladar wanted to carry Elavar: he wanted to tell his father he did, but one look at his eyes and he handed his brother to him. Then the three of them were gone in a swirl of mist. He was left standing alone upon the bank, ignored, forgotten.

They had not treated Elavar so when he had brought Eladar to them, so many years ago. He could not bear their coldness. He wanted desperately to leap into the River, to let its calm strength embrace him when his family would not. Instead he followed them, aware of hundreds of pairs of unforgiving eyes upon him.

When he arrived in his mother's chambers he could hear she was already beginning to treat Elavar. Her song sent a shiver up his spine as memory flooded him of being so injured, so helpless, so frightened. They had wept for him then.

Elanara turned on him, dry eyes accusing, voice laced with anger. "What are you doing here? This is your fault! You did this to him! Where were you? What were you doing? Why didn't you come back? Where's Talon? Did you decide to go off and play in Ardock instead of meeting him? Do you have any idea how afraid Elavar was for you when you didn't come back? He begged Father to let him look for you, but Mother swayed Father against it. She said you would never grow if we did not let you, if we did not trust you to do such a simple task as meeting Talon. When you were three days late returning, Elavar left anyway. Father was furious when he realized it. Elavar....” Her voice broke on his name. “Elavar had never disobeyed him before. Never! Look at what you’ve done! Look at him!” she yelled, grabbing him and shaking him.

Their mother’s song faltered and stopped. Their father turned to Eladar angrily. “Haven’t you done enough? You must truly be trying to kill him. Get out of my sight before I decide to banish you from the kingdom as well as this room!” he commanded harshly.

Then he turned to Elanara and his voice softened. “Go, my gentle daughter. You should not see your mother and brother suffer so.”

Eladar looked at his father, stricken. Then he turned and fled. They would not listen; they hadn’t even asked what had happened. They all assumed he had shirked the responsibility, that he had done wrong. They had expected him to fail. He ran toward his own rooms. There were whispers all around him: the Guard, the courtiers, all of them.

He shut himself away from them, the accusing voices, the glaring eyes. He had never before felt so alone. Always before, Elanara or Elavar had come to comfort him, to encourage him when things had gone wrong. But this time no one came, and he had done well, even Talon had said so....

Talon. He had forgotten. The Guard! He must tell them Talon and Beryl were coming; they must help them to enter. His people were all so enraged now that it would be terribly dangerous for Talon and Beryl if he did not warn them they were coming. He felt despair. The Guard would not listen to him, not now. But they would listen to Elanara.

He steeled himself and opened his door and went to her door, hoping she might be inside her rooms. He knocked hesitantly. She did not answer, but he could hear the sound of sobbing from within. He gritted his teeth and entered. He approached his sister hesitantly. He would not be able to bear it if she were to start screaming at him again. “Elanara? Sister, please. I need your help. They must be allowed inside and the Guard will not hear me now if I tell them.”

She looked up angrily, tears streaking her face. “My help?” she asked, outraged. “Where were you when Elavar needed yours?”

“I was there, by his side. I found him. I saved him. I carried him. I held him in the River. I did nothing wrong,” Eladar said desperately.

“Nothing wrong? You did nothing right! You never do! You think it’s all a game! You think everything’s a game! Well it’s not!” she screamed.

“Elanara, please! Not for me, don’t do it for me. Do it for them. The Guard won’t let them in unless you tell them to; they might kill them. You can't let Talon and Beryl die, especially not Beryl: he's only a child. I did meet them, I swear on our River I did. Talon was late, a whole week late, but still I waited. I was in the right place at the right time, I waited, and he finally came, but he wasn't alone. He brought his cousin Beryl with him. Caramore's fallen. Talon's people have scattered to the winds; he's sending Beryl here for sanctuary. Only Beryl was so cruelly injured in Ardock, he cannot even walk. I told them to come by boat…," he said in a rush.

Elanara's eyes focused on him. She saw him, truly saw him. "Eladar, stop, you're babbling," she said, unknowingly echoing Oberas. "What do you mean Caramore's fallen? Who is Beryl? If you met Talon, why isn't he with you? From the beginning, Eladar; tell me everything that happened, from the beginning, from when you left here."

Eladar took five long, shuddering breaths and began telling her all that had happened.

As ELANARA listened the scowl left her face. Surely not? Surely this could not be her younger brother talking! He had done everything right. He had decoded the Marker's message to get the location of the meeting; the meeting time and date had been prearranged, but the location never was. He had waited at the right spot. He even saved the life of a Man, when he could just as easily have let him drown. When Talon had set the obearn free and risked angering the trappers against their people, he had seen to it that the blame would be placed on a fox. How haunted he looked, telling her of killing him! He was still a child, and he had killed to save the lives of Men and perhaps his own people.

Then they had gone to the City. They should never have entered Ardock, already so delayed, but he had done it for Beryl. Beryl had lost his home, he was about to be isolated from his remaining family, his people, and it had been such a small kindness. Eladar spoke with such compassion for him. And the woman Eladar had sung to, just so she might die at peace, with her wish fulfilled.

It was Talon's fault Beryl had been injured, not Eladar's. Then he had watched over Beryl, so Talon might recover the symbols of House of Eagles. And when Eladar had left Beryl to protect one of his own people, he hadn't even known it was Elavar, and he had still ensured Beryl's safety. He had even granted mercy to those terrible Men, but then, when forced to, had killed one.

A Man, he had killed a Man, when he was as fascinated as Mother by them, though not so infatuated as she was. Elanara had never understood why their mother was so entranced by them. Mother had once said that they burned so brightly because they died so quickly, that their acts were so much greater because they had so short a time in which to achieve greatness.

Eladar had humbled himself before Oberas, when Elanara knew how much he despised him. He had ensured Beryl was safer still and that Beryl and Talon would come to Riviera. Eladar had done all he could to care for Elavar. He had come, knowing they would blame him, but still not prepared for such utter, total rejection.

Eladar was trembling, now that he had said all he needed to say. His eyes held such loneliness, but no tears; he had kept his composure throughout his tale. He was still such a little boy, needing to feel accepted, to be loved.

Her heart went out to him, and she embraced him. That is when he broke down and began sobbing against her, loudly and violently, when she finally showed her love for him after being so cold and cruel before. She did her best to soothe him, to calm him.

"It's all right, Eladar. Can you forgive me for what I thought of you? I will tell the Guard. I will ensure Talon and Beryl are safe. And I will see that Father is told what really happened, that he understands, that Mother does, that our people do. I will tell them myself or I will stand by your side when you do."

ELADAR clung to her. He could not let go. He had so desperately needed to be held. He drank in her scent of hyacinth and rain and knew that he was home. She soothed him as if he were still a little boy. But he was not.

He pulled away awkwardly, wiping the tears away with his hands. He had not meant to cry. He had not thought he would. But her gentle kindness, her compassion after such coldness, had been overwhelming.

"I will come with you to instruct the Guard," he said. He was still Prince; they must see it, acknowledge it. He almost convinced himself it was for that and not because he could not be so alone while she was gone.

Elanara hugged him again, impulsively. "Oh, Eladar! I am so glad you are safe! I was so afraid you might not be. I was angry with Mother, for convincing Father to send you. I screamed at her for it, at Mother! I didn't think you were ready. I thought you'd be hurt.

"Mother still loves you, Eladar, Father does also. That is why they are so angry, so hurt. But we will tell them, once Elavar is safe, once he is well, once they might listen. When the Guard, the people, see and hear, they will not shun you as they do now, you'll see. Come, we must hurry. Talon usually travels with surprising speed. Only something as disastrous as the destruction of his city might have made him be late."

As they walked toward the River, Elanara said, "I have been looking forward to meeting Talon. Elavar always speaks so highly of him, and he is almost as difficult to impress as Father. Mother cannot help but admire Talon, of course, although she said there is something odd about him. He is guarded in what he says—all his kin are—but it is more than that. There is great passion but also great tension. There is more. But now I am the one who is babbling.

"It is so quiet, I cannot bear it. It should never be so quiet here. The whole kingdom has its breath held. But Elavar will be all right; he must be. He cannot die now that he is with Mother."

She hugged him again. "Thank you for finding him, for saving him. Had you not been in that inn, had the innkeeper not overheard, not cared enough to tell you...."

Her eyes fill with tears again. "Men are so cruel! Mother says they are also wonderful, but I have not seen it. But the innkeeper, the minstrel, I must remember them also. Even Oberas. Oberas! We must go to the boat. We must be sure the Guard has let them out. They might not even think to with what's happened."

They went to the boat. The Guard had let them out from below decks, though they were still in the boat. "See that our guests are taken to the Palace and treated with all courtesy," Elanara commanded.

"Yes, Highness," the Captain of the Guard replied.

"And Captain, there will be a second boat coming, with Men on board. They will need to be escorted here. They will not be able to even find the entrance to our branch of the River. Talon and his cousin Beryl, both Captains of the Watch, will be on the boat. Eladar, please describe them to the Captain, so he knows whom to expect," she said smoothly.

Eladar did so. She could tell he was forcing himself not to squirm under the Captain's cold gaze.

"It will be done, Highness," the Captain of the Guard said to Elanara, ignoring Eladar, and turned from her.

"Captain, you forget yourself. My brother did not yet dismiss you from his presence," Elanara said, her voice ice. "Surely you do not forget that after the Crown Prince, he is the Heir to the Throne, not I?"

The Captain looked at her in surprise at such support and then appraisingly at Eladar. Eladar stood tall, with the bearing of a prince. "I forgive you your transgression, Captain. We are all under duress, for our concern over my brother, and my mother, who tends him. You may go."

"Yes, Highness. Thank you, Highness," the Captain said, and there was a note of respect in his voice.

Once he was out of earshot, Eladar released the breath he had been holding. "Thank you, Sister." He again fought the urge to enter the River, though it was beckoning to him. Now, if only Talon and Beryl came. If only they might both be safe.

TALON shifted uneasily. There was trouble at the docks. There were a number of City Guard and many fishermen, boatmen, and others, milling about, talking nervously.

They soon overheard why. Two dead Men had been discovered in one of the warehouses. One of them had two Elven arrows in him, one in his wrist and a second in his heart. The other had apparently died by a blade.

Lunahr's eyes widened. "Surely not Sylvan or Eladar?" he asked in Amontirin.

Talon looked grim. "I do not think it might have been Sylvan, from what was described of his injuries. Those Men, the bodies, I must see them. I fear I know who they are, from what was told to us. Remember those trappers we aided? How the one, Tan, wished he had an Elf he might send into the pits?"

Lunahr looked ill. "No, it couldn't have been! Talon, if it was, then it's our fault, what happened to Sylvan! If we'd not released the obearn, they would have left with her; they would not have kept hunting."

Eladar had warned him; he had all but begged him not to do it. But Talon had not listened, when perhaps he should have. "You stay here with the others," Talon said.

A short while later he returned, grim-faced. He'd used his Power on the City Guard, and he'd seen the Men. "It was them, Sev and Tan. It is my fault, mine alone. If Sylvan dies...." He could not finish. Elavar was like kin to him; he had seldom met someone who understood him so well. And though his kin all loved him, as fiercely as he loved them, many of them were also more than a little afraid of him for his Power, for the Madness. Elavar had not been, though he knew of neither his Power, nor the King's Madness that afflicted him because of it.

"He won't die. His mother will save him. She must," Lunahr assured him.

"He might not have lived to reach her," Talon said, agonized. "And he was so injured... she might have to sacrifice herself, in order to save him." He would never forgive himself if Queen Naraena died in aid of Elavar. Worse, King Laranela would never forgive him, and he was second in power only to High-King Laedrin. Their alliance with the Elves could so easily be shattered over this.

Talon felt himself falling, the darkness closing in around him, even in the light of day. He could scarcely breathe for it. Then he felt a surge of warmth, of love, across the bond from Lunahr, and the day was day again, and he could breathe.

"Laren, please don't send me away!" Lunahr pleaded in Amontirin. "You need me! I've seen how much. I thought you would be well again, but you are not, not fully. I can fight beside you. I have learned how to. I know I can! When they attacked Caramore, I did not falter."

"Ah, Lunahr, brother-of-my-heart," Talon said, embracing him. "You will fight beside me, always. We are bonded. Wherever I go I will feel you. I will know you are with me."

"But what if they do not want me in Riviera? I am only a Man. At best the Elves are annoyed by us. Many of them despise us. I love them, I cannot help it, but what if they see it and are insulted by it? What if they mock me for how I style my hair after theirs, for what I eat, for who I am? When our kin teased me, I could feel their love for me. Their jests did not hurt," Lunahr said sadly.

"Lunahr, Lunahr, Eladar is not like that. Neither are his brother and sister, and especially their mother is not. Her love for Men is the mirror image of your love for the Elves: she is infatuated with us. She is warm, caring, and gentle, so like your own mother was in those ways. They will soon learn to love you as we do, Lunahr, you will see. Come, we must find a boat. It will not be easy, now, I think. I cannot imagine many might want to go anywhere near the Elves after this."

Talon turned to Logan and Willis and said in Common, "I have a little more than eighty gold with me. I do not know if it will be enough to purchase passage for four, but do your best."

He lifted Lunahr from the cart and helped him to sit upon some empty wooden crates on the dock. "Thank you, Alroy. And thank your father again for me. And do not forget about Alnas and Hardred. I am grateful again that your father will be sheltering them."

"Take care, sirs. I wish you both well," Alroy said and drove the cart onward.

A while later, Logan and Willis returned. "Well, we've done it. I'm afraid it will take almost every coin you have, though. They are asking twenty gold per man, and Willis and I never carry so much with us: I have seven gold, and Willis has three. It's absurd that they are asking so much! Oberas will be livid. We usually pay less to go all the way to Seaview, but we were lucky to get the offer. No one else was even daring to set sail, at any price."

"I will pay your fares as well," Talon said. He sighed. He would leave the Elves a pauper again. At least he was not dressed like one. Poor Lunahr was, though, in his torn and bloodied shirt. He had wanted to get him new clothes to replace the ones that were stolen from him, for when he met the King and Queen, but perhaps this was best, after all, that he appear a poor orphan waif, although Lunahr would not choose to be pitied.

"I hear my name in your thoughts, Laren, but thoughts of me have never filled you with such despair before. I am sorry I have been such a burden to you this trip. You will be glad to be rid of me," Lunahr said in Amontirin and tried to smile, but his eyes filled with tears instead.

He could not do this! He could not abandon Lunahr amongst the Elves. Talon took a deep breath, then two. After five, he could speak.

Talon hugged Lunahr tightly. "Lunahr, brother-of-my-heart! Of course I feel despair, to know that for the next seven years at least, we must try somehow to live without your songs and your smile to strengthen us, to lift our spirits when they have fallen. I do not want to leave you with the Elves. You must know I do not! But I must be king first and man second. As much as this will pain us almost beyond bearing, it is preferable to the alternative. Were anything to happen to you, we would die as a people," Talon said in Amontirin.

LUNAHR was shocked to hear Talon say that after all they had endured, all those they had lost, that the loss of one man, of him, might signify their end. "Laren, no! You are the one we cannot lose, that we would not survive losing. I can't bear the thought I won't be beside you, to help protect you. I am only able to go because I am bonded to you. You are right. I will still be with you, wherever you go. I might still aid you. Our bond is so strong! I am only now beginning to understand the potential of such a bond. I love you, Laren—you know I do—but I wanted to say it here. It might not be proper to say it in front of the Elves."

"I love you, Lunahr," Talon said, holding him tighter then releasing him, his hands lingering upon his back for a moment, as if it was hard to let go. "Come, we've a journey before us again."

A long while later, they were docked at the Elves' pier. Lunahr and Talon emerged from the hold of the boat. Logan and Willis were still below decks; they had not yet been summoned. Talon had his arm around Lunahr. Lunahr could walk a little with his aid.

Lunahr's face lit with joy. Riviera! It was the most beautiful place he had ever seen. Crystal waters flowed everywhere, in streams and magnificent fountains. Graceful buildings of white and pink and peach marble seemed to grow up from the ground, as if they had been formed by nature rather than sculpted by the hands of the Elves, almost like the formations inside of a cave.

Only there was forest as well, all around them, and he could see the sky, the sun.

But for all its great beauty, Lunahr could instantly tell something was terribly wrong. There was no joy here or laughter or music. The Elves they saw were somber and silent, and they saw few, other than the Guard.

Talon looked as if he were in pain. He was in pain; Lunahr could feel it across the bond. "It is not supposed to be like this. It is because of Sylvan," he said in a whisper, not so that he would not be overheard—he spoke Elvish, not Amontirin—but because it did not seem right to speak loudly.

Then two other Elves approached, and Lunahr's face lit with joy. "Eladar!" he called out, forgetting himself.

THE Guard beside him glared at him for it, shifting his spear threateningly in his hands. "You will not speak his name, and you will address his Highness with proper courtesy!" he reprimanded in Common, his tone harsh.

Lunahr's face darkened in shame and he knelt, while Talon steadied him.

"Highnesses," Lunahr muttered softly, eyes downcast, when he desperately wanted to see his friend.

"Rise, Lord Beryl," Eladar said, his voice stiff and formal. Lunahr did so and looked at Eladar. Eladar was looking back at him expressionlessly, as if he were beholding a stranger.

The woman beside him must be his sister. They looked alike enough to be siblings. Lunahr's face flushed, just from looking at her, though she did nothing to encourage such a reaction. She was the most beautiful woman he had ever seen. Her silver hair cascaded to her feet. Her eyes were a piercing blue, like Eladar's, only they were cold as his now, rather than laughing and twinkling, as Eladar's usually were. Fragrant blue flowers were woven into her tresses, and she wore a filmy blue gown that glittered like sunlight upon the water. To Lunahr's surprise, Talon bowed to her and then to Eladar, and then he straightened.

TALON eyed Elanara intently. He had heard so much about her, from Elavar, but he had never before met her. She was a vision of loveliness. His heart, which he had thought long ago immune to the charms of the Elves, fluttered wildly upon seeing her, although he was confident that outwardly he gave no sign of it. "Highnesses. If we might speak privately with you?" Talon suggested.

"Of course," Eladar said coolly. He turned to the Guard. "We will require no escort, Captain. These men, Lord Talon and Lord Beryl, are to be shown the courtesy of their station while they are here, and it is my understanding that Lord Beryl will be with us for some time. Neither they nor their people are in any way responsible for my brother's injury. Is my meaning clear?" Eladar asked in Elvish, his voice imperious.

"Yes, Highness," the Guard said, the animosity he had previously shown immediately gone from his features. "I will so inform my men."

"See that you do. Dismissed," Eladar ordered, and the man spun smartly upon his heel.

"Follow," Eladar commanded Talon and Lunahr, and he and his sister began leading them.

LUNAHR leaned heavily against Talon, his heart pounding. He could not live here, not with such coldness! He would go mad. He would fall to despair. He felt hundreds of frigid eyes upon him, and he shivered. There was a reassuring wave of warmth from Talon, but he felt dizziness overwhelming him, even with Talon's support. He collapsed against him.

"Highnesses, please wait," Talon said. "If it would not insult you, I must carry my cousin the rest of the way. He still cannot walk."

"Of course," Eladar said coolly, but there was the shadow of concern in his eyes. Lunahr almost cried out, seeing it. It was the first sign Eladar had shown that he truly knew them. To Lunahr's embarrassment, Talon scooped him up and carried him. What the Elves who were watching must think!

"Perhaps one of our healers might aid him," Elanara said emotionlessly, as if she were discussing the weather.

"We would be grateful for such aid," Talon said, just as stiffly.

They turned and began heading in a different direction.

ELANARA was surprised by Talon. He was not whom she had expected him to be. He was stiff and formal, as regal as one of her own people, but the compassion in his voice, his eyes, when he spoke of his cousin was so powerful. And he was watching her. His eyes had not left her since first he saw her. He did not insult her brother by ignoring him, it was not that, but his unwavering gaze made her feel strangely uneasy.

Beryl, on the other hand, was so warm and young and afraid, completely in awe of all that was around him. And completely enraptured by her. She had seen it. She must be extremely careful around him. He could lose his heart so easily to her, were she not vigilant. Beryl reminded her so much of Eladar that she could not help but instantly like him. She must be sure that any affection she might show to him was that of a sister for a brother. And he so desperately needed affection. He was wilting before their coldness. She feared he did not understand, that he might think the formality now was all there was to them.

THEY entered a building of cool white marble. Incredibly, a stream ran through it. "Why is there a stream here?" Lunahr asked Talon softly, in Elvish, not Amontirin, lest he offend their cold hosts.

"This is the Healers' Hall. I have been here once before. The stream is for the injured, so the water might strengthen them and speed their healing," Talon explained.

Lunahr felt foolish for having asked. He knew that River Elves drew strength from their River somehow, and from all water, to some degree.

A male Elf glided up to them. "Highnesses? How might I serve you?" the healer asked, though he was eyeing Lunahr.

"Two days ago Lord Beryl was attacked by thieves in Ardock and injured. He was struck in the back of the head. He was unconscious for a time and when he awoke, at first, he would vomit when he tried to move. He has no memory of the attack. He is still dizzy and cannot walk nor even stand unaided. I would have you heal him," Eladar explained.

"Of course; place him upon the bed, there, so I might examine him," the healer said, his voice warm with compassion.

He turned to Lunahr. "I will try not to harm you, but I must examine the injury," he said in Common.

"I understand," Lunahr replied in Elvish.

"You speak our tongue?" the healer asked in surprise.

"Yes. Lord Talon taught it to me," Lunahr said, and then he winced in chagrin as he felt Laren's dismay flow across their bond, though outwardly Laren showed no sign of his displeasure. Lunahr remembered too late that though the Royal Family knew Laren spoke Elvish, few others suspected he might, and that Laren had told him one often overheard much of value when those around you did not know they could be understood.

The healer gently probed the wound. Lunahr tensed with the pain, but did not cry out, though he felt faint.

"I HAVE tended to it, as well as I was able," Talon volunteered, telling the healer what medicines he had already used.

The healer looked at him in surprise. "You are Elven taught. I had thought all of us had given that up as folly long ago. Were I anyone else, I might tell you that I could do no more for him than you have already done. Yet I have some small magicks that will aid him further still. You may leave him here with me. I will tend to him."

"I will return for you. I will not leave without saying good-bye," Talon said softly to Lunahr.

Talon could feel that Lunahr desperately wanted to hug him, but the wave of warmth he sent across their bond was enough to soothe him. Lunahr watched them go as the healer began preparing an elixir.

Talon walked with Eladar and Elanara, his thoughts in the Healers' Hall with Lunahr. By the time they reached the Palace, he sighed. Lunahr was asleep; he felt it across their bond. Lunahr would heal now, and he would be able to concentrate upon his negotiations with the Elves.

On the way into the Palace, they met Oberas exiting, with Logan and Willis beside him, surrounded by six Elven Guard.

"Highnesses," Oberas said, bowing to Eladar and Elanara. "I am pleased to see you. I had wanted to say good-bye and to thank you once again for the hospitality you have always shown me. Please give my regards to your mother and father and brother, when they are able to receive them."

"You are always welcome amongst us," Eladar said formally. "Even by me, now," Eladar added in a whisper, eyes sparkling with the smallest hint of mischief.

Oberas looked at him in surprise, and then smiled. "And I would truly welcome seeing you again, if ever you find yourself in Ardock again, Highness," Oberas said.

"Oh, and Talon, isn't it? This is for you. My guards tell me you paid their passage here. I'm grateful that you did so. I would indeed have sorely missed having guards to escort me home." Oberas handed him forty gold.

Talon took it in surprise and relief. "Thank you, Oberas. Farewell and thank you, Logan, Willis. I truly appreciate your aid."

The three men left for the pier, still surrounded by the Elven Guard. Talon and the others proceeded not to the throne room, but up graceful steps and down a long corridor to a door Talon had never seen before.

Eladar opened the door and entered and after Talon and Elanara had followed, closed it with a sigh of relief. "I wouldn't want to have to do that again anytime soon. Of course, I'll have to as soon as we leave here," Eladar said, sourly. He turned to Talon. "These are my private chambers. We can speak freely here. Would you care for some wine? I would. I would care for at least a bottle of it, all by myself. Sister?"

"I will even pour it," Elanara said sweetly.

Eladar sighed. "Then it will be a goblet apiece, I fear."

They sat upon a cluster of cushions, about a small table. Elanara followed with a glass bottle of wine and three crystal goblets. She filled each and sipped her own appreciatively.

"How is Elavar?" Talon asked

Eladar's face creased in pain. "Alive. It will be days before he is fully healed. Mother will, of course, recover sometime thereafter," he said softly.

"But he will recover fully? And your mother is in no danger?" Talon pressed.

"Elavar will recover, as will Mother," Eladar confirmed. "Although his injuries were so grave, she might have succumbed to them, were there not three other healers here with at least some trace of healing ability to them, who were beside her when first she began healing him. She collapsed. She stopped breathing, for a time."

The hand holding the glass shook, so violently that the wine spilled upon the table. "But my sister tells me the same thing happened when Mother treated me so long ago, so I should not be concerned by it," he said softly, and then added, his voice thick with anguish. "Not be concerned! That I have almost killed my mother, twice, and now my brother!"

"Eladar, she will be all right. They both will be," Elanara said, hugging him. Eladar was trembling, his whole body shaking. "You must not blame yourself. It is not your fault, this time." She looked accusingly at Talon.

Surely they could not know about the trappers? Eladar had not been there to hear them. Talon could not tell them, not out of fear for himself. They might not care for Lunahr if he did.

"Talon would not have been late had he a choice, Sister. He would certainly have preferred that Caramore not be taken. As usual, the Enemy did not think to consider his preferences in the matter when he attacked them," Eladar said, forcing levity.

"Forgive me," Elanara said to Talon. "It is a terrible thing, to see those you love suffer and not be able to protect nor aid them."

"How well I know that. Of course I forgive you. I would do anything you might ask of me," Talon said intently and then his face darkened in a flush at his words.

Eladar looked at him in surprise and speculation.

"I AM betrothed, to the High-Prince," Elanara said defensively, shocking herself for having mentioned it and knowing she shocked her brother even more so. "It is my station to dispense forgiveness," she added lamely, trying to recover from what she had already spoken. Talon's eyes! They were blue, but dark, intense, mysterious, as if they could bore into her mind, her very spirit, yet neither reflect nor betray his own.

"You are here to speak to us about sanctuary for your cousin, I believe," Eladar said, eyeing both of them.

"YES," Talon said, breaking eye contact with her in relief, turning to Eladar. He had felt himself drawn into her eyes, falling into them. He had never thought he might be so affected by someone he had only just met. His father had told him that it had been that way when his grandfather first met his grandmother, in the days before there were so few of his people that there were no strangers amongst them, but he had not truly understood his meaning, until now.

"Neither our father nor mother are available to discuss such matters," Eladar said. "But my sister is of age and station where she can. She might assume the role of guardian to Beryl, now, before my parents are free to speak. That way, no matter what Father's feelings toward Men might be after this, Beryl would yet find sanctuary here."

"I cannot have Beryl stay where he might be despised by all who saw him," Talon said.

"Not all. Eladar and I certainly do not," Elanara said. "Eladar has already confessed Beryl has become brother-of-his-heart, even in the short time he has known him. He might become as such to me, also. Already I like him. I found myself wanting to protect and console him. It was not easy for me, either, appearing so cold before him, when I could see he did not understand. You should have warned him, Talon," she scolded.

"I was ill-prepared for it myself," Talon said, surprised by the familiarity she had shown him by stating his traveling name without title. From what Elavar and Eladar had told him, he had thought Elanara prized formality.

Elanara: such a beautiful name. He felt a sudden irrational urge to speak his own given name to her, even his true name, and wondered at such feelings. He was drawn to her in a way he had never been drawn to one of his own kin. There were so few women amongst them, none of such surpassing beauty or such spirit.

"COLDNESS ill suits you, Highness. There is such warmth and softness about you, yet strength as well. The High-Prince has been gifted beyond all naming to have been promised your hand," Talon said, his voice tinged with regret, and perhaps even jealousy.

Elanara's face flushed. She all but squirmed under his gaze. She had never before felt so unsettled by any man of her own kind, let alone by a Man.

"We were speaking about Beryl," Eladar said, reminding the two of them.

"Of course we were," Elanara said. "It would be my honor to be named his guardian by you, Lord Talon. Are you familiar with the ritual?"

"No. I must confess that I did not read that portion of my father's book carefully enough, but it is not something I ever thought I might need to know."

"Your father's book?" she asked, curious.

"Yes. I have brought it with me, actually. I had hoped I might entrust it to your care as well, your family's, I mean. I fear it might be all too easily destroyed or lost, now that we are without a home," he said, removing it from his pack.

She looked at it curiously. It was thick and heavy. She opened the cover, curious. The title page was written in a bold hand, in Common, Elvish, and another language, which must be Amontirin. *"Understanding Elves: One Man's Perspective,"* she read aloud.

"My father did not understand all about you, of course. We never knew of Nalea while he lived, of the Elven Navy and Army, of the five years you each train. He had always wondered why your coming-of-age ritual was such a secret. We realize now, of course, it was your graduation and assignment as either a Reservist or active member of the Guard or King's Guard. I am sure there is probably much else that is not contained within these pages. It is impossible to capture an entire people within a single volume. Will you care for it for me, Highness?"

"Yes, I will. Might I be permitted to read it? I am curious to see how accurate your father's notions of us might have been," Elanara said.

"It is not a privilege I grant many, but you may, Highness. In fact, I would be honored if you did. Please also correct any inaccuracies you find. My father would not have wished otherwise," Talon said.

"Thank you. I am honored. Now, let me be sure you understand all of the ramifications of my being named guardian to Beryl," Elanara said and began telling Talon in detail.

LUNAHR awoke and stretched languidly, luxuriating in the feeling of the softness of the silken sheets against his naked body. Naked? He sat up suddenly, in panic, his calm shattered. Where was he?

"Calm yourself, Lord. You are safe," a kindly voice said.

Lunahr's face flushed darkly as he recognized the Elven healer who had tended him. He had thought for a terrifying moment that the Enemy had somehow captured him.

"How do you feel?" the healer asked.

"Feel? I feel wonderful!" Lunahr said, enthusiastically. "Clean and refreshed and… there is no pain, no dizziness at all! It is gone," he said in wonder, then feared anew. "How long have I slept? Lord Talon hasn't left, has he?"

"You have slept but a single night, Lord. You did not even need to sleep so long to heal, but you needed the rest. I have some new clothes for you here, to replace those you wore. I have already bathed you."

Lunahr blushed at the thought. "Thank you." When he saw the clothes laid out for him, he said, "Oh, but I couldn't! These are much too fine for me."

"Nonsense. They are quite appropriate to your station," the healer said.

Lunahr dressed, marveling at the feel of the Elven silks against his skin. No wonder the Elves were so known for their lasciviousness! How could they be otherwise, with clothes such as these caressing them as they walked?

He slipped on the boots with special joy. He had always worn his leather boots reluctantly, for the animals killed to make them, when the fabric ones he had tried to make failed to meet his needs. But these would not quickly wear, and would protect his feet from the cold and wet. He stood and walked in them to try them, then stopped, stunned. "I can walk!" he said, a grin lighting his face.

"Of course. I would hardly have called you healed could you not," the healer said.

"Thank you!" Lunahr said, kneeling to him. "My sword is ever at your service!"

The healer shook his head and smiled. "Men are such curious creatures. If you truly will be staying with us for an extended length of time, it will prove most interesting for us, I think."

"YOU want me to tell her my true name?" Lunahr asked Talon in surprise a short while later, his gaze flickering to Eladar and his sister. "But you told me I must never tell anyone outside our own kin. I would have told my given name and even my true name to Eladar days ago if I was permitted!"

"We need it, in order to perform the Ritual of Guardianship," Talon said. He took a deep breath. "As your current guardian, I will be telling them my own, as well."

Lunahr's eyes widened in shock. "But you cannot! No one must ever know it, lest the Enemy learn it. If that's what is required, then I cannot have her become my guardian," Lunahr said firmly.

"The Elves are our allies. They have trusted us with the secret of Nalea, which also the Enemy must never learn. It is time we returned that trust," Talon argued.

"I am afraid. What if the Enemy learns of it somehow? It would be because of me, that you would be made so vulnerable. I cannot, Talon, I won't. Hunter would never allow it, were he here," Lunahr said. Farad would never allow Laren to be so endangered.

Talon sighed. "Hunter is no longer Protector and King's Friend, Beryl; he cannot be, as Heir to the Throne. You know our laws. It is not in Hunter's power to allow or disallow. Nothing is more important to me than your own safety, Beryl. Surely you must know that? If someday I might fall because of it, then that is the price I am willing to pay. There can be no compromise in this. Their laws are clear upon the point, and are many thousands of years older than our own. Besides, they have sworn to me they will only tell their parents and brother. I fully trust the five of them with my life as well as yours."

Eladar's face flushed, and Lunahr realized it was in pride to be so included, after what his cousin had first thought of him.

"All right, Talon, if you're sure," Lunahr said reluctantly, and the ritual began.

Chapter 8

Feast Day

"HELLO. We're Hardred and Alnas. We've friends staying here, Talon and Beryl and Fisher. They told us we could share their room," Hardred said to the innkeeper at The Fatted Pig.

"Ah. They told us you'd be coming. They had to leave the City unexpectedly. A friend of Fisher's was injured. He had to bring him home," the innkeeper said, giving Hardred a conspiratorial wink for some reason. "But they told me you'd be coming and had me save the room for you. My name is Royden. With what Fisher paid me already, I'll not be charging you for it, either, for tonight at least, nor for dinner, and dinner's five silver apiece around Feast Day."

"Could it be brought to the room? I'm not supposed to be walking," Hardred said.

"O' course. Will you be needing a healer? I know one," Royden volunteered.

"No, but thanks. I've seen one already."

The innkeeper led them to the room. Negotiating the stairs on crutches wasn't easy, but Hardred managed, with Alnas carrying his pack for him.

"One of my sons will be up in a little while with your meal," the innkeeper said, leaving them to their privacy.

Hardred settled on the bed and propped his foot up on one of the pillows. He smiled at Alnas. "I'd be hard-pressed to say whether I'm better or worse off than this morning. I'm without a sword again, but not out the coin for it. I can scarcely walk, but at least now we've a roof over our heads. Although it will likely be a few days before I can start trolling in the Square for another caravan and perhaps longer than that before one might wish to hire me."

Alnas had been thrilled to see Hardred smile, but now he looked at him in dismay. "But Hardred, you can't! I was hoping I'd convinced you that you can't! You almost didn't make it. I still can't believe you survived. Do you think Seneth might have let you live, for the aid you gave Oberas? That maybe She was the one who sent Fisher to save you, when by all rights you should have drowned?" Alnas asked hopefully. "Maybe you need not run from Her any longer."

"Perhaps," Hardred said, sounding doubtful.

"Let's not talk about it anymore tonight. The innkeeper's son should be here soon. Let's just eat and then get some sleep," Alnas suggested with feigned calm. The thought of sharing a bed with Hardred, even just to sleep, sent his heart thumping wildly, but he could see Hardred was nowhere near ready to hear him say so. He likely never would be.

They washed their hands and faces with the cold water in the basin by the bed, making liberal use of the strongly scented soap and coarse but clean towel. "I could do with a bath, after dinner and before bed, to get the salt from my skin and hair," Hardred said.

"I could use one as well. I'll go down and tell the innkeeper, so he can start heating water for it, if you'll lock the door after I've gone," Alnas said.

"I'll be safe until you return," Hardred assured him.

Dinner was hot and filling, and the mead was better than expected, as was the bath. By the time they lay down in the bed, Alnas was feeling relaxed enough that he thought he might actually be able to sleep after all, until Hardred lay down beside him. All thought of sleep vanished. Alnas tried to put as much distance as possible between them. He was sure to keep at least a single layer of blanket between them as well.

Hardred, who was worn to the bone from his earlier exertions in the Arena and all the walking he'd done while injured, quickly succumbed to slumber, but Alnas lay awake a long time, listening to Hardred's deep even breathing, imagining all the wonderful ways he might wake him.

ALNAS could tell it was late when he woke the next morning from how rested he felt, even after lying awake for hours, listening to Hardred. He'd been tempted to light the lamp, so he might see him as well, but he'd been afraid of waking him. Alnas lay in bed without yet opening his eyes, reluctant to face the day. He had so few days left with Hardred, from what he'd said. But for that very reason, he should not waste them.

He opened his eyes and was startled to see Hardred already awake, lying abed facing him, as if he'd been watching him sleep. "You should have woken me. Today is Feast Day. I'm sure we've already missed a number of events, not to mention breakfast. I feel rested enough that it must be near lunch."

"You needed the sleep. And I made good use of the time. I've been thinking about all you've said during our journey, but especially what you said last night. I think you might have the right of it. Perhaps I am safe, here, safer than I'd likely be, if I headed downriver, at any rate. Oberas pretty well offered me a job after I aided him with the boat. I've decided to take it, to stay in Ardock. On the condition that he hires you as well, if you're of a mind to work for him. If not, we'll see what other positions we can find together in the City."

Alnas gaped at him and then grinned. "Hardred, that's wonderful!" he said, hugging him joyfully and then pulling quickly away, blushing darkly. "Forgive me! It's just that I was so relieved to hear."

"I hope you're still as eager for me to stay after you've seen me at my worst, Alnas. But even then, I think you might still be able to befriend me. You're too naturally happy for me to drag you down with me when I get in one of my doldrums. I'd not stay with you, otherwise. I value you too much as a friend to hurt you," he said softly. "I've not had a friend since Julian, and he was my only true friend my entire life. I never thought I might have one again, until I met you. But I'd rather live the rest of my life alone and die that way than to ever harm you by our friendship."

Alnas was surprised and moved by Hardred's words. He'd not realized Hardred cared so much for him. It should be enough that Hardred valued him as a friend, but still, he wished for more. Patience, he must be patient. He'd not risk scaring Hardred off; not now, when he was at least willing to stay in Ardock, and more, to stay with him. "You've no idea how greatly honored you make me feel by what you've said," he said sincerely.

Hardred nodded solemnly. "Come. It sounds as if Feast Day is a day not to be missed. We should not spend it abed or confined in the inn."

Alnas knew he dared not spend the day alone with Hardred, in that room with the bed tempting him, but he wouldn't see Hardred strain himself, either, and risk worsening his wound. "I'll only agree to it if you let me carry your pack as well as my own, as I did before. And if your leg starts paining you worse, or you feel you should come back here, you're to tell me. You must promise you will, or I'll not go with you," he said, holding out two fingers to seal the bargain.

"Agreed," Hardred said, crossing his fingers with Alnas's.

They brought their swords and Alnas's bow as well; they'd not risk any of their belongings being stolen by leaving them in the inn, regardless of how friendly the innkeeper seemed.

The streets were all remarkably empty, until they neared the Arena. Then they were so crowded they could barely move. Alnas had to fight to stay beside Hardred, who had to fight to keep on his feet. They would have turned back, but the crowd of people swept them toward the Arena as if it were a current.

Once inside, the crowd was sorted into different areas. There were still two boxes available for the wealthy, at thirty gold apiece. Other than that, there was only standing room left in the bleachers at the very top of the Arena, for a silver. When Hardred saw the view the boxes offered and learned the box included lunch and dinner for two, and a separate privy for the box holders, that decided it for him.

"Hardred! You can't be serious!" Alnas protested, when he heard Hardred say they'd take a box. "That's almost four times what we each made on our trip here!" They'd each been paid five silver a day, with a five gold bonus at the end of the journey, not counting the extra gold from the thieves they'd killed. "That's almost two month's work, for a single day's pleasure! And we've already missed almost the entire morning."

"You've not missed much," the ticket seller said. "They keep the best events for after lunch. Many of the folks who rent the boxes don't even bother to show until just before lunch. You're in luck, too. The other box has a pillar right in front of it that's hard to see around. You'll get a good view."

"I'd rather pay it than fight my way back to the inn through this crowd, Alnas. Besides, people come from everywhere to see this: they cross rivers and mountains, perhaps even the sea. I'll not miss it. Who knows? Next year we might compete in it. Don't worry. I'm paying for it," Hardred said as he dug for the coin in his pack. He didn't have nearly so much in the purse at his side.

They were escorted to their box. Alnas figured it was to ensure they went to the right one; there were larger boxes still vacant for the moment, which he assumed cost more.

Alnas brightened when the food came a short while later. They'd not eaten breakfast, and the lunch was well portioned and smelled delicious and came with ample mead. He suspected he'd be just as glad for the semiprivate privy later.

Alnas and Hardred both sighed in contentment once lunch was done. The food had been top quality. Alnas leaned back in the comfortably cushioned chair. "I could get used to this. It's times like these I wish I was born the son of a rich merchant or a nobleman, rather than a farmer, much as such a life would surely drive me mad!" he added, laughing.

"But you'll not have trouble being a guard for a rich merchant?" Hardred asked. "I plan to go to Oberas's shop tomorrow."

"Don't forget we'll have to buy you another sword before we go to work for him, or whomever hires us," Alnas said.

Hardred sighed. "I'll never find another like the one you returned to Talon. But I'm glad I was the one to have bought it, so Beryl might get it back. I only wish I might have been there to protect the boy, so he'd not have been harmed and lost it in the first place," he said, the beginnings of a scowl forming.

"Oh no you don't! No dark moods today, my friend. Talon said Beryl was recovering. You know they'll take good care of him. And he's gotten his blade back," Alnas reasoned.

Hardred sighed and smiled at him. "All right, you win. Hand me the rest of that mead, will you? That will serve to cheer me up, if anything does. Then you'd best watch my pack while I head to the privy. I'll not want to risk missing the beginning of the Games by going later."

When the events began again, Hardred and Alnas watched eagerly. There were wrestling bouts and archery contests, horse racing and jousting tournaments, sword duels and even a complex battle, where two teams of fifty men each staged a mock war to seize a crown. The man who did so won a purse of one hundred gold, while his teammates were each awarded ten. More than a few combatants were taken from the field upon a stretcher, some with blankets pulled over their faces.

From their vantage point, they could see the betting on all the events was fierce everywhere, but the amounts being wagered and lost and sometimes won in the boxes were staggering. Hardred and Alnas enjoyed listening but were not foolish enough to join in.

There was an intermission announced following the mock war, after which the water sports would begin. Hardred and Alnas stretched. "Do you still think we might compete next year?" Alnas asked Hardred.

"In some of the bouts, sure. I'd like to try my hand at the wrestling, and you might fare well in the archery. But I'd certainly not risk my life in the battle for the crown. I can't imagine dying or being permanently maimed, as some of those men were, for such a thing. Many of those men were quite brutal, when they'd no need to be," Hardred said. "Although I suppose part of it must be the women. I'm sure all of those who are wearing the blue of the winning team are already surrounded by more women now wishing to bed them than they might be able to handle in a single evening."

"I'd certainly not mind trying my hand at the archery, but you're right about the rest of it," Alnas agreed.

The water sports began a short while later. There were swimming and diving contests, the divers leaping from progressively higher boards. Then the pearl diving contest against the sharks was announced, and the constant conversation around them lowered to a murmur. Word had spread about the sharks and the man who'd been taken by them. Twenty names were called for the contest, with the men to stand before the tank, so they might be assessed and wagers made. But of the twenty names called, only eight men appeared, the rest apparently having thought twice about the feat they had planned to attempt.

The first man to show when called, Morgas of Ardock, was huge, a mountain of a man, his bare chest and arms so hairy they were almost black, with a thick, unkempt, bushy beard. He wore loose pants and no shoes and carried a spear taller than he was. "That's not a man, it's an obearn!" someone near them cried, and there was laughter and other appreciative comments. The crowd "oohed" and "ahhed" as he flexed his muscles and strutted for those in the stands, and the odds against him were announced at one to one. A furious round of betting ensued.

The second man to appear, when the sixth name was called, was not nearly as impressive, but of solid build. His odds were called at six to one. He carried a trident and a net, and he also played to the crowd.

And so it went, until the twentieth name was called. "Devan of Delthos!" the crier for their area read from the paper in his hand. The eighth and final man stepped forward, and there were guffaws of laughter. The man was tall but slim, leanly muscled. He had a neatly trimmed blond beard and golden hair, which was tied back in a ponytail that ran down the length of his back. He wore only a loincloth.

"Where's his weapon?" more than one voice called.

When Devan bent and pulled a dagger from a sheath on his calf and showed the crowd his knife, the arena burst into roars of laughter and several calls of condolences for the man's family. But he just smiled at them, bearing it all with good grace. The odds for him were announced at twenty to one.

The group of four men accepting the wagering for the boxes came by, bypassing Hardred and Alnas, heading for the next box, having learned it was a waste of breath to ask the two swordsmen for a wager.

"Here, bet taker! One hundred gold on Devan of Delthos!" Hardred called loudly. One of the men turned in surprise, examined the ten ten-gold pieces Hardred held out to him skeptically, and actually scratched each with the point of his knife and then tasted the metal to make sure they were genuine. Satisfied, he handed Hardred a chit for the wager.

Alnas moaned. "Hardred! I thought we promised each other we'd not bet on the Games. And so much!"

Hardred grinned. "It's not truly a gamble when you know you'll win. Have faith, Alnas. They gave his name as Devan of Delthos. Delthos is a port city, just under four hundred miles from Meria, if you take the Coast Road. One look at the man and you can tell he's a mariner: he's the hair and beard of one and carries a sheathed knife, as I do. He's got the muscles of a swimmer as well. I'm sure he's an expert at it, though few enough are."

"Then why wasn't he in the earlier diving or swimming contests?" Alnas challenged. "All of them but that first man were. Jerson took the purse in the diving and Venton in the swimming, and all the rest placed."

Hardred looked thoughtful. "Perhaps Devan didn't want to risk injuring himself for the smaller purses. The winner in each took only ten gold. The winner of this takes one hundred pearls. Good ocean pearls sell for as much as a gold apiece, at least in Logareth they did, though river pearls might be less. I've not heard them say which these are."

He grew grim. "Also, he must follow Her, for who he is. He'd not want Her to think he was too arrogant or confident. She might let him win the other contests, then pick the shark tank to teach him a lesson. He must know that," Hardred reasoned.

"Then maybe you shouldn't have bet upon him, Hardred, if the Goddess truly does hate you. She might make him lose to punish you, to see that you lose your wager," Alnas said without thinking, then cursed when he saw the look of horror upon Hardred's face. "Elmoth, I've a loose tongue! Forgive me, Hardred! Pay me no mind. You know what a fool I am."

"No, Alnas, I'm the fool, and now a good man may well die for it," Hardred said despondently. Hardred gripped the arms of his chair tightly as the contest began.

The eight men stood around the rim of the huge tank and at the clang of the bell, dove in, all except Morgas, who entered feet first with a terrific splash. Devan dove neatly, entering the water with scarcely a ripple. Ten men stood at the edge of the tank with poles and ten others with spears.

The water at the surface began to still and then broke again, and there was a gasp from the crowd, but it was just Morgas, apparently coming up for air, already out of breath. He disappeared again.

Suddenly, the water grew darker, as if someone had released ink into it. Then something bobbed to the surface, lying still in the water. There were screams from the audience and yells from the men around the tank as they realized it was a severed arm.

More cries flowed from those close enough to hear, all the way up the stands, for those too far away, as the water began churning violently. Five men bobbed to the surface, all screaming and yelling, with hands frantically grasping for the poles that were being lowered to them in the tank.

Two of the men with poles were yanked off their feet by the frantic men and fell into the tank with the others. One of those men was pulled out by a fellow pole man, and three of the divers were pulled to safety as well, but then the other two divers and the other pole man who'd fallen were suddenly yanked downward, disappearing from view. Devan had not surfaced at all.

Hardred was clutching the chair tightly, shaking and swearing softly under his breath. He'd not pray. He'd not risk calling attention to Devan by letting Her know that Devan's life, in particular, mattered to him.

Then suddenly another man appeared. It was Devan! He held something in his teeth and had his arm about another man, and Hardred realized it was the missing pole man. Devan hoisted the limp form up toward his fellows, and the man was pulled out of the water. The crowd gasped and there were more screams. The man had only a single leg; there was a bloody stump where the other had been.

He was lowered to the ground, and a number of the men clustered around him as Devan grabbed a second pole and climbed to safety. He joined the cluster of men around the fallen man, kneeling down until he disappeared from view.

A short while later he rose again. He removed the thing he had still held in his mouth and began talking to the men standing about the tank, shaking his head, his face grim. To Hardred's incredible relief, he appeared unhurt.

Then there was a surprised exclamation and a cheer and a roar as one of the men standing with Devan thrust his hand with what he'd been carrying in his mouth into the air. "He's done it! The pearls—he has the pearls!" The yell carried upward, echoed by hundreds of throats.

Hardred was shaking violently. He recognized it for what it was: the unspent surge of energy from his concern for Devan had seized him. He'd known he was too far away to help and too injured, but his heart had still begged him to. The dinner intermission was called. The pit fights would begin after dinner. "I've seen more than enough blood for one day and have no appetite. But I'd speak to Devan, if we can find him down there, amidst that crowd."

"Of course," Alnas said. "I'll come with you."

"No, Alnas, you'll miss your dinner, and it's sure to be a treat, from the lunch they served. I've not tasted finer in my life," Hardred argued.

"But before you see Devan, you must collect your wager," Alnas reminded him.

"I'd not do it, were it for myself. But the coin's for Riana," Hardred said and waved the bet takers over to him.

"We'll be a few moments. That's quite a sum that's owed to you," the man said, shaking his head in bemusement.

He left but returned sooner than Hardred expected. The man shook his head in disbelief as he paid out the two thousand gold, carefully guarded by the four armed men around him. Hardred was certain there must be bowmen about as well, perhaps behind the pillars, guarding the coin.

"No wonder you'd not wagered before! Why waste your time with petty bets when you might win so much? I'd thought you impoverished by the cost of the box, but it's obvious I was mistaken. Spend it in good health, away from the water. I'll be hard-pressed to even take a bath after what I've just seen, and I've been working the Games for the past ten years.

"It will be a good half hour at least until they serve dinner. You'd be smart to stretch your legs. That bout ended a lot quicker and bloodier than they'd realized it might. It will take a while to clear the field from it. They'll be trying to recover what they can of the bodies from that tank and slay those cursed things, now that that part of the show is over."

Hardred nodded, not mentioning they wouldn't be returning. He and Alnas made their way down the stands toward the arena floor, keeping a careful eye out for thieves. When they reached the bottom, it was easy enough to find the man they sought from the swarm of men and women around him.

The pole men were standing protectively around Devan, apparently guarding him for his aid of their fellow. "Move along! He's no interest in anything but a night's rest, and he'll be doing it alone; he has a wife he's trying to get home to," one of them called loudly to the throngs of eager women.

Finally, Hardred got close enough that he might speak with Devan as the disappointed women began to look elsewhere for company. Devan was clothed now, dressed in a faded red tunic, patched black pants, and worn boots.

One of the pole men stepped between them. "Hey, you, back away! Can't you see—hey, wait, I know you! You're the one that dove into the tank, yesterday, after that boy that was dragged in! It's thanks to you and Devan here that we was able to save poor Jonas tonight. Devan kept him from bleeding to death, but he weren't breathing at all when we pulled him out. But I seen what you done to the boy, and the Guard said it weren't wizardry, so I thought I'd give it a try. It surprised me as much as the rest when it worked, but I got him breathing again. The healer's with him. He thinks he can save him, even with his leg gone." He turned to Devan. "He's the one I told you about: the one I saw do it."

Devan eyed Hardred curiously.

"I'm Hardred of Meria. I'd like to speak with you, if I might. Mariner's Code I'll not try to rob you of your prize."

"Devan of Delthos. It would be my great pleasure to speak with a fellow mariner, although just hearing your voice makes my heart ache all the more for home. And I must learn more about what you did yesterday, and how you learned it, and make sure I know how to do it properly. I was too intent slowing the bleeding; I missed seeing it when they revived Jonas."

"We've a box up above, if you'd care to share it, so we might speak more privately," Hardred suggested. "And they've a fine dinner for us, and I've not the appetite for it. You're welcome to it, if you'd like."

Devan grinned. "Aye, I'd welcome dinner! I've not eaten in three days now. I've not had the coin for it, and though this purse of pearls will see me safely home, I'll have to change it for coin first, and that's not something I'll do easily tonight."

"I might know someone who can do that for you as well, perhaps even tomorrow. His name is Oberas. He's a Master Trader. He might have interest in buying the pearls," Hardred said.

They made their way back up to the box, some of the pole men coming with them to be sure they got there safely. "When you's ready to leave, you just tells me, like I said," one of the men told him. "We'll see no one robs you."

"I'm grateful to you for your aid," Devan said. "May Seneth bless you for your kindness."

Hardred winced at hearing Her name; he couldn't help it. He saw that it didn't escape Devan's notice. Hardred grimaced and said, "So you are so far inland, so far from your home port, yet still enjoy the Goddess's favor? I'd dared hope you might. I've a favor to ask of you, one I'll pay you for doing, of course, as you've no ties to me for doing otherwise." Hardred was relieved the man sported a beard and that his eyes were blue, not the green of the sea. For his voice and build and manner, he already reminded Hardred painfully of Julian.

A golden brow raised. "First I would hear what it was you might have done that would have caused you to lose the Goddess's favor," Devan challenged softly.

Hardred took a deep breath and exhaled just as deeply. "I lived. I lived when I should have died with my shipmates. She took our crew, or most of it, at least: thirty-seven of the forty who manned our ship. We limped back to port a ghost ship. My best friend is the one who saved me, but She took him, like the rest. He was to have married my sister, Riana. He'd promised himself to her before leaving port. Riana blames herself for it, the *Silver Gull* dying as she did. She thinks the Goddess was jealous of her, for Julian's love of her," he added, then looked appalled at what he'd admitted.

Alnas looked at him in surprise, and he realized Alnas hadn't known that part of it.

"I've tried to convince Riana that the Captain or all us crew must have offended Her somehow, that it couldn't be for her love of him."

"The *Silver Gull* out of Meria? I'd not heard she was lost. I knew her Captain, Brennan. Was he one of the other two to have lived?" Devan asked hopefully.

"Nay. He was one of the first to be taken. We were struck with illness, ten days after setting sail for home. Then, when we'd lost more than half the crew to it, when we'd thought the rest of us spared, a storm came, when it was too late in the season for there to be one," Hardred said, voice and face haunted by the memory of it. "And you?"

"My tale is quite different. I'm from the *Leaping Dolphin*, out of Delthos. Our last port of call was Seaview before heading home. We'd had a profitable trip; I've no doubt the rest of the crew is doing quite well for it. I was in a tavern, The Slippery Eel, with my shipmate Laris, my wife's brother, spending some of our coin on a hot meal and oushka. They've the best meal on the docks, and you know what it's like, eating ship's fare for a month. We ate and drank until we could scarcely walk. Usually, I have more sense than that, but Laris kept calling the serving wench over; I'm sure he was hoping to bed her. Well, he got his chance and took it, which left me all alone to head back to the ship.

"It was as I was cursing my stupidity for letting him talk me into being his leave partner, when I know he wenches and I don't, that I was set upon by four men. I don't know whether they followed me from the tavern or marked me on the street. I started running; I knew I'd not stand a chance against four.

"They chased me and finally cornered me on the pier. That's when I started to fight. I don't remember much of what followed. I saw a hand holding my purse, and there was pain and blood. I remember smelling it, tasting it," Devan said softly.

"I remember dragging myself along toward the water. I could smell it, hear it. I knew if only I could get to it, I'd be safe, that She'd take care of me. I remember asking Her to save me and then falling off the edge of the pier, hitting something that wasn't water, then darkness." He grew silent.

"Forgive me for asking, Devan. You need not continue," Hardred said.

"No, it's all right. I need to tell it. I awoke to a sharp pain in my hand, to feeling as if I was on fire, to the feel of the water beneath me. Truly the water. I'd fallen into the hold of a barge. She was leaking, and there was water in the bilge, washing over me. The pain was a rat biting me; there was more than one of them upon me, gnawing on me. I yelled and struggled and began crawling to what light was coming from the grate to the deck. They heard me, those above decks, and came with knives in hand, to see what was going on. I was half-mad with fever. I remember seeing their knives, their faces, and the sun shining so brightly. Then everything went dark again.

"I was lucky. Many a Captain might have labeled me a stowaway and just thrown me over the side, injured and ill as I was and not wanting to be bothered to care for me. But Captain Bertram was a fine man. He had his men tend to me as they made their way upriver, though of course, I didn't know it at the time. They even washed and mended my clothes.

"I was ill for weeks. By the time I'd regained my senses and health, we were already past Alridge, on our way past the Elves' wood, nearly at Ardock. That's when I found out where I was, who they were. Captain Bertram is one of two men the Elves let sail their waters. He's the one who came with the sharks and the tanks full of saltwater for the Games.

"He let me stay on board the first night, four nights ago, while he oriented me to where I was. I'd hoped he'd be going downriver after Ardock, so I might ride back down with him, but he's on his way upriver to Logareth, and it will be weeks before he starts heading back down again. Meanwhile, the *Dolphin* has sailed without me.

"Larissa—she's my wife—will be thinking I'm lost when they come home without me. She'll know I'd not have jumped ship and left her; she's pregnant with our first. I have to get home. So I told Captain Bertram I was going. He knew I'd not a coin to my name. He was kind; he gave me a gold piece. At the time, I thought it quite generous. I thought I'd have coin enough to eat and to have a roof over my head for a time. So I left them.

"I thought I'd find a boat to take me downriver again from Alridge so I might sign on with another ship heading for Delthos. I thought that I'd travel the road to Alridge, maybe get guard work to pay my way there. But I was told by more than a few men that no caravans would he heading south to Alridge until after Feast Day, but then there would be a number of them and plenty of guard work to go with them, as well as lots of boats heading downriver from Alridge. They said that I might easily stay with the same group that hired me from Ardock. When I asked how I was supposed to eat until then, I was told there was coin to be made in the Arena, before and during Feast Day. So I thought I'd try my hand at it, to tide me over until I could find honest work.

"I went looking for a meal and an inn to sleep in. I finally found a spot on the floor of the common room of an inn all the way on the other side of the City for five silver a night. Five silver! It shouldn't have been more than two. Feast Day was three days away, so that meant I'd have shelter, but nothing to eat, unless I won some of the trials to see who competes on Feast Day.

"Fortunately, I was too tired to eat that night. The dinner was expensive. They wanted another five silver for the basest meal they had. I thought I'd save my coin and have a hearty breakfast, knowing breakfast is always cheaper. But that first night in the inn, I had a dream. The Goddess came to me. She told me that if I competed in any of the Games before Feast Day,

She'd be angry with me and would ensure I lost more than the Games. But if I waited until Feast Day itself, She'd see I won, that I would earn enough coin that I could return to Delthos and even live in comfort for a time.

"Well of course I knew enough to listen. So I came to the Arena, but only to watch. I soon realized I'd not be able to compete in any of the events on Feast Day, if I didn't compete in the trials beforehand, but then I learned about the pearl diving, that they took all comers. That's when I knew what the Goddess had planned for me. So I watched and waited.

"I've been having the strangest dreams, the other two nights. I've still not been able to fathom their meaning. At least I've had a roof over my head, though I've been powerfully hungry, I can tell you."

As if on cue, their meals were brought. The steward was cross with them, at first, for having three in a box meant for two, until he saw who the third was. Then he was quite congenial. To Hardred's surprise, the man returned a short while later with a third meal. "For saving young Jonas. He's a wife and new baby who will be glad to see him come home."

Pain crossed Devan's face at mention of it. "I've a baby on the way as well. I was supposed to have been back in time for the birthing. Now I won't be. I fear for Larissa, when the ship comes to port without me aboard her, that she'll lose heart when she most needs to keep it." He looked forlornly at the plate of food.

"You'll not aid her any by taking ill again, this time for not eating," Hardred scolded. "I'll even eat with you, since they went to the trouble of bringing the third meal. I've never felt comfortable wasting food when so many go hungry so often."

Devan nodded and began to eat.

Hardred eyed him thoughtfully.

"You've been wanting to ask me something since you first spoke to me. I've seen it in your eyes. What is it?" Devan asked.

"I'd not realized how urgently you needed to return home. I was going to ask that you might deliver something for me, to Meria, but I can see that you can't, now," Hardred said, sighing.

"I can't at first, that's true. But once I see Larissa and know she's well, once I see the baby and spend time with them, I'll be heading out to sea again, when the *Dolphin* does, if I've not lost my place in her crew for abandoning her midvoyage. We sail to Meria as well as Seaview and elsewhere. What had you wanted me to deliver?"

"It's nothing you should trouble yourself with, not with a new baby. It's just some letters I hoped to get to my sister," Hardred said.

Devan stopped eating and looked at him intently. "Ten letters? Sealed with blue wax?"

Hardred eyed him strangely. "How could you possibly know that?"

Devan swallowed the bite he'd been chewing; it looked like he had a hard time getting it down. "You hadn't also been planning to give me twenty golden seagull eggs in a blue purse, had you?" he asked, as if fearing the answer.

"Why would you say that?" Hardred asked as a shiver ran up his spine.

"It was from my dream, the one last night. In it I'm a dolphin. I'm swimming along in the ocean, but I've got something in my mouth. It's a sheaf of letters and a heavy blue purse. I swim for many days, until I reach the shore, only it's not the sandy beaches of Delthos but the sharp cliffs of Meria. I swim past all the docked boats, up to a pier.

"Sitting on one of the pilings is a seagull, but she's not gray as she should be. Instead, she's silver, as bright as pallenteum, so that it almost hurts my eyes to look upon her. It hurts more to see the tears streaming from her eyes. Seagulls can't cry—I know they can't—but she is. She's standing in a puddle of her own tears, looking toward the cliffs above the sheltered bay and calling out, not with the raucous call of a gull at all, though. It's more like she's a songbird, like she's singing. Even The Sisters, Seneth protect me from them, couldn't sound so sweet," he said, sketching the sign of a wave of protection before him in the air with his hand. Then he continued.

"Then suddenly she looks out at the water, right at me. She flaps down into a dingy that's floating beside me. And I thrust up out of the water and release what I'm carrying: the sheaf of letters and the blue purse. The gull pulls at the twine about the letters with her beak and reveals that there are ten, all sealed with blue wax, imprinted with the image of a gull. Then she pulls open the purse with her beak, and pulls the sides of it down, revealing what was inside: twenty seagull eggs. Only they shine as if made of pure gold. Then she cries out. And then I woke up."

Hardred breathed deeply and opened up his pack. He pulled out his sheaf of letters to Riana, tied together by twine. "There are ten of them, sealed with blue wax, with the image of a gull. It's what I planned to give you. Also, if I truly felt I could trust you, if you'd swear by the Code you'd see it safely to her, I planned to give you coin to take to her. I made a substantial sum today, betting some of what I'd earned upon you for the dive. I planned to give you two thousand gold, with a hundred for yourself, to ensure you delivered it to her. I've no choice but to do so now and hope that you might take it to Riana, for I'll not anger the Goddess further against me by ignoring such a vision."

Alnas looked at him, eyes wide with disbelief. "But Hardred, you can't! No offense, Devan, but Hardred, you don't know him! How can you possibly trust a stranger with such a sum?"

"If Elmoth sent you such a vision, Alnas, would you risk angering Him by betraying the man who gave you the coin and stealing it when He instead showed you giving it to whom it was intended for?" Hardred asked. "Besides, I've seen the caliber of man he is from the dive in the tank. He saved the pole man, Alnas. He didn't have to. He could have died for it, but he saw him safely rescued first and then climbed to safety himself. And he didn't seem to care about the pearls at all after the others were hurt and killed for them. It was the man beside him who showed us all he'd claimed them. Between that and the Code, I'm sure he'll do it."

"I only wonder what it means for me. Perhaps the Goddess does not hate me as I thought She did. Yet still, She does not show me returning home. Maybe it is Riana She yet loves, that She wants to see her well cared for after taking Julian from her. I like to think the Goddess might yet watch over my sister. I should never have left her alone."

There was an announcement below, and Hardred sighed. "The Games are beginning again. I'd not planned to stay for the pit fights."

"I wonder how anything they have in the pit fights might possibly top the sharks," Devan said.

The first fight was six hunting dogs against a pumar. The dogs chased the great saber-toothed hunting cat and cornered it, and then the pumar attacked them. The battle was violent and bloody. At the end, only one of the dogs survived it. It was let out of the pit, but the bodies were left there.

"A pumar! And that's only the first of the three fights," Alnas said, whistling. "What could they possibly have to top that?"

The second fight was a pack of six wolven against an obearn. Two separate gates opened, one letting the obearn out and the second the pack. The obearn was an enormous beast, at least twelve feet tall when it reared. It made short work of the wolven, tearing them into a pile of mangled flesh and fur. Then it bellowed and roared and ran, leaping at the edge of the pit. There were screams of fear from the audience, but it was unable to get out: the walls of the pit were too high. It fell back, roaring its fury.

Then it was time for the third and final fight. One of the gates opened again, and the crowd gasped as a new combatant was released into the pit where the obearn still was. "I don't believe it! An ogre! It must be! What else could it be? Look at the size of it! How did they get it into the City, let alone the Arena?" Hardred asked in astonishment.

The monstrous creature was a brutish mockery of a man, at least ten feet tall and twice as broad at the shoulders as the biggest man Hardred had ever seen, filthy and hairy and nearly naked. Ragged scraps of animal hide were tied about its loins, and its thickly matted chest and arms and legs were marked with bare patches showing numerous scars and revealing corded masses of bulging muscle.

When it clenched its massive hands into fists and bellowed defiantly at the crowd, it revealed sharp teeth four times larger than those of a man, and the sound echoed from the very tops of the Arena. Dead silence filled the stands in the wake of its fury as the rolling waves of sound gradually dissipated while the monster glared about in hatred. Hardred's blood froze at the wild gleam of crafty intelligence he saw in the creature's pitiless gaze as it looked out at the sea of terrified faces. Then the second gate opened.

"What in Elmoth's name is that?" Alnas asked in a hoarse whisper, riveted by what emerged. The creature that now entered the Arena through the barred door was even more terrifying than the ogre. It had the head and forepaws and tail of a pumar, but giant wings like those of an eagle, and its hind feet were monstrous talons, while its back and belly were green and scaly, like a reptile. The creature immediately sprang into the air, and there were a number of screams, but there was a thick collar on the beast's neck and a heavy chain which led into the still open door. The creature roared in frustration as it jerked to a halt in midair, flapping furiously, the chain stretched taut.

The obearn, which had been seemingly as cowed as the spectators by the ogre's appearance, bellowed in rage and lunged for it now, apparently viewing it as the lesser threat. The ogre swatted it with one meaty hand, and it crashed against the wall and lay still after the single blow.

Ignoring the flying creature, the ogre lifted the body of the immense obearn as if it were nothing and placed it against the base of the opposite wall. Then it lifted the pumar's body and stacked it on top of the obearn's. Then it lifted one of the wolven and did the same. Then a second wolven.

"The fools! Are they blind? Don't they see what it's doing? It's trying to climb out!" Hardred cried.

He wasn't the only one to realize it. The crowd was screaming in pure panic now, and those in the lower stands began scrambling from their seats, trampling everything and everyone in their way to get to safety as the archers vainly tried to get a proper angle to shoot down into the pit. The ogre was staying close to the walls, as if purposefully using them to shield itself.

Those in the upper standing area and the boxes watched in horrified fascination as the ogre continued to stack the wolven bodies and then the dogs, darting out and back with each prize. All the while the flying cat-creature made no move against it. Then, unexpectedly, the ogre ran to the base of the chain which held the cat-creature captive, grabbed both ends in its meaty hands, and yanked, hard. Muscles along its back and shoulders rippled and bulged from the strain. The spectators in the upper stands and boxes, realizing they were about to be endangered as well, began screaming and scrambling for the aisles. A flurry of arrows hailed down into the pit but bounced ineffectually off the hide of the cat-creature, which was now effectively shielding the ogre.

Hardred cursed and drew his knife as he had only his broken sword. Devan drew his knife as well. Alnas snatched up his bow, grateful he'd strung it earlier to carry it easier, and nocked an arrow as the chain twisted and stretched, then snapped.

They watched in horror as the ogre released the broken end of the chain, freeing the nightmare creature, which shot into the air with a chilling hunting roar, heading directly for them, for all the boxes in the upper area of the arena.

Arrows began flying across the Arena, now, as the bowmen desperately tried to bring the monster down, but the arrows often fell short of their mark, more than once hitting spectators, as the Arena dissolved into utter pandemonium. Some few impressive shots hit the creature yet were again deflected off its scaly back and belly as if it were wearing armor.

Hardred saw that the ogre took advantage of the diversion and climbed the mountain of bodies it had made and grabbed the edge of the pit, pulling itself up and out to freedom. Then he lost sight of it as the cat-creature dove straight toward what Hardred had earlier heard called the Governor's Box.

Alnas released an arrow, and it flew true but glanced off the creature's scaly back. Some of the figures within the boxes cowered while others ran, many screaming as the shadow of the monster fell upon them.

Then a figure in a red cloak with a tall wooden staff leapt into the Governor's Box from the aisle beside it, standing upon one of the chairs within. His long white hair whipped about from the wind of the flapping wings of the beast as he raised his staff and pointed it at the monster.

Red lightning crackled forth from the staff, slamming into the beast. It roared in pain and fell from the sky, just short of the Governor's Box, instead crashing into the box directly in front of it. The screams of the people below it were abruptly silenced as it thrashed about upon them, furiously trying to rise, raking them with its claws and crushing them beneath it.

The wizard raised his staff again, but this time both his arm and the staff shook. A second, smaller arc of lightning flared out, and the creature convulsed then lay still. But the wizard toppled over as well, falling to the floor of the box he had stood in.

"The wizard has saved us all. We must go to his aid, for few else might," Hardred urged.

"Aye. They'd sooner trample him in their flight, now, than aid him," Devan said in disgust as the rich men about them fought their way through the aisles in terror—pushing, hitting, and trampling those who didn't move fast enough.

ALNAS looked below for signs of the ogre, but it had vanished. Both the lower and upper stands were a writhing mass of terrified men, women, and children. He shivered thinking how many must have already died from the panic of their fellows. Far more than ever might have from the ogre or monster.

He put his arm about Hardred and aided him to the Governor's Box, leaving his crutches behind, but taking their packs upon their backs.

By the time they reached it, there was no sign of the Governor or his entourage. The wizard was there, though, fighting to struggle to his feet. There was a gash on his forehead, leaking blood. He eyed them warily, squinting one eye against the blood, and raised one end of his staff toward them, though it appeared he could scarcely lift it.

Hardred raised his hand upward in a gesture of peace. "Peace, Master Wizard. We come to aid you, not harm you. I swear by the Mariner's Code."

"I also swear myself to your aid by the Code, Honored Sir," Devan said.

"And I'll swear the same, Revered One, but by Elmoth, for I'm neither a mariner nor a follower of Seneth," Alnas said.

"Seneth… that's a name I've not heard in a long time. You may approach me," the wizard said, his voice deep and yet powerful, for all his body seemed to have failed him. He lowered his staff.

"I have some small skill at healing, though no supplies with me," Devan said. "Where are you injured, besides your temple?"

"First you must check the chimaera, to be sure that it is dead. They are crafty and dangerous. It might only be feigning death, though I have at the least seriously injured it, if not mortally," the wizard said.

"Hardred, you stay here with him. Devan and I will check it," Alnas urged, hoping to keep Hardred safely away from the monster, lest the wizard's words prove prophetic.

HARDRED nodded reluctantly. Injured as he already was, he'd be more of a hindrance than a help. The others left him, and he turned back to the wizard and knew fear.

The wizard's eyes were no longer gray but instead glowed as red as his robe. "**YOU CANNOT ACT AGAINST ME, FOUL CREATURE OF DARKNESS. BEND OVER ME SO YOU MIGHT REVEAL YOUR MASTER'S SECRETS TO ME,**" the wizard demanded in a voice too soft for the others to hear, sitting up suddenly. He reached out to touch Hardred's face as Hardred leaned toward him, unable to resist the voice which commanded him, much as he struggled to.

The wizard's brow crinkled in puzzlement. "You are not what I thought you to be. They called you Hardred. I thought you had sought to deceive me. I had heard your name spoken here; they said you rose from the dead and that you turned another into a Revenant. I had not known how you could, when only He should have such Power. But I sense neither the taint of the Enemy nor Power about you. You appear only a Lesser Man.

"I will know the truth from you, but there is no time. The others even now return. I will take your strength, for I have great need of it, but I will not take your life, at least not yet. **YOU WILL FORGET ALL I HAVE SAID TO YOU. SLEEP,**" the wizard commanded, and Hardred collapsed.

ALNAS and Devan returned to the box. The wizard greeted them with a look of concern. "Your friend has swooned. I can see he has been recently injured. He has strained himself coming to my aid," he said, his voice warm with compassion.

Alnas knelt beside Hardred, fighting panic as he tried to rouse him but could not. He felt his heart, his hand shaking, and was relieved to feel it beating strongly. "The healer said he was not to leave his bed. I knew we shouldn't have come here. I should never have let him leave our room," Alnas said, voice filled with self-recrimination.

"The chimaera is dead?" the wizard asked.

"Aye. I drove my knife through its eye to be sure," Devan said.

"Excellent. By now, the City Guard should have dispatched the ogre. The immediate danger has passed. Your friend and I both must rest. I am but newly arrived. Do you have lodgings?" the wizard asked.

"Yes, at The Fatted Pig, near River Street, we have a room," Alnas said.

"Very good," the wizard said, standing, leaning heavily against his staff. "I believe I am recovered enough to walk. If you can carry your friend to the street, I am sure we will be able to find a cart to carry all of us the rest of the way."

"Alnas, you wait here. I'll get his crutches from your box," Devan said, heading off toward it.

"How is it your friend was injured?" the wizard inquired conversationally.

Alnas looked at Hardred in concern. "A boy was pulled into the shark tank yesterday. Hardred jumped in after him, to save him. Hardred found him and pulled him out, but one of the sharks bit Hardred's leg. The boy wasn't breathing, he'd drowned, he'd died. Hardred saved him a second time; he breathed for him until he began breathing on his own again, but the crowd almost killed him for it," Alnas said in bitter remembrance. "They thought…." He trailed off. He couldn't say that they thought he was a wizard and that they'd wanted to hang him for it, not to a true wizard.

"I sense no aura of wizardry about him. How is it he was able to achieve such a feat?" the wizard asked with an amused expression, as if he might have known what Alnas had been thinking to say.

"The Elves taught him. Well one Elf, really, Fisher. Beryl told Hardred that Fisher was a Prince of Elves," Alnas said.

The wizard stiffened. "Beryl? A slender youth with long blond hair and green eyes, with the look of a Wood Elf about him?" he asked intently.

Alnas swallowed and stepped back from the wizard, his hand fingering his sword hilt nervously. "Why is it you want to know? I'll not let you harm him. He's been harmed enough already," he said, fighting to keep from shaking. His sword would be no match against a wizard who could wield lightning, and the wizard no longer looked nearly as weak and helpless as he had only a short time ago. He looked dangerous.

"Harm him? Of course I would not harm him. I have come to Ardock looking for him, for all his people. **YOU MUST TELL ME WHAT YOU KNOW OF BERYL AND THOSE HE TRAVELS WITH, QUICKLY, BEFORE DEVAN RETURNS,**" the wizard commanded.

"We met Talon and Beryl and Fisher on the Southern Road, near the River, on the way to Ardock. Fisher saved Hardred's life after he'd drowned in the River. The three of them went off together after seeing Hardred safely to us. But then, in Ardock, I met Talon again, yesterday, outside of the Tower where they were holding Hardred for wizardry. Talon saw I was carrying Beryl's sword in Hardred's pack. We hadn't known it was Beryl's when Hardred bought it. Talon said Beryl had been robbed and badly injured, but he was recovering. I returned Beryl's sword to Talon and Talon invited us to spend the night in their room, as all the inns are full. But after the Guard released Hardred, when we got to the inn, the innkeeper told us the three of them, Talon, Beryl, and Fisher, had all left to go to Fisher's people, to the Elves, in aid of an injured friend. That's all I know of them."

There had been a complex play of emotions and expressions across the wizard's face as Alnas had spoken. "**I HAVE NEED OF A HORSE, I**

HAVE NEED OF MANY. DO ANY OF THE THREE OF YOU HAVE ONE?" the wizard asked.

"No, none of us do," Alnas said.

The wizard sighed. "YOU WILL NOT MOVE. Then I must take of your strength as well," he said and touched Alnas' face. "YOU WILL FORGET WHAT WE HAVE SPOKEN OF; YOU WILL THINK IT WAS ONLY OF MY CONCERN FOR HARDRED."

Devan returned with the crutches. "The crowd below us has been thinning out, but it will still be some time, I think, before we'll be able to leave here easily. The streets were packed before. With this, they must be madness."

Alnas nodded, sitting. "That's fine by me. I would rest here, before we move on. My battle surge has left me and I suddenly feel as if I'm the one who fought the battle with the chimaera. That was what you called it, wasn't it, Master Wizard? Never have I even heard of such a creature!"

"It is a creature of darkness, born of the Enemy. There are many of them in the Dwarven Lands. This is the first time I have fought one in the Lands of Men, though it will not be last," the wizard said with a sigh, sitting as well.

"At least Hardred doesn't seem to be in any danger," Alnas said. "He is so strong, or tries to be. But still, I am surprised he drove himself to exhaustion without saying aught to me; he swore he would."

"Let me tend to your cut, Master Wizard, as best as I am able to here," Devan said, pulling out a kerchief and his water skin.

The wizard had stooped and picked up a corked glass bottle, miraculously unbroken in the flight of those who'd planned to drink from it. He read the label and smiled. "I would have you use this, instead." At Devan's puzzled look he said, "Alcohol will keep the wound from festering far better than water might. Or so the God Jarnath teaches us," he said, smiling as if at a private joke.

"You are both wizard and healer?" Devan asked, sounding surprised, as he poured some of the liquid upon the cloth.

"I am many things to many people. We must not let the rest of this fine liquor go to waste. We must wait here until the chaos below clears. We'd not be able to help in any case. Those people are too terrified to listen, and seeing a wizard would no doubt not serve to calm them," the wizard said, smiling again. "This is fine oushka, even to my discriminating palate. You must share a drink with me, Alnas, Devan, for your aid of me. Few would come to the aid of a fallen wizard."

"Drink with a wizard?" Alnas said. "Never in my life did I expect I might!"

At the wizard's look, Alnas swallowed. "I didn't mean that as it sounded. I don't choose my words carefully enough, especially when I most desperately should, just ask Elmoth. I'm sure many of my prayers have been a source of amusement to Him, for the things I've told him, or worse, asked of him," Alnas said nervously.

"Ah. Then no wonder the God cherishes you enough to keep you safe. Even a God needs to smile, to be amused," the wizard said, as if speaking from experience.

Alnas shifted nervously. He wished Hardred were awake. He was sure Hardred would not feel at all in awe of this wizard, that he might say just the right thing in just the right way. Alnas was afraid of angering the wizard. He wished he'd leave, now that he no longer seemed in need of their aid. Instead, he was drinking with them!

He yawned, his face flushing darkly. Elmoth, he was tired! He had trembled, in the past, when his battle surge left him, but never before had he felt so exhausted, so weak. That he would now, before this wizard!

The wizard was watching him, as if he could hear his thoughts. Alnas swallowed, the hairs on the back of his neck rising.

The wizard handed him the bottle. "You are looking peaked. You must drink," he said, but the concern of his voice was not reflected in his eyes. His eyes... they seemed to look right through him, to his very heart, his spirit.

Alnas tilted the bottle back and took a mouthful of the liquor into it. But he did not gulp it down quickly, as he'd meant to. This could not be oushka! Never had he tasted anything so fine. The oushka he had drunk in Logareth, which he'd thought so fine, was swill when compared to this!

He let the liquor sit upon his tongue and slowly swallowed, once, twice, thrice, savoring it to the last. A burst of fiery warmth glowed in his stomach. He passed the bottle to Devan. "Devan, you must try this! It is amazing!"

Devan sipped cautiously, then drank appreciatively, savoring it as Alnas had. "I had thought I knew the taste of aged oushka, but never have I tasted such fine liquor. I've no doubt the cost of this single bottle is more than I might make in many months' travels upon the sea."

They sat drinking, watching the chaos below diminish.

Devan looked out over the Arena. "I think it will be safe to try to leave now, without being trampled. More people are starting to enter now than to leave, to aid those who were injured. I will carry Hardred, for a time, at least, Alnas. You truly do look weary, and having eaten, I find myself invigorated."

"I will not argue with you. I almost feel in need of Hardred's crutches," Alnas said. "I fear I will be leaning upon them instead of carrying them."

Devan and Alnas looked at the wizard in surprise as he stood without apparent effort. "Magicks such as those I wielded against the chimaera can be momentarily quite draining, but the adverse effects usually dissipate rapidly. You need not worry that you might have to carry me as well."

They began the climb down. Alnas was again grateful Hardred had paid for the box. They had not nearly as many stairs to negotiate as they might have. He felt so weak! He was grateful the climb was down the stairs, not up, at least. He'd not have been able to make it, if it were. As they neared the floor, they saw dozens of still forms draped in blankets and more than a hundred others writhing on the ground in pain, with City Guard and other men tending to them. When they reached the floor of the Arena, one of the City Guard in a torn and bloodied uniform came over to them.

"Is your friend injured or dead?" he asked, wearily.

"He has only collapsed from his earlier injury, Guardsman Farion," Alnas said, recognizing the man now that he'd spoken. He was the one who'd brought Hardred safely to the Tower. "He doesn't need a healer. We were going to leave."

FARION'S eyes widened in concern as he realized Hardred was the downed man. He'd seen so many injured, he hadn't recognized Hardred's friend when he first saw him, and he'd barely glanced at Hardred at first.

He looked from Hardred to the red-cloaked figure, eyeing his staff warily. "You look suspiciously like the wizard who was hurling lightning about a while ago," Farion said carefully.

"And if I were?" the wizard replied, his voice shading from amused to threatening within the few short words.

The hair on the back of Farion's neck stood out at his tone. "We are under orders to bring the wizard in for questioning, about the deaths a few nights back, near River Street and at Baker Street. I'd argue the same as I did when they accused Hardred of wizardry, that since he saved a life, it makes him a good wizard, not a bad one, that there might be two wizards loose in the City. You slew the beast. Yet the light the witnesses saw was red, like your lightning. I've never seen lightning to be red before, leastways, not that what comes from the sky. You wouldn't happen to carry a sword upon your person, would you?"

"What need would a wizard have for a sword?" the wizard countered, sounding more surprised than defensive.

"I asked that myself when they first told me a wizard was suspect," Farion said. "But the men who were slain were all killed by a blade."

"You realize that even speaking to me about it is foolhardy? That if I did not wish to be questioned, nor caught, you could do neither? That I could turn you to ash where you stand, were you to think of acting against me?" the wizard asked softly. The cold sorrow in his voice was terrifying.

Farion swallowed. "Yes. I've seen enough to know you could. But surely you realize in turn that, were you to do so, it would prove you are indeed a danger to the City, and the rest of the men here would do their best to capture or kill you," Farion said bravely.

"They could not hope to stand against me. They would be slain to a man," the wizard said, and Farion braced for battle.

"So it is fortunate I am not whom you fear me to be," the wizard said, smiling. "However, I am indeed on the trail of the other wizard, and would know all you have heard about the incidents near River and Baker Streets. But I would not speak of it in front of others. Will you walk with me there, where we will not be overheard, in full sight of your fellow Guardsmen?"

Farion neither liked nor trusted this wizard; every instinct in him screamed the man was a deadly threat to him, but neither did he want to see these men injured or killed, especially not Hardred, after saving Alarion. "Of course," he said coolly.

"Then it is here I will leave you." the wizard said to Devan and Alnas. "I thank you for your aid of me, Alnas, Devan, and Hardred as well, though he cannot hear me. I will not forget it."

Farion watched in relief as the two men carried Hardred toward the exit.

Farion began walking with the wizard, fighting the urge to finger his sword hilt. He could tell the man before him was as dangerous as he had threatened to be. Yet he was still breathing, when the wizard might easily have already slain him.

He was glad it was him facing the wizard and not Anorion, not someone with a wife and child who needed him. Farion sent another quick prayer to Ragnar that his brother and his family had not been here. He knew they wouldn't have been, for Alissa's illness, yet still, he'd checked carefully amongst the fallen. Alarion was not supposed to have been at the Arena before either, and he was so little, he'd have been crushed easily.

Most of the dead beneath the blankets were children who had been. Alissa could never have run; she couldn't have breathed deeply enough to. He'd pictured her falling, gasping, as dozens of feet crushed the life from her, or Anorion falling beneath them, trying to save his wife and son as other men had fallen here. He was shaking and fought to stop, lest the wizard think it was fear of him.

Farion looked bravely at the wizard but the wizard gazed right though him. "**TELL ME ALL YOU KNOW OF THE RED LIGHT, THE**

DEATHS YOU SPOKE OF," he commanded, and Farion did so, in detail he never would have revealed of his own free will.

"Then there is no question I must make haste to Riviera. "YOU WILL THINK YOU ONLY TOLD ME AS MUCH AS YOU SHOULD HAVE. YOU WILL AVOW TO OTHERS I AM NOT TO BLAME FOR THE DEATHS. I RELEASE YOU," the wizard said.

"Well, it's plain to see you've done no wrong," Farion said, greatly relieved. "Thank you again for your aid of us, Honored Sir."

The wizard smiled at him. "It is my duty to aid those who are in need of it. Now, if you will excuse me, I must be on my way. It is getting late."

"Of course," Farion said, heading back into the stands to look for more casualties.

HARDRED awoke to the feeling of a soft bed beneath him, and a warm body beside him. Intrigued, he turned to look at who lay with him. The effort it cost to turn his head was almost beyond him. He rolled back in relief. It was Alnas, and he was sound asleep.

Hardred tried to sit, but after a few moments struggle, gave up the attempt. But Alnas's eyes opened.

"Hardred! I'm so glad to see you awake! You've frightened us. We were going to send for a healer if you didn't waken this morning." Alnas sat up and then put his hand to his head. "Although it can't truly be morning, can it? I feel as tired as when I lay down last night."

"What happened? I can scarcely move my head, and I tried but I cannot even sit," Hardred said.

Alnas looked at him in alarm. "Your leg must be festering. The healer warned you. I'll need to check it," he said, and began removing Hardred's pants. "The bandages appear clean from the outside," Alnas said, relieved. "I was afraid how they might look." He began unwinding them.

"Here, let me do that," a voice said from the side of the bed, and Hardred tensed as a figure rose up from the floor, then he relaxed when he saw it was Devan. "Alnas, are you ill as well? You look unwell," Devan said in concern.

"I feel as if I might swoon like Hardred did," Alnas said, slumping back onto the bed abruptly.

Devan unwrapped Hardred's wound and looked at it, puzzled. "It's healing well. There's no sign of sickness upon it."

He looked from one to the other of them in concern. "If I were ill as well, I might almost think the wizard had done this, somehow. I will go downstairs and get the two of you some breakfast, something hearty. You're certainly both in need of it," he said, then stopped at the door and looked sheepishly at them. "I forgot. I'll need some coin for it. Have I your permission to enter either of your purses?"

"Permission? Devan, you could rob us both blind and slit our throats and we'd not be able to stop you," Alnas said.

Devan shook his head. "You were right in what you told the wizard, Alnas. You are a fool, to say such a thing, the position you are in. The two of you are lucky I'm as honorable as I seemed to be, upon our meeting, and will nurse the two of you back to health instead of slaying you where you lie."

He went to Hardred's purse, and took out two gold coins, turning to him in concern. "Hardred, I can't see how you might have been robbed, with the bolt upon the door and us sleeping beside you, and so much coin yet here, but there is certainly not two thousand gold in your purse. Although now that I think upon it, I cannot see that it would fit."

"That gold is elsewhere," Hardred said.

Devan grinned at him. "You might learn something from him, Alnas. You'll note he hasn't told me where! Your friend's no fool, that's for certain. You are lucky to have him."

"Aye, don't I know it! I praise Elmoth every day, that He's seen fit to give me such a friend," Alnas said.

"I'll not have you think I don't trust you, Devan. The gold is in my pack. I trust you enough to know you'd never think to take it," Hardred said.

"As I said, you're no fool. You've judged me as well as you thought you had, Hardred. Now, I will be back shortly with breakfast for two, in bed," Devan said, grinning, and left.

"We were terribly lucky he came with us to our box. I shudder to think what might have happened to us and our coin, with both of us so weak, otherwise," Alnas said.

"Aye. Though I am sorely troubled by this strange malady that afflicts us. Where has the wizard gone?" Hardred asked.

"He left us in the Arena. At first it sounded as if he intended to return here with us, but fortunately, he had other plans. He frightened me. I did not feel safe beside him. And to think, I drank with him!"

"Drank with him?" Hardred asked in surprise, and Alnas explained.

"Then if you and Devan were afflicted, I might think it was the oushka. You know the rumors of eating and drinking with Elves. A wizard must be much the same, I think. I'd not ever want to drink with one," Hardred said.

Alnas looked afraid again. "You don't think he's put a spell on me by it, do you?"

"If he has it wasn't the drink, Alnas, or I'd not be so weak as well and Devan would be. It might have been that creature, that chimaera, he called it. Who knows what foul sickness a beast like that might carry? I only hope food and bed rest might cure whatever it is that ails us," Hardred said.

Alnas sighed. He had been imagining for nearly three weeks now what it might be like to have Hardred in his bed, but this was not at all what he had been hoping for. But at least Hardred was alive, safe. If he was lucky, and blessed by Elmoth, perhaps the rest would yet come with time. Right now he could scarcely move, in any case.

"And here I thought myself nearly an invalid before, when I could yet walk," Hardred said wryly. "But still, I feel I am blessed, for I am better off by far today than yesterday. Today I have two friends, when yesterday I had only one. Although your friendship alone was all I could want, Alnas, more than I had any right to expect. I was truly blessed even before Devan came. I would not want you to think I felt otherwise."

"I feel the same," Alnas said sincerely.

The two men lay together in quiet contemplation and camaraderie until Devan returned. "Breakfast is served," Devan said with a grin, entering the room with a huge tray. "I will repay you later for what I eat, for I took the liberty of getting enough for three." He set the tray by the bed.

Alnas and Hardred both struggled to sit. The smile left Devan's face. "You truly are weak as newborn pups, aren't you?" Devan asked in concern, helping them sit upright.

Hardred said, "I will at least be able to feed myself, though I will undoubtedly ask for you to hand me things."

"Here is the kakla first, then," Devan said. "I hope you like it strong. I do, fortunately, for that's what they have here. There is also sausage and eggs, bread and roasted potatoes. The innkeeper is quite solicitous of the two of you, or at least of your friends. He couldn't stop telling me about them when he learned I didn't know them, only you. It seems they were quite generous, but also, it appears the innkeeper was more than a little entranced by the Elf who traveled with them."

"I'm not surprised. Fisher was rather overwhelming," Hardred said, remembering how the Elf had shamelessly tried to seduce him. Hardred drank the stout brew and then began eating, slowly, but with great appetite. He was surprised to realize he was ravenously hungry, as if he'd not eaten in days.

"I had hoped to go to Oberas today," Hardred said between mouthfuls. "But I would make quite a poor impression upon him as a potential guard, weak as I am. In fact I doubt I might be able to rise from my bed today."

"Then we will go tomorrow, or the next day. It is not like we do not have the coin to see us through this dry spell," Alnas said.

Alnas looked at Devan. "I know you're in a hurry to get home, Devan, but do you think you might stay with us a day or two, until we're feeling better?"

Devan looked surprised. "Of course! Do you think I'd planned to do otherwise?" he asked, truly sounding surprised.

Alnas looked both relieved and sheepish. "I'm not used to being ill, to feeling so helpless. It frightens me."

"Believe me I know how you feel, after this past month. I'm only glad that whatever is ailing you has bypassed me, at least so far," Devan said fervently.

They spent the day in their room, with Devan bringing their meals to them, although Alnas, at least, was able to rise from his bed for part of the day.

By the next morning, Hardred was able to stand, though even the simplest tasks exhausted him.

The following day, Hardred insisted he was well enough to head to Oberas's shop, though he'd yet to buy a replacement sword. He didn't remind Alnas that he needed one. He didn't feel hale enough to shop for one and still have the strength needed to make the journey. Reluctantly the others agreed.

He was able to walk without the crutches now, at least; his enforced convalescence had helped his leg heal. It was slow going, though, and by the time they reached the shop, Hardred was leaning on Devan, though he straightened when they entered the shop.

Logan came out to greet them. "Hardred, Alnas! Willis told us you'd stopped by days ago. We'd thought you might come by again before this." He looked at Hardred in concern. "You look done in. Have you been ill?"

"Aye, since Feast Day, but I'm better now," Hardred said, fighting to remain standing. He lost the battle, as the shop tilted crazily. Alnas and Devan both caught him before he fell.

"Here, we'll take him to the kitchen. I'll lead you," Logan said, his face creased with worry.

Hardred sat, and Alnas sank gratefully into a chair as well. "We hate to trouble you, but do you have something we might drink?" Alnas asked.

"Will mead do?" Logan asked, smiling, and returned with three cups. "You've not introduced me to your friend," Logan said, handing him one of the cups.

"I'm Devan of Delthos."

"Logan of Logareth," Logan replied and then laughed. "It's funny. I've lived here five years now, but I still say Logareth when someone asks." He turned to the others. "Oberas should be back shortly. He's at the Market."

"When we were on the road, Oberas told me he might hire me as a guard, if I were willing, once my coin ran out. It hasn't, but I'm interested in the work just the same. But I'd not want to work apart from Alnas. Do you think there's any chance he might hire the both of us?" Hardred asked.

Logan looked thoughtful. "He's certainly in need of one of you. Curtis left his employ rather abruptly a short while ago, and he's not started looking to replace him, yet, out of hope you might stop by again. Normally, he only keeps four guards. But it's certainly possible he'd hire you both. Anything's possible with him, really. I gave up trying to fathom how he thinks long ago."

"Also, our friend Devan here has some pearls he'd like to sell, but none of us are traders. Do you think Oberas might be interested, that he might get a fair price for them from him?" Hardred asked.

"Pearls? I thought the name sounded familiar!" Logan said to Devan. "Only if you might be able to convince Oberas you're neither a fool nor a madman. He heard about the tank of sharks. The whole City has been talking of it. He's been raving about it for days, that and the chimaera. For the first time, he wishes he'd gone to the Games, so he might have been there to help fight that monster. Although more, I think, to fight the wizard that slew it."

"Fight the wizard! And he'd call me a madman!" Devan said, appalled. "You'd have to be completely daft to go against him."

The shop bell rang, and Logan said, "Excuse me," and went to the front room.

A few moments later, Oberas entered the kitchen, Logan and Devrik in tow. "Hardred! So, you've come to take me up on my offer?"

"Yes sir, if you wish to have me and if you're in need of two guards, not just one. Alnas and I have become as close as brothers these three weeks past. I'll not part from him. He's a fine guard, honest as I am, and a better swordsman by far. He's a good shot with the bow as well and has a good head on his shoulders," Hardred said.

"Hmm. As of now, I've only a need for a single guard. There are a few arrangements I'd need to make. Where are you staying?" Oberas asked.

"At The Fatted Pig, near River Street. We've a room there. Do you know it?" Hardred asked.

"Yes and my men are familiar with it as well. They were there only a few days ago," Oberas said. "Talon, that man you met on the road, and his friends had been staying there."

"I know. It's their room we are in. They've left, though," Hardred added.

Oberas grunted and nodded, looking lost in thought.

"Also, this is our friend, Devan of Delthos. He has some pearls he'd like to convert to coin and we thought you might be interested in them," Hardred said.

"Pearls, is it?" Oberas asked.

"Aye, sir, I've come into possession of a bag of a hundred pearls that I'd like to sell for a fair price," Devan said.

"You've intrigued me. You sound neither a fool nor a madman, as first I thought you must be, and I doubt Hardred would have much patience for either. So tell me, what possibly possessed you to dive into a tank of sharks?" Oberas asked.

"I did it for the pearls. I had need of earning coin in a hurry so I could return home. I ran into trouble that brought me here. I've been gone far too long as it is. My wife is gravid with our first and must think me dead by now. I fear for her and the babe," Devan said, face creased in concern for them.

"We'll not keep you any longer," Hardred said. "Once you sell the pearls, you're to head to Alridge as you've planned. Alnas and I will be fine without you, now." He turned to Oberas. "Perhaps, Master Oberas, you might even be able to see Devan safely on his way, if you know of any caravans heading to Alridge. And he'd like to take a boat from there, to Seaview; it will be faster and safer than the road."

"What do you mean, fine without him?" Oberas asked, scowling.

"Alnas and I took ill at the Arena. We're not sure if the wizard or the chimaera might be to blame. Both of us weakened so suddenly, when we'd been fine before. Yet Devan is unhurt, and he was with us and was the one who stuck his knife through the chimaera's eye," Hardred said.

"I thought the wizard was the one who slew the beast—with lightning, from what I've heard. Are you telling me Devan killed it and the wizard took the credit for it? I'd not put it past him, if it's who I think it is. Arcanus has done far worse in his miserable life. If it is him, you're lucky to have escaped with your lives. Many others have not been so fortunate. I only wish they might have killed each other," Oberas said, his face darkening in anger.

Hardred eyed Oberas in surprise. "No, the wizard slew it, all right. But he was weakened by it and he fell. We went to his aid, as we knew no one else might. He sent Devan and Alnas to make sure it was truly dead as I couldn't walk easily. They'd have to tell you the rest. That's when I swooned, and I didn't awaken again until the following morning at the inn."

"Tell me, was this wizard tall and thin, with gray eyes and long white hair, and wearing a red robe? Did he have what looked to be a warm smile, until you saw his eyes looking right through you? Did he recover?" Oberas asked.

"That's him, all right," Alnas said, shuddering. "He was nothing but courteous to us, yet something about him was unnerving. And he recovered far more quickly than I expected him to."

"Of course he did. My past is coming back to haunt me, it seems," Oberas said sourly, but softly, as if to himself. "First the Elven Princes and now Arcanus and even a chimaera. What next? Will an army of Revenants and all the rest of the enemies of the Dwarven Kingdoms storm Ardock?"

Hardred opened his mouth to ask him more when Oberas turned to Devan. "You've the pearls with you? I'll need to see them before I name a price."

Devan nodded and handed him the bag. Oberas poured some of them out into his cupped hand. "Ocean pearls, of a good size and conformation, all white. If you'd come in off the street, I'd have offered you five silver a pearl, thirty-three gold and five silver total. Considering you're with Hardred, I'll need to count them, of course, but if they're all here, I'll pay seventy-five gold for the lot of them, a solid price, no haggling. That's more than a fair price, one that will allow me a twenty-five percent profit, though of course, that's not something I'd normally have told you," Oberas said.

"Aye, it sounds fair to me as well, from what I know of their price on the coast and what Hardred's told me of their value inland. I'll sell them to you," Devan said.

Oberas carefully poured the bag onto the table and began counting them. "There's one hundred all right, all of good quality, as the others were." He turned from them, took his purse from his side, and counted out seventy-five gold, then turned back. "Here's the gold. Now, if the three of you will excuse me, I've work to do. I'll send someone by The Fatted Pig tomorrow with a message for you," he said to Hardred.

"Thank you, sir," Hardred said, rising from the chair. The others rose as well, and they began heading for the front of the shop. But Hardred only made it as far as the kitchen door when he swayed again, sagging. Hardred cursed as he collapsed against Alnas, and Alnas and Devan caught him, one on each side of him.

"Been ill, you said, yet you're still so weak that you can't cross a room without falling?" Oberas said. His voice wasn't scornful at all but instead full of concern. "I'll not have you returning to The Fatted Pig, not like this. That inn's fair enough, but that part of town is too dangerous, the condition you're in. Logan, put him up in one of the spare rooms."

"No, Oberas. I thank you for your concern, but I'll be fine," Hardred said.

"Nonsense; any fool can see you're in need of aid. A guard who can't even stand on his own is of no use to me," Oberas said, and Hardred's face flushed. Alnas looked like he was about to argue in his friend's defense when

Oberas continued. "You'll have no choice but to do as I say when you're hired, so you're hired. You're to replace Curtis. I'll have no arguments about it. I order you to rest until I tell you otherwise." Then he turned to Alnas. "You're looking peaked as well, for all you've been trying to help him. Are you up to performing guard work yet?"

"No sir, not today, not yet, but by tomorrow…," Alnas began.

"We'll take it as it comes. You're hired as well. You'll share the room with Hardred, for now at least," Oberas said.

Hardred said cautiously, "It's customary to inquire about the wages before accepting a position."

"Three silver a day, same as all my guard who live here with me. Five silver a day if you live elsewhere, as I wouldn't cover your room and board then, but I've need of at least one of you to live here."

"But that's the same as we got for guarding the caravan!" Alnas said in surprise. "Is guarding you as dangerous as that?"

Oberas snorted. "Not usually, except when I'm on caravan myself, and there's bonuses for that. I'll explain them to you later. But you'll be helping in the shop as well; there are many duties you'll perform. Logan, Devrik, and Willis will tell you. So, do you accept?"

"Yes, sir," Hardred said.

"I do as well," Alnas said.

"All right then. Devrik, you show them to the room, after they've had a chance to say good-bye to their friend. Devan, I'll be talking to you about that caravan and boat you need. After I'm done, Logan, I've a matter to discuss with you," Oberas said.

Hardred and Alnas said their good-byes to Devan. Devan tried to pay them for the meals he'd eaten and for a share of the cost of the room at The Fatted Pig, but they wouldn't accept. "You keep your coin, Devan. But if you're willing, there is the matter of the delivery to Riana," Hardred said. He turned to Oberas, "I'll have need of Devan myself for a short while, then I'll send him out to you, if that's all right, sir."

"Very well then; Logan, we'll be having that discussion now," Oberas said. "Get the oushka and two glasses."

Logan looked surprised but did so.

Hardred, Alnas, and Devan were led to the back room by Devrik, who saw them settled, and then he left them to their privacy. Hardred looked about. The room was nicer than the one they'd left, and not nearly as expensive as the equivalent at two silver a day. Far less, he realized, as Oberas had mentioned that staying at the shop included meals.

Hardred unpacked his pack, emptying it completely. He counted out the two thousand gold and wrapped it in blue cloth, put it at the bottom of the blue pack, and added the sheaf of letters. He handed it to Devan. "You'll be in need of a pack and this will make it easier and far less conspicuous to carry," Hardred said. He counted out one hundred additional gold and handed it to Devan. "And this is for you."

Devan shook his head. "Nay, I'll not take it. I do this as your friend, Hardred, not for the coin."

"You must, Devan. I'm taking you away from your family, and you'll have expenses on the trip as well. If you won't take it for yourself, take it for the baby; give it to him or her when the child's old enough to have need of it. Otherwise, I'll take back the gold and the letters and find someone else to carry them," Hardred threatened.

Devan sighed and accepted the coin. "For the baby, then," he said, then grinned at the thought of the child he'd yet to see.

Hardred smiled at him. "My sister's name is Riana. When I left Meria, she was to have gone to the The Salty Squid to stay, and to work as a minstrel for her room and board. If she's gone elsewhere, you can ask Derek or Kessel, or just about any other mariner in the City, and they should know where to find her. This is what she looks like. I'd give this to you so you might recognize her more easily, but I have need to keep it. But study it, so you'll know her."

Devan looked at the small statue that Hardred held out to him. "She's beautiful," he said, amazed. "So is this. Did you carve it?"

A look of pain lanced across Hardred's face. "No," he said quietly.

Devan looked at him in concern then back to the statue. "I think I'll know her, now, upon seeing her. She looks like kin to you, and there can't be two women of such great beauty in Meria," Devan said, handing the statue back to him. He smiled. "I can say so without feeling guilty for it, for my Larissa is the most beautiful woman in Delthos." He looked at Hardred and Alnas. "I will truly miss you, my friends."

"We'll miss you as well. We wish only joy for you, Devan; you're deserving of it," Alnas said.

"May the water be calm and the wind at your back, on your voyage home," Hardred said. "And may the Goddess watch over you always," he added softly.

Alnas looked at him in surprise.

"I wish only happiness for the two of you," Devan said. "May Seneth protect you both, always," he said. The three friends clasped arms, and then Devan turned and left the room.

Hardred sighed. He tucked his spare set of clothes into a drawer of the bureau, along with the gull pipes, the writing materials, his purse, and the statue, and then sank gratefully onto the bed. "Hired as a guard, when I can yet scarcely stand," he said, bemused.

"You'll be well again soon enough, Hardred. I truly feared for you, before, for both of us. But I've the feeling we'll do well here, with Oberas," Alnas said.

"Aye, I've the same, or I'd not have accepted the position so readily. I've been ordered to rest, and I've no trouble following that order," Hardred said, removing his boots. He stretched his long, lean frame upon the bed, and pulled the covers up over himself.

"Nor I," Alnas said, removing both boots and sheathed sword and lying beside him. They were both soon asleep.

Chapter 9
The Test

ALISSA was asleep, her breathing labored and wheezing, even sitting in her rocking chair. She had gotten worse rapidly, ever since Feast Day. Anorion stroked Alissa's hair and kissed her brow, then gently shook her. "Alissa, honey, it's time for Alarion's test. You can go back to sleep in a few moments, after you give him his good luck kiss," Anorion said, painfully remembering the last time he'd told her so. He'd thought her so ill before, but she could scarcely move now, scarcely breathe. She'd not eaten anything but soup in days, and scant little of that. She'd choked too many times trying to swallow even the softest of foods.

SOMEONE was calling to her, from so far away. Alissa awoke slowly and reluctantly. What a wonderful dream she'd been having. She had been singing by the river, with the Elf, Fisher. The two of them had been singing "River's Ballad of Walker," the way he'd taught it to her. Rion and Anorion had joined their two voices to hers and his, and they'd been a perfect quartet. Then her father had come, walking along the riverbank, calling to her as he had when she was a little girl. She'd turned and seen him and run to him and was just about to embrace him when she heard the voice.

She was so tired. She just wanted to stay here, by the river, with her father, but she recognized the voice: it was Anorion. But hadn't he been here with her? He sounded so far away.

She looked around and saw Rion and Anorion and Fisher weren't there after all, only her father was. Then he spoke to her. "It's all right, Alissa. Your mother and I can wait a little while longer to be with you. You go back to Anorion and Alarion now. You've a fine husband and a fine son. I wish I'd had the chance to get to know them."

She left the river with a sigh and opened her eyes. Anorion was looking at her so anxiously, as was Rion. He was so small and pale and frightened. "Forgive me, I had forgotten for a moment why you might have been waking me," Alissa apologized. The dream had seemed so real.

"FATHER, please! I can go alone. I know the way. Stay here with Mother," Rion begged. He was terrified. His father had had to shake her so vigorously to waken her, and there had been such fear in his face.

"HE'LL do nothing of the kind, Rion. I'm fine. I was only sleeping. I promise you both I will still be here when you get back," she said, sitting up straighter in her chair, realizing they'd been afraid she wouldn't be, that she'd not waken this time.

Rion started to cry, tears streaming down his face, and he hugged her, clinging to her.

"Oh my sweet boy, my strong young man; you mustn't worry about me, not today. You have to do well on your test. But first, listen to me, Rion. This is important. I know you have somewhere you need to be, but there is time for this.

"I know I've been trying to convince you and your father that I'll be fine, that I will get better, when it is easy to see that I won't. I have little time left, I think. That is why it is so important for me to see you enter your apprenticeship now. Not just so I know your future is secure. But because I've seen how terrible it is for you to watch me suffer, when you know you are helpless to save me. I'm not going to try to deceive you any longer; I should not have tried to before. I'm dying, Rion, I know I'm dying."

Rion looked at her in wide-eyed fear.

She continued, her voice soft and soothing, the way it used to be before she took so ill. "Everyone dies, Rion. Dying is a part of life. But dying is not the end of life. People who know how to love and how to be loved live on forever, in the hearts and minds of those who are loved by them and who love them. When my own father died, it hurt terribly, but he gave me such a wonderful gift before he died. He spoke to me, only a few nights before he left me forever and he gave me his smile. He told me that any hardship in life can be overcome, as long as you never lose your spirit, your smile. That the people we love live on in memory; that they are always with us.

"He told me that everyone dies, Rion, but not everyone truly lives. So many get so ensnared in old grief, or loss, or failure, that they let their whole life slip away unlived. I don't ever want that to happen to you, Rion. I love you too much. You were born to smile and to laugh. It is one of your greatest gifts, and you have so many gifts! Some of them you and I and your father could never guess. It's up to you to discover all your gifts. And the only way to do so is by trying when everyone else tells you that you will fail, by pushing forward when it might seem the only way is to stop, or to go back, by never losing your integrity or your spirit or your desire to do good, to help people, to mend their injured hearts, to aid everyone you see who might have need of you. It's going to be up to you and your Uncle Farion to heal your father's heart, Rion, and up to them to heal yours.

"Now give me a kiss and a hug. I need to speak with your father. And I swear to you, Rion, I will still be here, awake and alive, when you return from your test. I just needed to tell you all this while I could speak so clearly. I think... I think Meloneth might be aiding me; I haven't coughed once this entire time. Wait in the kitchen, Rion," she said, hugging him tightly and kissing him.

RION didn't want to let her go, but he did.

A short while later, Rion's father entered the kitchen, his eyes bright with unshed tears. "Come, son, we've still time. We're not late yet. She swore she'd greet us when we return. She's never once broken a promise to you or me, Alarion. She'll not do so now," his father said, gruffly but with conviction.

"And you remember what she told you, Alarion. I know you can, though I've never understood it. I swear you remember every word you ever hear, every sight you ever see, and your eyes see much—far more than most people's." His father put his strong arm around Rion and guided him out the door.

How could he possibly take a test and do well on it now, when his head was swimming with all his mother had told him? He wished that something might keep Oberas from testing him today as well. He wanted to go home to spend the day with his mother. They had so little time left together. He started to cry again on the way to Oberas's shop. He couldn't help himself.

"Alarion, please, you have to calm down. Not for yourself, for your mother. She'd be devastated if you didn't do well because of her. This is so important to her, Alarion. Please, you have to try," his father urged.

Rion sniffed and nodded and was able to stop crying by the time he reached the shop. The door was open, this time, and the sign by the door said they were open as well. "Alarion. Whatever is the matter?" a concerned voice asked.

Rion looked up. "Hardred?" he asked in surprise. Hardred was wearing the livery of Oberas's guards. "You work for Oberas now?"

"That I do. He hired me this past week, while I could still scarcely stand," Hardred said.

"I'd thought your leg might have healed by now," Rion said, his face showing his concern.

"It has, Rion. I took ill afterward, not because of the bite. Alnas was ill as well," Hardred said.

Rion was more alarmed at the thought that it wasn't just the injury, that both Hardred and his friend Alnas were ill.

"Don't worry. I'm fine now; we both are. All we needed was bed rest, it seems. Come, Alarion, you need to wash your face. It won't do to have Oberas see tears. I know you're nervous, but it's not worth crying over," Hardred said.

"Oh, but it's not that. It's Mother," Rion said, and sobbed speaking her name.

"His mother's been ill. She's worse this morning," Anorion explained.

"I'm sorry to hear that. Why don't you leave the lad with me? Oberas will be more impressed by him if he doesn't see you hanging about here with him," Hardred said.

"All right. That's what I'd planned to do. Alarion, I want you to walk straight home once the test is done. Good luck, son," his father said and clasped him on the shoulder, as if he was already a man.

When Anorion had left, Hardred said, "Oberas was delayed. He won't be here for a while yet. More of the applicants will be coming throughout the day. I wonder if you'd mind helping me a bit. Oberas is having me check over some inventory figures for him. But his other guard went home ill this morning, and I'll never catch up with all I need to do before the other applicants come. Could you help me?"

"Of course," Rion said, brightening. He liked helping people. "What do you need me to do?"

"First, you'll wash up," Hardred said, and led Rion to the washroom. Rion felt much better after he'd washed off the tears. He was eager to help Hardred.

When he came out of the washroom, Hardred led him toward the back of the enormous shop, through the main aisle of the large open area where samples of different goods were neatly arranged in racks, on shelves, and on tables, for customers to peruse. Rion was amazed at the diversity of the wares on display, though he only caught a tantalizing glimpse of a fraction of them as he passed.

There were bolts and rolls of colorful fabrics in every hue of the rainbow and in the most intricate patterns imaginable, with textures that looked so rich he ached to touch them. Statuary in every metal and stone known to Man, ranging from hand-size figurines to life-size pieces that were fine enough to grace the halls of a Palace, were artfully arranged in the next area. Then there were half a dozen stepped racks featuring elegant vases and bowls, some made of the finest ceramic and others carved from stone or exotic woods. Rion had known Oberas was rich, but the wealth on display along this single aisle was staggering.

Hardred escorted him to a windowless office. A tremendous oak desk dominated the room, with a massive leather padded chair behind it, but there was a second, smaller desk against the right wall with a correspondingly sized wooden chair. Set into the wall on the left were racks of shelves containing a hundred or more leather-bound books.

Hardred indicated the smaller desk, which currently held a sheaf of paper, a pen, ink, and drying sand. "I've an inventory here that I was working on, but I can't get the figures to come out properly. I know there's something wrong on each of the ten pages. I just can't figure out what. Can you take a look and check my sums for me?"

"Of course," Rion said. He sat down and eagerly began working on the sums. "Oh, I see what you've done here. You wrote one hundred sixteen, when it should have been one hundred six. And this one should be one hundred five, not one hundred fifteen." He quickly found and corrected all the mistakes.

"Thank you! You've no idea how long I stared at those pages without seeing that. Now, if you wouldn't mind, read this list to me, there, so I know what to pull from the shelves without having to climb up and down the ladder," Hardred said, handing him a list he took from the larger desk, and leading him to a storeroom further back, past the office. Rion glanced at the list as he followed Hardred. It was a list of spices. At least he was pretty sure they all must be: he'd never even heard of half of them before, but he was familiar with the rest.

Rion's eyes widened as they entered the storeroom. It was nearly as large as the front one, but the dozens upon dozens of racks of shelves were packed solid with things in wooden crates and metal bins, practical, rather than pretty, though everything was neatly organized.

Hardred led him to one of the racks, slung a basket over his arm, and climbed the wooden ladder beside the shelves. Rion read from the list, speaking loudly and clearly, waiting for Hardred to find what he read before reading the next item, sounding out the words he didn't know as best as he could.

After Hardred was done, he climbed down and set the full basket onto a cart. Then he pointed at a pair of crates and said, "Would you be able to move those two crates from here to there? They're more than a bit heavy, and the healer said I'm not supposed to do any heavy lifting, yet."

"I'll do my best," Rion said, eyeing the large crates critically. He crouched and tried to lift the first crate. It was indeed quite heavy. "I think I might be able to push it across the floor, but I've not the strength to lift it more than a little," Rion said, apologetically. "Can you hand me that mat over there?"

Hardred looked at him curiously. "Why the mat?"

"Because it will slide easier on that, and also, I'd not want to scratch the floor. It wouldn't do at all for me to leave gouges in it. Oberas might get angry with you for it, when I'm not here to confess to it," Rion said.

Hardred handed him the mat, and Rion tilted the crate just enough to slide the mat under, pushing it with his foot to get it all the way under, while he used both hands to lift. He was sweating. He pushed and pulled and slid the crate across the floor. Then he went back for the second one, moved it as well, and then replaced the mat.

"Well done! I don't know about you, but I could sure use some kakla right about now, but I don't have the time to make it. You don't happen to know how to, do you?" Hardred asked.

Rion grinned. "I can brew kakla or tea, if you prefer. I've even learned to cook some, because…." His face fell as he thought of his mother again.

"Let me show you to the kitchen," Hardred said. He did so, and Rion looked in wide-eyed astonishment at the tremendous mess. The entire rest of the shop, from the display area to the office to the storeroom, had been so clean and well organized he never expected the kitchen might be in such an atrocious state.

Dirty plates and utensils and pots and pans overflowed the sink and were stacked haphazardly on the counters to either side of it. The refuse bin was overflowing, the stove was caked in grease and spattered with food stains, the open oven was full of ash, and the woodbin beside it was noticeably empty. The kitchen table and six chairs set around it were the only tranquil island in the sea of chaos around them.

Hardred sighed as he looked into the six buckets on the dirty wooden floor. "Oh, I forgot! We've no water, other than what was in the washroom, or I'd have already taken care of this mess. As I said, the healer said I'm not supposed to carry things yet, and Willis was supposed to have drawn the water from the well, but he's ill. And I can hardly leave the shop unguarded besides. Two of the buckets hook onto the yoke, there. The well's only a block away to your right, if you leave through this back door. I don't suppose you'd be able to fetch some water?"

"Of course," Rion said, concerned that Hardred had already been working so hard when he was ill. "Why don't you rest while I'm out? Once I get back, I'll clean the stove and get the kakla brewing, and then get a start on the dishes while it heats," he suggested.

"You're a fine lad," Hardred said with an approving sigh as he sank into one of the chairs.

Rion headed out with the buckets. He'd welcome the water. He'd already dirtied his hands and his new shirt helping Hardred, and he wanted to look his best for Oberas.

Rion headed purposefully down the street to the well and then looked wide-eyed as he approached it. There was a juggler not ten feet from the well, and three acrobats, doing all sorts of tricks. He sighed. He had no time for that, now. He dutifully got the water and with a last wistful look returned to the shop. He was panting by the time he made it to the shop: the full buckets were heavy.

"Excellent, Alarion; you were quick without spilling too much. A message came while you were out. Oberas has been further delayed. I'm touched you offered to do the dishes, but I'm going to get a start on them. Instead, I know it's a lot to ask of you, but do you think you can go to the Market for me? Oberas has left some coin for me to purchase some things we need, but as I've said, I can't leave the shop unguarded, and frankly, I'm glad not to have to make such a long walk. I'm about done in as it is. I can hear the bell from the kitchen, if anyone enters the shop while you're out. Here's the list and the coin," Hardred said. "Try to remember what you paid for each item. Oberas likes to know. There's a cart here for you to use. Just knock once you're back, as I'll be locking the door after you, since you'll be gone a while."

"Of course! But please, Hardred, you should rest. I can do the dishes once I get back, as Oberas has been delayed." Rion looked down at the coin Hardred held out to him with the list, and his eyes widened. Ten gold! Rion had never held so much coin in his life!

He clutched it in his hand, pushing the cart before him, and headed for the Market. He'd not risk putting the gold in his purse, for fear a cutpurse would rob him. He eyed the list intently. He'd never bargained for some of the things on the list before. He stood outside several of the stalls to get an idea of what he might expect to pay, before he tried to buy anything. He was surprised how high the asking prices were for some of the items. He realized to his dismay that he'd not have enough coin to get everything. Well, then, he'd have to buy what he could, getting the most he could. Presumably the things at the top of the list were more important that the things on the bottom, as they didn't seem to be in any other sort of order. What an odd assortment of things, too.

He grinned. He'd start with the lily; he'd buy it from the same flower merchant he'd haggled with before. He was sure he could get a good price for it. He hoped if Oberas came back while he was out, Hardred would explain where he was. He wondered briefly how his mother was doing, then forced thoughts of her aside and got to work.

Once he was done he returned to the shop, the cart loaded and heavy. He knocked as instructed and then entered with it. "I'll be back in a few moments and then you can help me unload the cart," Hardred said. "Meanwhile, if you wouldn't mind, you can empty the sink of the dirty dishes."

"Sure!" Rion said. He began emptying the sink, sorting everything into the four empty buckets on the floor, so they wouldn't make a worse mess. At the very bottom of the sink under the rim of the final bowl, he caught a glimpse of something surprisingly shiny. He lifted the bowl, astonished at what he found. A ring! It was beautiful. He picked it up and set it into his palm, admiring it. The band was narrow and silver, inlaid with fine filigree, and there was a faceted blue stone that sparkled like water lit by the sun. He'd always wanted to buy his mother something so fine.

Who would have imagined that such a treasure might have fallen into the sink and not been missed? He certainly didn't want it to get lost again. He opened his purse and tucked it safely inside with the change he'd brought back for Hardred. Then he filled the kettle with water and lit the stove to heat water for the dishes, located the dishrag and soap and drying towel, and set the stack of plates from the first bucket into the sink to soak.

By the time Hardred returned to the kitchen, Rion was done with the first bucket of dishes, which were dried and stacked neatly on the table. "I started on the dishes, but I left them on the table, as I wasn't sure where to put them. All the dish cupboards are empty, and I didn't want to put them in the wrong place." He'd noticed there were some sheets of blank paper and pen and ink and drying sand on the table, now, and figured that Hardred might have planned to do some more of the inventories, instead of more physical tasks.

"Excellent! How did you do at the Market?" Hardred asked, eyeing the full cart.

"Pretty well, though I couldn't get the last two things on the list. I didn't have enough coin."

"I didn't take a good look at the list, but I'm not surprised Oberas didn't leave enough for everything. It did seem pretty long. How about you write on a new sheet what each thing cost for Oberas? There's not room enough on this one to do so neatly."

"Of course!" Rion said, relieved that Hardred didn't seem overly concerned that he'd not had enough to purchase everything. Rion sat at the table and used the supplies there to do so, careful to make his lettering as neat as possible. He made a column for the items, another showing what the asking price was, and a third column showing the final price he'd paid. He put an "X" in the columns for the final two items that he'd not bought. He totaled both columns as well, and wrote the amount of change.

Hardred glanced at the completed list. "Are you sure you only paid six silver for the lily?" he asked, surprised. "Oberas warned me he can never get them for less than ten this time of year."

Rion grinned. "Ah, I had an unfair advantage, you see. The flower merchant, Mikkel, likes me. I purchased something from him a while ago, and he gave me some advice on how to haggle. I used it against him today. I had told him before I was apprenticing to a merchant. I told him today was my test, that I was at the Market to buy things for Master Trader Oberas, and I hoped I might be able to get a good price on things, so maybe I could impress him, even though it wasn't part of the test, that I was just doing a favor for one of his guards, who wasn't able to make the trip to the Market himself.

"Mikkel said he purchases the lilies for four silver each, in bulk, and never sells them for less than eight and never sells them to Oberas for less than ten, but that he'd do me a favor this time and sell it to me for six. I didn't even have to go back and forth with him over it. I told him I'd be sure to mention his kindness to Oberas, and he said, 'Don't you dare! I've the finest flowers in the market, but still, I'll never get him to pay ten silver again if you do, and I enjoy watching his face go dark red when he can't get the price he wants.'

"He told me, 'I usually ask him four silver more for things to start with than anyone else, just to watch the show!'" Rion said laughing. Then he grew serious. "Oh, but you mustn't tell Oberas! I wouldn't want him to hold it against Mikkel. He's such a nice man."

Hardred grinned at him. "I'll not say a word about how you made the bargain, only that you did."

Once Hardred was done looking at the list, Rion said, "I've got the change for you. And Hardred, I also found this at the bottom of the sink," he added and handed him the ring in addition to the change.

Hardred looked at it in surprise. "This was in the sink?"

"At the very bottom."

"Really? Well, it's been in there over a week now, at least, and I've not heard Oberas mention it was missing. Even if he realizes at some point, he won't know where or when he lost it," Hardred said with a wink, and slipped it into his purse.

Rion looked at him in surprise. Surely he didn't mean to keep it? "But Hardred, it's not yours."

"Who's to say? Or do you mean it's yours, for finding it? Look, if you don't say anything about it, I'll split what I make with you when I sell it," Hardred said.

"That's not what I meant at all. I'm surprised at you, Hardred. I'd not have ever thought from what I'd seen of you so far that you'd do something so dishonest," Rion said in dismay. The warm feeling he'd had from earlier had faded completely away.

"Oberas has more coin than he can ever spend. Why not have a little more for my own?" Hardred said.

"I don't think I want to speak to you anymore, Hardred. I'm going to wait in the main room for Oberas, for my test," Rion said miserably. He didn't dare tell Hardred he would tell Oberas about the ring. Hardred had a sword. He might decide to use it, though he doubted he'd take the risk, for his father being a City Guard.

Rion sat to wait, looking nervously back at the kitchen, and was surprised when a moment later Oberas emerged from an aisle at the left of the shop. He recognized him easily from when he'd seen him with his father.

Rion looked fearfully at the door to the kitchen then approached him. "Sir, my name is Alarion. I'm to take your test today. Forgive me, but before we begin, you need to know something. I feel terrible having to tell you, when I owe Hardred my life, but he might someday become a danger to you. I found a ring, sir, in the sink. I gave it to Hardred for you, but he's put it in his purse. He told me he plans to sell it. I thought you should know he's not as honest as he seems to be, sir," Rion said, wishing it weren't true.

"Is that so?" Oberas said coolly. "Hardred!" he bellowed.

"Yes, sir?" Hardred said, coming out from the kitchen.

Rion swallowed and took a step back from him, afraid he might seek retribution against him for betraying him to Oberas.

"Alarion tells me you've something that belongs to me," Oberas said imperiously.

Rion tensed. Hardred asked innocently, "Who, me?" Then he grinned and pulled the ring from his purse. He tossed it in the air and caught it, then held it out to Oberas. "That I do, sir. He passed every test! I have to show you and tell you how well he did on some of them, the part you didn't get a chance to see or hear from where you were hiding. You'll not believe how fast he was, or how well he did or how thorough he was."

Rion looked from one to the other, puzzled, then his eyes widened in surprise. "You can't mean I've already taken the test? That finding the ring was part of it?" he asked in growing understanding.

OBERAS was well pleased with the boy. For all his diminutive size, he was head and shoulders above the rest of those he'd tested so far. "That you have, taken and passed. That doesn't mean you get the apprenticeship, mind you. Others might still pass also: we've three left to test. We had to test each of you with different things, of course, since not all of you can read, nor do sums on paper. Some of the lads had more physical tests, lifting crates, sorting them, other tasks."

Hardred said, "So far you're the only boy who did all I asked without knowing it was for the test. Some of them weren't willing to help at all until we informed them and others balked after the first few favors I asked of them.

"Physically, you're actually the weakest of those we've tested so far. The other boys were all able to lift those crates, even though some had to struggle at it. But even there you didn't give up: you found a way to move them efficiently without lifting them. Putting the mat under them was especially impressive to me. The first boy was trying to show off and lifted too much at once, he had a stack of smaller crates and they fell every which way and three broke open, damaging the contents.

"You're one of the smartest. You did all the sums correctly and quickly and you read well. Also, you're responsible. You didn't stop to watch the juggler and acrobats and then move so quickly you spilled out all the water, as the first boy did. You bought more than we thought you might. The lily is really a bargain, I'll tell you the price he paid later, Oberas.

"And Alarion remembered the final prices and didn't cheat on the change, as the third boy did. The second boy didn't buy a thing, when he realized he didn't have enough, he came back to ask what to do. Then, when we sent him back out, he let himself be talked into getting twenty pounds of kakla rather than five, by a merchant who knew a fool when he saw one. Of course, he could then buy less of the other things on the list, but to make matters worse, he'd paid an exorbitant price for stale beans and thought he'd done well!"

Oberas listened to his new guard in bemused exasperation, without chastising or silencing him, as the normally quiet man accurately summarized Alarion's performance and went on to list the flaws of the other candidates in remarkable detail. The boy had had the same effect upon him, but to a lesser degree. His friendly, open nature invited such honesty. As a merchant, Alarion could learn to use that to his advantage when dealing with customers and suppliers. It would give him an edge bargaining, particularly if he could learn to exaggerate the value of his merchandise, while continuing to seem to be completely forthright.

Hardred continued to praise the boy. "Oberas needs someone who can think, and make decisions for himself, and make the right ones. Plus you wrote well and neatly. You even wrote the asking price, doing more than I'd asked you to, rather than less.

"And then to top it all off, you turned the ring in upon finding it. I had to find it for that second boy, he was so oblivious! I moved it three times and he still never spotted it. The one who tried to cheat Oberas on the change snuck the ring into his shoe. It took us a while to figure out he definitely had it. Oberas had me search him for it. You, on the other hand, didn't let even my saving your life sway you from what you knew to be right. You held honesty above all else," Hardred said, grinning as proudly as if the boy were his own son.

"Go home now, Alarion. We'll come by tomorrow and let you know whether you've gotten the apprenticeship," Oberas said, his expression contemplative.

RION beamed in pride and headed home with a light heart. He'd done well! And Hardred wasn't dishonest after all. He was as pleased about that as by the rest. He walked straight home as his father had told him to and knocked. His father could tell from the grin on his face he'd done well. Rion was delighted to see his mother was awake, as promised. They listened eagerly to everything he told them.

"WHAT was that about you saving the boy's life?" Oberas asked Hardred, as soon as Alarion had left.

"It was at the Arena, what they accused me of wizardry for. I told you about it."

"You didn't tell me it was him, though. Are you sure you judged him fairly, that you're not favoring him over the others for having saved him?" Oberas asked critically.

Hardred looked at Oberas seriously, the smile fleeing his face. "No. Not at all. If I'd known you'd doubt my assessment for it, I'd not have let you have me test him. Let me show you how well I think he did, and then you determine whether or not I've overly praised him, or judged him fairly." He proceeded to tell Oberas what Alarion had done.

Oberas was even further impressed. "That's better than any of the three who previously were my apprentices did at such a young age. Except for him being so weak and small. But he has wits and enthusiasm, determination and honesty. I'll take that over brute strength any day. You and the other guards might just have to help a little more shifting stock, for a time, until he grows a bit. I'm very pleased, not only with him, but with you, Hardred. I'd not want you to start to think otherwise. Enjoy the compliments while you can. I dispense them rarely enough—just ask Devrik or Willis. To my mind, they're worth far more then, the times I bestow them."

There was a knock on the door to the shop. "All right, that will be the next one. Go to it, Hardred. I'll be watching from the back again, as before. And none of these last three can read, so make sure between them they clean that kitchen: the stove, oven, floor, dishes, all of it. I want it spotless, or you and the other guard will be doing it. I can't wait any longer for an apprentice to, even if I do accept one tomorrow. There's not a clean dish left anywhere in the shop, save for the ones Alarion washed."

HARDRED nodded and headed for the door, secretly hoping the rest of the applicants would do poorly. He liked Alarion. He reminded him much of Alnas, sunny and cheerful and friendly. The apprentice Oberas accepted would be able to give the guard orders. He'd not chafe under Alarion, that was for sure.

THE day seemed endless to Rion. He wondered how the other applicants were doing. He could tell Hardred hoped he'd get the apprenticeship, but he wasn't sure whether Oberas might. But his worries about the test paled when compared to his worries about his mother.

She was having a terrible time of it tonight. She'd started coughing after dinner and hardly stopped at all. His father finally left him with her and went to fetch the healer. But when the healer came, he said there was nothing he could do, that nothing he might give her would ease her cough, nor aid her in sleeping, that she was far too weak for him to risk it. He felt so bad for not being able to aid her, for seeing Rion's eyes, and his father's, that he didn't even charge them for the visit. When Rion finally went to bed that night, he couldn't sleep. He lay awake the entire night, listening to his mother coughing, terrified she might suddenly stop, and what that might mean.

Finally it was morning. It was scarcely an hour after dawn that the knock came. Rion answered the door, fighting down a yawn as he did so. It was Oberas, and Devrik was with him.

"I've come to speak to your father, Alarion," Oberas said.

"Yes, sir!" Rion squeaked and went to get his father.

"Master Trader Oberas," Anorion said courteously, as he entered the room.

"Guardsman Anorion. It is my pleasure to inform you that I have selected your son to be my new apprentice," Oberas said, without any preamble.

"That is wonderful news, sir," Anorion said, relief upon his face, rather than joy or surprise. "If you'll excuse me just for a moment, I'd like to tell my wife. She's very ill and this news is sure to comfort her."

"Of course," Oberas said. When Anorion went to the family room, Oberas said, "Alarion, if you'll show me where I might sit to write?"

"Yes, sir. This way, sir," Rion said. He led him to the kitchen. "Would you like some kakla, sir?"

"Yes," Oberas said.

Rion noted he didn't thank him for the offer. He turned to Devrik. "Would you like some as well, Devrik?"

Devrik seemed surprised to have been asked. "No, but thank you, Alarion. I'm working now."

"Oh. I'm sorry, I hadn't realized you shouldn't be offered some," Rion said, feeling nervous. He filled the kettle to boil the water. He wished they had some honey cake. He thought Oberas might enjoy it. From his impressive girth, he figured he must enjoy sweets.

Anorion returned. "Please forgive me for having taken so long," he said, sounding distracted and not at all contrite.

Oberas pulled out a lengthy contract, and began reading it out loud, from top to bottom, line by line. Rion saw his father kept looking toward the family room, and realized that he was listening intently. Rion could hear his mother coughing too.

Oberas was halfway through when the kakla was ready. He sipped it while it was still scalding hot. Rion waited for him to comment on it, that he liked it, or even that he didn't, but he didn't say anything. He kept reading until he was done. "If you agree to it, sign there."

Anorion put his mark where Oberas had indicated.

Oberas looked surprised. "You don't write? Then how did the boy learn to?"

"My wife knows how. She's the one who taught him. Her father taught her. It never occurred to him what a waste it was for a woman to learn to, though she doesn't think learning to read and write was a waste. Of course, it's thanks to her that Alarion knows how, so I suppose there was some use to it, after all," Anorion said.

"Well, have the boy come to my shop at dawn tomorrow. And be sure he's not late. He was prompt to the test and promptness is important to me," Oberas said imperiously.

"Of course," Anorion said. When Oberas was gone, he turned to Rion. "Go to your mother, Alarion. I'll join you in a moment."

Rion crept into the family room, thinking his mother would be asleep. She wasn't coughing now, but he could hear her labored breathing even from the kitchen. He saw that she was awake.

His father joined him, and put his arm around him and his other around her, and they huddled in a threesome. "It's done, Alissa. Alarion leaves in the morning. You can rest easy, now. You must get some sleep. You didn't have any last night. Are you sure I can't get you some broth?"

She shook her head, and he realized she dared not speak or she would start coughing again. Then she looked at Rion intently. Her eyes were so bright, almost as if she were feverish. Rion touched her cheek, afraid she might be, but she wasn't. She was cold, terribly cold. "I love you, Rion," she mouthed. "I'm so proud of you."

"I love you too, Mother," he said, breaking from his father's grip and hugging her tightly and kissing her forehead, as she sometimes kissed his. "Please sleep now, Mother. Then tonight maybe you'll have enough of an appetite that we can celebrate over dinner."

She smiled and nodded, then closed her eyes. Still smiling, she began to hum, "River's Ballad of Walker." Rion recognized it.

Her breath was coming in such terrible, wheezing gasps now, between the humming. Rion turned to his father, worried at how bad she sounded. Rion was startled to see tears streaming down his father's face.

His father was holding his mother's hand in one hand and Rion's hand in his other. Suddenly he squeezed Rion's s hand so hard, he thought it might break. At the same moment, Rion realized his mother wasn't humming anymore, or wheezing. For one brief moment he thought she was asleep, as his father let go of his hand and his mother's and kissed her gently on the mouth. His father had hugged her but never kissed her in front of him before.

"Good-bye, Alissa," his father said, his voice scarcely a whisper, and Rion's eyes widened in terror.

"No! No, she can't be!" Rion cried in denial, turning to her. "Mother? Mother!" he cried desperately. Then he fell to his knees, sobbing at her feet.

His father knelt beside him, hugging him tightly, and the two of them cried in each other's arms for what they had lost.

ALNAS was looking forward to seeing Alarion again. He'd never seen Hardred so enthusiastic about anything before as he'd been since Oberas told them he was accepting Alarion as his apprentice. When just at dawn there was a knock on the door, Alnas opened it, expecting to see Alarion's eager young face. But it wasn't Alarion at all; instead it was the City Guardsman Farion. His eyes were red-rimmed, not as if he'd been drinking, but as if he'd been crying. He didn't look like a man who might cry easily.

Farion's eyes widened in surprise. "I didn't expect to see a familiar face. I've a message for Master Trader Oberas."

Alnas paled. "Has something happened to Alarion?" he asked, dreading what he might hear, how it might affect Hardred.

Farion nodded, swallowed visibly and then spoke. "His mother died yesterday, just after Oberas left. She'd been ill for some while. We knew it was only a matter of time, but it doesn't make it any easier to bear.

"Alarion needs to be home with my brother Anorion today, probably for the rest of the week; they need each other. But we don't want to risk Alarion losing the apprenticeship because of it. It meant the world to his mother, knowing Alarion was apprenticed to Oberas to become a merchant, that he'd not grow up to be a City Guard, as we are. We don't want this to affect his apprenticeship. That's why I've come to speak with Oberas. Anorion would have come himself, but...."

"Of course. I'll take you to him," Alnas said, his heart going out to Farion as well as Alarion and Anorion. It was obvious Farion had been close to his brother's wife.

FARION had been concerned that Oberas would not be sympathetic at all about Alissa. Oberas didn't have a reputation for compassion—far from it. Farion was surprised when Oberas was, in fact, very understanding.

"Of course he must stay with his father. I'd certainly not try to separate them now. Have Alarion come to me next week, the same day and time, if he's ready. If not, send word. I'll give him a full month, if need be, but the sooner he's able to get to work, the better for me, of course," Oberas said. "Besides, nothing dulls the pain in your heart like hard work. And a change of scenery. Him hanging about the house without her there will only make it worse for him."

"Thank you for your understanding," Farion said, genuinely pleased by it. He'd had his reservations about the apprenticeship ever since Cedric had told him and Anorion about rescuing Oberas from some angry swordsmen when he'd gotten so drunk he'd almost been at the center of a brawl at The Painted Pony, but now he thought it might work out well after all.

RION had done his best to be strong and brave, to stem the tide of tears. He'd been touched by how many of the City Guard led the procession to the graveyard. His mother had been placed in a wooden coffin, in a cart strewn with flowers. His father had put her mandolin inside with her. Rion had agreed he should. Rion had carried her potted flower with him all the way to the graveyard, and after she was buried, he'd pulled it out of the pot and planted it carefully on top of the grave, remembering what his mother had told him about the Elf planting the lily upon her father's grave. No one thought it was magic this time, but even his friends had cried when he did it.

Rion had been worried about Drew, who'd been almost hysterical. Rion realized he'd been flooded with memories of burying his own mother. Just as he had when Drew had lost his mother, Rion spoke to him about it, and this time, it eased the burden of his own heart, too.

He remembered what his mother had told him when she had truly told him good-bye, before the test, about helping people and not letting himself be consumed by his grief. He could hear her say every word still, and it helped hearing her comfort him when he most needed her to.

He was even able to help his father, at least a little, he knew. He'd make sure his father didn't lose himself to his grief, either. It helped, having such an important job to do, helping his father and Drew. Uncle Farion was invaluable, of course. And Rion's friends helped too.

Farion and Cedric, Darhew, Justin, and all Father's friends and their wives took turns stopping by and bringing food. Father was excused from duty for two weeks. But after the first week, he was desperate to go back. Rion could see he was.

His father spoke to him about it. "I need to work, Alarion. I keep expecting to see her or think I hear her cough or sometimes, when I'm fortunate, hear her sing. I expect to see her smiling face and—I want you to begin your apprenticeship, Alarion. I think it would be best for you to be working hard too."

"Only if you promise to try to do what Mother told me to, also. I'm not saying right now, not yet, but someday soon. You have to smile, Father. And laugh. Don't do it for yourself; do it for me. More, do it for her," Rion said, smiling at his father in encouragement.

"I'm so fortunate to still have you," his father said, hugging him tightly. "You've my eyes, Alarion, but you've Alissa's smile. I've always loved that most about you." He smiled weakly at him, even as a tear ran down his cheek.

"I'm proud of you, Father," Rion said. "And I love you. I'm so glad you're still with me. But she's with us too. She'll always be in our hearts, just like she said. And we'll always have her music to remember her by."

When Farion stopped by to check on them, to be sure he should tell Oberas Alarion needed at least another week, he was surprised to hear otherwise. "Are you sure about this, Anorion? And you, Alarion? You're not hurting yourselves thinking you're helping each other by it?"

"I'm sure, Farion. I'll be reporting to work with you in the morning, as soon as I've escorted Alarion safely to Oberas; I'll not take any chances that he gets there. We've already packed the things he wanted to take from his room and made sure his clothes are all clean and ready. But, if you wouldn't mind, it would help if you'd stay here with me for a few days. The house will be too empty otherwise, for at least a little while yet. I'll be fine during the day. It's the nights that have been the hardest for me."

"Of course; for as long as you need me," Farion said.

The next morning the three of them headed to Oberas's shop. Rion was pleased that Hardred was the one to answer the door.

"I've come to get started on my apprenticeship, Hardred," Rion said.

"Alarion, are you sure?" Hardred asked. "You know Oberas said you could take more time."

"I know. But Mother wouldn't have wanted me to delay it further. I'll be fine, Hardred, really." He turned to his father and uncle and impulsively hugged them each tightly. "Good-bye, Father, Uncle Farion. I'll see you when I can get away."

"Take care, son," Anorion said. "And remember, I love you, and you've always a home with me, if you need it."

Rion nodded and smiled, though his eyes were bright with unshed tears. Then he closed the door and exhaled. "Hardred? Do you think you might call me Rion?" Rion asked wistfully. "Mother always did and my friends do. Only my father and uncle and their friends use my full name and I suspect Master Trader Oberas will as well."

Hardred smiled at him. "Of course, Rion. Come, let's tell Oberas you're here."

THE next morning Hardred looked at the sleeping boy, sorry he had to wake him. He had a smile upon his face in his sleep. There had been such sadness in his face yesterday when he'd come. Not that he hadn't smiled as well, but he'd almost come to tears more than once. He was yet so young to have had his mother taken from him and to be parted from his father so soon after. "Rion, the sun's up. It's time for you to be, as well," Hardred said softly, shaking him gently.

Rion awoke slowly, yawning and stretching, hissing at the pain in his arms as he did so. Had he been ill? Then he saw the face above him, lit by the light spilling in from the hall. It wasn't his mother or his father. "Hardred!" he said, sitting up quickly, wincing at the pain in his shoulders as he did so. "I haven't overslept, have I?" Rion asked in concern.

"Not at all. I was told to wake you at dawn, and it's only just dawn now," Hardred said.

"Thank you, Hardred. I'll just wash up and get dressed." Rion swung his legs over the bed. His muscles cried out in protest. Oberas had shown him around the shop, but then put him immediately to work. He said it was best to learn by doing, that he'd work doing different things until he knew everything about Oberas's business.

There had been a lot of bending and climbing and lifting and carrying yesterday. He wasn't used to such work, although Hardred and Alnas had helped with the heaviest things. Rion had been concerned about it, at first, until Hardred told him what he'd said about not lifting things had just been a ruse for the test, though he really had been ill for a time. Rion was relieved Hardred was well now.

Rion liked Alnas immediately. He was glad both of them were there. He'd liked Logan, too, but he was no longer there. Hardred had told him Oberas had only needed four guards so he'd released Logan from his service when he hired Alnas. But Logan wasn't upset about it. Oberas had aided him in opening a tavern, as Logan had planned to, once he left Oberas. Logan just hadn't planned to go yet; he'd planned to help train the new guard. But Oberas said he could see that Hardred and Alnas both would need little in the way of training and that it was time Logan left him. Hardred, Alnas, Devrik, and Willis guarded Oberas now.

Rion washed and dressed quickly and headed for the kitchen. Hardred grinned at him. "That was quick. Now then, you need to make Oberas his breakfast," Hardred said, describing what to prepare.

Rion was astonished. "Really? All that, just for him?" he asked, then blushed. *No wonder he was so portly*, he thought.

"Not all for him. You and I and Alnas will be eating, too, though you're to serve him first and eat afterward in the kitchen with me and Alnas. Oberas dines first and alone."

"Serve him? All right, I'll do my best," Rion said, trying to keep the doubt from his voice as he went to work.

"Good morning, sir," Rion said, when Oberas appeared a while later.

"Hmpf," Oberas grunted, sitting. He looked at the platter of food. "Did you cook this?" he asked Rion, eyeing him intently.

Rion swallowed. "No, sir, Hardred did most of it. I cooked the sausage all right, but I made a mess of the eggs. I've never tried cooking those before. And I burned the potatoes. We've a different sort of pan at home; yours heated much quicker and hotter than I expected it to. But I'll get the hang of it sir," he said bravely.

"Hmpf," Oberas grunted again, sipping the kakla. "I can tell you brewed the kakla," he said, his voice harsh.

"Yes, sir," Rion said in dismay. He'd hoped he'd at least gotten that right. "I made it the way my father likes it. I don't drink it myself, yet. Hardred warned me it was weak, sir, when he tasted it, but I already heard you coming. I'll brew more now, if you like, and make it stronger," Rion said, fighting tears.

"You'll do nothing of the kind. Hardred makes a decent egg, but he's astonished me with the kakla he's made. This is fine, just the way I like it," Oberas said.

Rion grinned in relief. "I'm glad I've pleased you."

"You're relieved you mean. Surely Hardred's warned you about me? I've a reputation for being hard to please, but I'm not, not at all. All I expect is perfection in everything you do, and then we'll get along fine. What's that you're wearing?" Oberas asked, scowling at him.

"My clothes, sir; I'm sorry, but these are the best I have. I dirtied my blue shirt yesterday, with all the crates we moved, and I've not had a chance to wash it yet," Rion apologized.

"You mean to tell me you've only the one decent shirt? Unacceptable. We'll go to my tailor today and have suitable clothes made for you," Oberas said.

Tailor? "Yes, sir," Rion said.

Rion was relieved that Alnas and Hardred ate with him in the kitchen, after Oberas was done. "I heard him tell you he prefers your kakla to mine," Hardred said, smiling.

Alnas laughed. "He's not the only one! Honestly, Hardred, I can't see how you can drink what you brew." He turned to Rion. "On the road, I'd fill half my cup with kakla and the other half with the water the others had boiled for tea, and then it had been drinkable."

"You'd never make a seaman, Alnas," Hardred said, laughing.

"So you keep telling me," Alnas said, laughing with him.

Some of the tension left Rion. "Alarion!" Oberas bellowed from the shop.

"Coming, sir!" Rion said, leaping to his feet, knocking the chair over in his eagerness to please.

"What was that?" the voice bellowed.

"Nothing, sir! I mean, no damage done. I just knocked the chair," Rion said, scrambling to right it, then running to the other room.

Hardred shook his head in sympathy. "I wish he'd go easier on him."

Alnas laughed. "He probably thinks he is. He'd likely tell you he complimented the boy on the kakla, isn't that enough? He so seldom gives anyone a word of praise."

Hardred nodded. Oberas was difficult to work for, but not terrible, at least, he'd yet to be.

WHEN they set out for the tailor a short while later, Rion was in his blue shirt, dirty as it was. Oberas had insisted he wear it. Hardred was the one guarding them. Hardred had told Rion that Oberas never left the shop without a guard. They walked to Tailor Street, to a shop with a sign reading: "Wilton's, Clothier to Gentlemen." There was no picture on the sign. Rion suspected the shop had no interest in serving the needs of any who couldn't read, that they'd not fit their criteria of gentlemen.

They entered the shop, and a little bell set over the door announced their arrival. A young man approached them, eyes flicking quickly over their clothes. Rion saw the disdain in his eyes as he looked at him, and his face flushed darkly.

"How might I assist you, gentles?" he asked Oberas, his tone more haughty than helpful.

"By showing proper respect for my apprentice and fetching Wilton for us; tell him it's Oberas," he said, bluntly, glaring at the man.

The man looked nonplussed, but recovered quickly. "Of course, sir; one moment," he said, walking toward the back of the tailor's shop.

Oberas had noticed the look he'd given him too, Rion realized. But he was astonished Oberas had taken the man to task for it.

An older man came from the back, smiling in the superficial way Rion disliked. "Master Oberas! Welcome, welcome. Please forgive Manfred: he's my sister's boy and has yet to learn his place."

"That's obvious enough. I've a new apprentice, as you can see, Wilton. His name's Alarion. I need proper clothes for him. You're to take his tastes into consideration. He'd not look right in what Kenneth wore. He's not the build for it, yet."

"Of course," Wilton said, turning his artificial smile to Rion. "I've samples of different styles that would be appropriate that I can show you, young sir."

Rion looked at Oberas nervously. "Sir? I don't mean to bother you, but I've never shopped for such things myself. My father and mother picked this shirt for me. I… I'd not want to embarrass you, sir, by picking the wrong thing."

"Wilton knows his business, Alarion. You are to have four acceptable outfits, but I've business of my own up the street. We'll swing by later to pick you up. You're not to leave here without a guard. From now on, while in my service, you are always ever only to travel guarded, understand?" Oberas said sternly.

"Yes, sir," Rion said, swallowing nervously.

Oberas and Hardred left.

"Now, young sir, here are the styles I think might suit you," Wilton said, showing Rion a number of different designs.

Rion looked at the samples in dismay. "Don't you have anything similar to the shirt I'm wearing?" he asked. He began looking at other samples of the tailor's work, asking about the price and properties of the different fabrics. He could tell the tailor was getting quite frustrated with him. He selected fabrics for three different shirts but four pairs of pants, as he already had the one good shirt.

"Master Kenneth always wore what I selected for him," the tailor said in a huff, after trying to talk him into something else for the fifth time. "He was Master Oberas's last apprentice. You'd do well to be as much like him as you can. Master Oberas was quite pleased with him."

"Oh. Well, what is it he wore?" Rion asked, and the tailor again showed him the shirts and pants he'd thought inappropriate. Rion wavered for a moment, then thought of what his father or his mother might say. His eyes welled with tears at the thought of her, and he wiped them angrily away. "No. I've shown you what I want, what I like. Master Oberas said you're to take my tastes into consideration, that I'd not look right in what Kenneth wore, that… that I've not the build for it yet," he said, face flushing darkly.

"Very good," the man said, stiffly.

Rion swallowed, hard. The tailor was showing him no more respect than his nephew had.

The door opened. It was Oberas and Hardred. Rion forced a smile in greeting.

"All finished? Good. Now, show me what the boy's picked, Wilton," Oberas said, after glancing at Alarion.

"Yes sir," Wilton said. "I was hoping you'd want to review his selections. I don't think you'll be at all pleased with them." The two men began discussing the clothes.

Rion stood by Hardred, shifting from foot to foot.

"It can't have been as bad as all that," Hardred said softly, so Oberas wouldn't hear.

Rion's eyes swam with tears, and he fought a sob. "Rion, what did he say to you?" Hardred asked in concern, but Rion just shook his head. If he tried to speak, he knew he'd start crying, and he was trying so desperately not to.

"Alarion, come here," Oberas ordered.

Rion hurried over to him. "Sir?" Rion asked meekly.

"Tell me why you chose this fabric over that one," Oberas commanded.

Rion looked at the two in dismay. "I'm sorry, sir. The other one is fine. Master Wilton suggested it to me several times. As I said, I've no experience in...."

"No, that's not what I told you to do, Alarion. I asked you why you chose this one over the other," Oberas said.

"Yes sir," Rion said, voice trembling. Then he took a deep breath and spoke his mind. "This fabric is stronger, sir. The other would tear far too easily, with the work I was doing yesterday. The color is much better for me as well, the blue matches my eyes, but more importantly, the green is far too light and would show the dirt far too easily. Also, the price, sir; it cost less than half what the other did. I thought the other would have lasted half as long for twice the price, that you'd be spending a fortune in new clothes for me, when you needn't, if I picked better.

"I picked the charcoal gray for the second shirt and the taupe for the third, because they would look good on me as well, and the fabric has the same properties, but also sir, I've noticed you like to wear such bright, flamboyant colors, particularly oranges and yellows, so the colors I chose were more muted. I was concerned the reds and greens might clash strongly, were I to be standing beside you, or at least, detract from the effect of your own wardrobe. I thought that the brass buttons would add brightness enough for me."

"There! What do you say to that, Wilton?" Oberas asked the tailor triumphantly.

Wilton looked at the boy in surprise. "Here I thought you were just being unreasonably stubborn. Why ever didn't you say as much to me?"

Rion swallowed. "I tried to explain the first few times, sir, but you hadn't wanted to listen. I could tell you were annoyed with me, that you thought I was trying to tell you your business, when I really hadn't meant to be at all. I could see my opinion didn't really matter to you," he said, then blushed darkly, afraid he'd said too much.

"I think we can assume he had equally valid reason for choosing as he did with the pants. So then, you have his measurements, you'll make them up exactly as he asked you to, without further complaint to me about it?"

"Of course, Master Oberas. Forgive me for implying otherwise," Wilton demurred. A few moments later their business was done, and Rion followed Oberas into the street, breathing a sigh of relief upon leaving.

Oberas turned to him. "You did very well, Alarion. Far better than I thought you might," he said, then turned from him before he had a chance to respond.

"Thank you, sir," Rion said to his back, stealing a glance at Hardred. Hardred was smiling affectionately at him. He smiled back in return, and this time, his smile wasn't forced at all.

"You'll need new undergarments and socks to go with your fine new clothes and then it's off to the cordwainer. You've need of a fine new pair of boots as well," Oberas said.

"Yes, sir!" Rion said, far more enthusiastic about the boots than he'd been about the clothes.

THE week passed quickly. Rion was kept very busy. He woke at dawn and went to sleep long after dusk, working by oil lamplight well into the night. It became harder each day to wake him. Rion picked up his new clothes the morning of the sixth day. By that afternoon, Rion had fallen asleep four times: twice while doing the inventory, once doing the laundry, and even while sweeping the floor.

Hardred finally confronted Oberas about it. "Sir, you're working Alarion too hard. He's going to hurt himself if this keeps up."

To Hardred's surprise, Oberas nodded. "I know. I've seen it today at least. I was wondering how far I could push him, and I see he's reached his limit. I'd thought he might have complained about it himself by now; we've seen at the tailor's that he's not afraid of speaking his mind, but he hasn't. So tell me, how many nights have you heard him crying in his bed for his mother?"

Hardred looked surprised. "None; I hadn't realized he had been," he said in concern. "From what I've seen, he's been falling asleep quickly and deeply."

Oberas smiled. "Good. I thought maybe he'd been trying to hide it from me, but I can see it's worked as well as I hoped it might. There's nothing worse for grief than idleness, Hardred. It gives you too much time to think and leads to sleepless nights and even illness. Backbreaking labor is the best thing for him right now, but now that I've seen his limits, I'll be able to ease up on him a bit. Don't worry; he'll get his rest, now that I've seen he needs it. I plan to send him to bed early tonight and to let the boy go home to his father tomorrow and spend the day with him; it's Anorion's day off. But it's a surprise, so don't tell Alarion. I plan to do so myself tonight, at dinner."

"That's different then. Forgive me for saying something, then," Hardred said.

"No, I won't. It pleases me you're taking such interest in the boy, Hardred. I want you to feel you can speak to me about him any time you feel the need. Not that I'll necessarily follow your advice, mind you, but I'll at least listen to it. Alarion's a fine lad. I'd not want to harm him when I'm meaning to help him," Oberas said.

"I'm very glad I impressed you as much as I did, that you asked me to work for you, sir. I've never had a finer employer than you," Hardred said sincerely. "And you know me well enough by now to know that's not an idle compliment," he added, at the look upon Oberas's face.

"Yes, that I do," Oberas conceded. "Back to work, Hardred," Oberas said, gruffly.

Hardred smiled. "Yes, sir."

When Oberas told Alarion that he'd be spending the next day with his father, he received a grin in return for the news. "Thank you, sir!" Rion said effusively, four different times, before Oberas finally ordered him to stop thanking him.

THE following morning, Rion was awakened at dawn and he and Hardred cooked breakfast for Oberas, as usual, but then he was told he could leave for home, that he'd have the rest of the day to spend with his father. He was to return to the shop after dinner, to sleep. Oberas told him Hardred would escort him to his father's house, but that he'd trust his father to escort him back, as he was a City Guard, and from what he had seen and heard, a competent one. "Remember, you are never to walk about the City without a guard, understood?" Oberas asked.

"Yes, sir," Rion said sincerely.

Rion fidgeted in his new clothes on his way home to his father. He was wearing his new blue shirt and black pants and boots. It felt odd as well, having Hardred escort him as his personal guard, as if he were a rich merchant himself, or a lord, although he was certainly glad for the company.

He was surprised by how many people took interest in him out on the street, some looking at him in respect, others in curiosity, some in obvious resentment, and still others as if they were wolven and he a deer. He could tell those last were assessing whether it might be worth the risk to check and see if he had a full purse to go with his fine clothes. Hardred always noticed the latter. A simple move of his hand to his sword hilt and a single stare, and they'd turn away, without disturbing them. To Rion's surprise and embarrassment, there was even a pair of girls walking with their father who eyed him appreciatively, giggling and blushing prettily. Rion squirmed even more.

Oberas had told him he should look straight ahead as he walked, that he needed to develop a certain aloofness to those around him, that it was a mistake to make eye contact. Oberas said it invited beggars and thieves and all sorts of unwanted attentions. He'd tried to do it, but he liked looking at people. It didn't feel right, pretending they weren't there, or that they somehow weren't as important as he was. Still, Oberas expected it of him. He decided to practice it again.

He walked two whole City blocks without looking at a single face. He saw Hardred tense, then relax, as a group of three torsos with six legs between them headed purposefully toward him.

"Rion? Is that truly you? I scarcely recognized you!" a familiar voice said, from almost in front of him.

"I told you it was him!" another said simultaneously.

"You would have walked right on past him!" chided another.

Rion eagerly shifted his eyes upward at the familiar voices. "Ric, Matt, Drew!" he called out, excited to see his friends. Rion realized Hardred must have already recognized them as his friends, from near the tank before Feast Day.

Ric scowled at him. "For a moment there, I was afraid you might just snub us, that you'd walk right on by, even if we called out to you. Just what is your Master teaching you, not to talk to your friends, anymore, that sons of the City Guard aren't good enough for you?" he asked sourly.

"No, of course not," Rion said, his welcoming smile faltering on his face, surprised and hurt by Ric's words. He'd been so happy to see them! He felt the start of tears. He cried so easily, now, with Mother gone. At the thought, his eyes shone more wetly, even as he fought to keep the tears at bay.

"That was fine work, idiot. Now you've made him cry," Matt said in concern.

"Don't mind Ric, Rion, you know what an ass he can be," Drew said, his hand going to Rion's shoulder. "He's just jealous of you, that's all, seeing you in such fancy clothes. Have you been all right?"

"Of course," Rion said, forcing a smile. "I'm all right, really I am. I've been kept too busy to think about things, much. Mother, I mean. I think about the three of you all the time. You've no idea how much I've been missing you."

"Elmoth, Rion! Drew's right. I forgot for a moment... well, you know.... Will you forgive me?" Ric asked, his hand going to Rion's other shoulder.

Rion smiled at him in relief, the smile genuine this time. "Of course! Oh, Ric, Matt, Drew, this is Hardred. You remember, from... from the tank, before Feast Day."

Hardred smiled at them and they smiled back.

"So where are you off to, dressed so fine?" Matt asked.

Rion blushed. "To see my father; I've the whole day off to spend with him. It's a surprise. Oberas told me that Father's off shift today. I hadn't known that, but he had.

"Oberas isn't nearly so bad as people say he is," Rion confided. "Difficult to please sometimes, and strict of course, but not mean-spirited. He yells a lot, but he's just sort of loud in general, very forceful, it's just his way. He's not raised a hand to me once, yet, although he's not been angry with me yet. I've not given him cause to. But I don't think he ever might, though of course he has the right to. I've always thought that it's wrong that a Master can beat you, that it's all right as long as he stops short of killing you," he said, shuddering.

"They don't beat you in the City Guard," Ric said. "I'd not want to be an apprentice to anybody."

"Do you think you might have some time to spend with us later?" Drew asked.

"Of course!" Rion said. "How about you stop by my house in the afternoon?"

"Done!" Drew said, holding up two fingers to conclude the bargain. Rion grinned and touched his own to them.

"We'll see you later, then," Matt said.

Rion smiled at them as they left and began heading again toward home, his heart lighter again. He no longer tried not to look at the people he passed. It just wasn't right for him not to. He reached the familiar green door and knocked.

A moment later a voice called out, "Who's there?" The smile fell from his face, to be replaced by a look of concern. "Uncle Farion? What are you doing here so early, when Father's off shift? Is Father all right?" he asked through the closed door, his heart hammering in sudden fear.

"Alarion?" his uncle asked, as the door opened. His eyes widened when he saw him. "My, don't you look fine!" Then seeing his expression, he clapped him on the shoulder. "Your father's fine, Alarion, he's just asked me to stay with him a while, that's all. I was just starting the kakla to brew." Farion turned and called out loudly, toward the stairs, "Anorion, you have a visitor come to call!"

"What, so early? I'll be down in a moment," his father's voice called back wearily.

A moment later, Rion saw his father's feet and then legs appear. He didn't even wait until he saw his face. He ran for the stairs and up them and launched himself onto his father. "Father!" he cried, hugging him.

"Alarion!" his father called in surprise, sitting back hard on the stairs. "You almost knocked me from the stairs," he scolded gently. "Whatever are you doing here? Is everything all right?"

"I've come to visit. I've the whole day to spend with you. Oberas told me I could!" Rion said eagerly.

His father smiled at him in joy for a moment, but then his face clouded over again in pain. "I've missed you fiercely," he said, hugging him tightly.

"I've missed you too, Father. I was worried when I saw Farion. I'd forgotten you'd asked him to stay with you," Rion said.

They walked down the last few steps together, arms around each other's waists.

"Hardred, isn't it? Would you like some kakla?" Anorion asked.

"No, sir, I can't, I'm working," he said, smiling. "If Master Alarion will dismiss me, I'll head back to the shop now," Hardred said, grinning as he prompted Rion.

"Oh! Of course. You're dismissed, Hardred. My father will see me safely back to the shop tonight. Did I say that right?"

"Almost. Next time, don't mention my name, then it's just fine," Hardred said, grinning at him. "Now I'll speak out of turn. Have a good time, Rion. I'll see you tonight," he said, grinning, and then headed for the door.

Farion locked it after him. "Hardred's a fine man. Now, you must tell us all about this past week, over breakfast."

Rion grinned. "Of course! I didn't eat anything at the shop. I was too anxious to be coming here, though I was sure not to rush Hardred. We eat together, me and the guards, in the kitchen," he said, as he begun to tell his father and uncle all about his apprenticeship.

THE day passed all too quickly, both happy and bittersweet. It was hard, being home and not seeing his mother there, where she belonged. It helped, at first, when his friends came by. But his father insisted on walking with them to the Market; he said he'd not let his son walk around dressed so fine without someone to guard him, that he might too easily be robbed or even held for ransom. Rion started to argue but then remembered that he'd promised Oberas exactly that.

He managed to have fun with his friends anyway, despite the odd looks he received for walking with the other boys, who were obviously "inferior" to him. They'd felt just as odd about it. He parted company with them and headed back home earlier than he'd meant to. Farion had gone out while they were away, for his shift. It was just him and his father for dinner. Then it was time to head back to the shop. His father escorted him.

At the door, Rion hugged him tightly. "I'll see you again when I can, Father, though I don't know when that might be. I love you."

"I love you, too, Alarion," his father said, and then he knocked on the door.

"Who's there?" Alnas called out.

"It's Rion."

The door opened, and Alnas grinned at him. "Welcome home, Master Alarion!"

Rion felt a flash of panic. Home? This wasn't his home! Home was with Father, with Mother. He forced his face calm. "Goodnight, Father!" His father nodded, eyes bright, then turned and left quickly. Rion fought not to call out to him.

"Rion? Are you all right?" Alnas asked, concerned.

Rion nodded and then ran for his room, unable to stem the tide of tears now that his father was gone. He ran inside, closed the door then flung himself onto his bed, sobbing.

A moment later there was a gentle knock. "Rion? Rion, it's me, Hardred. Can I come in?"

Rion couldn't answer. He was crying so violently he couldn't speak. He heard the door open, then close again, and felt someone sit upon the bed beside him. "Rion," Hardred said, gently. Rion flung himself into Hardred's arms, sobbing wildly.

HARDRED held him and rocked him and soothed him, remembering all too vividly his sister holding him and rocking him like this, so many months ago, when he should have been the one trying to comfort her. The lad was homesick, that much was obvious, though it wasn't clear how much of it was for the mother he'd lost and how much for the father he'd just parted from. Hardred held him and talked softly to him, doing his best to comfort him.

At one point he heard the door open and he looked up. It was Oberas. Oberas watched them for a moment and then closed the door again, without a word. After a while, Hardred said, "You're tired, Rion. Here, let's take your boots off. It's time for bed."

"No, not sleep, I can't!" Rion said, the weary crying replaced by a fresh burst of hysterical tears.

"All right. But at least let me take your boots off," Hardred said, reaching down and gripping his boot, slipping it off, then his other. Then he held him again.

A long while later, Rion finally cried himself to sleep in his arms. When Hardred was sure Rion was asleep, he laid him gently back upon the pillow and tucked the blanket up around his chin. Then he dimmed the oil lamp and left the room, heading for the kitchen.

"It's about time. How is he?" Oberas asked. There was a glass bottle of oushka on the table beside a single glass, and it was obvious Oberas had partaken freely of it.

"He's homesick and still in mourning for his mother," Hardred said, eyeing the bottle of oushka wistfully. "Sir, I've not been on duty for some time now. If it's all right with you, I'd like to go out drinking. Alnas has early shift tomorrow and I'll not be late for my own." Seeing Rion's grief had brought his own sharply back. Julian's face was haunting him, his voice, the sound of the waves, the feel of his hands being torn away.

"Nonsense. I'll not let you out to drink, upset as you are. You'll stay here where it's safe and do your drinking. I'll do mine in my room," Oberas said, lifting the bottle and glass. He pulled a flask from the cupboard and handed it to him. "This flask cost me a gold. I'll sell it to you at cost. That's far less than a tavern would charge you for it. I'll dock it from your pay. Save the rest, in your room, for when you've need of it," Oberas said. Then he abruptly turned and left.

Hardred sighed. He'd not wanted to drink alone out here or in his room. He'd not wanted to drink alone anywhere. Devrik was on duty tonight, though, and Alnas had early shift tomorrow, although Oberas usually matched their shifts with one another, so they could work together and spend their free time together. But since they'd be staying in the shop, Alnas might drink with him, a little. He might keep him company, at least. Hardred desperately needed Alnas's company. The waters had risen, suddenly and violently, and were threatening to close about his head again. He went to his room, the flask and two small metal cups in hand.

OBERAS poured another glass and downed it quickly, cursing. He shouldn't have chosen the glass bottle: the liquor was far too fine. It had fire, but only as a comfortable hearth does, not the raging inferno he needed.

It was the tears that had done it: Alarion's fair face torn by anguish. He never should have chosen Alarion. He was far too pretty, like Terhannon, like Kenneth. Kenneth had at least lived. He'd not drunk like this since the night he'd gotten Kenneth back from those evil men who'd taken him for ransom, only a month after he'd first started his apprenticeship.

They'd have killed Kenneth, he knew, had he not escaped from them. They'd have killed him, too, once he delivered the ransom to them; he knew that, but he'd have done it anyway. He'd have done anything to try to save that boy. It was his fault Kenneth had been taken. He'd let him leave the shop unguarded. Kenneth had only just been going down the street; he'd not thought it dangerous. The boy should only have been gone for a few moments.

Oberas shuddered at the memory. They'd seen Kenneth, those horrible men, in his fine clothes, all alone. They'd abducted him in broad daylight, right off the street. They'd carried him off to a storeroom. They'd forced him to tell them who he belonged to, so they could ransom him. But they'd not been content at the thought of taking the coin. They'd taken the boy, as well. They forced themselves upon him, brutalized and beat him, all six of them, careful only not to mar his pretty face in case Oberas had insisted upon seeing him before surrendering the coin to them.

They'd thought him unconscious, left him poorly guarded. Kenneth had worn through the ropes, stacked the crates, and climbed out through the window high above him, falling into the alleyway, and then dragged himself along it to the street. A woman had screamed, and the City Guard had come running. But those evil bastards, those men who'd done it, had never been found; they'd gotten away.

For months afterward, Kenneth would awaken screaming from his nightmares, from his memories. He refused to leave the shop, no matter how well guarded. He'd cowered when anyone touched him, no matter how gently, and started sobbing if anyone spoke too harshly to him.

Oberas would have sent the boy back to his parents, had he any, but he'd been living with his aunt and she'd married as soon as he was out of the house and left Ardock for Logareth. Her new husband was a merchant from there; they'd met while he was on caravan. So Oberas had cared for Kenneth, as best as he was able. Kenneth recovered from it, finally. Oberas still remembered the first smile he'd seen upon his face, nearly a year later.

Kenneth had loved him, blindly, for the care he'd taken of him, like Terhannon before him, but for a far different reason, a far different kind of love. Kenneth had loved him in place of the father he'd never known. Terhannon had loved him as a wife might have, were he ever to want one. He never would. He and Terhannon had been *lythenia*. He'd never love another, not like that. His heart had died with Terhannon.

Kenneth refused to acknowledge it was Oberas's fault he'd been harmed, that he'd all but died because of him, that for a time his spirit had. Every day Oberas had spent with Kenneth had been torture, knowing he was to blame for his torment.

Now Kenneth was in Seaview. He was prospering, thriving. He even had a wife, now, and a babe on the way, when Oberas never thought he might, after all that had been done to him. Kenneth had sent letters to him, but he'd not answered any of them, not yet. He'd not known what to say.

Oberas had tried to find another apprentice after Kenneth. But each of them reminded him too much of him. They were all so young, so vulnerable. He realized he'd driven two of them away and found excuses for ridding himself of the other two. He never should have taken Alarion in. His mother was dead, but he still had a father. He could force the boy to leave his service.

No, no, he couldn't. His father was a City Guard. If the boy lost his apprenticeship, his father might not try to find him another. He'd grow up to be a City Guard, then, small and gentle and friendly as he was. He'd never last as a City Guard. He'd be hurt, killed, all too easily. Oberas remembered Terhannon's blank-eyed stare, before they'd closed his eyes for good. His beautiful face, as he lay in the hole they'd dug for him, the sight of the first of the dirt covering it.

Oberas howled in anguish, grabbed the bottle, and began drinking from it, chugging the liquor down as if it were mead. He glared at the empty bottle and threw it, shattering it against his wall, the force of the throw unbalancing him so that he crashed to the floor. He'd warned his guard not to enter, and they didn't. He lay panting on the floor, too drunk to rise.

Finally, blessedly, the drink took him, and he passed out upon the floor.

"RION, it's time to get up," Alnas said, shaking him gently and yawning as he did so. He hated to have to wake Rion. Alnas was glad he'd asked Devrik to waken him. He'd been up late into the night, drinking and talking with Hardred, though Hardred did most of the drinking and he'd done most of the talking. Elmoth, he was tired, and worried about Hardred.

"FATHER?" Rion said, then his face flushed. "Oh, Alnas. Is it morning? Thank you, I'm up now." He flushed darker as he realized he'd slept in his clothes. His face felt stiff from all the dried tears upon it. He didn't know how he'd be able to face Hardred.

He washed and dressed quickly in his gray shirt and navy pants, then headed to the kitchen to begin making breakfast. He took special care with the eggs, since Hardred wasn't there to help him. Still, he could tell he'd all but ruined them. And he'd managed to burn the sausage this time, for his concern over the eggs, though the potatoes looked all right. He fervently hoped Oberas wouldn't yell at him for it. He was afraid he might start to cry again if he did.

He was surprised and a little worried when Oberas didn't appear for breakfast as he normally did. "Perhaps I'd better go wake him," Rion said hesitantly.

"No, Rion, I think you'd best let him sleep. He was up drinking last night," Alnas explained.

"Drinking?" Rion asked in surprise.

Alnas looked sheepish. "Hardred was as well, though not with Oberas. I'm the one who kept Hardred company. They were both worried about you."

"Worried about me? They were drinking because of me?" Rion asked, shocked.

"Not exactly. I think it was just seeing you so sad reminded them of sadness of their own," Alnas tried to explain.

Rion looked distressed, and Alnas sighed. "You're not to blame, Rion. You've enough of your own troubles. I'm glad to see you're looking better. Hardred told me how upset you were."

"I didn't mean to cry like that. It's just… I'd been so busy before, I'd not had time to think about it, but yesterday, being back home, seeing Father and my friends…." Rion felt a lump in his throat and the tears coming again.

"Come have some breakfast, Rion," Alnas encouraged.

"No. I'm not hungry, really, and there's so much to do. There's that restock and inventory Oberas was working on. I think I'll begin on that. I'm pretty sure I know what he wants done with it." He headed for the new stack of crates. He picked up the pry bar, glad the crates were still sealed, setting to them with a vengeance.

A LONG while later, Rion wiped the sweat from his brow and went to the table and cleared the uneaten breakfast from it. He set about making lunch. Neither Oberas nor Hardred had shown themselves yet. He made beef hash, the way his mother had taught him, hoping it was something Oberas might not mind eating. At least it was something he knew how to cook that might be edible when he did. Normally Oberas told him what to make.

The shop bell rang, and Rion took the pan off the stove, covering it so the food would neither burn nor get cold. He dipped a towel in the washbasin and washed his hands and face quickly with it, then headed to the front room, mindful not to run.

Alnas was speaking to someone.

"Master Wilton!" Rion said in surprise, recognizing the tailor. "How might I serve you, sir?"

The tailor eyed Rion. "I'm looking for Master Trader Oberas. Your guard here tells me he's out."

Rion was glad Alnas was the one who'd lied to him. He'd never been good at lying. "Perhaps I might help you, sir? I can at least give him a message for you."

The tailor eyed him from head to toe. "I can see now why you insisted upon the more rugged fabric. You are indeed rough on your clothes, Apprentice Alarion."

"I was opening crates, sir. Forgive my appearance," Rion said sheepishly.

"It's because of you I'm here, actually," Wilton said, and Rion fought not to show his dismay.

To his surprise, the man smiled at him, a genuine smile this time. "Don't worry. I've not come to get you in trouble with your Master; quite the opposite, actually. When you were in my shop, going over my fabrics so intently, you found fault with the quality and price of some of them, comparing them to ones your Master had.

"This morning my supplier had only half of the selection I had ordered and informed me he was raising his prices yet again. I've worked with him for years, but I've not been pleased with the fellow for some time now. He has begun to take my business for granted. I thought I might take a look at what your Master has and see whether I might perhaps be better pleased by him."

"Oh! I'll certainly give him the message. Although if you would like, sir, I can show you the fabrics we currently have in stock; I've been spending all week working on them. You'd need to speak with Master Oberas directly, regarding price and quantity, if any of them please you, of course, but at least you'd feel the trip here was more fruitful," Rion said.

The tailor eyed him speculatively. "Very well; show me your wares, then, Apprentice."

Rion fought his nervousness. Perhaps he should have waited for Oberas? Well, it was too late now. He took the tailor to the shelves where the rolls of fabric were. "If you'll tell me what it is you are looking for, by color or fabric type, I will pull it for you, sir."

Wilton began listing a number of different types, as Rion listened intently. He stopped. "Aren't you going to write this down?"

"No sir, I'll just remember it. Afterward, once you've ideas of what you'd like, I'll write it down for Master Oberas."

The tailor eyed him skeptically. "Very well; now, where was I?"

"On the third cabinet, sir, the second shelf from the top, the navy blue wool," Rion said.

"Yes, that's... how in Aralyn's name do you know I was going according to cabinets or which one?" the tailor asked in surprise.

"Because I saw them, sir, remember? You showed almost all your stock to me, I think, or at least everything you had in blue, once you saw my mind was set upon it. I'd wanted to ask you, sir, but hadn't wanted to annoy you further than I already was. Whyever do you keep the gray silk beside the navy blue wool? I really didn't understand your system of organization," he said, quickly adding, "although I could tell it made perfect sense to you." He hoped he'd not just insulted him.

"I always match bolts of linings to outer fabrics that way, so the customer can picture it more easily. The rolls in the back are organized by fabric type and color, as you no doubt expected to see them. I can see I must have perplexed you nearly as much as you frustrated me," he added, smiling.

Rion's face flushed in embarrassment. "Not at all, sir. I'm terribly inexperienced, that's all. I'd never been to a tailor before. Until this week, I knew very little about fabric, actually," he admitted, then blushed again. "Oh, but I am learning, sir. I know I'm far from knowledgeable yet, but I am at least beginning to understand the basics."

"You sell yourself short, lad. Had you not told me, I'd never have guessed you hadn't been dealing in fabrics for years. I'd have thought your mother a seamstress for you to have.... Aralyn, boy, what's wrong?" he asked, as Rion's eyes filled with sudden tears.

"Oh, forgive me, sir! It's just... my mother, she passed away two weeks ago. I've been fine, really, it's just I was just back to see my father, yesterday, and it's made it all very vivid, again."

"You needn't apologize, then, lad. My father died when I was a lad of eight. I know what it's like, to lose a parent. I'm not in such a hurry as I'd continue to trouble you when you are so upset."

"Oh, no, please, sir! Working helps—it takes my mind off of it. We'd just seemed to have developed a rapport, sir. I'd not want to lose that. You're my first customer, you see, although I suppose I shouldn't have told you that. Unless, I can understand if I'm doing a poor job at it and you'd rather wait for Master Oberas," he ventured.

"Not at all. I'm quite comfortable speaking with you, Young Gentle, far more comfortable than I have ever been speaking with your Master, actually, although please don't tell him so. I can't imagine why I told you that. I'd certainly not want to risk insulting him and losing his business."

"Oh, no, sir! I know you meant well by it."

"Then let us continue, shall we? I believe we were up to the third cabinet, the navy wool?" Wilton said, smiling.

Rion smiled back at him and continued listening intently. Then he began showing Wilton their stock, extolling the virtues of each type of fabric.

THE tailor had only left a few moments earlier, and Rion had just begun writing what they'd discussed, when Oberas bellowed. "Alarion! Where's the kakla?"

Rion jumped, spilling the ink, and righted the inkwell, blotting at the puddle, snatching the paper away, before it was damaged by it. "Coming, sir," he said, taking the cloth with him and wiping the ink from his hands.

"Look at you, boy! How have you gotten so dirty?" Oberas roared.

"I'm sorry, sir. I opened the crates we'd gotten in yesterday and had started to unload them," Rion said, swallowing. He'd never dreamt Oberas could look so angry.

"Unloading? Were you inventorying them as well?" Oberas asked sharply.

"No, sir. I mean, I plan to, but I'd not had a chance yet, sir," Rion explained.

"Then why is there ink all over your hands?" Oberas challenged, glaring at them.

"I spilled it, sir, when you called me just now. I was writing up Master Wilton's order and you startled me, sir. I was concentrating," Rion said, realizing how clumsy he'd seem.

"What order? What are you blathering about? You mean the order we gave him? He's filled it already. Why would you write it?" Oberas asked as if Rion were stupid.

"I wasn't, sir," Rion said desperately. "I mean, I was writing the order for the fabric. I suppose order isn't quite the right word, as he's not agreed to buy anything yet of course. He can't, until you negotiate the prices with him. I was hesitant to mention prices to him. I didn't want to quote any that might be too low, or too high."

Oberas held both hands to his temple. "Stop! I need kakla, without the sweet cream. Make sure it's hot enough to burn my tongue upon, understand?"

"Yes, sir," Rion said, swallowing, hurrying for the kitchen.

Rion returned a short while later with a steaming mug and set it before Oberas. "I've made lunch as well, sir, if you're hungry. I'd just need to heat it, I...."

"Lunch?" Oberas growled. "What about breakfast?"

"I'd made that too, sir, but that was a while ago. It's afternoon, sir, so I took the liberty of making beef hash for lunch. I've no idea if you like it, but I'd not done very well making breakfast without Hardred to aid me and I know how to make the hash and...."

"Silence! Not another word until I ask you for one!" Oberas roared.

Rion nodded mutely, wide-eyed.

OBERAS exhaled and tasted the kakla. It was scalding hot and dark. He drank it gingerly, until he felt calm enough to speak without yelling. He could see the boy was nervous, but at least he wasn't trembling. He wasn't afraid of him. "Now then. Tell me about your morning, from when you awoke."

"Yes, sir," Rion said, relieved to see Oberas had mastered his anger. He told him everything, about the shipment he'd uncrated first, and then about Master Wilton's visit and the result of it.

"Do you have any idea how long it usually takes for an apprentice to speak to a customer, even with me standing there beside him?" Oberas asked.

"No, sir," Rion said meekly.

"Six months to a year, depending on the boy. Three years, before I trust one to speak to one without me standing there beside him. You've been here just over a single week!" Oberas said, flabbergasted.

"Yes, sir," Rion said in a small voice.

Oberas eyed him incredulously. "Thirty-six rolls? He wants to purchase thirty-six rolls? And he told you we'd become his main supplier if they pleased him? Do you have any idea what you've done, boy?"

"No, sir," Rion said tremulously.

"I have been trying to get that old goat to buy from me for the entire twenty years I've been getting my tailoring from him! At least once a year I try to sway him. You say he came to us for your criticizing his stock? I've been complaining about it to him for two decades, for all the good it's done me!"

"Yes, sir. He mentioned that to me, sir," Rion said. Wilton had also told him that Oberas had the worst fashion sense of anyone he had ever met, that the color choices he forced upon him to craft clothes for him were enough to make his eyes bleed, that Oberas often brought his own fabric to him for tailoring, because he would not be caught dead having such garish colors in his shop, and a few other choice things, but Rion had sworn he'd not reveal any of that to Oberas.

Instead he said, "He was quite impressed with the Thenalonese silks, sir, for the brightness of the hues, particularly the blues and greens, which he favors," he added quickly, for what Wilton had said of the orange and yellow fabrics Oberas obviously favored. "It was fortunate you'd told me so much about them. I was able to sound far more knowledgeable about them than I otherwise might have."

"Tell me, then, from what you've learned this past week of prices and what you think he might tolerate, how much you would charge for each of the rolls you've listed to me," Oberas said. "No, don't tell me, write the list you'd begun and write the prices on a separate paper, with the same spacing, so I can place the two side by side and they line up correctly."

"Yes, sir!" Rion said eagerly. He returned to the table in the back and wrote out the list of what the tailor had been interested in purchasing, then the prices he would charge. He thought long and hard about them, keeping in mind the prices he'd seen at the tailor's shop as well as the figures Oberas had quoted earlier in the week. Then he wrote a third list, of fabrics the tailor had mentioned he would like to see in the future. He returned to Oberas with all three lists.

To his surprise, he saw Oberas was eating the hash he'd made for lunch. One of the guards must have heated it for him; he could see the steam rising from it. Oberas held out his hand. "Give me only the list of what he's planning to order and pen and ink. Don't give me the price list yet."

Rion gave him the list and went back for the pen and ink and gave it to him. To his embarrassment, his stomach started to growl. He'd not had the stomach for breakfast before, but the smell of the hash was making him hungry. Oberas seemed not to have heard, at least. He began writing prices next to the list.

When he'd finished Oberas said, "Now hand me your list of prices," and Rion did so.

Oberas lined the two sheets up and started comparing. He grunted and slid the two to Rion. "Take a look," he said.

Rion did so. To his embarrassment, he saw that he had been ready to charge the tailor ten to fifteen percent more per roll than Oberas had. He knew that might well mean he'd have lost his business. He'd been so sure he'd judged the prices correctly!

Rion looked up, discouraged. To his astonishment, Oberas was looking at him proudly. "You've done well, boy. Remarkably, in fact. The prices I show take into account a ten percent discount I'm giving him for ordering more than thirty rolls, and I mean to tell him as much. You were within five percent of the pricing I'd suggest without the discount on all but three of them, and square on the mark on twenty-four of the thirty-six. If you learn the other parts of my business as well as you're learning the fabrics, you'll do quite well indeed. As long as you understand you are never again to speak to a customer without my permission."

"Yes, sir!" Rion said brightening.

"Good. Now, lunch has been edible, at least. Why don't you go inside the kitchen and get your own? I've heard your stomach complaining. I know you're in need of it," Oberas said.

Rion blushed and went to the kitchen to eat.

A short while later Hardred emerged from his room looking grim and sad. Rion blushed darkly upon seeing him. "Forgive me for last night, Hardred. I feel like such a child!"

Hardred shook his head. "You are a child. And you've lost someone you love, Rion. You've every right to mourn her."

"But I'm sorry I got you so upset by it. I had no idea I might! That's the last thing I'd ever want to do. It helps to talk, Hardred. Alnas is worried about you," Rion added. "He hasn't said so, of course, but I can see he is."

Hardred sighed. "I warned Alnas he'd yet to see me at my worst. I've still yet to show him. I couldn't sink so far, last night, for his company. How was breakfast?" he asked, changing the subject. "Did Oberas find too much fault with it?"

"No, but only because he didn't eat it," Rion admitted and then grinned. He began to tell Hardred all that had happened, and to his joy, Hardred smiled hearing it. "Well done, Rion. Very well done. I couldn't be prouder of you were you my own son."

Rion's eyes welled with tears at that, but in joy. "You were father enough to me last night, Hardred," he said, then blushed again.

Hardred was moved to hear him say so and pleased he'd helped him. He smiled affectionately at Rion.

"I should have known!" said Alnas, coming in from the main room of the shop. "I spend half the night with Hardred without noticeable effect, and you have him smiling within a few moments," Alnas complained happily, seeming incredibly relieved to see it.

Rion laughed at the look Hardred gave him.

"Oh well. I've not eaten yet and I hear you make a decent hash," Alnas said, heading for the pan.

Rion grinned and got out two more plates. He'd been worried before that Oberas might not have been pleased with him, but now he felt sure he'd be able to do well for him.

Chapter 10

Amongst the Elves

LUNAHR fingered the mountain dulcimer lovingly. His own, much as he missed it, paled in comparison to this one, as did all the works of Man, when compared to those crafted by the Elves. He had chosen a secluded spot, an isolated one, so that he might play under the sun and trees yet not draw attention to himself.

He had yet to hear Elven music played by Elves. The only Elf he had ever heard sing was Eladar, though he already knew a total of thirty-two Elven songs, from before he'd ever heard an Elf sing. He'd learned them from a book which had been gifted to Laren when he first began negotiations with the Elves of Erenia. To Laren's frustration, they had insisted he learn all of them, before they would deign to speak with him further.

Lunahr had eagerly helped Laren learn them. It was Arcanus who had been able to translate their musical scale into the one with which he was familiar, so he might be able to read them. He smiled at the memory but then sighed wistfully.

Laren had not sung since the negotiations began, and they had concluded years ago. And no one here would play when the Queen herself could not, not until she and the Crown Prince were fully healed. But Elanara had finally given him permission to play today at breakfast, as his guardian and for her station. She had that right. She had seen the desperation in his eyes, after having lived here an entire week without music. He had felt as if he was going mad, even though he had spent the entire time ensconced in his chambers, composing.

He had been thoroughly enchanted with his chambers. True to his word, Eladar had provided him with one of every instrument his people possessed, though he had apologetically explained that he would not be able to play them yet. Lunahr would have been content to instead spend the time with Eladar, if he could have, but he and Elanara were both burdened by their official duties, which had increased exponentially while their parents tended to Elavar.

But now, at long last, he had been given permission to play. He closed his eyes as his fingers caressed the strings, and his heart filled with joy, finally at peace, with the first sweet notes.

The last note faded to quiet, and he opened his eyes and blushed darkly. He was surrounded by Elves; there were dozens of them all around him. He was astonished to find they were not glaring at him, nor did they look disapproving. Instead they looked hungry, starving, but not for food. They had been drawn to him as moths to a flame.

"Please, Minstrel! The Princess told us we might find you here. She said that you would play for us, when we cannot. We had not dreamt we might more than tolerate it. We had thought anything that might bear some semblance to music would be better than none. We are astonished that a Man might know how to create such beauty. We have had ample reason to think ill of your kind. Play us another melody, Minstrel?" a male Elf asked hopefully.

"Of course. I have one I think you might find equally astonishing. I would first hear what you think of it before I reveal it to you." Lunahr tuned his instrument far differently and changed his style of play completely and began. When he was done, he looked at them expectantly.

"I can scarcely believe it is the same instrument! Tell me, what is it called? What master of music amongst Men has written such a piece, that we might praise him for it? Seldom has my heart been so moved," another Elf said.

Lunahr grinned. "It was not a Man at all. What I have just played you is Dwarven. It is a courtship song. I learned it in the Dwarven Lands."

"Dwarven? Truly? But they are so base! I had not known they understood the concept of music or of courtship!" another said surprised, and some of the others laughed. Then he sighed. "It is a great pity you are not yet of age, Minstrel, nor am I, for I would enjoy teaching you some courtship songs with which I am familiar."

Lunahr's face flushed, and his heart started to hammer. One of the other Elves scowled at the one who had spoken and reprimanded him harshly, leading him from the fountain.

Lunahr felt suddenly self-conscious. "Perhaps I had better stop," he said. But immediately he was overwhelmed by voices denying it.

"No, you cannot, not after only two songs!" one said.

"I cannot live another moment without hearing such beauty! I will go mad!" another said.

"Play for us, Minstrel. We have been withering. You cannot deny us what might sustain us," a third said.

Lunahr hesitated. Perhaps Elanara had an ulterior motive for allowing him to play? She had told these people that he would be here. They were those who seemed to need music as he did, as much as the others needed the River to live. This way, they might find their need fulfilled without insult to the

Queen or her family. Elven politics and ritual were both incredibly complex, far beyond anything he yet understood. "Then certainly, I shall play more," he said, and the crowd instantly stilled and awaited his next song in breathless anticipation.

JUST before dusk, Elanara came down to the fountain and listened with the rest of Lunahr's audience. Then she made her way to Lunahr as his current song was ending. She looked at his hands intently and was greatly relieved. She had feared they might be bleeding, now; his hands were so delicate, and he had been playing since just after breakfast without a break, she suspected, and the sun was about to set.

"Beryl, you must have dinner with me," she said, loudly enough for the others to hear. "He has my permission to return in the morning, if he wishes it, though tomorrow I think he might sing for you instead, or perhaps play his flute, or both, so that his fingers might be given a chance to rest."

"Thank you, Beryl, for restoring our spirits. Thank you, Highness, for sharing the beauty you guard amongst us," Riverstone said.

LUNAHR smiled at him. He had learned three dozen names today, ones that he could match faces to when he closed his eyes. The coldness of the past week, the loneliness, the despair, had vanished. He had friends here now, in addition to Eladar and Elanara. He had many.

He told Laren eagerly all about each of them over dinner in Eladar's chambers, until Elanara finally had to command him to silence and threaten forbidding him to sing, if he did not eat.

TALON laughed heartily at how quickly Lunahr began eating, tremendously relieved to see it. He had been terribly worried about Lunahr, who had been so forlorn before.

Talon had stayed with Lunahr. He could not yet leave. He knew Elavar should awaken in two days' time, and his mother, Queen Naraena, would be recovered perhaps a few days afterward. King Laranela had not left their side. Talon would not leave without seeing all of them.

He forced himself to eat as well, though he had little appetite. He feared with Caramore lost to them, the lean times his people had experienced in the past would pale in comparison to the deprivations they might now face. But he partook of the sumptuous fare mechanically, without tasting it.

He had spent most of the week in the Healers' Hall, supplementing his knowledge of their craft as much as he could, though it would be to little avail in the foreseeable future. With his people scattered amongst all the Cities of Man, he would not be there to tend their injuries or illness. He would be powerless to aid the few that remained. No, he must not think such things, true though they were, lest he fall to despair, and he'd not see Lunahr dragged down with him when he was so happy again.

And Elanara was here also. He was a fool. He was wasting a rare opportunity to speak with her. Resolutely forcing a smile, he turned his attentions to her.

Two Days Later

"TALON, my friend! You are still here! I had heard you had been here, but I had thought you might have left long ago," Elavar said, smiling warmly at him.

"Elavar!" Talon said, clapping his hands upon his friend's shoulders, fighting the urge to hug him, as he would one of his own kin. Elves did not like being touched by Man; he already dared far more contact than was customarily permitted.

"I could not leave without seeing you well again," Talon admitted, his relief all but bringing him to his knees. He released Elavar and continued bravely, knowing Elavar would never allow his touch again. "I could not leave without confessing to you what I did. I won't ask you to forgive me for it, how could you? You will not be able to help but hate me for it. I will confess before your father, as well, though I fear he may well decide to execute me for it."

Elavar looked at him in astonishment. "Surely not! You are a king in your own right, Talon, though you insist upon the title of Prince, to those few of us who know the secret of your birth, though none of us yet know your true name. My father would not dare to act against you. You are favored by Arcanus, Talon. You are under his protection. Even my father would not be so bold as to incur the wrath of the wizard who counsels you."

Talon took a deep breath. "Your sister and brother both now know my name. I had to tell them. Elanara has become guardian to my cousin, Lunahr, known to most as Beryl. Caramore has fallen. Though he has not yet come-of-age, I have named Lunahr Lord of House of Eagles as he is last of his House, and Heir to the Throne, should I fall, if Hunter should not return.

"I would hope that my death might not be at the hands of your people, Elavar, but you know I will do anything to preserve the alliance we have formed with your people. My people cannot hope to stand against our Enemy without your people's aid. If it requires my death to preserve our alliance, then so be it.

"It is my fault you were injured as you were. It is my fault you were almost killed, that your mother almost died saving you," Talon confessed, the admission tearing his heart.

Elavar looked at Talon in consternation. "Surely not! How could you be blamed for that?"

"Those evil men who caught you—we came across one of their traps in the woods, after Eladar met up with us. They had caught an obearn in it: a mother. Her cubs were with her. I wanted to free her. Eladar tried to stop me, but he saw nothing short of killing me might, I was so outraged. I freed the obearn and tended her wounds. Poor Eladar killed a fox to put in the trap in the obearn's place, so the trappers would think it sprang the trap. He had me maul the fox's body with the obearn's claws before I woke her.

"Later, by the River, when Eladar was off by himself trying to recover from what he'd done, four men came upon our camp. They were trappers: Tanran, Sevran, Dustin, and Raymond. Raymond had been mauled by the obearn I freed. He'd nearly died. They'd come to the River hoping to find a boat or caravan and a healer. Fortunately, my skills were sufficient to save Raymond. The trappers told us they were from Lethos, now, that they had been from Terleth originally, the village your father had destroyed for harming Eladar."

Elavar's eyes widened, but he kept silent.

"The one man, Tanran, had been a child when it happened and his brother Sevran not yet born. Their grandfather was one of the twenty-three men killed. Tanran saw him strung up on one of the drying racks, with an arrow through his heart. He watched your people drown his village. And that winter, their middle brother died. Tanran said he starved. He blames your people for that too. He says you kept the game away. He thinks your magic made the snows worse, though I know only a wizard might have done that part of it, if nature didn't.

"Tanran hated you, Elavar, all your people. He told me he wished he could see one of you in a pit fight, against an obearn, on Feast Day. He told me that and I just let him go. I let him walk out of our camp, with his brother Sevran, and they left us and found you and somehow caught you and beat you. They tortured you, and they would have killed you, if Eladar hadn't saved you.

"I'd sensed there was something important I had to find in the City, but I'd no idea where to look. I'd never dreamt it might be you! It's my fault that you almost died, Elavar, that your mother almost died," Talon finished, his voice raw with agony.

Elavar sighed and, to Talon's shock, hugged him. "Talon, brother-of-my-heart, you are wrong! You did not condemn me by freeing the obearn. You saved me, though you will not be able to believe it until I tell you," Elavar said, releasing him from his embrace. "I will tell Eladar and Elanara and my parents as well. They must know all that happened. Neither you nor your people, nor certainly the people of Ardock, must suffer for it.

"I was worried about Eladar, that he was going alone on the mission I should have been given, were it not for Mother's decision. Even then, I would have gone after him when he was first late returning, but she would not let Father allow it. That I went anyway, that I defied my father, my King, that alone is reason you should not be blamed. But there is more.

"Those men had set many traps, not merely the one you found. I was so intent upon looking for signs of Eladar as I traveled along the riverbank, after reading the Marker's message, that I failed to see the trap, the danger. I fell into a pit trap the trappers had constructed. It was over twice as deep as I am tall, and I had fallen poorly. I landed upon a large rock. I broke my shoulder in the fall. The walls were of loose earth, and they crumbled when I tried to climb one-handed. I feared I might bury myself alive. Injured as I was, I could not free myself.

"I was trapped, without the waters of the River to sustain me, without food or even water to drink. I was there for days, slipping in and out of consciousness from the pain, the lack of water. Finally, I awoke to a rope being tied around me, when I was too weak to fight it, too weak to even stand. They pulled me out, beat me, and then they carried me to Ardock, to the docks, to where Eladar found me.

"That is how you saved me, Talon. Had you not freed the obearn, they would have taken her instead, her and her cubs. They would never have checked their other traps. They would never have found me. I would have died in that pit. My people would never have found me in time to save me. They had not even begun to look for me, for my disobedience of my father's commands," Elavar said, clapping his hand upon Talon's shoulder.

"You need not ask my forgiveness. Those men hated me because of what my father did to their kin. Even so, the one, Sevran, was not an evil man. At the end, he tried to save me. I came so close to convincing him to release me, even with only my eyes. Had I not been gagged, all three of us might have been saved.

"I will see that my father understands. You know my mother will. Now come, I have heard even in my sickbed of your cousin's voice. You must introduce me to my sister's ward."

"Then I must instead ask your forgiveness for what I now do," Talon said, and he hugged Elavar. "I thought you lost to me, brother-of-my-heart, even though you lived! I dared not hope you might not be. My heart still aches for what you have suffered, but it also sings, to see you well again, to know that you yet love me."

Elavar smiled at him. "Your embrace I will forgive! Come, on the way to see Lunahr, you must tell me all about your time with Eladar. I have already spoken with him and with Elanara as well. She convinced Father that he had the right to see me. She argued quite fiercely upon his behalf, much to Father's surprise.

"You should have heard Eladar's confession of guilt upon seeing me and his emotional outburst afterward. Yet Elanara tells me he did well upon his mission. I was quite amazed by the pride upon her face from what she told me of it, yet I can scarcely credit that it was truly Eladar she was describing, for his actions were not those of the brother I know!" he said, eyes alight with unvoiced laughter.

"Then it will be my pleasure to enlighten you. He is little like the brother you warned me of, Elavar. He did well indeed. You give him far less credit than he deserves," Talon said, seriously. "It is hard to see those we know only as children grow, to become responsible adults before our eyes. Sometimes we cannot see it, no matter how hard they try to show us. You injure your brother with your words, Elavar. He so desperately wants you to be proud of him."

Elavar looked at Talon in surprise. "But I am proud of him, the times he gives reason for me to be. Surely he must know it?"

"From what I have heard, you are free with your criticism when he does wrong. I am sure you mean it constructively. But he seldom if ever hears a word of praise to balance against it. He feels that nothing he does is enough. You crush his spirit, Elavar. You wound his heart," Talon said, and then sighed.

"I can say such things, because he is not my brother. After speaking with Eladar, I fear Lunahr might feel the same. I think back upon all the words I have spoken to him on our trip here, and I wonder if he realizes how much I love him, how proud I am of him. I will tell him tonight; I must be sure he knows. It will be many long, lonely years until he might be with us again, as lonely for us as for him.

"He is our heart, Elavar. How are we to go on without him beside us? A single smile of his lights the room, a song brightens the most dreary of days. He is our last child. We are dying. There are so few women left. None I might name as Queen."

ELAVAR sighed. Eladar had told him Talon had smiled, more than once, that he had even laughed. He had so hoped he might see it. "Then perhaps it is time to look outside your own people. There are many Cities of Men, Talon, and a number of them have kings, many with daughters. Surely there must be some princess or noblewoman somewhere whom you might seek as a wife?"

Talon smiled, but only in that sardonic, self-deprecating way Elavar had seen in the past. "And what would I have to offer such a bride? A kingdom without lands, without treasure, without even people, but with a powerful enemy? Only a madman might betroth his daughter to a prince from such a kingdom," he said sadly.

TALON felt the darkness beginning to close around him again. Meditate, he must find a flame, he must... he breathed deeply and drank in the warmth and light that suddenly surrounded him. He sent an answering wave of warmth to his cousin, along the bond they shared, basking in Lunahr's radiance.

Talon smiled at Elavar; he could not help but grin, his heart was so full of love. "Pay me no mind, Elavar. Surely you must know by now my mood can change with the turning of the breeze."

"That is very true. However I have never seen such joy upon your face, such warmth," Elavar said, obviously baffled by his sudden, complete change in demeanor.

"Ah. I was thinking of Lunahr. Of a song he sang to me, the last time my mood was so dark," Talon lied adroitly, wishing that he need not, that he could tell Elavar of his Power, of his bond with Lunahr. "In fact, I hear him now. He must be at the fountain again. He has garnered quite a following. I only hope once your people can again sing and play they'll not all abandon him. He would be devastated if they did." Talon grew silent as they approached. He did not want to interrupt the song. But they were seen.

"Highness!" dozens of voices said in joy, and all those about Lunahr bowed in a single graceful wave, including Elanara and Eladar, both of whom had been listening with the others.

Lunahr stopped playing and bowed with them.

"Please, I would not have you stop on my account. Continue your song, Beryl. I would hear you play," Elavar said in Common.

"OF COURSE, Highness," Lunahr replied in Elvish and began to play and sing again, finishing the song which had been interrupted by Elavar's arrival. When he was done with that song he turned to Elavar again. "Is there some special song you might care to hear, Highness?" Lunahr asked formally in Elvish, careful to keep his eagerness at bay. He had been thrilled that he had not faltered. He had heard so much about Elavar from Eladar, and he was more than a little intimidated to be playing before him.

ELAVAR smiled at him. The boy spoke flawless, unaccented Elvish, as Talon did, in a properly courtly and restrained manner. He sensed his sister could not have chosen a more appropriate ward had she her choice of them. He saw Elanara smiling fondly at the boy, eyes bright with pride in him.

Elavar saw that Eladar had been smiling at Lunahr before, but was now watching his elder brother somewhat warily.

"I have been surrounded by music for many days, yet unfortunately unable to appreciate much of it. It would please me to hear 'The River Moves My Heart', in honor of my mother, who yet suffers for me. Do you know it?"

There was a soft whisper of comment, an expectant intake of breath. Elavar had named one of the most complex and cherished pieces ever written by their kind.

LUNAHR felt the nervousness that he had eluded before seize him. The song the Crown Prince had named was a love song, one of the thirty-two he'd helped Laren learn. Lunahr had never been in love before; he was still considered a child by his people as well as the Elves. He should not have been in love yet, especially not a love such as that. Yet he was afraid he might not have the depth of emotion the song required because of it. Worse, the song was meant to be sung as a duet, most often by a pair of lovers. Who might sing the other part with him?

"I would need someone to accompany me," Lunahr said bravely, looking toward Eladar and Elanara, concerned about the propriety of either of them singing before their people, for their station and particularly such a song, when Elanara was betrothed and his guardian and Eladar was underage.

ELADAR was angry with Elavar but fought to keep it from showing. In his typical manner, Elavar had specifically chosen a song that might embarrass Lunahr in front of all their people, those who had so respected his talent until now. Something that would embarrass him as well. Elavar must know Lunahr would look to him to accompany him. It would not be proper for Elanara to. Yet neither would it be for him to, for his age. If he offered to sing with Lunahr, it would be improper; if he did not, he would be failing a friend. Either way, Elavar would look upon him with disdain.

To Eladar's relief, Talon unexpectedly offered a resolution. "I would be honored to sing it with you, Beryl. I would take the man's part, if I may, as I have the depth of voice for it. You do as well, but I could never hope to reach some of the higher notes that will be required of you for the other part."

LUNAHR looked at Laren in relief and love and joy that he might sing before them. Laren seldom sang, though he had a wonderful voice. He seldom felt light enough of heart that he might. And he loved Laren, as a father, a brother, his cousin, his king. He could sing with the feeling required, thinking of him.

TALON moved to stand beside Lunahr and sent a wave of warmth and love to him and was met by an answering wave. Basking in each other's presence, they began the song, gazing into each other's eyes.

Then as the music swelled, they looked out at the audience around them. Talon's eyes met Elanara's as he sang the line which began, "You are like sunlight upon the water." Where his heart had fluttered before, the few times he had seen her this week past, now he felt it throb with passion, with longing, with desire, as the many decades of loneliness, of heartache thundered against his core like a river in spring flood.

ELANARA'S eyes widened and her breath caught as she realized Talon was now singing to her. She felt panic begin to build at the intensity of it, and fear that others might see as well. Then his eyes flicked away from her, as if she meant nothing to him, and he instead turned and looked once again at Lunahr, his eyes not straying from him again, so that she began to doubt what she had seen, what she had felt.

ELADAR fought to keep his face impassive, especially seeing his sister battle for control of her own features. He must not add fuel to the fire for any of the others who might have seen, who might have noticed as well. He eyed Elavar. He wondered if Elavar had seen, and if so, what he thought of it. Elavar's face was inscrutable, as always.

The last notes of the song died away, and there was absolute silence. Then the applause began, the praise. Many of the Elves around them had tears in their eyes and upon their faces. "Never might we have dreamt even you could sing it so well," Riverstone, one of Lunahr's most ardent followers, who was usually reserved, said to Lunahr with the enthusiasm of a child. Lunahr blushed, as others echoed him.

ELAVAR approached them. "My sister has indeed chosen well in naming herself your guardian, Lord Beryl, for you are a treasure even our own kingdom might wish to guard jealously." He turned to Talon. "And you have revealed a layer of yourself long kept hidden from me, my friend. Come speak with me, Talon, for it would not be proper for such a song to be followed by another." Elavar had not missed the look Talon had given Elanara. He needed to speak with his friend.

"Forgive me, Highness, but I fear my need to speak with Lord Talon outweighs your own," a deep voice said.

"Arcanus!" Talon said in surprise, turning toward the white-haired, red-cloaked figure. "I had not been told you were here."

"I only just arrived, and had yet to reveal myself to anyone, until now," Arcanus replied.

ELADAR eyed their visitor curiously. So this was Arcanus, the wizard who protected and advised the Amontir. He was old, his hair white and as long as Lunahr's. He wore a vivid red cloak concealing his clothes and frame, and he carried a knobbed and knotted walking stick of a dark wood.

Arcanus shifted his eyes, and suddenly they were focused upon Eladar. For a moment, Eladar could neither think nor move nor breathe, and then the feeling passed. Eladar shivered. There was such Power about him, such magicks—he'd felt it. His respect for Talon grew, that he had regular dealings with such a powerful being.

"Of course. Highnesses, please excuse us," Talon said, departing with Arcanus.

"SISTER, I would speak with you, as Lord Talon is otherwise occupied," Elavar said.

"Certainly. Beryl, Brother, if you'll excuse me?" Elanara asked.

"Of course," Lunahr and Eladar muttered in tandem.

Once Elavar and Elanara left, Eladar sighed, releasing a breath. "You did well, Lunahr, very well indeed," he said, looking about as if to ensure no one was within earshot. "Particularly considering what my brother tried to do," Eladar added angrily.

"What did he try to do?" Lunahr asked, puzzled.

"Never mind; it is not important. What is important is that you miraculously managed to pass his test, something I've seldom been able to do," Eladar said, sounding more than a little jealous.

Lunahr looked up at him intently. "You are too hard on yourself, Eladar. Your brother is proud of you, he must be. I will prove it to you later. You will speak with him. I will come also, if you wish; I've seen how nervous he makes you."

"Perhaps." Eladar eyed Lunahr, his scrutiny appearing speculative. "It takes a breadth of experience to sing that particular song correctly."

Lunahr blushed darkly. "If you are asking if I am in love with someone, or have ever been, the answer is no, Eladar." Lunahr's heart fluttered at why Eladar might wish to know, to his chagrin. He'd been trying so hard to think of Eladar as a brother. He'd thought he'd succeeded, until now.

"Actually, it is not you I was wondering about. I have never heard talk of a queen of your people," Eladar probed, to his surprise.

"Oh. That's because there isn't one, nor is there likely to be one. There are so few women left, and none are of the right House. We have to be so careful, you see, in who we marry. There have been so few of us for so long that many of us are too closely related." Lunahr sighed. "Had I been born a woman, I would have been destined to be Laren's bride, even though our mothers were sisters. I've wished, more than once, that I had been. He so needs someone to love him, to support him, to care for him," he said wistfully.

"You could still be *lythenia*, could you not?" Eladar asked.

"Lythenia? I've never heard that word. What does it mean?" Lunahr asked, as eager to learn a new word in Elvish as he was to know what Eladar was talking about.

"Truly, you do not know? I am surprised to hear it. It literally means 'heart's mate,' but it has come to mean lifemate; it is living as husband and wife, but for two men or two women. I was told the Amontir are not as inhibited as most Men in their choice of partners, and from what I have seen, I thought it was true. Have I been misinformed?" Eladar asked.

"No, we do take lovers within our own sex. For the men, it's much more common now, in fact, than ever before, out of necessity mostly. But it's not like that, it's just... well, two men, or rarely for us, two women, can certainly pair up with one another, but it's only a temporary thing. They can be lovers, but they could never live as husband and wife. I mean, no one would see them that way," Lunahr said, feeling increasingly flustered by the topic.

"Really? How odd! What a strange double standard," Eladar said. He looked at Lunahr and sighed. "You know, once you come-of-age here, you will have no shortage of those who would wish to partner with you, both male and female. They have already started vying with one another for the honor of being your first."

"What?" Lunahr asked, shocked by the wistful sounding declaration, blushing darkly at the thought. "But... but I've not yet come-of-age. I thought your people were as strict about that as my own."

"We are. No one would ever think to bed you now. But it's quite customary, the year before one goes to Nalea, to have a line of suitors set to wait for you upon your return. More than a few, of course, have been frustrated to find that the person they had set their sights upon found someone within Nalea to celebrate their coming-of-age with. I leave for Nalea next year. But I've no doubt no one might be waiting to so greet me upon my own return. Though I've heard Elavar had hundreds of suitors eager for his attentions, as did Elanara."

Lunahr felt the heat in his face and knew it was now likely a constant shade of dark red.

Eladar looked sheepish as he apologized. "Forgive me for speaking of such things to you! It's just... whenever I try to with Elavar, I receive a strict lecture about it, and I find I cannot even broach the topic with Elanara. It's something one normally speaks to a trusted friend about, but—well, I've never really had a friend, not a true friend, someone I might trust with things of such a sensitive and intimate nature. I had hoped—but I see now I cannot. Forget I spoke of such things. Please do not tell Talon I did so."

"Of course not. And Eladar, please, I didn't mean to scare you away like that. It's just… well, you surprised me, that's all. But I want you to feel you can talk to me about anything; I can see you need someone to confide in. It brings joy to my heart that you have so honored me. I was so afraid before coming here that I'd feel terribly lonely, completely isolated and alienated, both from my own kin and your people. But you've made me feel at home from the first.

"Truly, you can speak to me about such things. It's not as if I've never thought about them myself, you know. I've thought about it a lot, even knowing I'd most likely be matched with Ro… Heather, as she's not so terribly much older than me, and she… she's not too closely related," Lunahr said. He'd almost spoken her given name, Rowena, and mentioned that she had at least some Power. Their level of Power was just as important as the Houses, after all, in selecting a mate, though he'd so carefully not mentioned that before when speaking of queens for Laren.

"It's not that I don't like Heather, I do. She is fair of face, with poise and grace of body. She would most certainly have been a dancer, did our people have the time and freedom for such pursuits. It's just… she's never really interested me that way. I know everyone still thinks of me as a child, but if I were a normal Man I'd already be considered an adult. I certainly have the feelings of one, enough to know who I favor.

"Come, let's go to your rooms, where we can speak more privately. I keep looking about, for fear someone might overhear us," Lunahr said uncomfortably.

"That was an extremely subtle way of inviting yourself to my bedchamber, Lunahr," Eladar challenged mischievously.

Lunahr blushed darkly once more, and then laughed. "You're going to get us both into trouble, brother-of-my-heart, if you don't stop saying such things!"

Eladar grinned at Lunahr as they left the fountain, heading for the Palace.

ELAVAR walked in silence with Elanara to one of the Palace's private gardens. Then he turned to her. "I was surprised to see the way that Talon looked at you, Sister," Elavar said bluntly.

Elanara was as shocked by his directness as she was that he would mention such a thing to her in the first place. "Then think how I felt, that he did so," she replied, just as curtly.

Elavar's eyebrows raised. "Ah. Then his look was unexpected? He has been here for some time. I thought that perhaps you might have come to some sort of understanding with him while I was incapacitated."

"One of the first things I told him when I met him was that I was betrothed to the High-Prince," Elanara said defensively.

"Truly? How astonishing. It is not something that normally comes up within the course of conversation at a first meeting, one would think," Elavar said, sounding intrigued.

"It was an unusual conversation. After all, we were discussing my becoming guardian to Lunahr. I trust you are not implying I have behaved improperly, that I have acted with anything other than the honor of my position?"

"I would not have expected you to. Yet, I might have understood it if you did. The strain of my injury, of Mother's danger. In such circumstances it is not unusual for someone to seek comfort," Elavar suggested, as if he were encouraging her to confess her perceived transgression without shame.

"No. I did not. I would not. I am insulted that you might think such a thing of me. I have been betrothed to Aras since he was ten years old. In honor of that arrangement, I have kept myself chaste these thirty-two years past. Thirty-two years, Elavar! I am a scant few years shy of three hundred. Do you have any idea what it has been like for me, to have loved whomever I chose freely for over two centuries, and to then be treated as if I were again a child, a maiden, without the right to bed anyone, man nor woman? And you dare call my virtue into question over a simple look in a courtyard?" Elanara snapped, eyes flashing in fury. "You are fortunate Mother has worked so hard restoring you to health, my beloved brother. I would not undo such effort upon her part."

Elanara knew she was shaking and she fought to stop. Then she realized she had all but threatened her brother. She sat down suddenly upon the marble bench they stood beside, and began taking deep breaths. She looked up at him. "Forgive me, Elavar! You know I would never harm you. It is just… Talon upsets me. He frightens me. His eyes—I wish he were already gone. Already I am starting to love Lunahr as a brother, but Talon… he is so intense…. I did not realize he might be so passionate as well, until he sang, until he looked at me. The other looks he has given me since he came have puzzled me. I see now that he has hidden much from me. They were as nothing compared to that one!

"For the first time, I am glad to be betrothed to Aras, I am relieved to be. Of course, it is not that Aras is not someone I would want to marry. It is just that I have yet to even meet him. Although I am fortunate in that he sounds to be someone I could love. I know from what we have heard that Aras is sweet and warm and gentle, that he has been taught the healing arts by Jarnath, who surpasses even Mother in his ability, yet he is adept with sword and bow and dagger. He has not formally begun his training in Nalea, of course. He is not yet of age to. He is a year younger than Eladar. But we do know he was trained remarkably early by High-King Laedrin himself. He is fortunately, however, little like his father. Yet he has somehow remained one step ahead of the High-King for decades, in all his machinations. Ah, and of course, he has the delicate beauty of his mother."

Elanara sighed. "Apparently he has suffered greatly for it, over these many decades, for Laedrin's hatred of Ithelia. Surely the rumor that Laedrin had her secretly executed is true? Ithelia could not have fled for her own safety yet let her son remain, not when he was only eight and unable to defend himself against his father. Our father's agent in Nalea has told us much about Aras and Laedrin.

"It pleases me that once we are wed, Father's position will be more secure, that once the two families are joined by marriage, Laedrin might no longer view Father as a threat to his position. But also, I think Aras's own position will be made more secure by it, particularly once I have borne an heir to him.

"Although I know we must be certain, before I do. From what we have been told, Laedrin might well favor the child over the father. It would certainly not be beyond him to arrange some sort of accident for his son, once Aras is no longer sole heir, once Laedrin has a grandson," she said, face lined with concern that someone she might grow to love might be taken from her.

"It is not you who should seek my forgiveness. Forgive me, Sister! In all these many years of your betrothal you have voiced none of this to me, yet you have suffered such a burden of your heart. I have failed you as a brother," Elavar said in dismay.

"Failed? Elavar, don't be silly! You have never failed at anything in all your long life, least of all, certainly, at being a good brother. I have not been alone with my thoughts. I could not have borne to be. I have shared them with Mother. Who better to understand, after all the machinations she and Father had to go through to be together?"

"It eases the burden of my heart to hear you say so," Elavar said. "Yet still, I am at fault in this matter. I am the one who has only just begun encouraging Talon to seek a wife outside his own people. I never dreamt he might see you in such a light! I had spoken to him only of the Cities of Men. Yet it makes sense he might look to the Elven kingdoms. I must make sure he understands that, as much as I might be honored by his attentions to you, it is not possible that he might seek your hand, when it has been promised to another for so long.

"We are friends. He is as a brother to me, though I know you have always been puzzled by it, that I can feel so much closer to a Man than to the true brother of my own blood. But we are so similar, Talon and I. Whereas Eladar… ah, I must not speak against him. Talon has told me I must think hard about the effect of my words upon Eladar, before I speak them.

"I love Eladar, he must know that I love him, but he drives me to distraction! Yet still, he has done well. You have told me all he has done. He has even saved my life. Whoever would have thought that he might! I will speak with him again tonight," Elavar said intently.

Then he grinned mischievously, for a moment looking so like Eladar himself that Elanara almost gasped in her surprise. "If I can find him; he has hidden quite well from me, more than once, when he has known I have sought him," he said laughing.

"Oh, Elavar!" Elanara said, embracing him. "You were almost lost to us! I don't know what I might do without you. I hope I need never learn."

Elavar returned her embrace. "Ah, my sweet sister, I was a fool to ever have doubted you. I hope you might find the happiness you deserve with Aras. I think that you might. He is gifted beyond naming that you might be his wife. Would that I might ever find so worthy a bride," he said with a sigh.

Elanara smiled at him impishly. "I would be more than happy to assist you in finding one, Brother, as would Mother."

Elavar laughed. "No, please, not again! You might make a fine wife, Elanara, but you are not nearly so skilled as a matchmaker! I will find my own wife, someday. Though Mother might doubt it!" he said laughing. Then his face creased in pain. "She still suffers for her aid of me."

Elanara hugged him again. "Courage, Elavar. She would be the first to tell you her suffering was worth the price. She would die to save you, as would I, if ever there was the need."

"May such a need never come to pass, when one of us must give his or her life to save another," Elavar said passionately.

"Come, it is time you ate something, Elavar. I promised Father I would see that you did. Will you dine with me?"

"Of course," Elavar said, hugging her once more. "I love you, Sister. I realize it is not something I often say. I think it has perhaps been decades since I last did so. I am glad I have been given opportunity to say so again. I will tell Eladar the same tonight. He will, no doubt, spend the next many weeks thinking about what ulterior motive I might have had for telling him so!" Elavar laughed, his eyes twinkling again with merriment.

"You are truly terrible, Elavar. I doubt not you were just as difficult in your youth as Eladar has been in his. In fact, I think I will speak to Mother about your childhood. You lived through mine, but I would at least see yours through her eyes."

Elavar sighed. "Ah, I am doomed, then, for you have no idea how truly terrible I was, Elanara. You must never betray me to Eladar. It would only encourage him, and he has little need of such encouragement! Come, Sister. I am indeed hungry and nothing would please me more than to spend the rest of the evening in your company."

"I MUST hear all you know, Talon, starting with the fall of Caramore," Arcanus commanded as soon as they were alone. He did not dare speak Dewalaren's given name, even here, in seclusion, in the very heart of Riviera; he would not risk it. He seldom even thought of him by that name, lest the Enemy somehow hear. He never once thought of himself by his own.

"I had feared you were all lost to me," Arcanus said, unable to keep the pain and true fear from his voice, in spite of millennia of dissembling. Blessed Ragnar and Aralyn he was weary beyond all endurance!

He froze as he realized he had actually invoked the God and Goddess of his mother's people, for the first time in his long, lonely life. Yet even as the thought astonished him, he ached to embrace the false comfort they enticingly offered. He cast aside the foolish notion, discarding it with contempt. The God and Goddess were not real. Unfortunately, deeply flawed as he was, he was the closest thing this world would ever know to a God, though the Enemy yet denied it.

"We would have been were it not for your children, Arcanus," Talon said. Talon was looking into the water and fortunately did not notice Arcanus involuntarily stiffening at mention of them. "Though you might have told us of them! We nearly killed them ourselves, when they were so desperately trying to aid us, for the story of their identity was too bizarre to believe.

"I think, perhaps, that is why we did spare them, long enough for them to convince us. The Enemy would never have concocted such an unbelievable tale, that you had somehow sired an Elven child and a Dwarven one, that they were both wizards, as you are," Talon said, turning to face him, honesty, trust, absolute faith, and love shining from his normally guarded eyes. He had been counselor, advisor, and mentor to Talon for decades, almost as a second father to him, even before his father was killed. Fortunately his other children's rash actions had not shaken that faith.

They were alone here, it was secluded. None would dare disturb them. Arcanus prepared his core to touch Talon's, to learn all he knew, but primarily to feed upon him, as he had done so since Talon was a child of ten and his Power had first manifested so disastrously and spectacularly.

Arcanus had purchased six horses in Ardock. He had slain the first five just outside the City gates, within the wood, draining the life from each of them with a simple touch, as he had drained the life's energy—if not entirely the life—from Hardred and Alnas, though the temptation had been almost overwhelming.

He shivered at the memory of them. He had not fed from Lesser Men in a very long time; he'd not dared do so. He had limited his depredations to the beasts of the field when the Amontir could not suffice. But having tasted again of Man, the horses had not sated him as fully as he'd needed them to. He ached to feed off of one with Power, Power as Talon had. But he must be cautious. Talon's core was so weak, so fragile, that the slightest touch might drive him to Madness.

Arcanus put his hand in a fatherly way upon Talon's shoulder and then almost snatched his hand away in his surprise. He had extended a thread from his core to touch Talon's and found a new bond there, completely unexpected, bright and strong. And Talon's core hummed softly with Power. Who had dared bond himself to his king?

Cautiously, Arcanus touched the bond, careful not to disturb it. Such a bright light! And music, such music, coming across the bond! Lunahr? It must be! Yet Lunahr had not shown such ability before. Had the boy flared to Power while he was absent?

"I feared I had lost both the son of my body and the son-of-my-heart, Magus and you both," Arcanus said, needing to keep Talon distracted, needing to learn what he could. "I suspected Magus and Circe went to your aid, but I could not get close enough to be certain. The Enemy was everywhere, His minions swarmed about Caramore like a disturbed hive of hornets. You must tell me all that has happened, Talon."

"Of course." Talon told Arcanus of the two younger wizards' warning, how they'd flown into the City, nearly crashing into the sealed door to the one occupied building. Circe had flown, carrying Magus. They later revealed that Magus was the one who had done the scry revealing the pending attack.

"It was when Magus froze me where I stood, wrested Kathalanar from me, held the blade to my throat, spoke my true name and title aloud, then returned the Sword to me and released his hold upon me that we realized they must truly be allies, for otherwise I'd not have lived.

"The two of them remained behind, to cover our escape. We lost no one, Arcanus. All nineteen of us made it safely away. I tried to send word across my bond to Farad that Caramore has fallen, also, but I could not tell if he heard or understood.

"But at least we know Magus and Circe made it safely away. They joined us again, afterward, for a short time. It appeared they had drained all their strength away in the fight. After they landed, they could not even stand unaided. They could scarcely move. We tended to both of them for days, in the mountains by a stream, until they were strong enough to leave us."

"What possessed you to bring Lunahr away from the safety of your kin?" Arcanus asked.

"Safety? There is no safety amongst us, Arcanus. We can no longer protect him. We have seen we cannot. We would rather lose him for seven years than forever. Once he has come-of-age, only then might he rejoin us in our fight."

"Yet Lunahr was injured, in Ardock. He was robbed, he lost Loruthanar for a time, he was harmed. And you wielded the Sword, flaring red with Power, where others saw it," Arcanus accused.

Talon swallowed. "You know of that?" He breathed deeply. "Yes, Lunahr was robbed and terribly harmed. It was entirely my fault. Then I had to kill to recover Loruthanar. I did not wield the King's Sword lightly, Arcanus," Talon said, confessing to what had happened. "Would that I were a wizard, and perfect, that I did not make such mistakes."

Arcanus eyed him warily, but Talon had apparently spoken sincerely. "There is no shame in needing my aid, Highness, and as always, it is my pleasure to give it," Arcanus said. Talon had need of his support now, not his criticism; he punished himself for what had transpired already.

But Marcus and Selene were another matter entirely. With them he would not be so forgiving. They had risked revealing themselves to the Enemy; they had defied his every command regarding use of their Power. Yet in so doing, they had saved the Amontir, when they might have been lost to a Man.

"You must tell me also what has happened here. There is great tension in the air."

Talon explained about Elavar's injury and Eladar's rescue of him, of the Queen's endangerment for tending to her son. Then he hesitated. "Elavar has been speaking to me. Our people are so few and there are so few women amongst us, now. None who might be my queen. He suggested I might find a bride in the Lands of Men. Of course, he does not know of our Power, of the importance of it, as well as of our Houses. Men do not have such Power. But I have started thinking that, although the Elves do not have Power akin to ours, they do possess the ability to perform some small magicks. Some of them, such as Queen Naraena, wield greater magicks. Do you think, perhaps, Elanara might have inherited any of her mother's ability?"

"I sense no aura of Power about her," Arcanus said truthfully.

When he first came to Riviera, when he had first met the Royal Family, he had been astonished to find the King and Queen and both their sons were Latents. Elanara alone was an Inert; she alone did not possess their Power, though her children well might, particularly if she were to breed with Talon. He eyed Talon speculatively. It had not been an idle question. Talon was waiting to hear something. He was not sure what it might be. Unless he had somehow learned the Royal Family's secret?

"In Elanara's case, at least, it is a moot point. She is already betrothed, to the son of the High-King. I do not know his name. I did not even know the High-King had a son," Talon said.

"Ah. They are not on the best of terms. The High-King does not often speak of his son," Arcanus said. Arcanus was aware that Laedrin despised his son Aras. He had not known the boy was betrothed. He was surprised it would be to Elanara. Laedrin felt the same disdain for the River Elves that he felt for his own son. Could there be some sort of greater purpose behind such a union?

No, impossible. If Laedrin knew the secret heritage of the Royal Family, he would have slain them all without hesitation. He certainly would never have dared allow Laranela and Naraena to breed first, out of misguided yet justified fear and hatred for what might result from such a union. Laedrin had suffered greatly at the hands of his creations. So had they all.

"Even if she does not possess such magic, her children might," Talon said, unknowingly echoing his thoughts, hope in his voice. "We've seen it amongst our own people, time and again: a grandparent with great power, a parent with little, then a grandchild greater even than his grandsire." Talon himself had far outstripped his father's Power, even as a child, although his father had been the most powerful of all their kin.

"Talon, son-of-my-heart, you sound as if Elanara has already stolen your heart," Arcanus said in surprise.

Talon looked Arcanus in the eye. "I do not deny it. Already I have feelings for her that I have never had for another. I have kept them carefully hidden from her. Or I had. I fear I revealed myself when I sang to her. But it matters not how I feel. She will marry the High-Prince, and I will wander alone, always alone, ever alone," Talon said. Arcanus could see his heart sinking in despair. But then, unexpectedly, Talon smiled affectionately, the darkness that so often shrouded him perceptibly lifting. "No, not truly alone; Lunahr is always with me now. We are bonded."

"You are bonded to him?" Arcanus asked, feigning surprise, realizing Lunahr had affected the change in Talon through the bond they now shared. The thought of the Power the boy must now wield to be able to have wrought such a difference excited him. To have successfully bred another Latent! The thought that he might perhaps be more both thrilled and terrified him.

"Yes. Out of necessity, at first," Talon said, the smile fleeing his face. "I went mad again." His voice dropped to a whisper and he shivered at the memory. "This time, at least, I did not try to harm the others, only myself. Farad did not come across our bond when I needed him most, when I thought nothing might ever keep him from coming to save me. But Lunahr found me. He heard me screaming, he ran to me and embraced me, he began singing to me to calm me. The King's Madness just melted away before the music. He flared to Power as he sang. He wove the Power into his song as if he'd been able to do so his entire life. He healed me so gently.

"Lunahr's Power is greater than Farad's, Arcanus. It is greater even than my own, and you had told me mine was unparalleled in all our history. We can never lose Lunahr, for his Power, his song, his youth, his heart, his joy. All our hopes for the future lie with him, unless I find a queen, unless I sire an heir. But there is scant hope I might," he sighed.

"You must not surrender to despair, Talon," Arcanus chastised, even as his thoughts raced with the possibilities. "Have I taught you so little, these many decades? Where there is life, there is hope.

"I will speak to the High-King. I will see how strongly he feels about this betrothal, whether he might not consider altering it, whether the boy has feelings for Elanara. There are many Elven maidens Laedrin's son might wed. It should matter little to Laedrin which princess he chooses for his son." Arcanus was confident that he would be able to sway the High-King without using his Power upon him, though of course he would do so without hesitation should Laedrin not willingly accede to his request.

Perhaps it was time he told the High-King the truth about the Enemy the Amontir faced. Not the full truth, of course, but just enough so that Laedrin would realize it was a common enemy that approached, to ensure that the High-King would not hesitate to pit his entire forces against the Enemy. But he must be ever so careful. He could not risk that Laedrin might ever learn the full truth, that he might learn Arcanus's own terrible secret. He could ill afford to become an enemy of the combined remaining might of the Army of the *Aerta* and the Navy of the *Oceana*. Talon's voice dragged him back from his dark thoughts before he was too weakened by them.

"I will dare to hope then, Arcanus, for you have always signified hope to us. You have epitomized it. We would be lost without you, father-of-my-heart," Talon said, love shining from his eyes.

Arcanus smiled warmly at Talon. He was more father to Talon, to all the Amontir, than they might ever guess, though they must never learn of it. "Let us talk further. Then we must away. We must bid our good-byes to Lunahr.

There is much to be done. There was a chimaera in Ardock, at the Feast Day Games."

"A chimaera? And I did not find it!" Talon said, clearly appalled.

"Fortunately, I did. It is slain. But we need to return to Ardock, to find out who brought it. Why it was there is no mystery. Its target was Governor Jeffran. He is strong and intelligent. He is vital to the safety of Ardock. I cannot call him craven for fleeing before the chimaera, instead I call him wise. Few survive such encounters, as you well know.

"I fear the Enemy already turns His eyes toward the Lands of Men. He has begun testing to see how quickly their cities might fall. They will fall all too quickly, Talon, terribly quickly. At the rate He advances, He will have obliterated the last of the Dwarven Kingdoms within a scant ten more years or so. That is how long we have to find the King's Ring, to recover it. For once the Dwarves are gone, the kingdoms of Man and of the Elves will quickly turn to ash."

"Then we will find it. We must," Talon said with conviction. "Come, Arcanus. I will say good-bye quickly. Then it is off to Ardock and then Thenalon, Logareth, all the cities that now harbor my kin," Talon said.

"YOU'RE leaving? Already?" Elanara asked in surprise, fighting to keep the relief from her voice.

"I must. But before I go, I wanted to thank you, for taking Lunahr in, for doing more. I had thought I might only be finding him a safe haven here, amongst your people, but you and Eladar have already given him so much more. You have made him family. You have given him not a house, but a home," Talon said, sounding both grateful and wistful.

"I must likewise thank you for the care you have taken of Eladar, for the compassion you have shown him. We are grateful," Elanara said formally.

KING LARANELA had expressed the same sentiments to Talon, when he bid his good-byes to him. Talon was relieved that the King seemed as taken with Lunahr as Elanara had been, as eager to see him more than safe, to see him happy as well. Talon was confident that Queen Naraena would feel the same. He was sorry that he would not have the chance to see her this trip after all. He envied his young cousin, that he truly had a home here and a surrogate family that could not help but love him, while he was doomed to wander, to hide, even to flee.

"Farewell, Highness," Talon said formally to Elanara. Then, without conscious thought, he unbuckled his sheathed sword, fell to one knee at Elanara's feet and swore oath to her. "My sword is ever at your service."

ELANARA stared at Talon in astonishment that a king, even a king of Men, might kneel to her. "We accept you to our service," Elanara said, careful to use the royal "we" again, lest Talon think more of her reply than was intended. "You may leave our presence," she said, unable to keep the eagerness from her voice.

Talon rose, nodded, and departed without further word, strapping on his sword as he walked away.

"I have missed much while I was recovering," an intrigued voice said from behind Elanara. "I did not wish to intrude upon such a remarkable moment. I did not realize your opinion of Men had taken such an interesting turn."

"Mother!" Elanara said, hugging her in relief and joy.

"You must enlighten me, Daughter," Naraena said, her eyes sparkling with delight.

Elanara nodded, her face betraying the intensity of her emotion and began to speak.

"YOU'RE leaving? Already?" Lunahr asked, his eyes brightening with tears, though he was trying so desperately to be brave.

"I must, Lunahr," Talon said. "Arcanus has brought grave news. There was a chimaera in Ardock. The Enemy has already begun testing the Cities and Kingdoms of Men."

"A chimaera?" Lunahr asked, his concern for himself instantly subsumed by his concern for those in Ardock.

"ARCANUS slew it before it could carry out its mission, but time grows ever shorter. I cannot tarry here, much as I would give almost anything to stay." Talon loved Riviera, for its quiet beauty, but also for those who dwelt here: Elavar and now Lunahr. He had always liked the Queen, and he had even grown fond of Eladar. As for Elanara… he felt his heart flutter at the thought of her. If only Arcanus could truly sway the High-King.

"You stand before me, but you are already gone," Lunahr said sadly, and the tears that had threatened before came as Lunahr embraced him, his heart pounding rapidly. "Don't worry about me. I'll be fine, really. Please be careful, Laren! Take care of yourself, as well as everyone else. I know we are still bound to one another. I hope I might yet help you, but I'll be so far away and—Please don't forget me! I love you. I know you know I do, but I just wanted to say it and…." Lunahr began sobbing in his arms.

"I'm sorry, Laren… forgive me! I'm trying… so hard… to be brave… like you…," he said between sobs. Lunahr forced his arms down to his sides and stepped back from him.

"Oh, Lunahr!" Talon said, his finger tilting up his chin. "You are so very brave! And I am so very proud of you. I meant to tell you before I left how proud I am of the man you are becoming, how well you did on the journey here. I realized you might not know it, as Eladar had not realized how proud Elavar is of him. There is so much I wanted to say. But you were so happy singing and making new friends here, and I thought I had more time.

"Stay well, Lunahr. You are so very strong, so brave, and far dearer to me than you realize. I love you cousin," Talon said. Then he hugged Lunahr desperately, breathing in the scent of him, feeling the silk of his hair against his cheek. Talon released Lunahr and turned away quickly, lest Lunahr see his own tears as he began walking rapidly away.

LUNAHR watched Laren go, wiping at his eyes and sniffing until the trees hid Laren from him. But he could still feel Laren. He could hear his thoughts across their bond, and he could feel his heartache and desperate loneliness, even though he could tell the moment Arcanus joined him, even though Laren was not truly alone.

Lunahr began to sing the Elven song "You Are the Light That Guides Me," his voice breaking over the first few stanzas, but he had to try, for Laren's sake, knowing that if he lifted his own spirits, Laren's might lift with them. He realized too late that the song he had chosen was a duet, that without another voice he would falter.

Then, from behind him, he heard a clear, strong tenor join his own, singing the next line: "I will never be alone, for you will ever walk beside me." Lunahr turned in surprise, his heart lifting in joy and wonder at the sound of Eladar's voice harmonizing so perfectly with his own. Eladar smiled at him as he continued to sing and looked at him in such devotion that the pain in Lunahr's heart vanished, knowing that not only was Eladar with him, but Laren truly still was also.

Chapter 11

Terrible News

The Royal Palace, The River Elf Kingdom of Riviera

Five Years Later

"HIGHNESS, the King and Queen summon you. You must appear before them immediately," one of the Guard said to Elanara.

"They've returned?" Elanara asked, her voice weak with relief.

They had all been so frightened when the summons had come from the High-King so bluntly, so unexpectedly. Father was to make haste to Nalea and report to Laedrin on a matter of the utmost urgency. They had been afraid for him, though they could not believe High-King Laedrin would dare to act so openly against Father. Father told them he must go. He had meant to go alone, but Mother had insisted upon accompanying him. She hoped her presence might stay Laedrin's hand, whatever treachery he might be planning.

"I told you all would be well," Elavar said, rising from the cushions beside his sister, carefully hiding his own relief behind a proper mask of stateliness. Elanara stood as well, and the two of them began heading for the door.

The Guard's face flushed as he turned to Elavar. "Forgive me, Prince Sylvan, but you were not summoned. Their Majesties were most adamant that her Highness report to them alone."

Elanara looked at the Guard then Elavar in shock, that her parents might ever say such a thing.

"It would seem I spoke too soon," Elavar said, unable to keep the hurt and dismay from his face for being caught so unawares, even after centuries of practice. "All is not well. I will wait in the garden, Sister, for your return. I am hopeful you might at least be permitted to tell me what it is I have done that has caused Father and Mother to be so displeased with me that they do not wish to even see me after so long an absence. I had not thought I had ruled so poorly in Father's stead that one of our people might complain so bitterly to Father that he might wish to banish me from his sight."

Elanara hugged him. "Surely it cannot be something you have done! I will return as soon as I am able," Elanara promised.

Elavar nodded and walked to their mother's favorite garden, completely disconsolate, hoping Lunahr might be there and that he might find some comfort from the Man he had grown to love as a brother in the five years he had dwelt amongst them.

To his relief, Lunahr was there, and he was alone: Riverstone, Crystal, Driftwood, and the rest of his usual admirers were nowhere to be seen. But Lunahr was strumming such a haunting, mournful dirge that Elavar's own spirits sank even further, when he thought they could not. He struggled to recognize the piece and almost convinced himself it was a new composition when he realized Lunahr was playing "You Are the Light That Guides Me."

"Never have I heard that inspirational piece played in such a manner," Elavar said, his concern for himself instantly forgotten. "I came here hoping to hear your music, but that is not what I thought I might hear."

"HIGHNESS!" Lunahr said, his face flushing darkly, and he stopped playing. "Forgive me! It is just, Eladar has been training in Nalea these four years past now. I have missed him so terribly, but he has written to me often, as I have to him. But these past few months he has answered none of my letters. I have been so worried! Your parents promised to bring me word of him, but when I saw they had returned and I approached them, they would not speak to me and… and your father, he has been like a father to me also, these five years past, yet he looked at me as if I were an enemy. He glared at me with such anger. And your mother would not look at me at all. I could see she was upset also, but… please, Elavar, what have I done that might anger them against me?" Lunahr asked, his voice breaking and eyes bright with unshed tears.

Elavar said intently, "It is not you, I think, Lunahr, nor even me then. Something has happened, I know not what. They have summoned Elanara. She will learn what is wrong, I am sure she will tell us. Now please, sing with me? Never have I felt so alone. I would sing a duet with you, to know I am not. You are as a brother to me, Lunahr, surely you must know by now you are? Yet I do not know that I have told you so. It is like with Eladar. I forget you might not see it."

"Please, Elavar, then might you hug me? Just this once? Eladar has been gone for so long and it is not proper for Elanara to, for her betrothal, or anyone else to, for my age, and…." Lunahr was fighting a losing battle against his tears. It had been so terribly long since he'd felt even the most simple embrace. He and Eladar had secretly pledged to one another to become *lythenia*, as soon as they both were of age, but now…. Then Elavar's arms were around him, and his control shattered with his touch. "What if… what if something has happened… to Eladar? What if… what if he doesn't come back?" he sobbed.

"HUSH. He is fine, he must be. We would have been sent word, were he not," Elavar assured him. Then he shivered. Surely that could not be why Father was summoned? Had the High-King wanted to tell him in person of some tragedy involving Eladar, fearing the discord amongst the kingdoms a cold, formal letter might have brought?

Elavar had enjoyed the peace and calm of the first few months of Eladar's absence after he had left to begin his training in Nalea. But then he had felt his younger brother's absence keenly. The world was such a stiff, formal, even dreary place with Eladar gone. The thought of five years without him had begun to seem almost unbearable. He had been so relieved there was but a single year left of his training. The thought that he might now be gone forever was unendurable.

"No. No, it cannot be that," Elavar said, more to convince himself than Lunahr. "He will return; he must. Please, Lunahr, sing with me? The song you were playing when I came? I have heard you sing it so often with him. I would hear it as it is meant to sound, sung by two," Elavar said, releasing Lunahr.

Lunahr nodded, took a few deep breaths and began to play. Then he began to sing, and Elavar joined his voice to his, and they let the song carry the burden of their hearts away upon the wind.

THE Guard led Elanara to the throne room. "Majesties, I come as commanded," Elanara said stiffly, formally, curtsying, head bowed, eyes downcast.

"Guard, you are dismissed," Laranela said, and then his eyes panned the room. "All of you. You are to go, now. You are to lock the door and leave. You will await my next command outside the Palace. You are to take the servants and courtiers with you as well. No one is to enter here again until you are commanded by me or the Queen. Not even the Crown Prince nor Lord Beryl are to enter. Especially not them!" Laranela commanded angrily.

"Yes, Majesty!" the Guard intoned as one, quickly hiding their initial astonishment at the bizarre command. They marched stiffly from the room, and Elanara heard them scatter; she heard the sound of many feet, of anxious mutterings, as the Palace was efficiently evacuated.

Elanara stood with her head still bowed, unmoving, until there was absolute silence outside.

"Rise, Daughter, and approach," Laranela said.

Elanara did so. She was shocked to see her father was shaking, he was so angry, but then his anger seemed to burn away and she saw anguish replace it. "I cannot! I cannot tell her, now that she stands before me and I see her eyes, her love, her faith, her trust in me. I cannot betray her! There must be another way! Our agent in Nalea could smuggle him out," Laranela said desperately.

"Past the entire combined might of our Army and Navy? Beloved, he cannot! We have discussed every option and have agreed there is no other alternative. We must accede to his demands. Even were we to assassinate one or the other or both, their men, or surely Arcanus, would know we were the ones who had done so. They would exact their revenge, not just upon him, but upon our entire family, perhaps our entire kingdom," Naraena said.

Elanara stared in stunned disbelief. Her father spoke of betraying her, and her mother, who had never harmed anyone in her life, whom she thought never could, was calmly speaking of killing two people!

Elanara began backing from them cautiously while their attention was focused upon one another. What if these were not her parents at all? What if they were those she had been warned about—Resemblants, minions of the Enemy who had assumed their forms? They had ordered the Palace cleared, the doors locked; there would be no Guard to come to her aid if she cried out for it.

Her heart fluttered at the thought of what they might do to her, even as she resolved to fight them. She had her dagger—she carried it always—but she dared not reach for it, not yet, not until she was sure. She could not raise her hand against them until she was certain.

Her mother turned to her, eyebrows rising in surprise and concern. "Elanara, my child! You are afraid of us! Do not be, my gentle daughter. We are not agents of the Enemy, for all we must sound like it, though we are agents of despair. Although were your brother Elavar here, he might argue with me, did he know to whom we have been referring, for his love of one of the two of whom we speak. For that reason alone we could never harm him. We would not so injure Elavar by it.

"Nor sweet Lunahr. How could I ever have even thought such a thing, knowing how it would devastate one I have come to love as a son?"

Elanara's eyes widened in shock. Talon? They had been speaking of killing Talon? Surely not! But her father's eyes lit with a sudden wild hope.

"Lunahr! He is Heir to the Throne. Elanara loves him already, although as a brother, and he is like enough to us to truly be one of us. He is sweet and gentle as she is, as Aras is. We will dissolve the guardianship, we will find some justification. We need not assassinate either of them. We need only convince them to alter the betrothal once more, so that it be to Lunahr," Laranela said.

Naraena shook her head. "It will be two more years until he comes-of-age, and it is Talon that this is for. Arcanus loves him as a son. Arcanus would never agree to it," she argued.

"Father, Mother, please! What is going on? I cannot believe my ears that you might be speaking of killing Prince Talon! I do not want to even contemplate who the other person might be," Elanara said. Surely not High-King Laedrin himself? Yet who else could it possibly be?

Naraena sighed. "Forgive us, Daughter. It is fortunate we took the precaution of clearing the Palace so that we could not be overheard. We had thought we were ready to speak to you, but it was so hard to discuss this even circumspectly while on the way home, lest the Guard overhear us. Laedrin's spies are everywhere. Any of the Reservists might be one of his agents, save for you and Elavar."

She paused, then composed herself further before continuing. "We bear grave news, my child. Arcanus has somehow convinced High-King Laedrin to alter the terms of your betrothal. You are no longer to wed his son, Aras. You are instead to wed Prince Talon. You are to travel at once to Erenia. Rooms have already been prepared for you there," she said, cold fury marring her placid expression, that Laedrin had been so certain they would bow to his will.

"Prince Talon is to join you there within the month, to consummate his engagement to you as according to the custom of his people. You are to remain there until you are wed, sometime within the next year, or perhaps two at the most. He will need a quorum of his Lords in attendance for the ceremony, and it might take that long to gather them, for how scattered his people have become."

Elanara's eyes were wide with shock, but she forced herself to speak. "Marry Talon? But I cannot! It is not for him being a Man. I have learned to love Man as you do, Mother, or at least one Man. But I find Talon… unsettling. When he was here five years ago, when I met him… I cannot describe how I feel, I—there is a wrongness to him, he… he frightens me. Surely the High-King would not attempt to force such a union upon me? Surely, Father, you can refuse?"

Laranela looked at his wife in anguish. "I cannot tell her. I will not."

"Then I must," Naraena said softly, turning from him back to Elanara. "We refused the High-King, of course. We were polite but firm. We have learned much about Talon these past years. He is as cloaked in secrecy as he is in violence, yet finally we have learned one of the secrets he has kept from us, even from Elavar. He is unstable; more, he has a history of madness. I have always sensed the wrongness in him as you have, Elanara, for all Elavar cannot see it, for all he accepts him as he is. But Laedrin would not take 'No' for an answer.

"Arcanus has revealed something to him about the Enemy of Prince Talon's people, something that has enraged Laedrin against their Enemy and has made that madman Laedrin's enemy as well. Laedrin did not reveal it to us. But he was most insistent that you wed Prince Talon. He reminded us that... that training in Nalea can be quite dangerous... that accidents sometimes happen. He said that Eladar might receive special treatment, were we to agree to this, but... were we to disobey him, that... Eladar might not be so fortunate, that... that Eladar might never return to us," Naraena whispered, struggling to finish.

"No," Elanara said, horrified. "He threatened to have Eladar killed? He... he would do it, too, you know he would! We've all heard what he's capable of! He killed his own wife! We all know he did, for all he made it look like she disappeared without a trace when Aras was only eight. He...."

"Then I'll do it, or at least, I will agree to marry Prince Talon. I have no choice. I'll go quietly, meekly, to my exile in Erenia. I'll lay with Talon, consummate the betrothal. You said we were to be wed in a year or two. In a year, Eladar will graduate. He will leave Nalea. He will be safe. We'll make sure of it.

"Father, you have been talking about sending an ambassador to the Dwarves, you have said that if we are to fight this Enemy, why not fight him in their lands, before he ever reaches ours? You can send Eladar.

"He'll do a good job. I know he will. We've seen he can. And he'll be out of Laedrin's reach. Then let's see Laedrin or Talon himself try to force me to wed him," Elanara said, voice uncharacteristically hard.

"You were right to tell me in private. Elavar and Lunahr must not learn of Eladar being in danger and why. Let them think I am a willing bride. They can learn the truth later, once Eladar is safe."

"Are you sure, Elanara? To be exiled, to be forced into his bed," her mother said.

"I will endure, Mother. We all must do what we have to in order to see Eladar safe. And perhaps if we are fortunate, some day soon Laedrin will fall to an assassin of the Enemy, or of our own people. He is hated by many. Then we will not need to play this charade any longer," she said, eyes flashing.

"You are a wonder, Daughter," Laranela said, hugging her. "Now we must plan carefully what we are to say to Elavar and Lunahr and the others."

Master Trader Oberas's Shop, Ardock

OBERAS eyed the boy before him skeptically. Boy he was in his eyes, though Hardred had told him he was a man by law, well past sixteen, nearly seventeen. He could see he already sported much of a man's build.

"You, boy, stay here. You, Hardred, come with me," Oberas said, heading into the back room.

Once there he slammed the door and spun on Hardred. "You've worked for me for five years now, Hardred. In all that time, with all the many guards I've hired, have you ever seen me hire a guard as young as sixteen? Whatever possessed you to think I might now?" Oberas asked, incredulously.

"Because Tarrell is special. I know you scoff at the Feast Day Games, but you miss much by not seeing them. Tarrell outsmarted ninety-nine other men to snatch the crown and win the tournament. He's the youngest to ever claim the purse of one hundred gold, and it was bloodier than usual this year; there were a dozen dead and two full score wounded, twice as many as usual.

"But he also came in thirteenth out of one hundred in the sword bouts. Remember, these are the best swordsmen this City and the surrounding ones have to offer, the ones willing to compete, anyway. They weed out the poor ones well before Feast Day. I'm sure a number of his opponents underestimated him, not taking him seriously until it was too late, when they saw they would lose. I'm also sure once he has a little more length of arm, a little longer reach and the strength to go with it, he'll be able to defeat many of those who beat him.

"And, to top it all off, he can both read and write. So you tell me why you shouldn't hire him, when we've need of a guard?" Hardred countered.

Then he said more softly. "Also, he has Alnas's smile and Rion's. We could use a little more of that around here. You've still not gotten over the men you lost last year, on the trip back from Seaview. There's only me and Alnas and Elkrum, now, to guard you, since Derek left last week, though I'll admit, Elkrum is almost two men by himself, both for his size and ability.

"Please, Oberas! Tarrell's ready to hire on as a caravan guard all the way to Seaview, and they're taking the Southern Road, not the Methris. You've heard as well as I that trouble's been brewing to the south. If even half the rumors are true, something terrible is on the coast and starting to come upriver. You know what his chances of surviving that trip might be," he said, eyes filled with fear. "He'll not. None of them will.

"If it were up to me, I'd be heading north, not south, nor would I be staying here. I wish you'd do as your friends in Athanark have been asking you to do all these years, and move there. If you cared at all for Rion's wellbeing…," he said, realizing he'd gone too far, the moment he said so.

"Enough!" Oberas roared. "One more word and you're gone for good, you and Alnas both! I'll not have him working for me when I've released you. He'd not stay anyway."

TARRELL had been walking around, eyeing the goods in the shop curiously. He turned around when he heard a friendly greeting from behind. "Hello, sir. Might I help you?" He saw a boy who looked to be thirteen, richly dressed in a bright blue shirt with shiny brass buttons and tan pants and boots, with an intelligent, curious expression and a wide smile.

Tarrell grinned back at him. "You must be Rion. Hardred's told me about you." Hardred had also told him Rion had just turned fifteen. He was small for his age. Tarrell was a full head and shoulders taller than Rion. He was proud of his height and that he already showed much of the muscle and frame of a man, rather than a boy.

"I'm here trying to get a job, as a guard. Or I should say, Hardred's trying to get one for me," Tarrell said, laughing. "From the look on Oberas's face when he saw me, I'd say it's not likely I'll be hired."

"Oh, but you mustn't say that!" Rion said. "You have to be confident in front of Oberas if you want him to respect you. He's a wonderful man to work for, in many ways, especially for a guard. Very strict, of course, and he has a terrible temper, but you can learn much from him.

"Those who have stayed with him have done quite well for themselves: Logan and Devrik both opened taverns, Mathis opened a stable, and Stanton opened an inn. He actually encourages that, to have his older men quit guarding and find safer work. He provides references for those who wish to do so, he helps them pick their properties; he does more."

Tarrell was surprised by the genuine respect in Rion's voice.

"But if you were to guard for us, you'd have to like to travel," Rion continued, his expression intent. "Every year Oberas goes on caravan to Logareth or sometimes even all the way to Seaview. He takes the River, you see, when most take the Southern Road. Though he's not gone yet this year, when I thought he might.

"He never takes the same guards with him, of course, two years in a row. It's dangerous work and bad luck to guard too many caravans, I've heard, though Oberas always seems to do well. Except for last year, of course," Rion said, eyes suddenly filled with pain.

Then he forced a smile. "I'm sorry, I'm being too chatty. Oberas has tried to break me of it, but I've almost convinced him it's hopeless. Still, he likes a challenge, so he tries. Oh, but what I meant to say was, nothing. I mean, I meant to give you a chance to talk, if I can still my tongue long enough for you to get a word in edgewise," Rion said, looking up at him eagerly.

Tarrell laughed. "You'd certainly be pleasant enough to work for! Hardred told me you'd be giving me orders, too. I suspect when you do, though, they come out more like suggestions, am I right? You know, 'Could you help me with this,' or 'Would you mind doing that.' I'm sure Oberas's are the ones to sound like orders.

"That's all right, though. I'm used to people spouting orders all types of ways around me. I'm the third son of Varrell, one of the Governor's advisors, or he was one. He died two years ago," he said, his expression sad and wistful for a moment.

"My brothers have been caring for me since. My oldest brother, Darrell, is on the Governor's staff, in place of my Father, now, as he'd been trained to be," he said, and Rion heard the pride for him in Tarrell's voice. "Farrell, the second eldest, is a Captain in the Governor's private Guard. He wanted me to join him there, if I wanted to be a guard as well, but I've spent enough years having him boss me around, without wanting to have him for my commander."

He laughed again. "You see, I'm chatty too, when given half a chance. You're a good listener, Rion. Most people ask you a question and then fidget while you answer it. You know they never hear half of what you tell them. You're easy to talk to."

"So are you," Rion said, then laughed. "Although I don't seem to find anyone too difficult to talk to, just ask anyone!"

Tarrell grinned back at him. "You know, I wasn't at all keen on working here, when Hardred told me about it; I really only came to please him. But now, from talking to you and what you've told me about the caravans Oberas goes on, I'm glad I came. I truly hope he might hire me."

He laughed. "Though I doubt it, from the look he gave me! He thinks I'm too young, though I'm nearly seventeen; it's been just over nine months since I've come-of-age. Still, I can see why he'd be leery of hiring me. Most men don't start guard work until they're eighteen. I know I've not got my full build yet. I'll still be gaining height and muscle; at least I hope I might!" Tarrell said, laughing.

"You hope so! When I was ten I looked to be nine, and now that I'm fifteen I look to be thirteen. I'm a head and shoulders shorter than all my old friends, now, when I used to only be a head shorter. Sometimes it makes me feel I'm shrinking instead of growing!" Rion said, laughing. Then his expression changed. "Uh-oh. It sounds like Oberas is angry again."

They could hear Oberas bellowing at Hardred even through the closed door.

"He doesn't really mean it, does he? That he'll dismiss Hardred and his friend, all because he wanted him to hire me?" Tarrell asked, concerned.

"I don't think so. Oberas yells a lot. He threatens things all the time that he doesn't truly mean. Although sometimes he does mean them," Rion said, eyeing the door a bit anxiously.

"But he can't dismiss Hardred and Alnas both. That would leave us only with Elkrum, and we can't have but a single guard, not even if it is Elkrum. We need at least four: they work in shifts. One always guards us when we go out, one watches the shop, and the other two switch off with them when their shifts are done."

HARDRED came out of the back room, with a rueful expression upon his face. "Well, that didn't go quite as well as I'd hoped. I'm sorry, Tarrell. You'd best go home for now, or wherever else you'd planned to go today before I intercepted you. But please, promise me you'll not hire on to a caravan yet?" Hardred asked hopefully.

"Sure, I can promise that. Rion's swayed me into thinking you had a good idea after all, Hardred. Now all we need to do is convince Oberas it is," Tarrell said, obviously amused.

"I'm glad to hear it," Hardred said, grateful to Rion for having influenced him. "I'll try again later, once he's had a chance to calm down. He doesn't think straight when he's so angry."

OBERAS glared at the closed door. They'd be talking about him, of course. Well, he didn't care what they thought. Why should he take on a child, a sixteen-year-old, subject him to that kind of danger?

Only working for him wasn't so very dangerous, he knew, except for when they left the City, and of course he'd never bring someone so young with him. That boy would die all too easily as a caravan guard.

He'd heard Alarion's voice before. He could ask Alarion what he thought of Tarrell, except Alarion liked everybody. Well, almost everybody. Still, he was a good judge of character.

It would be good for Alarion to have someone closer to his own age here. All his other guards were older: Alnas was twenty-four, Hardred was twenty-three, and Elkrum was twenty-two. Alnas should be retiring from guard work next year, only he doubted he'd do so without Hardred. Those two men were inseparable.

Oberas doubted anyone but he knew the true extent of their bond. He'd been careful over the years to do all he could to aid them in concealing it. Hardred and Alnas were *lythenia* to one another; they loved one another with the intensity and passion of a man and wife, the way he still loved Terhannon. Twenty-five years gone, and the pain of his loss was still as sharp as a blade.

Oberas wondered sometimes how much coin Hardred and Alnas had, for the frugal lifestyle they led, though the two men were known to splurge now and then upon one another. Both Hardred and Alnas lived in the back of the shop, their two adjoining rooms separated by a door that Oberas knew was seldom closed. He knew they slept in one room or the other, in the same bed, though he maintained the two for them for the sake of propriety.

Oberas had always insisted at least two of his guards live with him, but now he had three. Elkrum did as well. But he also had room for a fourth.

Elkrum spent his coin freely: he refused to plan for the future. He only wanted to die fighting. Not that he took chances of course; he'd not have kept him on if he had. It was just that Elkrum had no interest in doing any work but guard work.

Tarrell could read and write. Once Hardred left, he'd need someone who could.

Pfah! He'd give it some more thought when he had a calmer head. "Alarion! Brew me some kakla!" he bellowed as he bent to work on one of his inventories. Hardred always made it so strong. He liked it better when Alarion made it, for all the lad couldn't cook to save his life, save for a few dishes. "And fetch me some…"

"… honey cake, yes, sir," Alarion said, sweeping into the room with a tray of it. "The water will be hot enough soon."

"So, what do you think of Tarrell?" Oberas asked, surprising himself by the question. He'd thought he'd set that issue aside for a while.

"I like him, sir. He's very friendly and he's intelligent. He's confident, without being full of himself. He's a bit cocky, but he's young yet.

"He's the third son of one of the Governor's former advisors: his father, Varrell, died two years ago, but his oldest brother, Darrell, is now an advisor in his father's stead, and his second brother, Farrell, is a Captain of the Governor's Guard, so Tarrell wouldn't be intimidated by the people you deal with. He might even be able to smooth some of the feathers you ruffled last year, and make it less difficult to deal with the Governor's staff. He's perceptive and he listens well.

"He wouldn't mind the caravans at all. I got the feeling he's eager to go. I didn't tell him you'd not let him, for a year or two, at any rate. I didn't want to discourage him from accepting the position, if you offered it to him," Alarion said, looking chagrined about it.

"Hmpfh," Oberas said. Alarion was an excellent judge of character. Oberas had never once known him to be wrong about anyone. Put him in a room with someone for a few moments, and he'd learn more than someone else might after knowing the person for months or even years. Even for Alarion, he'd given a favorable recommendation. Alarion was brutally honest about people, honest about everything. He'd have mentioned any shortcomings he'd seen, as he'd mentioned Tarrell's cockiness.

"Tell Hardred to go after the boy and tell him I need to speak to him," Oberas said. If his own opinion was favorable, perhaps he'd hire him after all.

Alarion grinned and ran from the room.

Oberas shook his head. He wore his heart on his sleeve, that boy. Someday he'd get burned terribly for it, if he wasn't careful.

"LIVE here? Why?" Tarrell asked Hardred.

"Because it's one of the conditions Oberas is requiring. He wants you where he can keep an eye on you. He feels responsible for all his guards, not just you, for being so young," Hardred was quick to add, at the look on Tarrell's face. "He's not like most employers. When something happens to one of his men, it hurts him deeply. When one of us dies…." Hardred looked intently at Tarrell. "He doesn't get over it, ever.

"His men usually fare very well, even on caravan. You're too inexperienced to know, and it's not something merchants go around advertising, or caravan Captains, but usually at best only fifty percent of the guards who start out with a caravan survive it, and often it's much worse. With Oberas, he usually averages twenty-five percent losses or less. He's had more than one trip where he's lost no one. That's why last year was especially hard for him to cope with," Hardred said, his expression grim.

"Usually he starts with four guards, for the shop. Then he hires on two new men, about three months before the trip. He leaves one of his most experienced men with one of the newer ones, and takes the other four with him. Then, at the other end, he hires new men, to replace any he's lost and to bring the total to eight, to guard the loaded wagons or boat he returns with, then he keeps the best of those who survive.

"He planned the same last year. Alnas was to have gone with him, with Ethan and Rheen, and Drake, one of the new men, and I was to stay here, with Sarnas, the other new man. Only Alnas took ill, terribly ill; so bad we feared for his life. Oberas couldn't delay his trip any longer. He left without knowing whether Alnas would live. Oberas took Sarnas instead. He only was able to do it because Rion's father and uncle are in the City Guard. They and some of their friends took turns filling in for Alnas's shifts, on their off shifts, while Rion and I and the healer nursed Alnas back to health."

Tarrell was watching Hardred intently. He could see the shadow of the terror over his friend's illness in Hardred's face.

Hardred continued on softly, so softly that Tarrell had to strain to hear. "Ethan had been with him for three years. He'd planned to open an inn after coming back from that caravan. Oberas had already helped him pick out the site for it. Rheen had been with him for two years. Both were fine men, and the two new ones, too.

"They all made it to Seaview without difficulty. Oberas hired on his usual four new guards. Elkrum was one of them; you've yet to meet him. They started back upriver. They were halfway back, just north of Lomas, when it happened. The boat ran aground, when it shouldn't have: the way had been clear and the pilot experienced. It was a trap; it was river pirates. They were taken completely by surprise, even Oberas, and he's not one to ever fall for such things."

Tarrell could see the pain in Hardred's face. "The pirates bungled it, though. The boats sank, both of them, theirs and Oberas's. Oberas's started to pull free, to get away, so the pirates rammed them to stop them. Only they rammed his boat so hard, they cut it clear in two. Oberas lost everything to the River, all his goods. He lost a fortune. He only kept the purse at his side, though he nearly drowned for the weight of it. But that wasn't what's been eating at him this past year.

"Many of the pirates died in the wreck, but so did many of Oberas's guards, and the rest drowned, those who didn't die fighting. When it was all done, all the pirates were dead, but of the eight guards, eight good men, two of whom Oberas had known for years, only one man survived, and only just: Elkrum. He and Oberas were barely able to stagger back to Lomas. Elkrum carried Oberas most of the way, though it nearly killed him, injured as he was and heavy as Oberas is. It took weeks for them to recover, before they could continue on.

"Alnas and I feared Oberas was lost for sure, this time, for not coming when we expected him to, but Rion refused to give up hope. Rion kept us doing business as usual, convincing all Oberas's customers and suppliers and buyers that he was acting on Oberas's orders, as if he were in contact with him, or following prewritten instructions. And then Oberas came back.

"When he saw the three of us, me and Rion and Alnas, especially Alnas, alive and well, when he'd been so sure he'd not be, he cried. He just fell to his knees and wept. We got him into bed. He grew feverish, and we tended to him, as we had to Alnas. It's thanks to Rion Oberas recovered as much as he did. He'd have died without Rion. But Oberas has changed. He was so arrogant before, so self-assured. That's all gone now," Hardred said softly.

"He should have left on caravan two months ago, but he hasn't. I think he won't this year. His business suffered terribly from the lost boat. If it weren't for Rion's handling of his affairs while he was away, he probably would have lost everything. As it is, he lost a number of buyers and suppliers. You might think him rich, but he's lost a full half of what he had. And I'm afraid he might not leave the City again. It took him weeks and weeks to hire a fourth guard, Derek. We saw he almost couldn't do it.

"That's part of why I wanted him to hire you, Tarrell. Not just for your own good, because you'd learn from him, you'd profit from working with him, but for his sake, also. Because he needs your smile as much as he needs a good guard. He has to put what happened behind him, but he takes every death personally. He blames himself for all of them.

"In the past, he's always been obsessed with coin, with the business, with profit. It's all to ease an old pain, a loss long ago that was too terrible to bear. I know a little about it, but I won't say more, I've said far too much to you already. Alnas would be shocked to have heard me speak for so long."

Hardred looked intently at Tarrell. "Please take the position, and more, agree to live here with us. All three of us live here with Oberas. I do all the cooking. I'm good at it, too: even Oberas eats in the shop many nights, now, instead of frequenting the inns he used to. Rion does most of the cleaning; it's part of his duties. We talked Alnas into doing the laundry long ago, somehow. Elkrum hauls the water from the well and prepares Oberas's baths for him, as well as does all the rest of the heavy lifting: he's got the build for it. We'll only ask you to help here and there.

"Mostly, I think, we'd like you to be a companion for Rion. I love him, of course. We all do, but he's almost a son to me. He's almost of age. He's almost ready to be a man, but he still has the body and heart of a boy. You're much nearer his age. What he really needs now is a brother, someone he might share things with, someone he might confide in."

Tarrell looked at Hardred in surprise. "Amazing. And here I thought you were worried about me, that I'd get myself hurt going to Seaview. I'd no idea you wanted me hired as much for Oberas's and Rion's sakes as mine! You're an interesting man, Hardred."

"Very well. I will tend to their hearts and spirits as well as their bodies. With Rion, at least, I'd have done so anyway; now that you've shown me Oberas has a heart, I'll know to take care of it as well."

Hardred clapped him on the shoulder. "I knew I'd chosen well in you, Tarrell. Come, let me introduce you to Elkrum. He can be a bit intimidating, at first glance. He's big and loud, but he's a fine man."

Master Trader Oberas's Shop, Ardock
Six Months Later

"LET'S see if you remember what I taught you last week," Tarrell said to Rion.

Rion was facing off with him in the back room, wooden practice sword held at the ready. He was eager to spar with Tarrell. They could only do so when Oberas wasn't about. Oberas didn't approve at all of Rion learning the sword. Rion would only do so when he was caught up on all the work Oberas left him. Unfortunately, that often wasn't until after Oberas returned. As a result, their practice sessions were disappointingly few and far between, for all Tarrell had been with them six months already. Rion wished he had a real sword to practice with, to wear when they went about the City.

"Good. Very good," Tarrell encouraged, as Rion parried the blows aimed in his direction.

It had been hard enough seeing Drew in a City Guard's uniform, six months ago. But just last week he'd seen Ric in his as well, in the Market. He'd not even known he'd joined. He'd all but lost touch with the two of them, and Matt as well, for all they'd been inseparable before he apprenticed. He looked and felt like a little boy, compared to them.

"Rion!" Tarrell cried, not able to divert the blow in time.

Rion had been so wrapped up thinking about his friends that he'd fallen for the feint to his chin and been completely unprepared for the thrust to his unprotected stomach. He was suddenly grateful for the padded armor Hardred had forced him to wear, when he'd first caught Tarrell teaching him the blade, even though they were only using wood. Still, he let out a "whuff," of air, as he fell back, hard, onto his bottom.

"Are you all right?" Tarrell asked, his face creased in worry.

"I'm fine," Rion said, struggling to his feet, the armor making him clumsy. He winced as his stomach muscles strained as he did so.

"Are you sure? I hit you pretty hard. I wasn't expecting to hit you, or I'd have pulled back on it. It's been weeks since you've fallen for a blow like that. What happened?"

Rion's face flushed. "I wasn't paying attention," he admitted sheepishly. "I was thinking about my friends in the Guard."

"Well, let's hope they never think of you like that, when they're out on patrol," Tarrell said. "Distractions like that can kill you in a real battle, Rion. Perhaps we'd better cut today's practice short."

"No! Please, Tarrell? We so seldom get the chance to practice. I promise I'll pay attention," Rion swore fervently.

"All right. How about you attack me this time?"

"Rion," Elkrum called from the main room. "There's someone here to see you."

Rion's eyes widened. He'd not heard the front bell. He quickly stripped off the torso pad he'd been wearing, and the cloth bucklers and kneepads, and ran his hands over his hair to make sure it was flat. Then, trying not to appear like he was hurrying, he went out to greet the customer. Only it wasn't a customer, it was Cedric. Rion hurried over to welcome him, but the welcoming smile froze on his face as he saw Cedric's eyes. They were brimming with tears.

Rion's heart started hammering. "No. Don't tell me. Not Ric? Has... has something happened to Ric?" Rion asked, fearful of what he might hear. He was oblivious to Tarrell, who had come up behind him.

"No. Not Adric, praise Elmoth. He was spared," Cedric said, putting his hands on Rion's shoulders. "I'm so sorry, Alarion," Cedric said, as his chin began trembling and the tears began streaming down his face.

Rion paled. "No. No, it can't be. Not... not Father?" Rion asked, looking searchingly at him.

"We lost seven," Cedric said, his voice a ragged whisper. "If it wasn't for Anorion and Farion and Justin, we'd have lost twice as many. They saved me, Rion, me and Adric and six others. You need to know they died heroes."

"No. No! Not Father and Uncle Farion," Rion said, looking desperately at Cedric. "Both of them? They can't be!"

"Come, Rion. I'll take you to them. You need to see them. You'll never believe they're gone if you don't. I still can't believe it, and I was there when they fell," Cedric said, voice haunted. "I tried to protect them. I swear I tried. It's a miracle any of us made it out of there alive."

Rion looked at Elkrum desperately and around at the shop. "I... I can't leave. Oberas left me in charge... I...."

Tarrell clapped his hands on his shoulders and looked him in the eyes. "Rion, of course you must go. Come, I'll go with you. Elkrum, close the shop. Lock the door behind us, until Oberas gets back. He'll understand."

Elkrum nodded. "Tarrell's right, Rion. You go. Leave Oberas to me."

Rion nodded numbly and headed for the door.

Cedric led them across the City to the guardhouse, then into the Tower and down a flight of stairs to a thick wooden door.

"Cedric! The Captain needs to see you," a voice called from down the hall.

"I'm with Anorion's son," Cedric replied.

"I'll stay with him. The Captain needs you, now. You're the only other Lieutenant who was there. The Lieutenant Governor's been called into it, for Governor Jeffran being killed along with all the others," the Guard said.

Cedric looked at Rion, agonized. Tarrell said to him, "It's all right. I'll be with him. Come back when you're able. I'll take good care of him until you can."

"You must be Tarrell. Anorion told me about you. I'm grateful to you. Alarion, I'll be back as soon as I can. You know I wouldn't go if I had a choice," Cedric said.

Rion nodded numbly, staring at the heavy wooden door. Reluctantly, Cedric left, and the other Guard unlocked the door and let them in.

Rion had thought his mother's death was terrible. But she'd been ill for so long; in his heart he'd known she would die. But his father should still be alive: he had still been so strong, so healthy, so young. He'd even learned to smile and laugh again, as Mother had wanted, though he'd never looked at another woman. He'd never had even a passing interest in any; he couldn't, he said. He'd never love another, after her. And now he was gone, Father and Uncle Farion, both at once.

Rion was alone now, truly alone. There was no one to comfort him this time. Even Hardred wasn't here; he was with Oberas. Hardred could have helped ease the terrible coldness and emptiness. Rion's shoulders started to shake as he began sobbing silently, looking at them both, the sheets that had covered them clenched tightly, one in each hand.

"Rion, I'm here. Lean on me," Tarrell said, wrapping a strong arm around him. Rion dropped the sheets, turned to him, and fell against his chest, sobbing, as Tarrell comforted him.

Rion realized Tarrell knew what it was like. He'd lost his own father. As soon as the tears abated enough that Rion could speak, Rion began to talk to

Tarrell, about his father, about Farion, even about his mother. Rion poured his heart out to him, knowing his heart was safe with Tarrell.

Tarrell had become like a brother to him these months past. He'd always wanted a brother. Mother had always been sorry that she'd not been able to give him one. She was an only child too, —her mother had died birthing her—but she'd seen how close his father and Farion were.

He began sobbing harder in Tarrell's arms, thinking of all those he had lost, as Tarrell held him and did his best to comfort him.

TARRELL remembered how it felt, when his own father had died so suddenly, how Farrell and Darrell had done their best to comfort him when their own hearts were breaking as well. It didn't seem to have helped them much that they were older. He suspected nothing ever helped grief such as that, other than having someone to hold you, to listen to you. He was glad he was there for Rion.

Cedric returned a short while later. Rion let go of Tarrell and hugged Cedric instead. "It's not your fault, Cedric. You must know it's not. I'm so glad you and Ric are safe." Tarrell was amazed at how quickly Rion was able to go from needing comfort to comforting his father's friend. "If it won't hurt too much, please, I need to know what happened."

"IT WILL hurt, terribly, but I'll tell you. You should know." Cedric told him the whole story: how they'd thought it was just another drinking brawl at the Gilded Stein, but how this one turned nasty, like that other, so many years ago, the one where his father had been hurt.

This one ended with a full-scale riot, much worse than that other time. It had spilled out into the street, and down the block, until four whole city blocks seemed to have gone mad, with Governor Jeffran's coach getting caught up in the middle of it.

"It was as if some evil seized those men. For a while, there, I didn't think any of us would make it out alive," he said, voice scarcely a whisper. Then he continued on more strongly. "Adric would like to see you, Alarion. He feels terrible about how distant he's grown from you. Can you come to our house for dinner this evening?

"No. Not tonight. I... I couldn't. Perhaps later, after... after the burial," Rion said.

"Of course. Tarrell, you'll be able to see him safely back?" Cedric asked.

"OF COURSE. Come sir, I'll see you get back to the shop," Tarrell said formally, adopting proper demeanor, guard to employer, with practiced ease. Once in the street, he said, "Would you like to come have a drink with me, Rion, to your father?" He knew Rion didn't usually drink.

"No. No, I just want to go home," Rion said, then stopped. "I... I meant back to the shop. When did it start becoming home to me? I saw Father so seldom this past year. I... I should have gone home more, seen more of him... I...." He looked at Tarrell in despair.

"No, Rion. You loved your father and he knew it. You've got nothing to feel guilty over. You can ruin your whole life with such thoughts, if you let them seize you. I've seen it happen, not to me or my brothers, fortunately, but to enough others.

"The past is the past, Rion. You can't ever change it. You just need to make sure you do your best living day to day as you can, so you don't have any regrets in the future. You need to remember how to smile and how to laugh, when you can bear to, when the pain dulls enough."

RION nodded. "My mother told me the same thing, before she died. It was important to her that her death not end my life, as well, or... or Father's," he said, eyes tearing. "But when she died, I had Father and Uncle Farion, and I still had my friends, but now... I'm all alone," he sobbed, then wiped angrily at the tears, humiliated to be crying on the City streets.

"No, Rion, you're not alone, never alone. You've me, Hardred, Alnas, Elkrum, and even Oberas to look after you, to comfort you. You're as much family to me now as my true brothers are. I'll always be there for you, Rion, whenever you have need of me."

Rion looked up at him, eyes bright. He didn't know what to say, he was so moved by Tarrell's words.

Master Trader Oberas's Shop, Ardock
Three Months Later

RION couldn't believe the changes to the City that had happened in the three months since his father died. He'd seen the tension continue to build as the first trickle of refugees from the south was followed by a steady stream and then a river and then a flood. Some had come all the way from Seaview, it was rumored, fleeing city after city, as the enemy chased them ever northward, as every haven they sought was attacked and burned.

"Alarion! Bring the oushka!" Oberas bellowed, while the shop bell was still ringing from the door opening.

Rion was surprised. Oberas had only drunk oushka once before in front of him, with Tarrell, two weeks ago, when he'd been mourning the anniversary of the death of an old friend, someone named Terhannon, and had gotten so drunk he'd fallen asleep at the table. Rion hurried into the front room with the bottle and two glasses. He almost dropped the tray when he saw Hardred.

"Calm yourself, Alarion, it's not nearly as bad as it looks," Oberas said, taking the bottle from him and pouring a generous amount of the expensive aged liquor onto his kerchief and dabbing at the blood on Hardred's forehead with it. "By Elmoth, will you sit down!" Oberas bellowed at Hardred.

Rion stared at Oberas, truly terrified now. He'd invoked Elmoth! He never spoke the God's name, and Oberas's hand was visibly shaking.

"Oberas, heed your own words. I'm all right. I swear I'm not about to die, nor even pass out," Hardred said.

"What happened?" Rion asked, wide-eyed.

"We were attacked, in the street, in broad daylight, in full view of two of the City Guard!" Oberas said in disgust. "It was the refugees. They just came boiling out of the alley. They had me on the ground before I even knew what was happening. If Hardred hadn't been so quick upon his feet, I'd have been dead," Oberas said angrily, then took a drink from the bottle of oushka in his hands.

"I'm a fool for staying as long as I have. I'm sending a message to Athanark tomorrow. There's no shortage of men leaving Ardock. I'll find someone trustworthy enough to carry it. I'm selling the shop. We'll take whatever goods we can't sell quickly with us and we'll start fresh in Athanark. There will be a month's travel, including a range of mountains between us and whatever evil's headed this way. It might be enough. If not, we'll head further north, and you can be sure I'll take my friends in Athanark with me.

"Elkrum, I want you to fetch a healer, despite what Hardred thinks," he said, glaring at him. "Where's Tarrell? I don't want him on the streets. If he's not here, you're to find him and bring him here, even if he's with that girl, Elsbeth is it?"

"It was, sir, but he's not seen her in months. I think he might be at The Painted Pony. I could go…," Rion started to say.

"No! You're not to leave this shop without my permission and at least two guards, Alarion, do you understand?" Oberas said harshly.

"Yes, sir!" Rion said. He'd never seen Oberas like this.

Oberas glared at Hardred. "And you. You're not to get yourself hurt in my service ever again, do you understand me? I'll not outlive another guard! I'll not lose another man, ever, not unless I go down fighting beside him. Is that understood?" Oberas growled.

"It's my job to protect you, sir. But even if it weren't, I'd do so anyway. You know that. Just do me a favor and try not to frighten Alnas, would you? He'll be upset enough when he hears we're to leave the City. Relieved that we're going, mind you, just worried for me. He's convinced himself I'll not survive another caravan. Although it's been almost six years since my last one, I doubt he'll be reassured," Hardred said.

Rion listened, wide-eyed. Leave the City? For good? He couldn't believe it. But what about Ric and Matt and Drew and their families? He'd try to convince them to go, but he doubted they would. They and their fathers would want to stay to protect the City.

And Tarrell's brothers? Tarrell saw them rarely enough, but Rion knew he still loved them. What if Tarrell decided to stay? Rion was deeply troubled at the thought he might.

Oberas said, "As soon as Alnas and Tarrell arrive for their shifts, we'll begin preparations. Depending on how much I can sell before we go, we'll need three to ten wagons for goods and supplies, horses to draw them, and four guards per wagon. We'll contact all our old guards, urge them to join us, and see if they have any trustworthy relatives or other men they can recommend. I've never before traveled with my known and trusted guardsmen so outnumbered by new men, but we've no choice."

Rion was greatly relieved when later that evening Tarrell seemed eager to go with them.

"But what of your brothers? Will they come too?" Rion asked, voicing his earlier concern.

"No, Rion, they won't. I know without asking them that they won't. But I'll ask them just the same, of course. It's folly to stay here, with what I've been hearing in the taverns. I won't tell you what I've learned. Your imagination is too great. You'd not be able to sleep at night with the stories I've heard. But you've seen the City changing. It's getting worse by the day. It's heading toward anarchy, toward tragedy.

"I'm only glad you'll be safely away from here too. I couldn't leave here, if you weren't going, but I'll not let you go without me to protect you, either. It's a harsh world out there, Rion, though neither you nor I have seen much of it yet. I doubt we've any idea of what we'll find, once we leave the safety of these City walls. But these walls won't hold the City safe for much longer, I fear," Tarrell said softly.

Rion nodded. He'd already seen and heard more than he wished to have, more than Tarrell probably realized. There had been more and more refugees, all coming from villages and towns and cities along the Methris, from the south: merchants and craftsmen at first, then the very poor and the very rich. And there had been stories he'd heard, terrible stories, of forests and entire cities burning and fighting, terrifying beasts and things that might have once been men, some even said the walking dead, come to life again.

He was glad Oberas had decided to leave. The Ardock he had known was already gone. He shuddered to think what it might soon become. He feared the enemy would not stop before it reached them, that not even the Elves might be able to fight such terrifying evil. He wondered if they would flee before it too, or if they would stand and fight. He wondered if what he'd heard was true, that Elves live forever, or whether they might be killed, as a Man might.

The River Elf Kingdom of Riviera

KING LARANELA looked about him at the breathtaking marble buildings amidst the crystal fountains surrounding him, thinking how fragile, how ephemeral they truly were. He had spent much of the past weeks in the Library, ever since they'd learned that the Enemy had defied all their predictions and left the last three Dwarven Kingdoms untouched, that he'd bypassed all their defenses by launching his attack against the Lands of Men from the coast and even now he was rapidly advancing up the Methris.

Laranela had been pouring over ancient texts and tomes, insuring that their defenses were as formidable as he could make them. Inevitably, in his research, he'd come across pictures of the world that once was, the Homeland his people, the Oceana, and their distant kin, the Aerta, had forever lost in a single final night of terror and fire, the last night of the War. And it was fire that was coming to claim them again, though thankfully not the fire of the Faeren. They were extinct, them and the Aerie, consumed by the madness they'd unleashed, though there was scant comfort in that knowledge.

Millions had died, their Homeland had been destroyed, and they'd doomed the Dwarven Homeland as well, one land lost to fire and the other to flood, though he doubted the Dwarves knew they were the ones responsible for their loss. He took a deep breath, forcing such thoughts aside.

He had prepared as well as he was able. And he had sent those he loved most to safety. Elanara was yet in Erenia, awaiting Prince Talon's return. Eladar was in Dorolingas, or perhaps Ironhand, in the Dwarven Lands, as an ambassador as he and Naraena and Elanara had planned, to protect him from Laedrin. He had warned Eladar against venturing into Malar, for their intelligence on that kingdom.

Only a few short weeks ago he had sent Naraena to Salenia by way of Tanieria, to visit their friends there on the pretense of being a courier for messages he dared not trust to anyone else regarding their plan to ally themselves with the Dwarves against High-King Laedrin's command.

He planned to send Elavar after her within the week, also on a courier mission, to follow in Naraena's footsteps. The messages would be genuine enough. He only hoped Elavar would not deduce that he was being sent away for his own safety. Elavar would never leave him nor his people were he to guess his father's true intentions.

He would send Lunahr away as soon afterward as he dared, either to join Eladar in the Dwarven Lands or Elanara in Erenia, he was not sure which yet, but he would not risk the life of the son-of-his-heart when the children of his blood had been sent to safety.

Master Trader Oberas's Shop, Ardock
One Week Later

OBERAS eyed Hardred and Alnas intently. They were safely tucked away in Hardred's room, and Elkrum and Tarrell were keeping Alarion distracted in the storeroom. "I've already spoken to Tarrell. He understands the part he needs to play if things don't go right on this trip. I've instructed him that if the situation is dire, if we are being overrun by bandits, or worse things, if a number of guards have fallen, he's to flee with Alarion to whatever safety he can find. He's to hide him, to protect him.

"What Tarrell doesn't realize is that I'm doing so as much for his protection as for Alarion's. I'll not see either of those boys killed. Tarrell's job is to protect Alarion. Yours is to protect the both of them. If they flee, you are to follow. It's your job to see the two of them safe from harm.

"You're not to think twice about me. Elkrum will protect me, along with the rest of the guards I'm hiring, and I'll be standing and fighting alongside them. I was as good and nearly as big and muscled as Elkrum once. I was a master wrestler. I was defeated only once in all my many battles, and I'm yet a deadly knife fighter. I've a blade again, and I've been training with Elkrum daily to hone my skills. So then, what is your job on this trip?"

"To see Rion and Tarrell safe," Alnas said.

Hardred shook his head silently, his eyes never leaving Oberas's.

Alnas tensed beside Hardred, obviously expecting Oberas to be enraged. But this was too important for fury. Instead, Oberas spoke softly, intently, from the heart. "Do you remember the night you drank with me, Hardred? You might have been too drunk to, so I'll remind you. I hate having to cause you pain by speaking his name, but you've left me no choice. I had a Julian too, Hardred. His name was Terhannon and he died in my stead, the way Julian died in yours. Only he was more to me. He was my Alnas. We'd consummated our love. We'd shared many days and nights in one another's arms, as you and Alnas have, though we were so blessed for a far shorter time than the two of you.

"You'll save Alarion and Tarrell in my stead, because you cannot save me, Hardred, no matter how hard you try. I'm already dead. I've been dead since the day Elmoth took Terhannon from me. My spirit has been, at any rate. But if anything happens to those two boys, my body will follow. I swear to Elmoth, if they die and I live, I'll cut my own throat. They're like sons to me, the closest thing I'll ever have, the two of them and the three apprentices before them.

"I can't save those other three. Kenneth was in Seaview, with his wife and children. I've scarcely been able to sleep for worrying about him, about them, since I've heard what's coming upriver. I've hoped that they either died quickly or somehow weren't there. If the Enemy of the Dwarven Lands and his minions... if...." Oberas swallowed hard, the thought of Kenneth ever being hurt like that again, only worse, paralyzing him.

He barely felt the strong hands on his shoulders, shaking him. It took all his will to focus on Hardred's anxious face before him.

"Can you hear me now? I'll do it, Oberas. I'll save Rion and Tarrell both for you. I swear to you that as long as I'm with them, they'll not come to harm.

"Forgive me. For all you know of my pain, I know little of yours. I've had Alnas to heal my spirit. I wish you might have found someone as well, but I know you cannot. Not if he was your Alnas. A man can only love so fiercely once in his life. It is both a blessing and a curse, but far more of the former, for those of us who are fortunate. Every day is a gift, to be cherished.

"But you yet have those who love you, Oberas, for all you might wish you did not. You've been like an uncle to Rion, and whether you realize it or not, a friend to me. I'll do my best to see you safe as well, but not at risk to Rion or Tarrell. You have my word. I swear by the Mariner's Code, I'll protect Rion and Tarrell with my life, for as long as I'm with you all."

Oberas nodded stiffly, satisfied, and headed for the storeroom, when weeks ago he'd have headed for a bottle. He had no time for drink. He'd spar with Elkrum instead. He'd be as ready as possible for the many potential dangers that lay ahead. And though no doubt more than a few would think him mad for it, despite the stories they were hearing in the taverns, he'd be sure to tell his guards both old and new of the true dangers they faced: chimaera, hippogryphs, and Revenants, and the ways to defeat them, if not slay them. No one could slay a Revenant. They were already dead.

Loessen had been the one to behead Terhannon, before they buried him, to keep him from being turned into such a monster. It was one of the many reasons Loessen had never forgiven any of them for losing him.

He forced the memories back down into the cairn in his mind, knowing they would rise up and haunt him until he drew his final breath. His only goal now was to see that no others were added to the ranks of the dead. Truly the ranks: an army was coming, inexorably, up the Methris: an army of the walking dead.

The Royal Palace, The River Elf Kingdom of Riviera

"MAJESTY, forgive me, I know you had not wished to be disturbed, but there is a visitor of some importance. Also, she has come from Tanieria, so I thought you would wish to see her," Minister Haravela said to King Laranela.

"A visitor from Tanieria? Send her to me at once," Laranela said. Could she have word of Naraena? Surely nothing could have happened to her? Or Elavar. Elavar should have only just left from Tanieria for Salenia.

Laranela greeted the smiling lady who sought audience with him in relief and dismay upon recognizing her. Tashira was a renowned healer, and he had no doubt that they would soon be in need of her services, but he would no more wish her to be here than he had wanted Naraena or his children to be.

Tashira was like a niece to his wife; Naraena loved her almost as a second daughter. She was the daughter of Naraena's first lover, Iradne. The two women had spent four decades together with one another and a host of shared lovers, before Iradne had fallen in love with the one man they could never share, Maratash. Naraena had gracefully stepped aside so that the two might wed and had remained close to the couple ever since. Why had Tashira chosen now of all times to come?

"Lady Joy," he said formally, not revealing Tashira's name to those of the Guard around him who might hear it and did not already know it.

"Majesty," she said, curtsying to him gracefully. Then she looked at him in concern. "They did not tell me you were ill."

Laranela saw his Guards look anxious at her pronouncement.

"I am not ill, merely a little tired," Laranela said, smiling at her. "But seeing you is as refreshing as a swim in the River. Come, walk with me, Lady Joy. I would hear news of Tanieria and of your parents in particular. It has been too long since your mother's last letter to Naraena," he said lightly.

Tashira seemed to realize he wished to speak with her alone and looked like she regretted speaking before the others about his health. "Of course, Majesty," she said, beaming, the carefree smile of joy for which she was known lighting her face.

Laranela walked to his wife's favorite garden, realizing belatedly it was not the sanctuary he had hoped for. "Beryl. I should have realized you might be here," Laranela said, eyeing the son-of-his-heart in compassion. Lunahr had been terribly lonely, with Eladar gone for so long, and then Elanara, and now Naraena and Elavar. Even his many friends and his music could not lift his spirits.

"Majesty! Forgive me! I had wanted to speak with you, but I see now is not the time, I...." He faltered before the frank gaze of the lady beside him.

"Ah, so you are Lunahr," Tashira said, her intelligent face creasing in dawning understanding. "Naraena told me so much about you when I saw her in Tanieria. Though I am pleased to meet one who holds her heart so strongly, I wish I had not. You should not yet be here, Lord of Eagles. The Watch can ill afford to lose you in what will no doubt be only the first of many battles in our lands."

Laranela felt a chill of foreboding. Naraena had realized the true danger, yet still had left for Tanieria without resisting his efforts to see her safe? It was a wonder, then, that she'd not come with Tashira, instead of continuing on to Salenia, as they had planned. He could only hope that she was indeed already safely in the west, that she would not instead return.

LUNAHR gaped at the strange Elf in unconcealed astonishment. She knew his given name and the Queen's, and she had spoken to him as if she were kin!

"You are suffering from the same affliction as his Majesty," she accused gently, her face creased in compassion and concern. "Not illness at all, but fatigue, and suppressed fear, many weeks of unending stress. I was right to come, despite Mother's misgivings. I am sure others of your people are suffering in silence also, Laranela. Your healers will have need of my assistance, with Naraena gone. All the more so once the attack comes, of course. I fear there might be many wounded who will need my aid."

At Laranela's flabbergasted expression and Lunahr's stricken one, she looked at Laranela, her own face betraying her shock. "Surely you have not been concealing the true extent of the danger from him? How could you... forgive me! You had planned to send him to safety as well, hadn't you?"

"I am such a fool! Mother has often told me I am far too frank and direct, that I have never learned the arts of circumspection and concealment we so cherish, but until today I never truly understood.... Perhaps I should not have come, but having done so, I cannot say I am sorry to have. I can tell what you are thinking, Laranela, though I cannot read your thoughts; you know my talent lies in other directions. You hope to send me safely away as well, do you not?

"You may save your arguments. I will not go. I will weather this storm with you. Together we will see your people as safe and well as we can make them."

"Then I was right as to why both the Queen and Sylvan have gone," Lunahr said in conviction, speaking Elavar's common name in case this stranger who knew far too much by some chance did not already know it. He walked from them pensively, forcing his hand not to go to his sword hilt as it ached to, then spun about and approached again as if to complete an accusation.

He timed his fall perfectly, making sure that Laranela was on the other side of the stranger and unable to aid him, managing to trip upon the path of smooth river stone he had walked hundreds of times, falling toward the lady, reaching for her to catch himself. He had been sure she would try to yank away, but she did not; she instead caught him.

Heart pounding in terror, expecting to feel a concealed blade pierce him at any moment, he reached out with his Power and probed her at the instant of contact. He expected to find her a Resemblant, one of the twisted agents of the Enemy that took the form of a trusted friend. Instead he found light and joy and laughter and healing and music, so strong that he was left truly reeling from it.

"Lunahr!" Laranela said in concern, looking at the lady in sudden suspicion.

"Majesty! No, it's all right. She truly must be who she appears to be.

"Forgive me, Lady! I had to test you I... I'm not supposed to speak of such things! How could I have forgotten? But never have I felt one such as you. I was not prepared for...." Lunahr forced his babbling tongue still, appalled that he had betrayed so much.

She was looking at him in amazement. "I did not know that any Man save for the wizard Arcanus might possess our magic."

"Magic? No, it is not magic, it is only Power, we—no, forgive me, I'm not supposed to say anything about it ever, I...." Lunahr stopped again, completely tongue-tied.

"WELL, now that you have seen I am not whom you feared me to be, an agent of the Enemy, no doubt, and now that I have seen your heart as well, why don't the three of us get some dinner? I can tell it has been many meals since either of you has last truly eaten. As a healer, I insist you join me. And don't think I won't tell Naraena if you refuse," she threatened Laranela with a mischievous twinkle in her eye, as he opened his mouth to oppose the idea.

She grinned as he closed it again wordlessly. "That's much better. I can see I am going to have a lovely visit, despite the intentions of outside forces to see to the contrary. Now I insist you feed me and then give me the grand tour of your kingdom again. It has been many decades since last I was here and I'm sure at least one rock or fountain might have changed during my absence," she said, laughing as if she did not have a care in the world, leading the two of them away, determined to do what she could to fortify them against the coming dark times ahead.

The premonition of doom had hit with the force of a hammer, the moment Naraena embraced her in Tanieria. Never before had her carefully concealed Power flared so strongly, in such an unexpected direction. It was all she could do to remain standing.

She was her mother's daughter, in that her true talents lay in healing. Perhaps someone who was fortunate or cursed enough to have precognitive visions might have seen what was to come more clearly. All she knew was that the woman she loved almost as a second mother was in deadly peril, as was her family, her kingdom, her people.

Later, when she overheard Naraena speaking with her mother, she learned the terrifying details of the danger coming up the Methris. Tashira was furious that the High-King had not already activated the Reservists, that he had not sent platoons of them to reinforce the defenses of Riviera and Loatia, to protect them.

Surely Laedrin had received the reports of the coming danger and calls for assistance that Laranela had sent? Surely Laedrin would not let his lingering anger against Laranela and Naraena for their defiance of him over half a millennia ago influence such an important tactical decision?

She was also an Oceana and a Latent, though Laedrin did not know the latter. As such, she knew she could not influence the High-King. He would never listen to her, even if she revealed what little she knew of what was to come and how she knew it, or she would have done so, even knowing it would likely cost her her life. So instead, she had come here, to do all in her power to save those she could.

The Southern Road, Northbound, En Route to Athanark
Three Weeks Later

"I CAN'T believe we're actually doing this again," Alnas said, their first morning on the road. "I, for one, am too old for this!" he complained, stretching his back, glad for Esular's smooth gait. What a horse he was! He'd sworn to Hardred that the horse must have the blood of the steeds of Aralon in his veins, both for his build and his gait. He'd been a true find, he and the other stallion and two mares purchased with him, almost worth what Oberas had paid for them, though he'd had to pay far more for the other guards' steeds than what they were worth.

"I'D ALMOST forgotten what it feels like to sit in the saddle day in and day out," Hardred said, but he smiled and patted Halahar affectionately. He was a high-spirited mount. Halahar and Esular reminded him of him and Alnas, for what the horse merchant had said of them. The man had been adamant that they could only be sold as a pair, that they'd not stand to be separated from each other, which was quite rare in stallions.

The two mares they'd purchased along with them, Janahar and Kaldahar, that Tarrell and Elkrum rode, were also exceptional mounts, and also had been sold as a pair. Their newer guards had not fared nearly so well, but no one had complained. They were to a man relieved to be leaving the City. They'd have walked if they'd had to.

It had taken them almost a month to sell the shop and liquidate much of Oberas's goods. They'd paid four times what the horses and wagons were worth, but Oberas had gotten twice what the shop was worth. You couldn't find a space on the floor of the most meager inn in the City; it was as if every day was Feast Day, except no one was smiling or laughing or celebrating now. Most had no coin to spend, either. Many didn't stay in the City for more than a night or two. There was a constant flow of people leaving, heading for the Velmar Mountains, for Athanark, Logareth, and Fenemal and even the cities to the west of them, over the Coroden Mountains.

Oberas had a total of twenty guards for this journey: Hardred, Alnas, Elkrum, Tarrell, and sixteen new guards, many of them younger brothers, cousins, and even sons of their former guards, as well as a few of their retired guards, guarding five wagons. Four hired men were driving four of the wagons.

Each wagon contained brightly colored rolls and bolts of cloth, shining objects of metal and other goods, as well as a fifth of their supplies. Oberas was adamant that everything be spread out evenly amongst the wagons, to minimize the loss in case they lost a wagon. But the final wagon contained all the jewelry and other smaller and more expensive items, and Oberas's, Rion's, and their men's personal possessions, as well as the last fifth of their supplies. Oberas drove that wagon himself, with Rion riding beside him on the bench.

On the very first day of the trip Rion began trying to convince Oberas to let him learn to drive the wagon, so he might help. Hardred was glad to see Rion smiling and eager. He'd been afraid leaving his home, his City, his people, might put Rion into despair. When they'd left, Rion had stared wide-eyed at the refugees they'd seen. They were ragged and hungry and dirty, and their eyes had been filled with terror and hopelessness.

RION was bubbling over with excitement when they made camp that first evening. He'd spent his whole life in Ardock; he'd never once left the City. Excitement turned to despair in a heartbeat at the thought of those he'd left behind, that he'd likely never see again: Ric, Drew, Matt, even Cedric. Ric's father had almost been another uncle to him. Farion! Father! Mother! They were buried in Ardock. He'd visited their graves and spoken to them there more than once since they'd died. The last time he'd come he'd been pleased to see that the blue flower he had planted upon his mother's grave had flourished and spread to cover Father's, Farion's, and Justin's graves as well, like a blanket of his love.

He swallowed, hard, fighting the homesickness that threatened to engulf him and purposefully dug in his pack for the blank journal Oberas had given to him to record his trip in. Oberas had ordered him to write in it every night, to chronicle their day's journey. Rion suspected it was so he'd be kept too busy to worry or be sad or afraid. He dutifully got out the book, his pen, ink, and the drying sand, his mind overflowing with all he'd already seen and thoughts of what tomorrow might bring. He had an entire empty book to fill!

He stared at the first blank page for only a few moments, organizing his myriad cascading thoughts, and then set pen to paper and began to write.

The Southern Road, Northbound, En Route to Athanark
Thirteen Days Later

HARDRED surveyed the men and wagons around him, weighed down by the burden he'd so far concealed from all but Alnas. They'd been on the road just under a fortnight, so far without incident despite the number of other refugees on the road. They'd fortunately left before the mass exodus of Ardock truly began. If all went well, they'd reach the crossroads tomorrow, where the caravan would leave the Southern Road for the Lost Road, to Athanark. Only it would be proceeding on without him and Alnas.

They'd be taking the Southern Road, paralleling the Methris River past Logareth, all the way to the Western Road, and then from there heading west all the way to Delthos. From there they'd go northeast on the Coast Road to Meria. The Goddess had spoken to him. She'd called him home.

Seneth had sent him dreams every night for the past six nights, visions, like the ones Devan had nearly six years ago, like the ones Breandon had, the year before that. He and Julian and all their shipmates hadn't heeded Breandon's warning, and they'd all paid a terrible price for it. He'd had a vision of his own right after, but he'd discounted it as a nightmare, though it had all but driven him mad for a time with fear for Julian. He'd not make such a mistake again.

He'd listened when the Goddess spoke through Devan. He could do no less this time, now that She'd spoken to him directly again, and so clearly. He prayed that in so doing, the others would be safe as well. He'd never have been able to go if he thought Rion, Tarrell, Oberas, Elkrum, and the others might be endangered by it, even if it meant risking Her terrible wrath once more.

He could scarcely believe he might get to see Riana again, and more, see her children. He'd had no word from her in all these years, no news until the visions, though he'd sent letters to her through other couriers than Devan over the years.

He still could not fathom why Devan might have wed his sister when he'd already had a wife he adored and a child on the way, but he was certain that's what his vision had shown him. He feared Devan's wife, Larissa, must have died in childbirth, and the babe along with her. The symbolism of the seagull and the dolphin in his dreams had been unmistakable. They'd looked so happy together, the two of them and the fledgling gull and baby dolphin with them. His niece and nephew? They must be.

He'd never dreamt his sister might find another to love after Julian. He'd thought she'd live out her days a widow who'd never truly been a wife. For her to have found love a second time was as miraculous as him having found love and happiness of his own.

He looked longingly at Alnas, once he was certain no one was watching. They'd not slept in one another's arms since they'd left Ardock. They'd been careful not to touch one another before the other guards; even in the dead of night, they'd been careful. After knowing nearly six years of Alnas's love, his touch, it was almost unbearable to live without it, even for a fortnight.

He was truly blessed to have found such a man, when for so many months he had thought himself cursed. He could not help the affectionate smile that warmed his face as he remembered their first awkward kiss, born more of frustration, desperate longing, and frantic hope on Alnas's part than passion. The panicked look in poor Alnas's face before Hardred had responded in kind, when Alnas feared he'd done the unforgivable, that he'd destroyed their friendship. Both his and Alnas's overwhelming relief and incredible joy when they each realized they were truly wanted, truly loved, that neither of them would want for such happiness again.

It was so hard, riding beside Alnas every day, lying beside him every night, yet not being able to touch him, not intimately like he was accustomed to, like he craved to. Alnas had become as necessary to him as the air he breathed, the water he drank. Never in all his pining after Julian had he ever dreamt how love like this would feel. He was blessed beyond measure to have loved so deeply twice, and this time, to have his love so fully returned.

It tore his heart, knowing he must leave the others behind, but he dared not stay. He'd not risk losing Alnas, ever, the way he'd lost Julian. The Goddess had spoken through Breandon, and he'd not heeded the warning: he'd not even truly heard it. This time he did. He only prayed the others might be safe, with him gone, all of them, but Rion and Tarrell especially. They were almost as sons to him, the only ones he would ever have. It would be so hard to explain his decision to them, but he had no choice. He'd pay any price the Goddess asked of him to keep Alnas safe. He looked longingly at the man he loved, needing to see him, to know he was yet safe.

Alnas looked over at him, as if he'd sensed his eyes upon him, and slowed his horse to ride abreast of him for a moment. "You mustn't look at me like that, Hardred, not after we've lain apart nearly two whole weeks. I can scarcely sit in the saddle, now, that single look has inflamed me so."

Hardred immediately schooled his expression. "Forgive me. I let my thoughts stray. I did not mean to tempt you, nor tease you. Although be assured I won't show such restraint tomorrow night, nor all the other nights of our lives."

"You're still planning on telling Oberas and Rion and the others tonight?" Alnas asked, unable to mask the fear in his voice. Hardred knew Alnas still could not believe they were risking such a long journey. Hardred thought it would have helped if Elmoth had reassured Alnas in his dreams that all would be well, but at least Elmoth had not sent dreams against it.

"I've no choice, Alnas. If Julian and I and my shipmates had listened to Breandon, we all might have lived."

"But twenty-one hundred miles, at least nine months on the road, and only the two of us!" Alnas said in dismay.

Hardred looked him in the eye. "Seneth wills it. I'll not go against Her. I'll not risk angering Her against me or you, or Rion, Tarrell, Oberas, Elkrum, or any of the others. Resume your position, Alnas. We've yet a ways to go before dusk."

"I love you," Alnas whispered.

"And I love you. Go, Alnas. All will be well, I swear it."

"I'm holding you to that," Alnas said, and then he pulled ahead once more.

OBERAS had taken the news far better than Hardred had expected, for losing two of his guards a fortnight from their destination. He'd listened without commenting as Hardred had requested, until he was done explaining. The eruption Hardred had expected had not come at all. Instead, once Oberas had learned of the dreams and heard it was Seneth's will, he'd insisted they go, in spite of Hardred's reluctance and Alnas's reservations.

"You're going. You've no choice. The two of you are released from my service, effective as of dawn tomorrow. I'll not risk angering Seneth against you, when you've somehow regained Her favor. Only an arrogant fool resists the Gods' will, and he does so in peril of his life, or worse, in peril of those he loves. Safe journey, the both of you. May the water be calm and the wind at your backs all the days of your lives. Now get back to work, the both of you. You're both on shift tonight, and we're not at the crossroads yet."

"Yes, sir. But our final shift doesn't start until after dinner, and we need to break the news to Rion. And Tarrell and Elkrum, of course, before the others hear," Hardred said.

"I don't envy you that burden," Oberas said. "Just be sure you let Alarion know it's for your safety and happiness. He'd never put his own before someone else's. He'll be able to take the news better, hearing it that way."

Hardred nodded. He and Alnas approached the campfire Rion was seated at with Tarrell and Elkrum. Fortunately, none of the newer guards were about at the moment.

Rion had been talking animatedly about Athanark, but as soon as he and Alnas approached, Rion grew pensive and silent. He stood, looking intently at them. "Something's wrong. You've told me it's nothing, but I've seen enough these past days to know that's not true. Is one of you ill?" Rion asked fearfully, looking anxiously from Hardred to Alnas.

"No, Rion. It's nothing like that. But you're right, we've been wrestling with weighty decisions these days past, and it's time now to share them, though it will be hard for you to hear and harder still for you to understand. Alnas and I aren't going with you to Athanark." Hardred exhaled heavily and continued resolutely. "Tomorrow at the crossroads, we're continuing north, while you go west. We're going to Meria. I'm going home, to my sister Riana, to the sea, to Seneth."

Hardred saw Rion deflate, as if he were a proud ship and he'd taken the wind from his sails, but the image the analogy brought only strengthened his resolve.

"But you can't! I can't have lost Ardock and the both of you too! How can you leave me?" Rion asked, stunned by the magnitude of the betrayal, as his eyes filled with tears.

"I have to go, Rion," Hardred said gently. "I've been thinking about her, dreaming about her, every night this past week. The creak of the wagons sounds so like a ship at sea. I miss the sound of the waves on the shore, lulling me to sleep at night. She's calling me to her, Rion. She's calling me home."

"Who's calling you? Your sister?" Rion asked, not understanding. Rion knew Hardred had a sister. Alnas had told him once. Alnas had mentioned he had a statue of her, and that he wrote letters to her, but Hardred had never spoken to Rion about her.

"No, Rion, not Riana. It's the sea that's calling me. It's Seneth," Hardred said, his face lighting in joy, his lips embracing the name he'd been afraid to speak and had seldom uttered for nearly seven long years.

"Alnas, please, tell him he can't! Not after what I've heard you say. You said he'd never survive such a trip!" Rion pleaded.

Hardred sighed. "I know it's hard for you to understand, Rion. But Seneth has sent me dreams, visions. The only danger to me, to Alnas, would be in defying Her will. As long as we go, now, as She commands, we'll be safe. I swear to you we'll be. You must know I'd never endanger Alnas, just as I'd never endanger you. I'd gladly die before ever bringing harm to either of you.

"Oberas understands. When he heard it was Seneth's will, he released us from his service, effective tomorrow at dawn. He knows I must go. I'm sorry,

Rion. I know you're not pious, that your parents weren't. I know you must not be able to understand," Hardred said sadly.

"Oberas understood?" Rion asked, amazed that he might.

"He did. He insisted we go, once he learned of the visions. Rion, you know I could not love you more, were you my own son. Surely you can't believe any but a Goddess might part me from you? Please try to understand," Hardred said, tears in his eyes.

Rion swallowed hard. "I'm sorry, Hardred, Alnas, forgive me! I don't mean to make this harder on you than it already must be, to be so selfish. And I do understand, a little. Mother and Father were never devout, but Uncle Farion was. He and Justin kept a shrine to Ragnar in their home. Uncle Farion replaced the candle religiously every night and kept it lit for decades. It was a special fire, a sacred flame brought by my father's mother all the way from the Temple of Ragnar in Logareth, the only such consecrated flame in all of Ardock, as far as we knew.

"And I knew something was wrong, I saw the two of you were upset over something. I'm just thankful it was this and not illness. It's just, I never dreamed I'd lose you both, and so soon! But I'm not losing you at all, am I? Not really. It's only distance that will separate us. You'll still be alive and well. I'll still be able to write you and you can write me back.

"Someday I might even visit you both in Meria. I've never seen the sea before. You've never before wanted to speak of it, Hardred. But will you tell me of it tonight? So I can picture you and Alnas on the shore? And maybe even play a song on your pipes for me?" Rion asked hopefully, his eyes shining brightly with unshed tears.

Hardred fought his own tears, seeing how hard Rion was trying to be brave, to be a man, when at heart, at least, he was still a boy. "Of course. We'll talk over dinner, all about Meria and the sea, and more after we've eaten, and then I'll play my pipes until it's time for bed," Hardred assured him, giving him a fatherly hug. "I love you, Rion."

"I love you too, Hardred. And you, Alnas. I'll miss you both, but I wish you nothing but happiness," Rion said, hugging Hardred back tightly, and then Alnas.

"Tarrell, Elkrum," Hardred said, clasping arms with each of them. "We're trusting in you to watch over Rion and Oberas. We couldn't leave without knowing you and their other guards stayed. You must know we'll miss you both terribly as well."

"And we'll miss you. But you needn't worry. We'll watch over both of them for you," Tarrell said. He turned to Rion. "I'll always be here for you, Rion. You're as a brother to me, the only brother I fear I might have left. I'll not soon be parted from you, if ever."

"And I'll be here for you as well," Elkrum said. "As will Oberas. Don't you two worry, Hardred, Alnas. We'll see Rion safe."

"Now then, let's all settle down to eat. Then I'll play and perhaps even sing for you," Hardred said, the burden of his heart lifting already, knowing how well Tarrell and Elkrum and Oberas would care for Rion, now that he and Alnas no longer could.

He began humming one of the songs they used to sing aboard the *Silver Gull*, the night before they'd come to port, before they came home.

Coming Soon

Descent of Kings
Book Two:
Heir to the Throne

"It would not be the first time I made such a grave tactical error. I have made many. It is not your responsibility to save this world from the evil that threatens to consume it, Aras. Do not blame yourself for my shortcomings."

—Prince Talon of the Amontir

When his bonds to his cousins Hunter and Beryl are unexpectedly severed, Talon is devastated, fearing his kinsmen dead. In his darkest hour, Talon succors a young Wood Elf, Aras, unaware of the crucial role his new friend is destined to play.

Prince Jargas thought he would never learn the secret of his grandsire's line and his lost heritage. He never suspected the answer might lie in a Dwarven dungeon or that it could cost him the life of his beloved twin sister, Jarina.

Young apprentice trader Rion and his guard, Tarrell, thought Athanark would be their new home until they met Talon and Aras.

Friends become enemies and enemies become friends as new alliances are forged, men die, cities burn, and kingdoms fall. Everyone has secrets, and no one is who or what he seems.

Coming Soon

DESCENT OF KINGS
BOOK THREE:
The Coming of the King

"The world is ending. It is a cruel place and perhaps it should end. But then, there is Rion and you, and the brothers, and Rarnak, and those like you, those I might still find reason to fight for. So I look for Jargas, so he might help me, for I can stand alone against the darkness no longer."

—Farad, Lord of House of Wolven

After risking all to come to the aid of Rion and his friends, Farad believes his only hope for sanity and survival lies with Jargas. Yet it is Jarina who will either destroy or save him, at the cost of a lifetime of faith and loyalty to Prince Talon.

Meanwhile, past the outskirts of Nalea, Aras and Leonas undertake a dangerous mission to parlay with the Hill People, never dreaming the fates of both their own people and Talon's rest upon the outcome. Ironically, consumed by suspicion and mistrust, believing Jargas to be the Enemy's minion and fearing Farad lost, Talon lashes out at Aras, with devastating results.

The Amontir see agents of the Enemy everywhere, where there are none, and fail to see those who are beside them, ready to strike.

Coming Soon

DESCENT OF KINGS
BOOK FOUR:
The Final Battle

"But I am just a Man! You all want so much of me! ...I am not a wizard. I am not even one of you. I have no magic. There is no fire in my eyes."

—Rion of Ardock

Rion wields a power of heart that touches all he meets. The wizard Circe once called him a lynchpin, a keystone of the world. When Rion is viciously attacked and maimed in Gosa, he believes Circe's family is retaliating for his betrayal of them to Crown Prince Elavar. Learning the horrific truth brings him to the brink of madness.

Rion's friends take him to the River Elves of Salenia for aid, but the Elves send them onward, to King Talon. The company's perilous journey to the Watchtower is fraught with danger and filled with tragedy and triumph, but their trials have just begun.

King Talon's army has been decimated by the Enemy's relentless attacks. After staggering losses, they are outnumbered ten to one and teeter on the brink of defeat—yet somehow their dwindling forces must overcome a being with the Power of a God.

MARIA ALBERT lives in the California Bay Area with her two daughters and several dozen friends, most of the latter of whom are still confined in binders on her bookshelves. She looks forward to releasing many more of them in the coming months.

Contemporary Romance from MARIA ALBERT

http://www.dreamspinnerpress.com